Better Get
to Livin'

Books by Sally Kilpatrick

The Happy Hour Choir

Bittersweet Creek

Better Get to Livin'

Published by Kensington Publishing Corporation

Better Get to Livin'

Sally Kilpatrick

KENSINGTON BOOKS
www.kensingtonbooks.com

KENSINGTON BOOKS are published by

Kensington Publishing Corp.
119 West 40th Street
New York, NY 10018

All Kensington titles, imprints, and distributed lines are available at special quantity discounts for bulk purchases for sales promotion, premiums, fund-raising, educational, or institutional use.

Special book excerpts or customized printings can also be created to fit specific needs. For details, write or phone the office of the Kensington Sales Manager: Kensington Publishing Corp., 119 West 40th Street, New York, NY 10018. Attn. Sales Department. Phone: 1-800-221-2647.

Kensington and the K logo Reg. U.S. Pat. & TM Off.

eISBN-13: 978-1-61773-573-8
eISBN-10: 1-61773-573-6
First Kensington Electronic Edition: June 2016

ISBN-13: 978-1-61773-572-1
ISBN-10: 1-61773-572-8
First Kensington Trade Paperback Printing: June 2016

10 9 8 7 6 5 4 3 2 1

Printed in the United States of America

To Tanya, who puts up with my writerly neuroses.
I've forgotten what it was like to write without you.
Please don't remind me.

To Romily and Jenni, who got more than
they bargained for with this one.

And to Anna, because Declan is her favorite.

Thanks, Ladies, for believing in me
when I didn't believe in myself.

Acknowledgments

Third book in, and the acknowledgments page still terrifies me! It takes a village, and I appreciate those of you who answer my wacky questions.

First, I have to thank my editor, Peter, who blessedly didn't say "This book is crazy and you are crazy for writing it." Thank you for making my stories better. Thanks, too, to Monique, who keeps me on my toes, and to Paula, who shares my love of nice pens and keeps my manuscripts so pretty. Thanks to all of my folks at Kensington—publicity, covers, all of it—you spoil me.

Tanya Michaels, Romily Bernard, Jenni McQuiston, and Anna Steffl were all instrumental in getting this book done. Nicki Salcedo gave it a read-through and lent her expertise, too, so booty smacks to her. Mom, my most faithful proofreader, and Ryan, husband and beleaguered expert on heroes, also contributed to the cause. Raymond Atkins was kind enough to give me a read-through and a charming blurb, as was Haywood Smith, who also happened to look at an earlier draft.

I owe a huge debt of gratitude to Linda Bendixen, who was a phenomenal beta reader, focusing on all of the aspects of the funeral business in particular. I can't begin to tell you how thorough and helpful her notes were. Jason Pendley took time out of his day to answer a million questions and to give me a tour of Mayes Ward-Dobbins Funeral Home. Any mistakes you see are mine and not theirs, let me assure you. Also, Jason and the nice folks at Mayes Ward-Dobbins are a thousand times more professional than my fictional funeral home family. I made up the bourbon parties, y'all. Made. Them. Up.

Jeanne Myers kept me on the straight and narrow with the design of my houses and what to do when the tornado damaged the funeral home. (Psst! Do NOT call a house a "Victorian." That is verboten.) The Old House Guy was kind enough to chat with me about octopus furnaces, among other things. Zachary from The Denver Hearse Association told me all about the hearse on the cover. If you see any errors in any of these areas, again they are liberties I took to make the story work.

When Anderson Funeral Home needed to look into adding a crematory, Shane Burton and Paul Boudreau assisted me in figuring out how much such a thing would cost and what kind of business plan my fictitious funeral home would need. Again, all mistakes are mine—mainly because the math isn't my strong suit.

Kevin Quigley, Beth Showman, and Jennifer Burress all contributed valuable opinions on things ranging from Sean and Alan's marriage to what kind of gun Caroline might carry. Thank goodness Holly Morris was willing to strike up a conversation with a stranger in Starbucks, because she helped me with some acting info as did friend and perennial adviser Gretchen Swales. Any mistakes? Still mine.

Special thanks to my aunt Dot for the apricot salad recipe in the back. Thanks, as always, to The Hobbit and Her Majesty for letting Mommy live in La La Land and write down the things she sees and hears. Also, there aren't enough words for all of my family, friends, and readers both new and old who keep showing up and keep supporting me. I say a little prayer of gratitude for each visit and each review. From the bottom of my heart, thank you.

Finally, this book wouldn't have happened without Fentress Casey. (Best funeral director name ever, right?) Mr. Casey not only presided over MANY a family funeral, but he also used to pull me out of high school sometimes to play "Taps" at military funerals. Nothing like sitting in the back kitchen of the funeral home listening to that crazy chime music to get your imagination going, let me tell you. Did I mention he pulled me out of school AND he *paid* me?

Presley

Camera flashes blinded me as a cool breeze whipped across my backside. I yanked my skirt out of my thong, but the damage had been done. I pushed through the small throng of paparazzi and made a break for my car. One asked for my comment. Another asked who I was.

Why, I'm Presley Cline, F-list actress extraordinaire. Do you mean you haven't heard of me?

But of course I didn't say that because, for once in my life, I didn't want anyone to know who I was.

That second paparazzo gave me hope until the next morning when my agent, Ira, called me at an ungodly hour. He skipped the hello as he always did. "Kid, you gotta get out of town and lie low."

"Do you think I'm out of the running for the lead in the godmother movie?"

He made that noncommittal Ira sound.

"But they say all publicity is good publicity, right?"

"That's what people with only bad publicity say. Parents like for their kid movies to have good role models, and most fairy godmothers don't get caught on the wrong side of a booty call with their pants down."

Technically, it was my skirt up, but I didn't correct him.

"Ira, I don't even know where to go," I said. My most recent boyfriend, Rob the wonder accountant, had found a newer, younger girlfriend and then absconded with a majority of my funds. A quick look out the window of my apartment showed at least one suspicious person outside waiting for me to emerge.

"Go someplace quiet. Real quiet," he said with a grunt. "I should have something to tell you by New Year's."

Then he hung up on me, which wasn't that big of a surprise.

"Someplace quiet, huh?" I let the curtain fall back and looked around for a duffel bag. It looked as though I was going to be spending Christmas back home in Ellery after all, and whoever said there was no place like home for the holidays obviously didn't have a mother like mine.

"I told you not to come home until just before dawn. The paparazzi are more likely to be asleep then."

I'm such a nobody, the paparazzi shouldn't have been there. Had Ira sold me out?

I did my best to ignore the ghost in the corner, a curvy brunette with bangs. Somehow she always had a cigarette and a plume of ghostly smoke winding around her. Sometimes I could even smell the Lucky Strikes.

I continued to pack, hoping Pinup Betty, the erstwhile inhabitant of my apartment, would go away. She didn't. I'd tried everything I could think of to exorcise her, but none of it had worked.

Ghosts gravitated to me, and Pinup Betty was more stubborn than most.

According to my mother, I was born with a knot in my umbilical cord, which was also looped around my neck twice for good measure. The knot, the loop, the fact she smoked throughout the pregnancy—one or all of those things meant I was born blue and lifeless. She told me she prayed when she saw me, for the first time since she'd found out she was pregnant, not saying amen until I gave a whimper then a cry.

Those eighty-seven precious seconds must've been enough to connect me to another world because I, like the little boy in the movie, could see dead people. In fact, I was looking at Pinup Betty in spite of myself.

"What're you looking at?"

"Just thinking about how happy I'm going to be to leave you behind," I said.

"Maybe I'll come with you. I'm getting bored of sitting around here waiting for something to happen." She took a drag on her cigarette. I braced myself for a coughing fit, but it didn't come. At least the ghostly smoke only carried the faintest whiff of the real thing.

"Don't even think about it," I said. "You got me into enough trouble with your so-called advice."

She waved away my concern. "It'll turn out all right in the end. You'll see. As long as you gave him a night to remember, then you'll get that part. It's not like things have changed *that* much since the forties."

Not that I was about to admit it to Betty, but I hadn't given Carlos *anything* to remember other than the memory of me running out of his house like my hair was on fire. Now the whole world was accusing me of something I hadn't done.

I zipped up my duffel bag. No need to pack too much because I'd be back before the new year. "Bye, Betty. Don't do anything I wouldn't do."

She grunted and went back to staring at the ceiling as I closed the door behind me.

Three weeks. I could stand anything for three weeks—even my mother.

Declan

Folks around town have always speculated that the Anderson men lived forever due to an overexposure to embalming fluids. Since great-granddaddy Seamus lived to be over a hundred, I couldn't prove them wrong. Sure, my father didn't make it that long, but there always has to be one, right? With the distinct possibility of dull decades stretching out before me, I did have to question my quality of life. After all, I was standing in the city cemetery at dusk on the night of the Ellery Christmas parade.

Christmas carols and jingle bells echoed over the graves, and I had a sudden and intense longing for a greasy cheeseburger from Burger Paradise. I could blame Grandpa Floyd for that one. After every burial, he'd do two things: go get a hamburger and kiss Grandma full on the lips the minute he got back. He said there was nothing like putting a body in the ground to make a man suddenly aware of his own mortality.

"*¡Oye, Jefe!* This look good?"

I looked away from the Anderson plot to where Manny leaned out the backhoe's cab.

"Perfect-o, Manny-o," I said. He grinned at my mauled southern Spanish. We both knew I could do better, but it was my way of telling him he was forgiven for last week's incident of driving a backhoe while intoxicated and thus knocking over two grave markers. Caroline, my stepmother and our boss, wanted to garnish his paycheck to get back the money his stunt had cost. So far, I'd been able to hold her back. After all, Manny was Armando's nephew and still reeling from the sudden loss of his wife. Cemeteries freaked him out, which was rather unfortunate for someone whose third job was digging graves.

Our most recent grave filled, Manny drove the backhoe up on the flatbed and hightailed it out of the cemetery. I reached into my pocket for a cigarette only to remember I'd quit. Again. I couldn't even look at puffs of my breath and pretend they were smoke because it was pretty warm for early December. Hell, it was the warmest December I could remember, and I couldn't get out of my monkey suit fast enough. Only my father's discipline reminded me that I was not to take off my suit coat until I was safely home and thus off duty.

"We have a certain reputation to maintain, son," he used to say. "A momentary discomfort on your part is worth making sure you do the job right."

Doing the job right. I snorted. Manny and I would've been gone already if I hadn't let the Latham family have such a late graveside service. They'd been holding off as long as they could in the hopes that a relative from Seattle would be able to make it despite a canceled flight. Dad or Sean would've easily talked them out of such foolishness with words like *decorum* or *extra fees after three*. But I was the soft touch. My traitorous tongue told them we would be happy to hold the service a little later and that, perhaps, a twilight service would be a touching and beautiful way to remember someone who worked the night shift.

What a load of horseshit.

Not only would I do just about anything to make people feel better, but I also didn't feel the need to always pass on extra fees due to extenuating circumstances, which explained why, at least according to Caroline, I was running Anderson's Funeral Home into the ground. To top it all off, she was still ticked at me for laughing at her unintentional pun.

What she didn't know, in this case, certainly wouldn't hurt her.

I was awfully close to paying off the loan from the chapel we'd added on a few years back. Sean, my younger brother, was supposed to be home any day now, fully graduated from Gupton-Jones and ready to take my place as soon as he dragged his punk-ass self back from Atlanta. After I gave her the loan pay-off for Christmas, I would still have enough to buy the old McHaney place on Maple Avenue, a great way to start my second career renovating houses. Yep, it was going to be a pretty merry Christmas.

Across the street from the old cemetery, I saw Manny pull his truck—complete with the offending backhoe—over to the only Mexican restaurant in town. He had made it to El Nopalito for his medicinal shot of tequila, but I wouldn't have to worry about him because his sister would make sure he didn't drive under the influence.

Manny swore up and down he could *feel* the ghosts while he was in the graveyard, which made his job as assistant to the cemetery sexton unfortunate. I called bullshit. Why would a ghost hang around a cemetery? What fun would that be? Not that I believed in ghosts because I didn't. I wasn't entirely sure I believed in heaven or hell or a god who sent people to one place or another. Best I could tell, you got what you got. All the rest was science we hadn't figured out yet.

Declan, my boy, life holds too much mystery to be explained by science alone. There are some things you have to take on faith.

Shut up, Dad.

I turned to my father's monument. I knew his voice was only in my head just as I knew I'd paused here at his grave and would have a hard time leaving it. Here in the quiet of the cemetery I could feel that connection with him and Grandpa Floyd and even Great-Grandpa Seamus—the old Colonel who'd started the whole family business.

"For once, Dad, we aren't in a mell of a hess," I said. "I'm about to pay off the loan, you know. I'm going to keep my promise to you and find a way to go into business with Uncle El. I won't be designing houses, but I'll get to fix them up."

All that's left is for you to find a good woman.

Where had that come from? It had to be my mind playing tricks on me because it sounded like something Dad would say. I wasn't about to repeat his mistakes, though. My mother hadn't been cut out for being the funeral director's wife, and she'd gone to her rest a long time before my father. I couldn't quite look at her grave since she hadn't loved me or my brother enough to stick around.

The throaty sounds of a muscle car made me look up, and I saw a classic Firebird roar down MLK beside me. Suddenly, it seemed silly to be standing in a graveyard talking to a headstone so I started picking my way through the unevenly laid out graves just as the security light hummed to life.

I had been hanging out in a cemetery after dark in a suit that was too hot for comfort because I didn't want to go home—now how sad was that?

Pretty sad, but I didn't plan to be sad much longer.

I actually started whistling as I rounded the shiny black hearse and climbed inside. As of Christmas, I was going to be free, but until then I would keep my promise.

Because an Anderson always keeps his promise.

Presley

So much for keeping my promises. Guilt had hit me hard somewhere around Amarillo, and it hadn't let up the rest of the way to Tennessee.

I'd told myself—and LuEllen—that I wasn't coming home until I'd made it big. Now here I was driving her vintage Firebird right through town.

Oh, you've made it big all right.

That picture with my skirt caught in my undies as I left a certain producer's beach house in the middle of the night had gone viral. To make matters worse, I shouldn't have gone over there in the first place because—at least according to some media outlets—the part had been mine to lose.

I really, really want that part.

Finally, after years of playing a corpse or mouthy hooker or sexy dancer, I'd found a role I *wanted* to play. Leave it to me to succumb to the casting couch for a chance to play a fairy godmother. Leave it to me to chicken out at the last minute but to still be caught by the paparazzi, thus making it *look* like I had actually done the one thing I'd sworn I'd never do.

Ira, for his part, had been subtly suggesting for years that I should at least flirt with various Hollywood power players, but it was Betty who'd told it to me straight: "Honey, you ain't gonna get nowhere unless you go over there and make it happen for yourself. And by make it happen, I mean bang him."

And that's what you get for listening to a less-than-subtle ghost whose idols are Ava Gardner and Lana Turner.

I couldn't tell my therapist about Betty, so I told her about Rob the Accounting Wiz instead. She, at the last session I could afford, had suggested my boyfriend's betrayal had created within me a desperation that might lead me to make poor decisions.

Understatement of the century right there.

I had panicked when I saw I had no money, and Betty's advice started making sense for the first time ever. But going over and over again how I'd come to that spot on a moonlit beach with my skirt tucked into my thong wasn't accomplishing anything.

"Face it, Presley, you're screwed." And then I laughed because I hadn't even gone through with the screwing.

I was still laughing—probably delirious from driving ten hours a day for nearly three days—when I turned right on MLK, but the sight of the cemetery sobered me up. For a split second, I thought about joining the people there. Surely, LuEllen had any number of pain pills lying around unattended.

Don't be ridiculous.

I gripped the steering wheel so tightly that my knuckles went white. So I'd embarrassed myself. And LuEllen. So I was back in town with my tail between my legs. It was three weeks. Ira said he'd tell me something before the new year, and I knew they planned to announce the cast list for *The Secret Lives of Fairy Godmothers* by mid-January. With any luck, my name would still be on that list, and I would go back to Hollywood and back to the life I'd had before. Once I got back, I could call in a favor or two for a modeling gig or a bit part and have enough to make the rent. Then I would start over.

And stay far, far away from handsome accountants who promised to make my investments grow.

In the meantime, it was time to face the music and admit to LuEllen that I was flat broke.

That last light of day had completely faded by the time I

pulled up to trailer number four of the Green Acres Estates Mobile Home Park. Green Acres was not the place for me. There were about a million other places I would *raaaather* be.

Weeds still grew around the battered trailer so thickly I couldn't see the faux-brick vinyl that covered the underpinning. The rickety porch looked as though it would fall in with the first strong breeze.

I rolled out of the '78 Firebird that had been a hand-me-down from my mother, and I stretched. I hadn't stopped any more than I had to, but that still meant five stops since Amarillo. My legs were jelly.

Either that or they wobbled because they were afraid of what I might find inside. Unseasonably warm air wrapped around me. Kinda felt warmer than Los Angeles, which was good because I didn't have a very impressive winter wardrobe.

One of the porch steps broke, and I thought I heard a hiss under my feet. Heart pounding, I hopped up to the landing, scratching my ankle on the broken step in the process. Great. *Snakes hibernate in the winter, you dork.* I didn't want to think about the last time I'd gotten a tetanus shot so I hoped that snag was all wood and no rusty nail.

At least patching me up would give LuEllen something to do.

When my mother met me at the door, I didn't recognize the walking skeleton with the orange leather skin. The woman who'd taught me everything I knew about curling hair and pulling it back into a hundred different styles had cut hers in a severe, straight bob with an awful dye job. The woman who'd spent hours teaching me how to properly apply eyeliner, mascara, and the perfect shade of lipstick now didn't wear a lick of makeup.

"Well, I was wondering when you would show up," she wheezed, pulling me in for an angular hug. "I guess I should be glad you're home for Christmas."

I might be an adult, but her disapproval stung just as much as it had when I was a girl. It was always about twirling the baton faster or singing a little louder or smiling a lot wider. I wanted to wish her a sarcastic "Merry Christmas to you, too!" and walk out, but I had nowhere else to go.

Instead I said, "LuEllen, you didn't tell me they put you on oxygen."

She stared at me, her smile sad. "Are you hungry?"

So that's how we were going to play it.

"I got something outside Memphis," I lied. Telling the truth would do no good because I already knew her cupboards would be bare, her fridge empty except for a rotted head of lettuce and maybe a block of government cheese.

That and the beer in the crisper drawer hiding behind the rotted head of lettuce.

"Baby, you're bleeding on the floor. When were you going to tell me about that?" She shuffled off to the bathroom before I could explain about the broken step.

In the end, I sat on a bar stool by the little counter that separated kitchen and living room while she huffed and puffed as she nursed my ankle. It wasn't as deep a scratch as I'd first thought, but the rubbing alcohol still stung like the dickens.

"There now," she said. For a minute I thought she might lean down and kiss the wound to make it better, but she didn't. Instead she got to her feet with a gasp and a grunt.

"Wanna watch some TV?" She gestured to the tiny set in the corner behind her, and I realized she hadn't even bothered to put up a tree. Nothing about the living room said Christmas.

"I think I might want to roll into bed."

LuEllen didn't have cable. She also didn't have much of an antenna, so my choices would've been limited to two channels, one of them PBS. Come to think of it, I might be able to watch TV without having to worry about seeing that damned picture of myself. Maybe later.

"Bed sounds good," she said with a yawn.

I made a show of stowing my lone bag in the bedroom that had been mine, even though I wasn't really ready for bed. When I unfolded the futon, dust clouded the air. My apartment back in California was a craphole, but it was still better than this place.

My walls were littered with teenybopper posters, complete
with statistics down the side. They were innocent shots of fully
clothed boy band members, but they still reminded me of how
I'd turned down *Playboy*. I still couldn't see myself sprawled out
for God and everybody to see complete with inane stats down
the side.

*Presley Ann Cline: blond hair, blue eyes. 5'10" and 125 pounds. She
likes baseball and long walks on the beach while holding hands.*

*She also has a jagged scar on her right thigh that you'll have to air-
brush out and a bunch of emotional baggage that you can't. Oh, and she
actually weighs ten pounds heavier than that, give or take.*

If I'd done that spread, as well as the photographer who'd suggested it, I might've gotten somewhere. Where exactly, I still
didn't know.

I reached for the corner of one of the boy toy posters, but I
couldn't rip it down. If I did, I was admitting to LuEllen that I'd
changed. I would admit nothing. I refused to feel guilty, considering she'd had me out of wedlock. Who was she to judge what I
did in my spare time?

My therapist's favorite topic had been how my mother had stifled my sexuality. She didn't think it was healthy. Come to think
of it, Rob wasn't too fond of it, either, which is probably why he
had a new girlfriend along with my money.

They could all kiss my sexually stifled ass.

I didn't need a man at all.

What I needed was a beer.

Next door, I could already hear LuEllen's ragged snores, so I
sneaked down the hall to the kitchen. No rotten lettuce, but a
shriveled apple and a petrified lime camouflaged a couple of
longnecks.

My stomach growled in protest, but I knew the buzz would
come on quickly and be enough to get me to sleep. Tomorrow I
would figure out how to move forward while I waited. Tonight, I
would have a beer and go to sleep—after all, going to bed tipsy
was a family tradition.

Declan

As I walked across the funeral home parking lot loosening my tie and looking forward to a beer, my cell phone rang. I looked longingly up at my apartment above the old carriage house but answered the phone anyway.

The nursing home needed me to pick up Mrs. Borden, and they'd prefer that I come right away while so many of their patrons were asleep, to avoid upsetting them. I assured the nurse I would be right over and sent a text to let Armando know he wasn't done for the night yet, either.

Just as I was adjusting my tie and heading back to the car, Caroline rounded the corner. "I thought I heard you, Declan."

"Yes, ma'am, but I'm headed out again. Nursing home called."

"A funeral director's work is never done," she said as she ran a hand through her short salt-and-pepper hair. "Not that you plan on doing that forever, as you've so often informed me."

"I'm going to keep working part time," I said.

"Mm-hmm. You're going to run off and leave me, just like that brother of yours."

Nothing left but to change the subject. "You've been working late."

"Oh, you know. Puttering about on the computer. Gotta make up for the Latham fiasco."

I didn't take the bait. No good would come of our rehashing the argument about the late funeral or the extra money the cemetery had charged us, a charge I hadn't passed on to the Lathams.

"Ginger Belmont passed away," she said. "Armando's on his way here."

"That explains why he didn't answer me."

I leaned against the hearse. Knowing that someone was dying never made it any easier. Not even when they told you each and every one of their final wishes beforehand. Several times.

Caroline cleared her throat. "We're going to lose our shirts on that one, too. Make sure you don't let the Bordens talk you into something similar."

"Look, we had to honor the policy Dad sold her. The Bordens don't have a policy like that, so you should get your money."

She shrugged. "You know full well that there's a clause in those old policies that allows us to make an adjustment for inflation. And you could've upsold the casket, too."

Always with the money. I knew she meant well. I knew she was concerned with keeping the business afloat, but still. "Why don't you do the removal and talk with the family then?"

She raised one eyebrow. "You know I don't do removals anymore because of my bad back. But if you're such a bleeding heart liberal chicken, why don't you tell Jessica to come see me in the morning about the particulars?"

"Gladly."

As fate would have it, I wasn't interested in the one woman interested in me. I had tried to talk myself into it, but she was too . . . sweet. All wide blue eyes and dark hair, she dressed like a younger version of June Cleaver, complete with the faux pearls. Long ago, at our high school's first annual Sadie Hawkins Dinner, she'd asked me to be her date. She'd caught me by surprise at my locker, and I'd made an excuse about having to work for my dad. Her face had crumpled, and I'd felt bad ever since. Avoiding her had become second nature.

"Chicken," Caroline said.

"And proud of it."

She sighed. "I really don't think she's holding a grudge, but you do what you need to do, and I'll see you in the morning."

"Night, Caroline."

She grimaced. She didn't like it that I called her by her first name, but she was my stepmother, not my mother. "Night, Declan."

She walked stiffly to her new Mercedes, leaving me to the hearse.

I'm running the funeral home into the ground, but *she's* leasing a brand-new Mercedes. She'd tell me appearances are important. I'd remind her that appearances can be deceiving, like how a business barely squeaking by allowed her to drive a Mercedes.

What-the-hell-ever.

As soon as Armando showed, we'd go to get Miss Ginger and Miss Sylvia. Caroline could handle Jessica Borden.

Thanks to some red tape, I didn't get back until one in the morning; then Armando and I did the embalming. This did not, however, absolve me from being back at work by eight thirty the next morning, an hour that came entirely too quickly.

My tiny carriage house apartment didn't have a stove that worked worth a damn, so I walked across the back parking lot to the funeral home to make breakfast. That morning, I remember stopping in the middle of the parking lot and looking up to a white sky framed by leafless trees. The winter sky didn't look right for the warm, muggy temperatures. Something was off, way off.

I shrugged away the feeling and unlocked the back door to the kitchen that had been built onto the classy old four-square house that had become Anderson's Funeral Home. As usual, I felt smothered the minute I stepped inside. Between the humidity outside and the weird cloying feeling inside, some instinct told me to run as far as I could.

I didn't listen.

I never did.

Instead, I put the coffee on and commenced the morning check, starting with the prep room.

"Morning, ladies," I said, even though I knew neither Miss Ginger nor Miss Sylvia could hear me. Then I walked down the hall, double-checking the doors that needed to stay locked and opening the ones that needed to be opened. Hell would freeze over before Caroline came in on time. She might be frugal, but punctual she was not.

By the time I ambled back to the kitchen, the coffee had finished dripping. I took off my suit coat and rolled up my sleeves to make some eggs. Caroline came through the back door, her cheeks pink with excitement.

"You look happy this morning," I said as I slid a plate of eggs and toast in front of her.

"Got some good news," she said.

I waited for her to share her news. Instead, she got a cup of coffee and sat down across from me. "Declan, you are going to make someone a mighty fine little wife someday." She frowned. "Well, if you ever start dating again, you will."

I let that slide. No way was I going to discuss my love life with my stepmother. She meant well, but she had no idea. I'd been out of high school for over ten years, but folks still called me "Cold Fingers." I'd tried dating in Jefferson or some of the other towns nearby, but it usually didn't go well—except for the goth girls. And the old ladies.

Unfortunately, the goth girls usually weren't in it for me—they tended to dump me because I was too straitlaced. I didn't find much mystery in death, having lived with it my whole life. As for the old ladies? They *said* they weren't interested in anything long-term, but with all of the advances in medicine I didn't want to take any chances.

Also? No.

"You know, your brother never had a problem finding a date," she said as she took a bite of eggs. "Maybe you could ask him for some pointers."

Right. As if I would ever ask my *little* brother for dating advice.

Besides, he wasn't the one who had been saddled with the nickname "Cold Fingers," so he had one fewer obstacle to overcome.

"When is he coming in anyway?"

"He didn't say." I took a seat across from her. "I would like to point out that *he* wouldn't have been able to cook you breakfast."

"True." She shrugged, but we both knew she favored Sean over me. When she'd married my father, I'd had a bad case of "You aren't my mama," but Sean had been young enough to embrace her. Caroline was the only mother Sean had ever known.

"Besides," I said, not willing to crush her dreams of grandchildren just yet, "according to Grandpa Floyd, I have at least one more year of freedom. He said he'd never known a funeral man to get married before thirty-three."

Caroline snorted. "That old coot! He got married when he was twenty. You don't need to put stock into anything he said."

She couldn't fool me. Caroline had always had a soft spot for Grandpa Floyd. There were times when I was growing up that I would've sworn she loved Grandpa Floyd more than Dad.

"Yeah, well the two of you got along so well because you already understood the business. There's not exactly a surplus of ladies working at funeral homes around here."

She frowned. I didn't know the whole story of how Caroline had defected from her father's funeral home to come to ours, only bits and pieces. Like her father, she believed in earning a living. Unlike her father, she didn't believe in taking more than she deserved.

"Is this more of that 'Cold Fingers' nonsense?" she asked when she'd finally mustered up a smile.

"You can call it nonsense all you want, but the fact of the matter is the girls I went to high school with don't want to have a thing to do with me. Even the college girls shy away once someone from town starts telling them stories."

"Ha! Jessica Borden would *love* to go out with you."

"Good thing for me she married Bart, then." Jessica had always seemed fragile, and fragile wasn't a good quality for a funeral director's wife.

"Beggars can't be choosers," Caroline practically sang. "You don't want to end up an old cat man, and she does make all of those picture-perfect desserts. I heard she makes a pretty penny on them, too."

I didn't need desserts, and we weren't in need of as much money as Caroline thought. I almost told her about my plan to pay off the chapel, but I stopped myself. "I'm not adding adultery to my list of flaws, and I don't think she would've been strong enough for this line of work anyway."

Caroline sat up straighter, no longer teasing me. "Declan, what your mother did . . ."

The doorbell chimed. *Saved by the bell—and just before we wandered into very-special-episode territory.*

"I bet that's Jessica Borden now." Caroline took her napkin and carefully dabbed around her lips before getting up from the table. I looked at her half-eaten breakfast, listening to her heels click down the hall.

I cleared the table, hesitating when I picked up her plate. I didn't want to toss her breakfast, but I couldn't leave the kitchen messy.

A pitiful mew from the other side of the door saved me from the decision. When I opened the door, a tiny yellow kitten sat on the back step. He waltzed into the funeral home as though he owned the place.

Old cat man, huh?

"Very funny." These were the moments I leaned toward the existence of God. Miracles weren't always so far-fetched when you considered the equal number of disasters, but these moments when it felt as though the universe was poking fun at me? That made it feel like Someone had a sense of humor.

I scooped up the kitten for any indication of who he was or where he was from—oops, where she was from.

"Declan Orion Anderson, what are you doing?" There stood Caroline in the doorway with the ever-persistent Jessica Borden. And I had a cat by the tail checking out her privates.

"Um, I wanted to know if it was a boy or girl."

"That doesn't tell me where you got a kitten! Put that thing outside," Caroline hissed. The look on her face took me back to my teenaged years when Sean and I decided to soup up the hearse. That hadn't ended well for us, but fun times before we got caught.

"Actually, Mrs. Anderson, I would feel better if the cat stayed." Jessica Borden sounded like Marilyn Monroe singing "Happy Birthday" to the president, but she looked more like a sedated Zooey Deschanel.

Caroline's lips disappeared into a thin line. "Fine. Keep it out of the prep room."

I arched an eyebrow and started to remind her it was Golden Boy Sean, not me, who'd given the puppy free rein in the prep room that time.

"I can take her over to the shelter," I said. Sensing the ambivalence in my voice, the kitten really got her motor running and was kneading her claws into my arm.

"No!"

Both Caroline and I turned to our eccentric client.

"I mean, I would feel better if you would keep the cat. Ancient Egyptians revered cats. Even mummified them."

Not so sedate.

I looked at Caroline, and she nodded. We knew all about mummies thanks to our coursework, but we weren't going to squash her childlike wonder on the subject.

"Then I'll take her to the pantry for now."

Jessica smiled, which made Caroline smile. "If the kitten really is a she, that's kinda rare. Most yellow cats are toms."

"Really? I didn't know that," Caroline murmured. "Would you like a new kitten?"

"Oh, no. I have four cats already."

Why am I not surprised?

I put the kitten down in the pantry, unable to resist scratching between her ears. If Egyptians mummified cats, then we could call this one Cleopatra—at least until we found her rightful owners. I couldn't keep her in here without a litter box and some food, but neither Miss Sylvia nor Miss Ginger was going to prepare herself. We had some sand in the garage for oil spills—that would probably do until I took care of my other duties for the day.

"Oh, and Declan," Caroline said as I walked through the kitchen on my way to get sand and a box. "Be sure to call Delilah. Jessica would prefer that she do Mrs. Borden's hair and makeup."

Oh, good. I loved talking to that old battle-ax.

Of course, if I'd known what talking to her might bring, I might've been a little more enthusiastic.

Presley

All I could find in the pantry was instant coffee and long-expired commodity peanut butter. Another beer would've been a more nutritional breakfast.

Even as I thought it, LuEllen shuffled through the kitchen in her robe and opened the fridge for a beer. I didn't say anything as I watched her pour the frothy liquid into an insulated cup, but my look must've been enough because she gave me a defensive "What?"

"Not exactly the breakfast of champions, is it?"

"You live your life, and I'll live mine."

Well, then.

She shuffled over to the bar stool and hoisted herself up, then reached for a pack of cigarettes with trembling fingers.

"You're on oxygen! You can't smoke!"

"Oxygen tank's in the bedroom," she said with a shrug.

"It's still dangerous to have fire anywhere near that thing. You could blow us up to kingdom come. Besides, smoking's the reason you have to drag around the tank in the first place."

She fumbled with the lighter but managed to get a flame, cupping a trembling hand around the cigarette as she lit it. Closing her eyes, she inhaled the tobacco with such vigor, her lips puckered into a hundred wrinkles. She let the breath go with a cloud of smoke that sent me off into a coughing frenzy.

Granny had always made her smoke outside.

And I'd forgotten just how much I hated for the smell of the stuff to permeate my clothes and hair. I was going to smell like a chimney even though I couldn't stand the darned things.

"Stop judging me," she snapped. "I'm your mother. Besides, you aren't so perfect, now are you?"

Now I stared, more stunned at the harsh tone than at her breakfast of hops, barley, and nicotine.

She took another drag, and her hand stilled. Her shoulders rolled back into a relaxed position. "And I know you swiped one of my beers last night, missy."

I'm not sure which bothered me more, that she smoked and drank before eight or the fact that she knew exactly how many beers were in her crisper drawer. That and she was calling me "missy." The woman was barely forty even if she did look twenty years older.

"I'll get you more when I go to the store. I might even pick up something for me."

She cackled, and the laugh turned into a cough. With great gasps she finally recovered her voice. "You'll have to go all the way into Jefferson if you want anything other than beer. This here's a dry town—no vices allowed."

"Um, know of any openings at the beauty shops?"

I thought it best to change the subject because we were headed down a road I didn't want to travel.

Her eyes widened. "What do you need to go working at a beauty shop for? I thought you were only here for a visit while things calmed down."

I grabbed the counter to ground myself. "Remember Rob?"

She exhaled, studying the ceiling while she thought. "Yeah, handsome devil, if I recall."

"He invested *my* money in *his* bank account and ran off with a younger woman. I am broke."

She started to say something, but I glared at her. She closed her mouth, but I could tell she wasn't finished with the conversation.

Sucking on her cigarette, she squinted as she thought aloud. "I reckon you could ask Delilah if she has any openings."

My fingers clenched the edge of the bar, but the trailer still threatened to spin around me. Delilah? As in the owner of the Holy Roller? "I'm pretty sure she hates my guts. Do you think Eliza Rhodes has anything?"

"She closed up shop a couple of years ago. So did that Wanamaker girl. Nope, your best bet is Delilah. You tell her that *I* sent you."

Something hard and fierce glittered in my mother's brown and otherwise bleary eyes.

"LuEllen. Mama. I'm not here to cause trouble. I've got to learn to get along with people while I'm here."

She reached across the counter and laid a leathery hand over mine. "Baby, surely you have enough to get you by for a couple of weeks here. You go ahead and hide for a while, lick those wounds. Then you go on back to California. Grandma Moses didn't start painting until she was . . . was, well, until she was really old. So you've still got plenty of time."

And Grandma Moses wouldn't be cast for anything short of a Depends commercial, either.

"Okay."

"That's the spirit!"

"You mean you aren't mad at me?" I didn't like how small my voice sounded.

"For what?"

She was going to make this hard on me. "For sleeping with someone to get a part *and* getting caught."

LuEllen went on a coughing jag, and I waited. Finally, she wheezed enough to catch her breath. "I'm not going to lie. I don't like the snickers when I go to the store, but I can't say anything about what you did. But why him? And why now?"

If we were the Gilmore Girls, this is the point where I would spill all my troubles and my plucky mother would have witty,

pragmatic answers for me. But what could I tell her? That I'd ignored her years of warnings? That I was tired of waiting? That I
was desperate after Rob left because I doubted my abilities and
was suddenly strapped for cash? "I really, really wanted that part,
and I was tired of waiting."

"Well, screw that." LuEllen had never been known for answers that were pragmatic or witty, much less both, but this one
was pretty close.

"Maybe I'll like fixing hair better." Even as I said it, I knew I
wanted to be a fairy godmother. Goodness knows, I'd always
wanted one.

"Don't you want to be a star? Don't you want more than . . .
this?" She threw out one hand to encompass the shabby trailer
around us, spreading ash from her cigarette as she did so.

"LuEllen, only a tiny, tiny number of people actually become
famous and make lots of money. There for a while I was making
a living, but I still sometimes made more doing hair than finding
bit parts. Heck, I'm practically over the hill by Hollywood stan-
dards. The last commercial I did, they put me in a cardigan and
had me pretend to be the mom of a teenager."

LuEllen winced. "That ain't right."

"No, it's not. I'm tired. And I'm hungry." *And I've hopelessly embarrassed myself with a certain influential producer, quite possibly ruin-
ing any chance I ever had.*

"Well. If you want to be a hairdresser while you're here, then
you are going to be the best hairdresser in Ellery." She patted my
hand so hard it started to sting. "So, you need to work with the
best."

"LuEllen," I warned.

"I know about the Homecoming fiasco, but that's water under
the bridge. You tell Delilah I sent you. She'll give you a job."

She took her hand from mine so she could curl it around her
cup of beer, and I saw something I hadn't seen before: LuEllen,
whether she knew it or not, was trying to kill herself.

It was as though she was out to damage her skin, her lungs,
and her liver—so much the better if she could get all three to

give out at once. That's the real reason she hadn't wanted me to come home. She didn't want me to see her slow march to suicide, and she had to be taking something to make her crazy if she thought for one minute Delilah was going to hire me.

About seven years ago, Delilah had screamed "Whore daughter of a whore!" at the Homecoming football game, her anger echoing over the hushed field while Roy Vandiver placed a tiara on my head. Sometimes I still woke up in a cold sweat, reliving the moment in my dreams. Some people had gasped. Far more had snickered. I had decided to leave town the day after graduation.

And now, at least according to the tabloids, I was proving her right.

"I don't think it's a good idea, so—"

"I don't give a rat's ass whether you think it's a good idea or not. You are going to march downtown and tell that woman that *I* sent you and she is going to give you a job."

I took a step back at her vehemence. It was the only flash of pride I'd seen from my mother in years. I had to do what she asked. Besides, what was the worst thing Delilah could do? Tell me no? Call me a whore again?

The woman had no idea how funny *that* was.

"All right. I'm going. Can I get you something while I'm out?"

She cocked her head to one side as though she'd never really considered that question. I thought of all the jobs she'd worked, most recently the convenience store off the highway, and how almost every cent went to me or Granny or keeping the lights on. At some point a few years ago she'd become "disabled" while moving boxes and those checks didn't go far. I still thought she'd mainly come up with the scheme so she could afford to stay home and keep an eye on Granny. By that time the old lady had dementia something horrible and was prone to wander off and get lost, but we didn't have the money for a nursing home or even a nurse to come check on her.

She smiled at the memory of something she'd once wanted, something that had obviously slipped through her fingers. For just a moment she looked her age, younger even, but then she trained her eyes on me. I expected something profound.

"You know, if you could swing some Bud Light instead of Natty Light, I would appreciate it."

Tears pricked my eyes, but I nodded and turned to go because I didn't trust my voice. I'd always had trouble with lines, but I was pretty darned good with cues.

"Presley Ann."

"Yeah?" I stopped at the door, but didn't turn around because I didn't want her to see the tear that had slipped down one cheek.

"You start with Delilah. You hear me?"

"Yes, ma'am."

The Firebird coughed and lurched all the way into town. I bypassed the parallel parking on Main Street and parked behind the buildings instead. I didn't want the Firebird to belch out smoke or, worse yet, backfire.

Everyone's going to know you're back and broke before sundown. No need to prolong the agony.

Still, pride's a funny thing, so I pulled into one of the far spaces in the back parking lot, knowing I could sneak into Delilah's shop through the back door. If I was lucky, she wouldn't even have customers yet.

Yeah, right.

I heaved the heavy car door shut, marveling at how warm it was. I didn't remember West Tennessee winters being this balmy. When I reached the salon's back door, I saw the soldier. He stood there in combat boots and camo fatigues with the name Banks over his chest. He didn't make a move to open the door for me. Odd. But once the hair on the back of my neck started to stand up, I knew.

He wasn't reaching for the door because he was a ghost.

"You can see me, can't you?" His blue eyes sparkled, and he grinned.

"Sure can." *But that doesn't mean I'm going to do anything about it. Couldn't if I wanted to. At least not on purpose.*

"Wait! You can't say that and just leave." He honestly looked confused. And handsome.

"Yeah, I can," I hissed. "I'm done with ghosts, and I couldn't help you if I wanted to."

There. I'd said it.

He tried to put his hand on my shoulder to stop me, but it went right through me, causing a full-body shiver.

"Don't do that!" I shrieked as I tried to shake off the foreign sensation.

"But you're the only person in town who can see me. And I keep walking away, but I always end up here again."

Over the years I'd learned that ghosts were often tied to one place or person. Gary in catering had loved his job over at the Universal lot so much that he hadn't been able to leave it. I'd actually liked Gary. Pinup Betty seemed stuck in my apartment. I still thought she should chip in for the rent.

But this guy? How long had he been standing here, stuck in the same loop? Did he even realize he was going through the same motions over and over again because there was something important that he needed to fix?

Unless he just *loved* hanging out at the Holy Roller back door.

Compassion got the best of me. "Here's the deal. You keep ending up here because something happened here that really bothers you, something unresolved."

"No shit. But how did you know that?"

"I'm a genius. Best I can tell, this is how it works: You figure out what's bugging you, get a living person to fix it, and bam! The light will appear and you can move on."

"That makes sense." He scratched the back of his head, and I wondered if he'd been shot there or if he was repeating a nervous tic from when he was alive.

"Get it? Got it? Good." I reached for the door, and he reached through me again.

"Will you stop that?"

"Sorry." He gave me such a sheepish grin, I couldn't be mad at him. Something about him looked so familiar. Had I graduated with a Banks who'd gone into the military?

"I'm gonna need you to help me."

"Oh, no. I told you I'm out of that business." The last thing I tried to "fix" went very, very wrong.

Or did it count if the ghost was the one trying to fix me?

"But you're the only one who can see me. If you don't help me, who will?"

"Fine. Whatever." *Please don't be a girlfriend I have to track down. Please don't be a girlfriend I have to track down. . . .*

"So my girlfriend was pregnant when I, well, when I died."

Oh, that's much better.

"I had a huge fight with my sister, too, so I don't think she's been looking after my kid. If I knew everyone was okay, I think I could, you know . . . be at peace."

Okay, that seems doable. "Who's your sister?"

"Delilah. She works here."

My breath whooshed out. "No can do. She hates me."

"Delilah?" He gave me a crooked grin. "She's all bark and no bite. A little bossy maybe, but—"

"Seriously. She hates me."

His grin faded, and he stepped backward, blending into the brick wall behind him. "Okay. I understand. Maybe if you can see me, someone else will, too."

I looked over my shoulder to see if anyone had witnessed my talking to thin air for the past few minutes. Blessedly, the back parking lot was empty. But the soldier was still there, and he looked as if he might cry. How could I walk off and leave him stuck there? I mean, he hadn't asked me to track down a stripper like that weirdo on Hollywood Boulevard that time.

"Fine. I'll do my best." *Even though she's not going to like it, and she's not going to believe me. They almost never do.*

He jumped forward from the wall, his ghost eyes bright. He couldn't have been more than eighteen when he died, not with that kind of enthusiasm. "I could kiss you! Just tell Delilah that Blake says he's sorry and he didn't mean any of the things he said. Got that?"

"Anything I could tell her that might make her believe me? Something only you and she knew?"

He thought about it for a minute and started to sing, something about having a sister whose head's like a rock.

"Is that Elvis?"

"Oh, yeah, it's 'Hard Headed Woman' but with different lyrics. That's how she'll know it's me."

"I'll tell her, but I'm not singing it."

He looked away for a second, and I would've sworn he was blushing. "Just tell her."

"And one more thing."

"No more things. I—"

"Just ask her to take care of my kid, would you?"

"All right. I'm going in, and you can go into the light or whatever."

He shielded his eyes. "I don't see a light."

"Maybe it'll show up after I tell her. The other ghosts tell me it's like a bright white circle that keeps getting bigger."

"I'll look. In the meantime, can I look at your Firebird?"

"Sure," I said. Wasn't like I could stop him. Or he could hurt the broken-down piece of crap.

"I knew someone who used to drive one a lot like that." I couldn't tell if his reverence was for the car or the guy who used to drive it. I was guessing the car. He looked like one of those guys.

I took several deep breaths to steel myself. Asking Delilah for a job was bad enough. Asking for a job and then telling her about her brother's ghost? That was a recipe for disaster.

I reached for the doorknob, but my hand dropped. I so did not want to do this.

My stomach chose that moment to growl, reminding me that I only had twenty dollars to my name and a mostly empty gas tank.

Okay, Pres. It's this or thumb it back to Hollywood and remind everyone of that less-than-kid-friendly thing you did.

I sure as heck didn't want to do that. No, I'd rather face Delilah than chance running into a certain producer.

My hand closed around the knob.

I am an actress.

I can act like Delilah doesn't scare the shit out of me.

And I entered stage right.

Declan

Caroline went to get a proper litter box and assorted cat paraphernalia, and I took care of Miss Sylvia and Miss Ginger. Once I had Miss Ginger ready, all I had to do was tuck her in the casket and close the lid. She had once warned me that she would haunt me for the rest of my natural-born days if I so much as thought about gussying her up and putting her on display. Miss Sylvia, on the other hand, had died rather unexpectedly and thus didn't get much say in the matter. She also didn't complain a bit, which is one of the reasons I sometimes preferred to work with the dead instead of the living.

I left the hair and some of the finer points of cosmetology to Delilah. She'd said she'd be around that evening after her shift, and I was more than willing to let her have the job. I mean, I *could* do hair, but I wasn't going to win any awards for it.

Satisfied that all was well in the prep room, I washed up and went to the kitchen. Caroline was at the table reading the paper with the cat snuggled in her lap.

"So. 'Throw that thing out,' huh?"

She had the grace to grin sheepishly. I poured a cup of coffee and topped off her cup before sitting down across from her. "Everything in place?"

Her smile faded as she folded the paper and put it down. "That Borden woman is . . . persistent. Polite, but persistent."

"Tell me about it. I went to school with her."

Caroline frowned. "She kept asking to work with you even after I told her you usually didn't work on arrangements. And she must have mentioned that Sally Hawkins thing at least twice."

"Sadie Hawkins." Since Ellery was positioned right in the buckle of the Bible Belt, dancing was not allowed because it might lead to . . . other things. For a couple of years, the Beta Club had sponsored a Sadie Hawkins Dinner to raise money for some charity or another. When Jessica Still, now Borden, had asked me, I told her that I would have to work visitation, which I couldn't possibly know yet. I did not tell her that I was still hoping Lacey Hutchens would ask me. Nor did I tell her that I wasn't about to go with a freshman. In retrospect, I probably should've just told her the truth because, all these years later, she was still having trouble taking the hint.

"Declan, she picked out the most expensive casket." She paused to let that information sink in. No one picked out the most expensive casket. According to Caroline, it was only there to help direct people to one of the models priced in the middle. I wouldn't have picked out the most expensive one for myself— and I could've had it at cost.

I took a sip of coffee. It was lukewarm. Time for another pot. "Now that you mention it, she did the same thing two years ago."

Caroline frowned. "She did?"

"Yeah. You were off at that funeral association convention in Nashville, and Sean and I handled the whole thing. I think that was for her grandmother, though."

"I remember that! Now she's left taking care of her parents. I've heard they're not doing well, either."

I felt another twinge of sympathy for adding to her grief.

"Now, Declan. You're always complaining about not being able to find a date, and the woman has been throwing herself at you."

"Well, now she's married. To someone else."

Caroline slumped. "I keep forgetting about that."

It was hard for me to forget, because she'd sent me an invitation a couple of years ago. Yet another awkward spot to be in, courtesy of Jessica Borden.

"So sad about her losing her mother-in-law so soon after her father-in-law."

We had just buried Mr. Borden a few weeks before, but life was funny like that. It wasn't unusual for spouses to die close together—especially if they'd been married for some time.

"Declan, why don't you hop across the street and ask Mrs. Morris if she's missing a kitten? We really shouldn't keep this little fella, and I sure don't want to hear any more about mummified cats."

And that's how I ran into Mrs. Morris and her run-over mama cat. As we stood in the middle of Maple Avenue looking down at the victim, her owner tried to be philosophical about losing the gray tabby. "She was a good cat, Declan."

I patted Mrs. Morris on the arm, a force of habit. "Do you want me to take care of her?"

Why in the blue hell had I asked that?

Because you are a sucker.

And because Mrs. Morris shouldn't be burying cats—not while still in her terry-cloth robe because she'd had a hip replacement last month and was still recovering.

"Oh, I couldn't possibly ask you to do that." As she said it, she brought a gnarled and palsied hand to her face.

The woman had watched Sean and me after school in the years between my mother's death and Caroline's coming. She made a mean coconut cake. I put an arm around her shoulders and pointed her back in the direction of her house across the street. "I'll put her in that little patch of grass behind the carriage house, how about that?"

"Declan, that would be so kind of you. I'll have to make you one of those coconut cakes you like so much."

Still a hit with the little old ladies. "You don't have to do that, Mrs. Morris."

"I know that, but I want to. Smokey was a good houser."

"Houser?"

"You know, one of those cats that keeps the mice out of your house."

Mrs. Morris often got words mixed up, a bit like Dad and his "mell of a hess." It was best not to correct her if I wanted her to do me a favor. Or bake a coconut cake. "Speaking of Smokey, did she have any kittens, by any chance? Maybe a yellow one?"

Mrs. Morris thought about it. "She had a litter a while back, but I've almost given them all away. Not a yellow one in the bunch."

"Oh. Would you like a kitten?"

She laughed. "Honey, I already have five, and I'm trying to get rid of two of them. Those cats eat more than I do!"

Well. I couldn't add to Mrs. Morris's grocery bill, now could I?

Woman had the audacity to reach up and pinch my cheeks. "You need a pet, Declan. You keep that kitten."

And with that she walked up the driveway with more pep in her step than the average elderly lady who'd recently had a hip replacement. Then she remembered she was supposed to be old and decrepit and slowed down while reaching for her back.

Well played, Mrs. Morris.

At least I was going to get a coconut cake out of the deal.

A few minutes later, I'd managed to carefully remove poor Smokey from the road and was shoveling dirt behind the carriage house. Now I was burying pets for free. This is what I'd come to.

I had a vision of wandering the streets with a wheelbarrow, shouting, "Bring out your dead!" just like in that Monty Python movie. I could be Dec Anderson, Pet Undertaker. Why limit it to pets? Hell, bring me that squirrel you ran over last week, maybe a possum who could sit up and say, "I'm not dead yet" in a British accent.

Clearly, I'd lost it.

Or had I? Hadn't I just been reading an article in one of the trade journals that talked about how some funeral homes were branching out into pet burial as a way to supplement income? We even had a little piece of property by the old Ellery City Cemetery that we could make into a pet cemetery.

Caroline was always looking for new ways to increase revenue, so . . .

Wait. That idea didn't work too well for the characters in that Stephen King book.

Of course, if Caroline didn't want to have any part of my ideas for installing a crematory, she wouldn't want to hear about pet burial. And wouldn't most folks want to keep Fluffy's ashes in an urn instead of taking him to a plot?

If so, then that crematory was sounding like a better idea all the time.

But we'd have to have *two* crematoriums, one for people and one for pets. We didn't have the money for even one.

At this point, I was sweaty, but I had a hole deep enough for dearly departed Smokey. I gently laid the old girl in the grave and felt compelled to say a couple of words on her behalf.

"To Smokey, an excellent . . . houser!"

When I smoothed the last bit of dirt over the cat's grave and surveyed my handiwork, I had a revelation: At least I could now add grave digger to my resume.

Presley

I passed through the darkened hall to the front of the Holy Roller. It seemed Delilah only used the front of the salon these days. She'd decorated for Christmas, adding garlands, lights, and a tree that was too big for the window. To my chagrin, she did have a customer, an elderly lady getting a wash and set.

I sucked in a breath at the sight of something else sitting in the front window: a HELP WANTED sign. At least I had an excuse. Maybe LuEllen had even seen the sign and that's why she'd sent me here.

"If you're looking for a haircut, I don't have anything open until later this week." Delilah didn't look up. Self-preservation made me hesitate before speaking. I didn't want to repeat the Homecoming incident.

"You hard of hearing, Miss Priss?" Her already thin lips stretched into a smaller line.

"No, ma'am. I saw the HELP WANTED sign in the front window, and I was wondering if I could apply for a job."

Finally, she looked up, her eyes widening then narrowing as she recognized me. She snorted and turned her attention back to styling hair, pulling so hard she was yanking the lady's head left then right. The lady said nothing. She was made of sterner stuff, a relic from the Greatest Generation.

Finally, Delilah took off the cape and shook it out with a snap that made me jump. She murmured niceties to her customer and took the money. We both watched the older lady's painful progress toward the door. The minute it closed behind her, Delilah turned on me.

"You've got a lot of nerve coming in here," she growled. "I may have an opening, but it's not going to the likes of you. I bet you only play-act at cutting hair."

I swallowed hard. "I went to beauty school in California. I have my credentials in my purse if you want to see them."

She stepped closer, and I willed myself to stand stock straight and not cower before her.

"I don't care if you studied with Vidal Sassoon and Paul Mitchell put together. I'm not hiring you. Ever."

Tears pricked my eyes, and my stomach growled. Damned if I didn't get teary when I was hungry. Deranged woman. It wasn't my fault I beat out her niece for Homecoming Queen. I turned to go, but some perverse part of me had to add, "LuEllen sent me."

Delilah's knuckles went white where she was holding the broom. Her face mottled with rage. "You tell LuEllen that I said she could go to hell."

I walked down the hallway at something just shy of a run. A few steps from the door, I saw the silhouette of my new friend the soldier.

He can tell her himself.

Stopping dead in my tracks, I sucked in a huge breath. But he wouldn't because he couldn't. And who else could help him?

That's not my problem, now is it?

But if I didn't tell her, he might start following me around. I wasn't going to tell him about this little exception to the ghostly rules of place, but he might figure it out. Lord knows I did not need another Pinup Betty on my hands. I'd had to go all the way to Tennessee to get rid of her.

And what difference did it make if Delilah didn't believe me? She was already mad at me anyway.

If I told her, she would probably tell everyone in town what a total psycho I was. Then I'd sure enough have a hard time getting a job.

Outside the soldier swayed a little. Did ghosts ever get tired feet?

"You gonna just stand there trespassing? I can call the police." *Old biddy.*

I wheeled around and stalked down the hall until I towered over my nemesis. "Miss Delilah, I have one more thing to tell you before I go. There's a man outside who wanted me to give you a message. He said he's your brother and he's sorry for what he said to you and he didn't mean a word of it."

She blanched and slumped against the broom she was holding. Then color flooded her face. "How. Dare. You."

She picked up the broom with shaking hands. For a minute I thought she might chase me with it. "Get out of here! What did I ever do to you?"

No one had ever reacted this violently. I started backing down the hallway. "I didn't mean to upset you, I swear. I don't even know why you hate me."

She advanced. I retreated.

"That's just what he told me. That and something about having a sister with a head like a rock. He sang that."

She froze.

Should I admit I knew her brother was a ghost? Sometimes I admitted that in sympathetic company. Delilah was the very definition of *un*sympathetic company. That said, Delilah was beginning to look like a believer.

Putting my hands up in surrender, I blurted out the rest so I could leave and never, ever come back. "He also asked you to find his kid and take care of him. But that's all I know."

"LuEllen put you up to this, didn't she?"

"No, ma'am. I mean, she told me you had an opening, but that's it."

"LuEllen's an expert in openings," Delilah muttered. Her beady eyes squinted to almost nonexistent slits as she searched down to my soul. "Based on the magazines at the store, looks like you are, too."

I flinched, and my stomach chose that moment to growl. Loudly.

Delilah looked down at it and back up to me. "But you're not much like her, are you?"

"No, ma'am. Not really."

My stomach growled again, this time roaring its displeasure.

"Hungry, are you?"

"Haven't had time to go to the store." *Or the money.*

Her thin lips curled up into a Grinchish smile. "I may have just the job for you."

"Oh?" She was hiring me? After threatening to beat me with a broom? This had to be a trick. My head throbbed from ghosts, angry beauty shop owners, hunger, and the teensiest bit of a hangover.

"You want the job or not?" Her nostrils flared. I flinched.

My stomach growled for a third time. I remembered that food service uniforms didn't flatter me in the least and I totally sucked at retail. "Yes, ma'am."

"Take that case over there and be sure you show up at the funeral home at six this evening. Consider it your audition."

Oh, good. Working with the dead. My favorite.

But even Pinup Betty was an improvement over an angry Delilah, and no one but me could hear any complaints from the dead. "You can count on me."

"Yeah, yeah. Make sure you go to the back door." She reached into her apron for something, then pressed the paper into my palm, her own hand still shaking with anger. I looked down to see a crumpled twenty. "Get something to eat, for God's sake. Consider it an advance."

Then she stomped down the hall, leaving me to wonder what had just happened.

Declan

By early evening, the wind howled and rain slammed into the house in sheets. I'd already sent Caroline home even though I had to pry her away from the computer. I had no idea that much accounting needed to be done.

I was beginning to wonder if Delilah would show. Usually, she called me if something came up, but the weather was bad. The temps were dropping and the forecasters were calling for thunderstorms and even the possibility of funnel clouds.

Someone rapped at the back door. "About damn time."

Instead of Delilah, an oddly familiar blond goddess stood on the stoop getting drenched. I resisted the urge to pinch myself. Presley Cline?

"May I come in?"

"Please." I stepped aside, willing words to come but, no, I'd lost the ability to word.

"I'm here from the Holy Roller," she said. "For Mrs. Borden."

"I thought . . ."

She winced. "Delilah was supposed to come, but I was looking for a job, and she sent me instead. I hope that's okay."

"Okay?" Great. I could only say one word at a time in this woman's presence. That was going to work out well.

"I can call her instead if you—"

"No! I just wasn't expecting you."

"You don't think I can do it. I'll just go. This was a stupid idea."

"No, no. I didn't mean that at all. Please stay. Let's start over." I extended my hand. I cleared my throat and willed it to use my funeral director tone. "Declan Anderson. Thank you for coming."

"I know who you are," she said with a grin that made my heart land somewhere around my feet. "It's me, Presley. As if I would forget the person who helped me pass geometry!"

Oh, dear God, she remembers.

"Oh, I remember you. I thought you might've forgotten me, you being famous and all."

"Famous?" She snorted, and even that was cute. "I did a few commercials, and I was really good at playing damsels in distress. And corpses."

Something pinched in my chest. I couldn't help but smile.

Her cheeks went pink, "I mean—"

"I know what you mean. As much as I'd love to talk, the weather isn't getting any nicer, so I guess we'd better get you to work."

Although I would love *to know why you're here doing this.*

She sighed with relief. "Yeah. They say it's only going to get nastier."

With my back turned as I led her across the kitchen to the prep room, it was easier to slip into funeral director default mode. "Have you worked with the deceased before?"

She laughed. "You don't have to be so formal. I did some work for a funeral home back in Los Angeles."

I opened the door for her and let her enter. "Well, the only catch is the daughter-in-law specifically requested Delilah since that's who used to do Miss Sylvia's hair. Think you can figure it out?"

"Oh, I'm sure I can," she said. She hesitated for a minute before she brushed past me. It was as though she saw something down the hall, but I didn't see a thing when I looked.

"Do you want me to stay with you?" I asked when she didn't make a move to step farther into the room. She shook her head no and walked to the table with squared shoulders.

"I can handle it. Pretty sure she isn't going to complain about my work."

I couldn't help but grin at her gallows humor. "I'll be across the hall finishing up some paperwork if you need me."

"No problem. Don't worry a bit. It's going to be just like getting ready for the prom," she said. "Yep, an old lady prom. For dead people."

Her shaky breath betrayed her, but I couldn't help admiring her stoicism. So many people ran screaming from the thought of styling a dead person's hair. I hadn't thought I could like Presley Cline any more, but I was wrong.

I turned but then had a thought. "Oh, Miss Ginger has requested a closed casket, so she's going sans makeup."

Presley arched an eyebrow. "Bold. I like it."

And I liked her. I couldn't look away from the gorgeous leggy woman who wasn't recoiling from my world.

"Think you ought to get started on that paperwork?"

"Ah, sure. Call me if you need me." I ducked down the hall with what little dignity I had left.

Smooth move, jackass.

I hadn't been that tongue-tied since Callie Westwood flashed me in junior high.

Without a bra.

Right before my presentation on Woodrow Wilson, who ended up not being the only woody in the room that day.

In my mind, Presley Cline flashed me, and it was spectacular.

Declan Anderson, you are one sad sonuvabitch. Maybe you need to get out more. Maybe get naked more.

And, in other news, snow was cold.

Yes, the dating pool in Ellery was shallow. At the moment, it kinda looked like a mud puddle and Presley was rising from it, like that *Birth of Venus* painting.

Just be cool.

I sank into my chair and attempted to focus on some paperwork. At the moment Presley was employed by Anderson's Funeral Home, which made me her boss and the situation dicey. Then there was the fact that she'd been splashed all over the rags at the grocery store. I could just hear Caroline reminding me of our reputation and how we didn't need to get mixed up with someone who'd been caught doing the walk of shame.

Even if Sean showed up to take over—and it was supposed to be any day now—any girl I dated might be saddled with a ridiculous name, like Mrs. Cold Fingers. That wasn't even counting the worst-case scenario of what had happened to my mother.

Leave Mom out of this. You're not going to put any woman—much less Presley Cline—in that situation.

But that pinch in my chest and that gasp of air when I saw her? That's what Dad used to describe. He'd say, "I took one look at your mother, and I knew."

The combination of the storm outside and thinking of my mother took me back in time to when I was eight and Sean was just a baby. Thunder woke me up that night, and I thought I'd sneak down to the kitchen for a glass of water, maybe sweet tea if everyone was asleep and there was enough in the pitcher that no one would notice in the morning. I crept down the stairs, stopping short on the bottom step when I heard voices arguing.

"Patrick, I can't do this anymore."

"Lucy, what are you talking about?"

"This." She paused for dramatic effect and I dared glance in the direction of the room where they were arguing. I couldn't see her, only her shadow from where she stood just inside the Freesia Room. "You told me I wouldn't have to raise the kids in this . . . this . . . death house."

"That was before money got so tight, darlin'. It's not so bad, is it? I was raised here. If things keep going the way they've been going, we'll get the down payment for a house soon."

"It's more than that. I hate this life." She broke into tears. "People in town look at me funny. It's always so gloomy in here, and you're out at all times of day and night."

"Darlin', these things have never bothered you before." I could tell from how they formed one blob of a shadow that my father had embraced my mother.

"It's good business," he soothed as the shadow in the doorway rocked gently from side to side. "It's business that needs to be done."

"The ladies won't let me bring a dish to the potluck because it would come from *this* kitchen."

"Oh, Lucy. Don't you think they're more worried about how busy you are with the new baby? I've never heard such a thing before."

"They say things about us, Patrick."

I couldn't hear the rest of what she said because her voice was all muffled sobs at that point.

Her complaints made no sense to me as an eight-year-old boy. After all, life in the funeral home was all I'd ever known.

Even as a grown man I couldn't understand why she did what she did. The doctor said she had a mental problem or some kind of depression. Caroline had once told me she thought my mom had had really bad postpartum depression but that people didn't know so much about it back then. People could call it whatever they wanted to, but that didn't make it any easier to explain.

I forced myself to focus on the paperwork. This is why I was destined to be an old cat man: I didn't want to find Presley Cline or anybody else hanging from one of the cellar rafters.

Presley

I looked over my shoulder to make sure Declan had left, then turned my attention to the two ghosts in the corner. Miss Sylvia rocked back and forth, wringing her hands almost as though she didn't realize she was dead. I had seen enough to be able to replicate her hair and makeup, but the rocking was making me nutty.

I crouched in front of her ghost self, careful not to touch her. "Miss Sylvia, are you okay? You're really making me nervous, and I need to know what shade of lipstick you want to wear."

She rocked on, muttering under her breath. "That damn salad. It had to be the salad."

"Miss Sylvia?"

"She's not going to answer you."

At the sound of that tart voice, I stood up straight and my hands automatically went to proper piano position. I only took four years of lessons, but those were the two things that my teacher preached the entire time. Sure enough, Miss Ginger Belmont, my former piano teacher, now stood in the middle of the room.

"Miss Ginger! You scared the bejeezus out of me!"

"Good. You were slouching. Besides, I can't help it if I'm walking through walls." She took a seat next to Miss Sylvia and turned to her. "You are going to have to snap out of this!"

"The salad. It had to be the salad."

Miss Ginger looked up at me. "Obviously, you can see ghosts. Have you ever seen anything like this before?"

"No, ma'am. I'm afraid I haven't. Have you?"

Miss Ginger pursed her lips. "Of course not! I've never been dead before."

I opened my case and went to work on the corporeal Miss Sylvia's makeup. "Me neither, but I've always been able to see ghosts. There's one who used to live in your house."

"Oh?"

"Handsome young man in a navy uniform. Used to follow you around wherever you went."

Miss Ginger cocked her head to one side, studying me in that way of hers. "That right?"

"Yep. He told me he'd go into the light if I'd fish some book out from behind the chifforobe in your bedroom. That's why I was back there that time."

Miss Ginger's mouth hung open. "That's why you were in there? That's where it came from?"

"Some old book of poetry," I said with a shrug. "I didn't mind that you didn't want to give me lessons anymore. I wasn't very good at playing the piano anyway."

"You sweet girl," she murmured. "I wish you'd told me."

"I don't think you would've believed me."

"No, you're probably right. But thank you. I always did think there was something special about you."

"Oh, Miss Ginger. I'm just trailer trash. I tried to go off and make something of myself, but it hasn't worked out so well." I looked from Miss Sylvia's body to her ghost and back again. Her ghost moaned piteously.

"You're about as bad as Beulah," Miss Ginger said.

I wanted to laugh at the comparison, but I didn't want Miss Ginger to think I was laughing at the infamous Beulah Land. To most people, she was the "good" girl turned "bad" while I was the "bad" girl turned "good." She was just enough older than me to have been one of my mother's cautionary tales.

"Silly girl. You never had to run off to prove anything, you know."

My hand holding the eyeliner jerked, making one of Miss Sylvia's eyes look positively Egyptian. I'd never really thought about it like that, but I supposed Miss Ginger was right. I'd always thought I had to prove something. Well, the earth didn't stop turning when I gave up and came home, now did it?

"Thank you, Miss Ginger," I said as I removed my mistake and started over.

"Just calling 'em as I see 'em," the older lady said with a shrug. "I would tell you life is short, but I made a pretty long go of it. Still, I wasted a whole lot of time trying to please other people instead of myself. Once I figured out I didn't have to please anyone but me, I was already shriveled up and out of energy."

Now *that* was a cautionary tale.

"I wasn't ready to go," moaned Miss Sylvia.

"As if any of us ever are," snapped Miss Ginger. "You need to get ahold of yourself."

Despite the harsh words, she was trying to pat Miss Sylvia's ghost's shoulder, not that it was working very well. I left any comforting to her and concentrated on my job of hair and makeup. While I worked, I had to wonder. I could see Miss Sylvia had been traumatized, probably by the suddenness of her death, but that didn't explain why someone as levelheaded as Miss Ginger was still sticking around. So I asked her.

"I don't know," she said. "I thought I was ready to go, or as ready as I'd ever be."

"Anything eating at you?"

She thought about it for a long minute. "I would say I'm here because I need to make sure that casket stays closed, but there is one thing I was too chicken to tell Beulah."

And that one thing was keeping her tethered to the earth. I sighed. I'd survived talking to Delilah. How hard could it be to talk to Beulah? "Do you want me to deliver a message?"

"Oh, I couldn't put you to any trouble," Miss Ginger said.

"You'll probably be stuck here as long as it bothers you."

She thought about it while I surveyed my handiwork and put away the tools of my trade. Finally, she spoke. "Guess I was too much of a coward to add this to my letter to her, but could you tell Beulah I said to make up with her mother?"

Oh, sure. That wasn't scary at all. Everyone in town knew Beulah's parents had tossed her out when she got pregnant. I took a deep breath. "Is there something I could tell her so she would know the message was coming from you?"

"Call her Beulah Lou," she said. "And tell her to do it for herself since I used up all the favors I wanted her to do for me."

"Okay. I'll do it."

I felt the light behind me, not daring to look over my shoulder because I knew it would blind me.

"Oh! Now that's more like it," Ginger said. "C'mon, Sylvia, you're coming with me."

Miss Sylvia moaned, but she didn't argue when Miss Ginger took her by the arm and dragged her in the direction of the light.

At the edge, my former piano teacher turned back, already looking younger, beautiful even, in her starched dress, bright red lipstick, and victory rolls that reminded me of Pinup Betty's. "You promise you'll tell her?"

"I promise."

"Well, thank you. Now get on home. I didn't like the sound of that storm."

"Good thing I just finished then," I said with a smile. "Take care, Miss Ginger. You, too, Miss Sylvia."

The portal closed and I blinked my eyes against the brightness that had been there only a few seconds before.

So much for not helping any more ghosts for any other reason. *It's not like Miss Ginger is Betty. Really.*

I zipped up the massive case that Delilah had given me that morning and padded down the hall to where Dec Anderson sat behind his desk. He was taller than I remembered, and more . . . dour?

He looked over the top of his reading glasses as if he'd heard what I was thinking. "Are you leaving?"

"I thought you might want to inspect my work first."

He nodded and took off the glasses as he scooted his leather chair back from the desk. I put Delilah's case on the chair by the door and walked with him down the hall.

"That was fast," he said.

"I work quickly," I said.

He whistled from the doorway. "You are good! I normally don't remember a lot of details, but I'd put money on that being just how Miss Sylvia looked the last time I saw her. How did you do it?"

"Lucky guess?"

He lifted a dark eyebrow and studied me as though looking for a different explanation. No doubt he'd learned how to do hair and makeup in mortuary school, but the last funeral director I'd worked with had been sure to tell me that just because he *could* didn't mean he *should*. I pegged Dec Anderson for being that kind of guy.

"Miss Cline, you are full of surprises."

You really have no idea.

He stuck his hand in his pocket, and his jacket inched backward to reveal a peek of suspenders. I sucked in a breath. I'd had a thing for suspenders ever since I'd met the ghost of a wannabe Rat Pack member.

"Let me get your check so you can go home," Dec said as he walked back to his office. "I can't believe such a warm day has turned so nasty."

I nodded, following him. He took out a binder full of checks and reached into a desk drawer for a pen. "Sorry to be so old-fashioned, but Caroline isn't into online banking or even running checks through the printer."

"No problem."

It occurred to me I didn't know if he needed to make the check out to me or to Delilah. I didn't even know how much I was going to get paid.

You are an idiot, Presley. You would be better off working for a company with applications and—

"What's that?" I asked as an eerie moan sounded somewhere outside the house.

"Surely not in December," Dec muttered. He put his pen down and reached for a small radio. It had to be a weather radio like Granny used to always keep with her.

At first all we heard was static, then, ". . . Giles, Cleburne, or Yessum County, you should immediately take shelter. Tornados have been spotted to the southwest of Jefferson. Again if you are in Crump, Giles, Cleburne or Yes—"

"Come on!" He grabbed my hand as his desk light flickered and went out. The moan of the siren mixed with the howl of the wind as Dec put the radio in his pocket. We ran toward the back door, but a crash outside made Dec stop.

I clenched his arm with my other hand. "What are you doing?"

"Cellar's safer, but we'd have to go outside to get there," he muttered before dragging me back to a closet beneath the stairs. He tossed aside a stack of coats and rolled out a vacuum cleaner. The hairs on the back of my neck pricked again, but I already knew a ghost was there and that Dec couldn't see him. I looked at the front door in spite of myself and the ghost of a man in a Confederate uniform stopped pacing long enough to stare through me. As a rule, ghosts didn't scare me, but the yellow-gray light from the transom window illuminating the hatred-fueled expression of a bearded man with an empty sleeve? That was enough to spook anyone.

Dec pulled me inside the tiny closet, and we had to shimmy inside to close the door because it opened inward. The small space smelled of mothballs with a hint of cedar. I tripped over something on the closet floor, and my hands instinctively flew up to Dec's chest while one of his hands splayed across my back to steady me.

My heart thudded recklessly. As much as I wanted to tell myself I was scared of the tornado, I knew it was something else. The last time I had been this close to a man, it had ended . . . badly.

"I'm sure it'll blow over," he murmured.

I closed my eyes and reminded myself that this was Declan Anderson. He was one of the people who'd been so kind when Granny died. He had also tutored me in geometry every Wednesday for an entire semester after he'd come back from funeral director school in Nashville. He'd been so subdued then.

Yes, I would think about those Wednesdays.

Back then my heart had beat so quickly because he was handsome and recently back from college, while I was a sophomore in high school. It's a wonder I could concentrate on anything he was saying because my hormones were out of control. That was back when attraction felt more like anticipation than apprehension, back when I still harbored hope of a romance with a fairy-tale ending. Declan had always been the perfect gentleman, never so much as letting his leg brush against mine. I blushed thinking about it, especially about how Kari Land figured out I had a crush on him and teased me about having a thing for Cold Fingers.

He must've seen you as nothing more than a little girl, Presley.

The house shook. A lot of somethings fell from the shelf above us. Dec pushed me deeper into the corner, grunting as his back took the brunt of the falling objects. Now one arm cradled my back while the other cupped the back of my head to keep it from slamming into the wall. He moved that hand gently to the wall beside my face. His whole body loomed over me in a way that should've scared me, but it was a delicate protectiveness instead.

The closet door rattled on its hinges, bringing me back to the severity of the moment. The roaring wind reminded me the tornado could lift off the roof and hurl us into the night sky in an instant. The closet door popped open into the closet, and I gasped. Dec slammed it shut with his foot. His whole body shifted forward until his stubbled cheek rested against mine.

Hysterical laughter threatened to bubble up, but I tamped it down. If I turned to the right just a little I could fulfill my fifteen-year-old fantasies and kiss him.

Heck, you should kiss him now. You could die at any minute.

My head turned slightly, my lips brushing against his rough

cheek. His breath hitched, and mine did, too. In my mind I begged him to turn his face a little, just enough for his lips to touch mine. If I were going out of this world, I wanted to go out in style.

But he didn't move. He held himself so still. Maybe he hadn't been a gentleman all those years ago. Maybe he wasn't attracted to me.

You have lost your ever-loving mind. This was what fear did to a person, wasn't it? I could not seriously be worrying about whether or not Declan Anderson thought I was pretty while we were stuck in a closet with the world going to hell all around us. And what if he did think I was pretty? It wasn't like I was sticking around town. I had no business stirring up any more trouble.

Then he turned his head slowly, his jawbone scraping against my lips. Just as his lips were about to reach mine, I turned my head, which left him with a mouthful of hair.

Declan

She saved you from yourself.

Even as I told myself I was grateful I hadn't actually kissed Presley, my pride smarted. I should've known better, though. No way a movie star would want to kiss a funeral director.

Although I would always be sharply dressed on the red carpet.

Well dressed, yes, but I'd look like her dad. I wasn't that much older than her, but I had tutored her in geometry. And I was, at least in the moment, her boss.

Her hair smelled of honeysuckle, and something about that combination of wild and sweet fit. I backed away from her as best I could, but the closet hadn't grown any larger, and I sure as heck wasn't ready to take a look outside.

The wind whistled and something above us popped, a sickening sound like a breaking bone.

"You're crushing me. A little."

"Oh, sorry." I'd drawn her closer at the sound. "Are you okay?"

"Fine. You?"

"Fine. Just trying to, you know—"

"Save my life?"

I shifted to give her as much space as I could. Less than a foot separated us. Outside it had gone eerily quiet. "I don't know about that."

"I do."

I wanted to kiss her. I wanted to kick myself for wanting to kiss her.

Take a hint. She's not interested.

"None of the stuff that fell hit you, did it?"

"No," she said, but she gave me a ragged sigh.

"Claustrophobic?"

"Something like that. Can we go?"

"Not yet."

She shifted, and I resisted the urge to reach for her.

"I don't hear anything. Please?"

"Give it a minute. We don't want to leave the closet only to get hit by falling debris. I remember once—" I stopped. She didn't need to hear any of my gruesome tales.

"Once what?"

"It's work stuff. I don't know why I started to tell you that."

"Go ahead. I need the distraction." She breathed deeply in a rhythmic pattern that told me she was struggling not to panic.

"Well, two years ago a tornado went through the trailer park on the other side of Harlowe Bottom. Sarge MacKenzie decided it was calm enough for him to check on things. His trailer had been ripped in half, but he'd been in the bathtub under a mattress. He steps out in nothing but a bathrobe just as a branch came flying through and took his head clean off. They found it in his back-yard."

"What'd you do?"

I searched her voice for disgust, but all I heard was curiosity and . . . compassion? I couldn't tell if that compassion was for me or Sarge, but I'd take it. "I can work miracles with wax, and shirt collars can be very forgiving."

"Well, I don't want to test your expertise, so I guess I'd better stay put."

She went back to those deliberate breaths, and I kicked myself for telling such a gruesome tale. "Are you sure you're going to be okay?"

"Don't have much of a choice, now do I?" she snapped.

I could understand not wanting platitudes, so I shut up. Beyond the door was an eerie calm, but I wasn't about to pull a Sarge.

"I'm sorry. I don't like tight spaces."

I reached for her arm and followed it down to her hand, which I took with a squeeze. "I think the storm has almost passed."

Her body vibrated. I wanted to pull her close until she calmed down, but that would be weird.

Weirder than almost kissing her?

I had to get out of there before I did something even more stupid.

I forced myself to let go of her hand and squeezed to the side so I could open the door. Some numb-nuts had put the hinges on so the damn thing opened inward. I made a note to fix that—assuming there was enough of the funeral home left to worry about such things.

"I'm going first. If anything knocks my head off, please tell Caroline to give me a pumpkin and pretend I'm the Headless Horseman."

She giggled, as I had hoped she would.

But then I stepped out into the hall.

The storm had blown the front door open, but the foyer was still intact. At least that's what I was gathering as my eyes adjusted to the total darkness of a world without electricity. I still had a roof over my head, that much I could see.

I walked toward the door to close it and looked to see what damage had been done to the newer chapel addition. A huge chunk of the roof was gone, its contents either blown away or scattered.

"Sonuvabitch!"

The roof on the portico had been peeled back all the way to the prep room. At least the prep room was still intact. That would've been more than we could handle. I know Grandpa Floyd used to embalm folks in their homes, but it wasn't a tradition I was looking to reinstate.

"What?" Presley poked her head out of the closet then ducked back in.

"I was just about to pay off the chapel, and now look at it." I rubbed my hand over my face. At least we were alive. At least we had insurance. At least the rest of the house was still there.

I walked to the front door and started to step outside, stopping short as I realized I didn't have much of a porch. Several of the individual porch boards had been pried loose. One of the slats had landed between two branches of the old oak tree in the front yard. Trees, branches, even a picket fence gate littered the street in front of me. Saddest of all, a garland of tinsel had blown against the oak tree, reminding us all of Christmas. Nothing bad's supposed to happen at Christmas.

But it often does.

Soft rain pattered the ground as if consoling the earth for the violence of a few minutes before. I closed the door on the world. Presley, stuck in a daze, followed me from room to room as I inspected the damage. The chapel was a mess, but the prep room was intact, Miss Ginger and Miss Sylvia included. The upstairs showed no damage from the inside, but I guessed the pop I heard earlier was a branch hitting the roof. We'd be lucky if the roof damage was only minor.

"Cleo!"

"LuEllen!"

We said the names at the same time.

"What?" Presley scrambled after me as I headed through the kitchen for the pantry. I could hear the kitten howling before I reached the door. When I opened it, she dashed out of the room but then backtracked to my feet and sat down to yowl at me until I picked her up.

Holding the trembling cat against me I saw Presley was standing at the back door, her mouth hanging open. I moved to look over her shoulder, not sure I wanted to see.

A branch might've hit my roof, but a whole tree had landed on Presley's car, denting the top and busting glass out of the windows. She shook. "That car's all I had, other than LuEllen."

I put down the cat and drew her close. "It's just a car, and I'll take you to find LuEllen. We'll go in my truck."

I took her by the hand and led her through the prep room to what was left of the portico, but the tree that had crushed Presley's car was also blocking my truck.

The hearse, on the other hand, sat under a half-demolished portico just as pretty as you please.

"Looks like we're taking the Caddy."

Presley

I was riding in a hearse to a trailer park through the aftermath of a tornado. *Please, God, don't let this be prophetic.*

Dec wound through town avoiding some streets and sometimes having to turn around to find a different way. He managed a U-turn that I almost applauded, but I was too worried about LuEllen. Even if the trailer had survived the tornado, it'd be a minor miracle if she didn't somehow manage to blow the place up. The first thing she would want was a cigarette. The first thing she would need would be her oxygen tank.

"It's number four," I whispered. I'd finally told him which trailer park even though I really didn't want Declan Anderson to see the craphole where I'd grown up.

Do you really think he cares that you live in a trailer?

The minute we topped the hill, I wanted to kick myself for such petty worries.

The first two trailers had been ripped open as if a giant had needed a new dollhouse. The third trailer sat in exactly the same spot it always had, unscratched. Trailer number four? Upside down.

"LuEllen!" I shouted as I ran to the opposite side of the trailer and tried to open the door. What should have been the top of the door was mired in the earth beneath it. I tugged and tugged, making a deeper jag in the mud but no progress. Dec touched my shoulders, and I jumped out of my skin.

"Sorry. I just wanted to give you a hand."

I stepped out of his way. "Thank you."

He looked at me curiously, seemingly hurt that I'd flinched when he touched me. I didn't have the time or the inclination to explain it to him. He pushed against the trailer with his shoulder while pulling on the door and managed to wedge it open enough for us to slip inside.

Popcorn ceiling crumbled underneath my feet, and I had to walk around the light fixture as well as the furniture that had fallen to the ceiling haphazardly. My eyes darted to the counter where LuEllen usually sat and then to the floor/ceiling beneath it, but I didn't see her crumpled body underneath the broken mass of stools. Down the hall I crept, wondering if at any moment I would see her ghost. Then I would know. Or had she already died and gone into the light without saying good-bye?

I choked back a sob at the thought and tiptoed down the hall, feeling as though I'd stepped through a broken looking glass. In the master bedroom, the bed lay with its feet in the air like a beetle on its back. A whimper told me LuEllen was under there somewhere.

"Dec!" The word came out strangled, but he must've heard. He was already there and lifting the bed enough for me to help LuEllen out. She held a limp arm to her chest and had a glassy-eyed expression that could've been shock. It also could've been a mixture of beer and sleeping pills. I went to hug her but stopped short.

My mother wore nothing but a gauzy red teddy that left nothing to the imagination.

I gaped at her, but she held her chin up high. Dec spied an equally transparent robe on the floor and lifted a corner of the chest to retrieve it. "You must be cold, Mrs. Cline."

Did nothing bother the man?

"Thank you," she said with a sniff. "I think I may need to go to the hospital for this arm."

I drew my cell from my pocket to call for help and went to search the closet for something more appropriate—a robe at least—but the bathroom next door had somehow flooded everything in her tiny closet. I picked up my duffel from the next room so I would at least have underwear then returned to find something for LuEllen.

"Let me step outside and see if I can get a signal," Dec said after I hung up for the third time to try again.

"Thanks!" I turned to LuEllen's dresser, but the flick of a lighter had me turning toward her. "What are you doing?"

"I need a smoke!"

"Where's your tank?"

"I don't know!" The cigarette fell out of her mouth, and the area under her bed caught fire. For just a sec I froze, entranced by the sudden sheet of flames.

Then I came to my senses and grabbed LuEllen's good arm, pulling her outside.

We squeezed through the door just as a boom happened at the back of the house. I leveled LuEllen with a stare and then turned to watch our trailer burn. Panting as though I'd run a race, I bent over to clear my head of the dizziness. Now I really had . . . nothing.

It's not like it's the first time. Pull yourself together.

"What the hell?" Declan said as he appeared beside me.

"My *mother* dropped her cigarette near her oxygen tank."

"Well, if you'd left me alone, then I wouldn't have dropped the cigarette." She turned on me, but I could tell her heart wasn't in it.

"I'm just glad you came out of both the tornado and the fire alive," I said, surprising myself when I pulled her close. "I was worried sick about you."

She chuckled. "I think I'm supposed to say that kind of thing to you."

She hadn't, and she never would. I might be the daughter, but I was the cautious one, the one who would never go to bed in a filmy negligee or wear holey underwear for fear of getting into an accident and having paramedics see it.

Thanks for teaching me the important things in life, Granny.

I was the one who didn't smoke and only occasionally drank, the one who'd been so scared she'd get pregnant that she still hadn't had sex before marriage. Sorta. Kinda. Mostly?

Red lights flashed through our smoldering, upside-down home, and the ambulance pulled up to where we stood.

"Fire truck's right behind us. Anyone inside?" asked the paramedic.

"We're all out," I said.

The paramedics took LuEllen in hand and Declan told them in a calm, measured voice that no one else appeared to be hurt other than Mrs. Dabney down in trailer seven.

He helped me into the ambulance so I could ride with LuEllen and Mrs. Dabney. "Call me if you need a ride."

The hysterical giggle bubbled up in spite of myself. "Keep your phone handy. I don't have a car. I don't have anything."

He squeezed my hand. "It doesn't seem like it now, but it's going to be okay. We have all the people, right?"

I chanced a glance over at LuEllen, who was covered with a blanket, her glassy eyes trained on the ceiling. Mrs. Dabney moaned behind me, and a paramedic squeezed past me.

"Yeah. We have all the people," I said.

The other paramedic closed the back doors to the ambulance. In the distance I could hear the sirens for the fire engine, but the last thing I saw was Declan bending over to pick up the duffel bag I had dropped when the ambulance showed up.

One lock of hair had fallen across his forehead, and one sleeve was coming unrolled. He turned to talk to a police officer while still holding my bag, and I realized two things. One, I trusted him with the few things I had left in the world, and, two, he was the first person in a really long time who'd stopped to help me.

Declan

Once I sent Presley and her mother off to the hospital, the nursing home called with news that the tornado had hit one of their wings. Armando and I had a busy night on call, going back and forth between Anderson's and the nursing home then embalming.

Once we finished, I staggered for the kitchen and reached for the bourbon but put it back on the shelf. One, the sun was shining through the kitchen window. Two, Presley would probably be calling me at any time to come get her. Three, we were expecting families to come by and make arrangements.

So, back on the shelf for the bourbon. I made a pot of coffee instead.

Cleo rubbed around my legs, and I wondered if she'd been fed.

"Hey, Caroline. The cat's saying you haven't fed her."

Caroline clicked down the hall and into the kitchen. "Well, the cat is a liar because I fed her when I came in at six."

"You came in early? Now, I'm inclined to believe the cat." I collapsed into a chair at the table, willing the coffee to drip faster.

"You did good work last night," Caroline said as she took a seat across from me.

"Thanks."

Odd. Caroline wasn't known for handing out compliments. Maybe she was fishing for something.

"What are we going to do about the chapel?" she asked.

"I was thinking we'd tape off that area, fix the porch, and have all of our visitations and funerals in the two rooms like in the old days. The Freesia Room used to be a chapel anyway."

She frowned. "Are we going to be able to handle it?"

"Don't know. Potter took three bodies. We've got four, two of which, strangely, are pro bono. Then we have the two ladies who are ready for today."

"All four from the nursing home?"

"Nah. That's the two pro bonos and Mr. Baker. Then Mrs. Tice from the trailer park."

"I don't see why that old man can't take an indigent or two," Caroline muttered. She well knew that her father refused to take any of the people too poor to pay for their own burial. Business practices like that were a large part of the reason she ended up marrying Dad. Once she started working for her father, she said she couldn't stand the way he did business. The straw that broke the camel's back, though, was when he left Caroline's mom for his secretary. That relationship had since ended, but Caroline had no desire to go back to her father's fold.

As for the indigents, Anderson's took almost all of those cases. The state paid us something, but we still operated at a loss— especially at a time like this when we had more paying customers than rooms.

I poured coffee for the two of us. This time when I sat down, Cleo jumped up into my lap. "Dammit, Cleo. You're shedding all over me."

The kitten turned around twice before lying down and revving up her purr engine.

"What are we going to do with that cat? What did you call her?"

"Cleo," I said as I rubbed just behind her ears. "You know, like Cleopatra."

Caroline groaned. "Oh, good Lord. We gotta get rid of this cat before that Borden girl comes around talking about mummy cats."

"Maybe we could give *her* the cat."

"I tried that already."

My phone buzzed, but I didn't recognize the number.

It was Presley calling from a pay phone, shyly asking if I could pick her up, as if we hadn't nearly kissed in a closet less than twenty-four hours ago.

"Who's that?" Caroline asked as I dumped the kitten into her lap.

"Presley Cline," I said. "Delilah sent her to do hair and makeup last night and we got caught in the storm."

If Caroline's eyebrow went any higher, it would become a part of her hairline. "Really?"

"Really. Before you get any ideas, I feel responsible since that's her car under the tree out there."

"Really?" Caroline repeated as I put on my jacket and reached for the keys on the counter. "*The* Presley Cline?"

"The Presley Cline. Now, if you'll excuse me . . ."

"Oh, you go be her knight in shining armor," Caroline said with a smile.

"Yes. I'll be the first ever knight in shining armor . . . in a hearse."

I had lots of time to think on the way to Jefferson.

Telling Presley that I would come to get her was no problem.

Knowing what to do when her trailer was upside down or when we had to find LuEllen? Also not a problem.

Knowing what to say to Presley Cline or how to treat her after sharing a closet and watching her trailer burn? A problem.

On the one hand, she hadn't yelled at me in that closet. On the other, she hadn't said anything else about the incident, so it could be she wanted to forget the whole thing. Or she could be in shock from losing her car and home and almost losing her mom. Or it could be she hadn't realized I was about to kiss her.

My gut told me she knew I had been about to kiss her. I could kick myself for doing it. I could kick myself for thinking even for a minute that she might be amenable to being kissed.

Unfortunately, my inner angst was doing very little to keep me alert, so I smacked both cheeks to stay awake and to punish myself for being stupid. The country road led me to the edge of Jefferson, but my eyelids had grown heavy, blinking down again and again. I rolled down the window for the fresh air and turned up the radio.

Damn, I couldn't handle the all-nighters as well as I used to.

I came to a stop at a four-way just as Axl Rose welcomed me to the jungle on the radio. The elderly lady at her mailbox glared at me. I smiled and tipped an imaginary hat.

Now what are you going to do? Talk to Presley about it?

Hell to the no.

Stop thinking about things that can't be.

Insurance would pay for the chapel. Sean would come home to take over my job. I would start working with Uncle El, and I would find a nice girl even if it meant I'd have to travel two towns over.

But now I couldn't get Presley out of my mind. Dad had warned me a long time ago that Anderson men were like bald eagles: They mated for life. Of course, he hadn't explained how he'd recovered from my mother's demise to marry Caroline. They'd always seemed affectionate, but I'd always thought of their marriage as one of convenience.

And who's to say you couldn't marry Presley Cline?

Right. My sleep deprivation had led to delusions of grandeur.

And grandeur had me thinking about Presley's very humble beginnings. I'd had no idea she'd lived in the Green Acres trailer park. It wasn't even the nicest one in town. I did remember having to meet with her at the library for our tutoring sessions. I'd thought that was odd at the time.

And I still wasn't sure what she was doing in town. Surely, she hadn't given up. She'd had some little parts on some big shows and done a commercial or two. She was still young. Still the most beautiful woman I'd ever seen, with those legs that went on for days and that grin and—

Someone honked behind me to let me know the first traffic light at the edge of town was green.

Sorry, dude. I'm operating on a little sleep and a lot of questions.

It wasn't long before I pulled up to the entrance of the hospital. Now I had one more really, really good question: *Once you've rescued your distressed damsel and her half-naked mother, what are you going to do with them?*

Presley

It took six hours in a chaotic emergency room before LuEllen was patched up. Even worse, someone had strung up those Christmas lights that blinked intermittently. Because that's what a room full of people in pain needed: the incessant blinking of multicolored lights.

At least there were enough real people that I could ignore the ghosts. And there were plenty of ghosts in the emergency room. Some of them didn't realize they were dead yet, but I could see the wounds that had brought them there, garish wounds that were open but didn't bleed. I looked away from one ghost in particular, a woman whose throat had been slit from ear to ear. She watched TV patiently as though someone would call her back and she could be stitched up.

No nurse was going to call her name. I debated speaking with her—the folks in the emergency room surely wouldn't notice if I talked to myself—but then the nurse called for LuEllen, and I left the ghost behind.

She'd figure it out.

Once LuEllen's arm had been prodded, X-rayed, and put in a cast, I called Declan. LuEllen was yammering on about how the doctor said all those relaxants in her body had probably kept her from being hurt worse and how she was lucky it was just a hairline crack without too much swelling so she could get a real cast that day and not have to come back later. I turned to lead her outside and realized she couldn't get her robe back on now that she had a cast, a hot pink cast that clashed viciously with her red negligee. I draped the robe over her and asked to borrow a hospital gown, but the nurse looked at me as if I had four heads.

So outside we went. LuEllen stood outside the door, her robe flying back to flash unsuspecting hospital patrons before she grabbed one corner and held it shut. The woman was even wearing marabou kitten-heel slippers, making it look like I'd taken her from a house of ill repute.

Then Declan pulled up for us in the hearse. Apparently, they still couldn't get his truck or the van past the downed tree.

An older lady took in the tableau and shook her head. A younger woman snickered and took a picture with her phone. No doubt we'd be ridiculed mercilessly in the land of social media. I practically shoved LuEllen into the backseat, standing between her and the girl with a phone. If LuEllen flashed the world, I didn't want it on the Internet where they could connect the picture to my own embarrassing photo. I could just see it: me with my skirt in my undies and LuEllen in her teddy with the caption, "Like mother, like daughter."

Pres, that girl probably just thinks the whole thing is funny.

"Thanks for coming to get us," I said as I slid into the passenger seat. One look at Dec confirmed my suspicions he hadn't slept last night, either.

"No problem. Sorry it couldn't be the truck. The tree guys said they'd be over as soon as they can, but they're going to be busy, I'm afraid."

"Anyone pull a Sarge?"

He smiled at our inside joke. "No, but the tornado did hit the nursing home. Looks like the nursing home and Green Acres were the areas hardest hit, but there's wind damage all around town."

His frown came back, along with way too many worry lines on his forehead.

"Oh. I'm sorry. I didn't mean to take you away from work."

"That's all taken care of, but I do need to know where you're going."

"Well, they said on TV that some of the churches had set up some cots. I was thinking we'd start with one of those."

He paused so long that I thought he was agreeing with my plan.

"We have some extra bedrooms in the funeral home. You're welcome to stay there. If you want to."

"That would be very kind of you," LuEllen slurred in her best Blanche DuBois. If she added anything about depending on the kindness of strangers, I would throw something at her.

"LuEllen, we really shouldn't impose on the Andersons—"

"It's not imposing. No one's living in the upstairs rooms. It would have to be better than a cot."

I opened my mouth and shut it. Was this an act of kindness? Was he wanting to pick up where we'd left off? Did *I* want to pick up where we'd left off?

"No strings attached," he said. "Just a spot to stay until you get back on your feet."

"Then I guess all I can say is thank you."

He carried on as if he hadn't heard me. "I don't blame you if you don't want to. Some people have funny ideas—"

About me.

He didn't say the last part, but I could feel it just as surely as if he had. I'd heard about Declan "Cold Fingers" Anderson since I was in middle school. Anytime it was cold outside, and someone put cold hands on you to make you squirm, you might say, "You been hanging out with Dec Anderson or something?"

Shame pooled in my belly. I regretted having ever uttered those words.

I studied his profile, trying to figure him out. My sum conclusion was that I never wanted to play poker with Declan Anderson. Instead I needed to change the subject, so I turned up the radio.

"What's this song? I like it."

"Led Zepplin. 'D'yer Mak'er.'"

"Classic rock station?"

"Of course," he scoffed. "How have you made it this far in life without hearing this song?"

"Very carefully," I said with a smile.

"We'll have to see what else I can introduce you to." He looked away from the road for a second, just long enough to give me a dazzling smile.

LuEllen cleared her throat from the backseat, and I flinched because I'd forgotten she was back there.

"True classic rock is Elvis," she said with a sniff. A love of Elvis was one of the few things Granny passed on to her daughter; also one of the few things they ever agreed on.

"I have nothing but love for the King," Dec said.

I rolled my eyes because he had no idea about the depth of LuEllen's love for Elvis. At least she'd had the sense to name me Presley instead of Elvis.

Rolling into the Ellery city limits put a damper on our light mood. According to the news, Yessum County had been hit hardest by the tornado. Nine people had died, but no one had an estimate on the number of injuries or the amount of property damage done. So far, it looked as though Green Acres and the nursing home had been hit the hardest, but I could see the damage on the other side of town.

Trees leaned away from the road, some snapped as easily as toothpicks. The roof to my right had a bald spot where some of the shingles had blown away. The whole town had bits of debris scattered in front yards as though someone had busted up a huge trash bag and scattered its contents.

Branches still littered the roads, even though the larger ones had been removed. Neighbors helped one another to put blue tarps over holes in the roof or plywood over windows.

"It looks like a war zone," I murmured.

Dec nodded. "So far, only nine dead that I know of, and one of those appears to be a heart attack that could be unrelated."

Only?

But to each of the families of one of those nine, that person was probably their world.

To my right a father put an inflatable snowman up while his daughter clapped in the driveway. It would've been a perfectly normal picture if not for the tarp on the roof and the nearby tree that had been pulled up by the roots.

"What can we do to help?"

Dec pulled into the parking lot where the chapel used to be and trained his almost black eyes on me. "You and Miss LuEllen—"

"I am not an old biddy. Call me LuEllen."

"You and LuEllen are going to freshen up and get some sleep. I'll walk over to the pharmacy and see if I can get this prescription filled for when you wake up."

My mouth opened to tell him he didn't need to do that, and, besides, I didn't have the money to pay for the prescription. The set to his lips and the expression in his eyes warned me he wouldn't take no for an answer. Instead, I helped LuEllen inside. We shivered at the lack of heat.

Dec sighed, and a puff of air surrounded him. "Looks like we have lights, but the furnace is broken again. Go look in the blue room upstairs, bottom drawer of the bureau, and you should find some sweats. Bundle up, and I'll see if I can fix the furnace when I get back."

"But you need a nap, too. Let me get the prescription, and—"

"Presley, I'm used to running on little to no sleep. I'll take a good long nap when all of this is over. Now, both of you have been out in the cold without a coat, so go get warm. You're welcome to a shower."

And clothes, in the case of my mother. Of course, he was too much of a gentleman to point that out.

"Go on," he said as a shorter woman with salt-and-pepper hair emerged from a side office. He held out a hand to stop her from speaking, and I was left with the Civil War ghost standing at the foot of the staircase. Maybe if I pretended I didn't see him, he would go away. I ignored him and placed my hand under LuEllen's good elbow to lead her up the stairs.

Once we reached the top, I could hardly move for all of the ghosts up there. The world swayed around me, and I almost lost my balance.

"Presley, what's the matter with you?" LuEllen hissed.

Oh, I'm just dandy with several hundred ghosts living in the space we're about to call home. It'll be great.

"Nothing. I'm fine," I lied. I ushered her into the first bedroom— the blue bedroom—ignoring the cold prickles from brushing too closely against someone in another plane.

I sure as hell wasn't taking a shower with all those extra pairs of eyes.

Declan

"What in the hell do you think you're doing?" Caroline spit the words out between her teeth even though she smiled. I had learned early on that all disagreements had to be handled in a corner while smiling at the other person. We Andersons were experts at looking like we were sharing charming anecdotes when we were actually cussing each other out.

"In case you haven't noticed," I said, pretty sure I looked like a possessed game show host, "there's been a catastrophe that has left several people homeless. Since their trailer burned down, I thought it was the least I could do."

"*You* didn't set their trailer on fire. Send them over to the church where it doesn't matter that *the* Presley Cline had an affair with some Hollywood big shot." Caroline smiled like a demented beauty pageant contestant.

"Maybe I will. After they've had at least one good night's sleep. Now, if you'll excuse me, I'm going to get a prescription for them, then see if I can fix the furnace."

She muttered something about everything in the place falling apart and then grabbed my arm as I tried to pass. "Dec, we have another couple of removals, too."

"Caroline, we're out of space! Where's Armando anyway?"

She wouldn't look me in the eye.

"Oh, no. You did *not* send him to get Uncle Hollis."

"I had to! We've got more work here than we can do by ourselves. Trying to arrange this many funerals is going to be a logistical nightmare. I have been meeting with families all morning long. We can use his help. Just because he gets a little confused—"

"But Uncle Hollis? Really? He's in that special assisted living for a reason, you know."

She was wringing her hands. "But he embalms like a champ and herds cats even better. I don't care if he talks to huge invisible rabbits as long as we get the help we need."

"You haven't heard from Sean, have you?"

"No." I pinched the bridge of my nose. Caroline didn't want anyone upstairs because she was bringing Uncle Hollis home, and we were hoping Sean would arrive any day.

"Besides, it's Christmastime!"

"All the more reason to lend a hand to those who need it!"

"The Lord helps those who help themselves," she countered.

"I can't talk to you right now. I'd swear Potter sent you here to sabotage the whole business if I didn't know better."

Her bottom lip quivered. "Declan Orion Anderson, that was a rotten thing to say."

She marched to her office to cry. No way would Caroline Potter Anderson ever let any of us see her cry. Not at my father's funeral. Not even when Sean announced he was going to Atlanta to school and didn't know when he'd be back.

And damned if she wasn't right about it being a rotten thing to say.

I opened her door and poked my head inside. She hurriedly dabbed at her eyes with a tissue.

"I'm sorry, Caroline. I didn't mean it."

"I am *not* like my father." She opened her mouth to add something more but waved me on instead.

If I'd had enough sleep, I would've been able to hold my tongue.

Any reference to Potter's Funeral Home was, and had been,

strictly taboo for years. To imply that Caroline might still feel loyalty for her father's business was like rooting for Alabama in the middle of Tennessee country. Sure, most folks thought Potter ran a swankier funeral home, but there were plenty of people who had been burned by him before. His clients weren't alone; Potter had tried on more than one occasion to find a sneaky way to undermine Anderson's.

Cussing under my breath because, as I'd been taught, funeral directors must always be beyond reproach and thus could not scream their curses to the sky, I put my shoulders into the wind and walked the two blocks to Main Street and the pharmacy. Dr. Giles took the prescription and gave me the side eye until I told him the whole story about LuEllen and Presley, complete with fireball trailer and emergency room. I left out the part about the negligee, but I did mention they were staying with us at the funeral home.

Some flowers might make a nice peace offering to Caroline.

"Mr. Anderson, here's your prescription."

I signed for the prescription and paid for it. Only my strict funeral director training combined with unbelievable fatigue kept my eyeballs from popping out of my skull when he told me the price. Dr. Giles then apologetically explained that LuEllen didn't have insurance.

Taking the little white sack, I thanked him and headed next door.

It didn't hurt that the florist was one of my favorite places to go. My mother's family had started the florist shop, and she used to work there. That's how she met my father—delivering sprays of flowers to the funeral home.

Eventually, she inherited the place. I had one particularly vivid memory of being in the store with her while she was pregnant with Sean. It must have been fall because she was humming as she affixed little gold footballs to mum corsages for the Homecoming football game and turned to where I sat on the floor behind the counter playing with toy cars.

"Declan, did you know you can tell a story with flowers?" And then she'd taken me around the shop showing me flowers that said, "I'm sorry" and ones that said, "I love you," and just about everything in-between.

She showed me flowers that said friendship and respect and innocence.

Then she paused in front of the striped carnations. "Now, these flowers can even tell someone to go—go—take a long walk off a short pier!"

I needed some "I'm sorry" flowers that day, but I'd probably need a striped carnation "go to hell" bouquet for somebody before the week was up. I pictured Presley's face and thought about ordering an "I want to kiss you" arrangement, but no.

As it was, I was about to have to turn in my man card since I could name flowers instead of pointing and grunting while saying, "Me man. Send pretty flowers to girl."

You know you're too old for her.

Surely seven years—or was it eight?—wasn't too much, was it?

Hell, seven or eight years probably seemed like a lifetime to someone who hadn't reached twenty-five yet. Besides, I couldn't imagine making Presley deal with the things my mother had complained about. And the funeral home wasn't the sort of place where you just dropped off the kids when you had to leave early for a Tupperware party. What were the kids supposed to do? Color while Daddy comforted the bereaved?

That's what you did.

Yeah, and I was so normal because of it.

"Can I help you?" Kari Vandiver's voice brought me out of the past and into the poinsettia-filled shop of the present. As usual, she sat behind the scarred wooden counter working. Today she deftly wrapped green tape around the bottom of a boutonniere, her wild, red, curly hair shading her face.

"Morning, Kari," I said.

"Don't you mean afternoon?" She looked up at me with a wry smile.

"Yeah, I guess it's afternoon. Kinda lost track of the time with all that's been going on. How're things at your place?"

"Thank the good Lord we are untouched, but I figure I'm about to be really, really busy. Heard about your chapel."

"We did. We're going to have to do it old-school and set up the visitations in the rooms downstairs. I'm thinking at least eight funerals."

Kari sighed. "That's too bad. At least most of them were at the nursing home, right?"

"Yeah, mostly folks who were suffering from dementia. One lady told me she thought it was actually a blessing because her mother hadn't recognized her in five years."

Kari nodded. Such "blessed" deaths never hurt any less. "Well, send anyone who needs flowers my way, and I might share some Gentleman Jack with you once we make it to the other side."

"Sounds like a plan. Say, do you have anything around here for an 'I'm sorry' bouquet?"

"Uh-oh. Whose heart did you break?" Her sly smile made me wish I'd done something stupid enough to be sleeping on a good woman's couch.

"I said something I shouldn't have to Caroline. Thought I'd get some flowers to make it up to her." I paused to give her a minute to think. When Kari's parents bought the florist shop, my mother's dog-eared notebook of flower meanings had come with it. Kari found the notebook in a back room when they were spring cleaning one year. Her mom was about to toss it in the trash when Kari rescued it. She was just a little girl, but she saw Mom's name and brought the notebook to me. I had scoured that notebook, looking for any explanation for why my mom did what she did, reading it through so many times I memorized the flowers and their meanings. In the end I didn't find any answers, so I gave it back to Kari since she kept calling me all the time to ask questions. She liked the notebook even if using the Internet to look for meanings might be quicker.

"Let's see . . ." She tapped the side of her chin. "I think you're stuck with the pink peonies of shame."

I winced. That was going to cost me. "No purple hyacinth?"

"I don't care what anyone says, a man who knows his flowers is sexy. Good thing for you I'm a happily married gal. No hyacinth, but I do have some pink peonies left over from the Madrigal wedding. Hothouse, of course."

"Make it so."

She hopped down from the stool and disappeared behind the curtain that led to the back. When she returned, she came carrying a glass vase full of pink blooms that would, with my luck, be bedraggled by the wind before I got back.

"It'll be—"

"Don't tell me. Just put it on my tab," I said as I picked up the vase.

"Just be careful who you give those to," she said as I reached the door. "In Japan those blooms mean masculinity and virility."

"Sure they do." *I'm gonna look real manly carrying these pink flowers two blocks in the bitter cold.*

Her laughter mingled with the bell above the door as it closed behind me.

I passed through the prep room with my peonies, irrationally expecting it to be warmer once I got inside. Once again, I was destined for disappointment. As I stepped into the hall, I almost ran into Presley. She stepped back, startled.

"Sorry about that," I said as I handed her LuEllen's prescription. "I didn't mean to scare you."

"I couldn't sleep," she said. "I know I should be able to, but I can't."

I nodded in agreement. I knew the feeling. Her eyes flicked to the peonies and back up to me. Did she expect me to hand her the flowers?

"Do you think I could make some tea?"

Apparently not.

"Help yourself," I said. "Kettle's on the stove, and the tea's to the right of the sink."

She headed for the kitchen but looked over her shoulder with a grin that made me feel like a fourteen-year-old boy all over again. "Nice blossoms."

"Thanks."

Masculinity and virility, huh.

I turned to Caroline's office. She sat behind the desk wearing her glasses while she typed on the computer, no doubt doing death certificates, invoices, and all the other things I didn't like to do.

Only, when I appeared, she minimized what she was working on. That was odd.

Whatever. I owed her more than a vase full of peonies.

"Wanted to say I'm sorry." I slid the peonies to the corner of her desk.

"Dec, you didn't have to do that," she said. Her glistening eyes told me otherwise.

"Yes, I did. And thank you."

"I need to apologize, too." Caroline took off her glasses. "You did the right thing by letting Presley and her mother stay."

I nodded. "Anyone would do the same."

"No, they wouldn't," Caroline said with a sad smile. "Besides, that Presley is a pretty little thing, isn't she?"

"Don't start matchmaking. I bet she's headed back to California any day now."

And she's not pretty. She's gorgeous. She sure as hell isn't little, either—not with those long legs.

Caroline threw her hands up in surrender. "All right, all right. I'm just saying, if the good Lord gives you a gift, it might be wise to take Him up on it."

And we were back to the faith stuff. Best to smile and nod.

"She's a person, not a gift."

Caroline cocked her head to one side, studying me. "Sometimes a person *is* a gift."

"And sometimes a person is just a person."

She sighed heavily as I left the office to figure out what was wrong with the furnace. At least that heap of junk didn't try to meddle. It did, however, go through igniters like it was going out of style.

Come to think of it, the furnace was probably going out of style.

I mentally added it to the list of things that needed to be replaced.

Presley

Tea. As if I really wanted tea.

No, I really wanted to get away from all of the *ghosts* upstairs. They were all talking at once, wanting something I couldn't give them. They kept speaking over one another and carrying on to the point that my head felt as if someone were splitting logs on top of it.

I squeezed my eyes shut and massaged my temples while my tea steeped. Sooner or later, I would have to talk to Declan about what happened in the closet, wouldn't I?

Well, today I had bigger fish to fry.

What was I going to do? We'd lost the trailer, and LuEllen didn't have any insurance on anything. I thought I had the job with Delilah—unless I'd lost it by not showing up today. Now even my car was a mess.

The hairs on the back of my neck began to stand up one by one. When I opened my eyes, I looked straight through the Civil War soldier.

"Stop following me," I hissed.

"So. You can see us," he said with a more genteel voice than I would've expected.

Might as well cut to the chase. "What do you want?"

"Young lady, that is no way to speak to your elders." Even in death he could give a stern glare. "My name is Colonel Seamus Anderson, proprietor of this establishment. Most people address me as the Colonel."

Like Kentucky Fried Chicken? I stifled a giggle.

"Nice to meet you," I muttered out of reflex. I almost offered my hand, too, but I didn't want the cold ghost prickles. "I'm Presley Cline."

"Oh, I remember the Clines. Good people. I think one of your great-great-granddaddies fought with me in the Second Tennessee."

I doubted that, but who was I to argue with a ghost?

"Sir, Colonel, what do you want?" I whispered as I looked over my shoulder at the back door. I certainly didn't want Dec to walk into the kitchen and find me talking to an empty chair. He would call the nice young men in the clean white coats to take me away.

Of course, that would solve my housing issues.

"Well, we're in need of a conduit, as it were," he said. "When they took my grandson Hollis away, quite a few souls got lost. You will be sending them to the other side."

"Oh, I will, will I?"

"Of course, that's what you do, isn't it? You make the light." He leaned forward, and I could see a hint of the handsome man he had been once before. In his ghostly form, he was older with a thick mustache, his left sleeve empty. But sometimes, his appearance would flicker to that of a younger, more intact man.

He caught me staring and chuckled. "Lost the arm at the Battle of Pickett's Mill. Almost made it through the war with all of my arms and legs. Almost."

"I'm going to have to be honest with you, Colonel. I don't know how to make the light," I said. "And usually I have to do something for a person before they'll go. You know, like deliver a message. That's a lot of people up there."

The Colonel nodded solemnly. "That's the problem. My wife was the one who could make the light. Not everybody needs it, but she had a way with spirits. Course, she passed on before me."

He looked past me, and I wondered if he was thinking of a

time when the kitchen wasn't full of modern appliances. Heck, since the kitchen looked like an add-on, maybe it didn't even exist back in those days.

"Anyway," he harrumphed and turned those intense eyes on me, Dec's eyes, I realized. "I've had a stern talking to with the people upstairs. Whatever didn't get done just didn't get done, and they are going to have to leave before the house explodes."

"Before the house explodes?" I slapped a hand over my mouth because I'd yelled it.

"Hey, now," Declan boomed from behind me, causing me to jump out of my skin again. "I'm not the most skilled handyman you'll ever find, but I think I can fix the furnace without blowing up the house."

I looked back at the Colonel, but he was gone. Note to self: Sit in the other chair by the pantry so you'll be able to see if someone enters the room. Following Dec was the ghost of a woman with long dark hair and a red dress. The minute she saw me, she vanished.

Who is she?

Trouble, that's who she was. I needed another ghost around like I needed another hole in the head.

But she had looked so sad.

Nope. She's on her own, whoever she is.

"Sorry," I said, willing my cheeks not to turn red. They didn't listen. "I think I'm delirious from lack of sleep."

"I know what you mean," he said over his shoulder while he washed away the grime from his hands at the sink. "Maybe I'll take a nap now that the furnace is working."

Sure enough, I heard the reassuring whoosh of air. He had fixed it. Was there anything the man couldn't do?

"It'll take a while to warm up, but we should be well on our way." He took the seat across from me. "Did your mother get settled in okay?"

"She's upstairs sleeping like a baby," I said. "Wish I could."

He chuckled and looked at my tea wistfully.

"Why don't you take this cup? I'll make another."

"I couldn't ask you to go to the trouble."

He had a small brown smudge of something underneath his eye. My fingers itched to brush it away.

"No trouble, really," I said. "Water's still warm."

I passed him my cup and turned the kettle back on. Sure enough, it didn't take long to whistle. It took longer for me to decide if I really wanted to ask Declan a certain question.

"So, Declan, have you ever seen anything . . . strange around here?"

He laughed out loud, a rich laugh that might have been attractive if it didn't mean he thought I was a few jokers shy of a deck.

"I'll take that as a no," I said as I fixed my tea and sat across from him.

"I was wondering when you would get around to the ghost question."

I pushed the tea bag down with my spoon. "Just wondering if you'd ever seen anything odd. That's all."

He frowned into his own cup. "Oh, I've seen things, all right. So far science has been able to explain them all."

Lucky you.

I wasn't sure science could explain the one-armed ghost colonel, but maybe that was just me. Maybe it was time to change the subject. "How's everything after the storm? Any more damage?"

"Nah, we're lucky. This old house has good bones, and we'll be able to fix the rest. In the meantime, we can use the rooms for visitations like we used to."

"So business as usual?"

"Well, more business than usual," he said.

"Anything I can do to help? You know, to earn my keep?"

He studied me intently. "You don't have to do that."

"But I want to. I've always been one to earn my own way."

"I'm sure we could use some help with hair and makeup."

I smiled. "That I can do."

His leg bumped mine underneath the table, something I used to wish for when he was tutoring me in geometry.

He cleared his throat. "So, about the other night."

Here it was. Would he want to forget it ever happened? Did he want to kiss me again? Would he expect certain things for offering me a place to stay? Better to make him speak first and see. "What about the other night?"

He opened his mouth to speak, and I leaned forward to hear what he was going to say. But a voice in the hallway boomed, "Oh, it's the Colonel! I've missed you, Gramps."

Dec's face paled, but my heart beat frantically. Whoever was in the hallway could see the Colonel! There was someone else out there who could see ghosts.

I didn't realize I was standing until Dec's hand rested on my forearm. "I'd like to apologize for my uncle Hollis in advance. He isn't quite with us here in the real world."

His mind could reside in Rhode Island for all I cared as long as he gave me some idea of this light business. Maybe he could teach me how not to see ghosts at all. The only other person who'd ever mentioned being able to see ghosts was a bag lady on Hollywood Boulevard. I didn't stop to ask her if they were real ghosts or something induced by whatever she was drinking out of her paper sack.

Wait. Wasn't Hollis the guy the Colonel mentioned?

"He sounds like a charmer," I said, craning to see if he would enter the kitchen.

"He's been in assisted living for folks with dementia," Dec said. "I think he's harmless, but you may want to steer clear of him."

Dec clearly didn't want me to meet his uncle Hollis. I sat back down and said a selfish little prayer. *Please send this Hollis to me.*

Whether through divine intervention or sheer force of nature, the booming voice started heading our way.

Dec buried his face in his hands with a groan.

In walked an almost skeletal elderly man followed by a portly Hispanic man. For a moment, I thought he would start belting "The Impossible Dream" because they looked so much like Don Quixote and Sancho Panza.

"Oh, hello, miss." Uncle Hollis stopped at the table and took my hand, bending over it with a kiss. "I'm Hollis Anderson."

"Presley Cline." I couldn't help but grin. I didn't care if Hollis was crazier than a betsy bug. Him, I liked.

"Armando Cepeda," the other gentleman said with a tiny smile. He opted to shake my hand rather than kiss it.

"I can't believe you," Dec said to Armando with a disgusted shake of his head. "I can't believe you let her talk you into this."

Armando motioned for Dec to follow him, and Hollis took the chair across from me. He took a sip of Dec's tea then winked.

We stared at each other, then I looked to where Dec and Armando were standing in the doorway having an animated sotto voce discussion with eerily smiling faces. I took a deep breath and screwed my courage to the sticking place. "So. You can see the Colonel, too?"

"Of course I can," he boomed. I shushed him frantically since he appeared to be proof that anyone who could see the Colonel would be institutionalized.

The old man reached across the table and took my hands before adding in a stage whisper, "They think I'm crazy, but I'm not."

The jury was still out on that one.

I took a deep breath. "The Colonel told me there are a lot of people upstairs who are stuck. He wants me to make the light, but I don't know how."

"Well, then we will have to teach you!"

Did the man have no volume control?

Then he stirred Dec's tea with his pinkie finger while singing a rousing rendition of "Goodbye Yellow Brick Road."

I *thought* I was sane. Was I? Was I destined to have whatever it was that Uncle Hollis had?

"Presley?" Caroline poked her head around the corner. "Delilah's on the phone and wants to speak with you."

Well, that couldn't possibly be good.

Declan

"Armando, I love you like a brother. Hell, most of the time I love you more than my own brother, but this is ridiculous. You know Uncle Hollis is a loose cannon."

The unflappable Mexican shrugged. "She's the boss. She said she'd handle him."

"That's what she always says," I muttered. Something rubbed against my legs, and I looked down. Cleo was making figure eights around my ankles.

"You are too strict. You need to lighten up," Armando added.

About that time, Uncle Hollis brushed past us singing the falsetto "la's" of "Crocodile Rock." Presley followed hot on his heels.

"Declan, are you listening to me?"

I turned back to Armando, but I'd lost myself in the sway of Presley's hips as she walked down the hall to Caroline's office. Well, that and wondering what I could do to stop her from following Uncle Hollis. There was no telling what he might say or do next, including, but not limited to, walking around in his boxers once the working day was over.

"Declan!" Armando punched my arm.

"Dammit, I'm listening, Armando!" He knew I'd been watching Presley's ass.

"No, you're not. You never hear a word I say."

Out of the corner of my eye, I saw Caroline stop Presley and hand her the phone. Breathing a sigh of relief, I turned back to Armando's glare. "Okay, fine. What did you say?"

"I was asking if you'd done the removals yet?"

I slapped my palm to my forehead. No, I hadn't done the removals. I'd taken care of Presley and her mother. I'd fixed the furnace and made nice with Caroline, but I hadn't done removals because, in my mind, Armando was on call instead of helping Uncle Hollis escape from assisted living.

"Let's go," I said. "But you're driving."

Potter had beat us to the punch on one of the bodies, which put Armando in a foul mood and was going to put Caroline in an even darker one. One of the families had called Potter when I didn't show up. I'd made profuse apologies and they'd said they understood, but we were still left looking unprofessional. Still, we were headed back to Anderson's, and I could finally get some sleep after that evening's visitation.

"This would not happen if I were in charge," Armando said. "Or if Sean were here."

"I don't want to hear another word about Sean, and if you would like to be in charge, it's possible we could arrange that."

"Really?"

And why hadn't I thought of that before? Why couldn't Armando take my place instead of Sean? "Really."

"I've never thought this was the business for you," Armando added.

Well, no shit, Sherlock. I never asked to be a part of the family business. I was told to man up and take my spot on the roster whether I liked it or not.

"Maybe next time I should go get Uncle Hollis, and you can do my job."

"You would've left him there, and I can't fix the furnace for shit."

"Maybe it's time for you to take on a few more responsibilities. I'll still work with the damned furnace."

"No me tomes el pelo, cabrón."

"I wasn't! I was thinking about getting out of the business."

"You tell Caroline that?"

"A few times."

"I'll believe it when I see it. This business? It gets in your veins just like the embalming fluid."

We rode in silence the rest of the way. I knew Armando deserved a promotion. I'd met him in one of my mortuary classes in Nashville. I'd just gotten back from studying a semester abroad as a part of my attempted architecture degree. He was still working on his English. No one wanted to be his partner in one of our classes, so I volunteered. Now his English was better than my Spanish, and his knowledge of the funeral business had always been greater than mine. Sure, there were a few odd looks when he first moved to Ellery, but I couldn't imagine Anderson's without him.

So the chapel had been destroyed, and I still hadn't heard from Sean. Armando deserved a promotion. He and Caroline could handle things now that Uncle Hollis was here. They didn't need me.

"You're too quiet, too depressed. You need a woman."

"Seems to be the consensus," I said as the hearse pulled into the funeral home. "Not many ladies who'll sign up for this gig."

"I wasn't talking about marriage. You. Need. To. Get. Laid."

"Good to see your English is improving," I muttered. He did have a point.

"My English *es perfecto*. Unlike your Spanish. What about the pretty girl in the kitchen?"

"Out of my league, man."

"Bullshit."

"What was that about your English, again?"

"I told you my English is perfect. Now have some *cojones* and ask her out."

Presley

Delilah chewed me a new one for not showing up. Apparently, in Delilah Land, neither tornados, nor fires, nor assisting your mother with a broken arm was a good reason to blow off work. Honestly, the thought that she'd open the shop that day had never crossed my mind. I offered to come in, but she grudgingly admitted it would be better if I waited until the next day.

When I handed the cordless phone back to Caroline, she looked up with sympathy in her eyes. "I could hear her yelling all the way over here."

"She doesn't like me that much."

Understatement of the year.

"For what it's worth, I told her you did excellent work on Mrs. Borden."

"Thank you," I said. "I appreciate that."

"You did especially lovely work on the nails. Do you think you could do mine one day?"

The nails? "I'm sorry. I didn't do her nails. She must've had that done in the nursing home. I'm not good at manicures and pedicures—just the hair and makeup."

"Well, darn! At least Mrs. Borden is ready for her visitation this evening. Goodness knows nothing else is. Speaking of, you might want to scoot along upstairs. Her visitation will start before too long."

She had the same smile on her face, but her eyes had changed from friendly to half-threatening. I decided I very much wanted to be out of the way during the visitation even if it did mean hob-nobbing with all of the spirits.

Once upstairs, I looked for Uncle Hollis or the Colonel. I saw . . . no one. Where had all of the ghosts gone?

Across the hall, I could faintly hear Uncle Hollis singing about how the doggies need to get along. Apparently he'd switched from Elton John to country and western. Light radiated from underneath his door in a way that told me the spirits had a new friend in town.

I started to knock on his door, but my phone rang just as I was about to rap.

Ira.

"Any news?"

"Nothing on the godmothers, but I do have something else that might interest you—got an address where I can overnight this script?"

"Sure. Hang on a minute."

I knew there was a stack of old-fashioned promotional fans complete with address in the kitchen, but this would mean violating Caroline's request that I stay upstairs. Maybe if I dressed up it would be okay, but I didn't have much to work with. I had rescued my duffel bag from the car earlier, but I only had one "nice" outfit: a skirt and a blouse. The skirt was mini, the blouse was hot pink. And the shoes? Black stilettos.

"Stay with me, Ira. I've got to go downstairs to get you the info," I said as I wriggled into the outfit and stepped into the shoes. "It's a long story."

"Well, I'd like to get out of the office, so get on with it."

I rummaged around in the closet—bingo! A blazer that must've been Declan's in his younger years. It didn't quite swallow me whole and matched the skirt enough that I thought I could sneak downstairs and lift one of the fans. Maybe I could get a sandwich while I was at it.

A look to where LuEllen snored on the bed confirmed she was still out cold from having taken double the dose of painkillers. I shook my head and put the bottle in my pocket. If she insisted on acting like a reckless child, then I supposed I would have to be the mother.

"Almost there, Ira. Promise."

Declan

I had been awake for thirty-seven hours, a few of which had used up all of my adrenaline stores. I still had an hour and a half to go.

You need a vacation.

An unbidden image of Presley Cline came to mind—she was frolicking on a white sand beach in the American flag string bikini she'd worn for the *Maxim* shoot.

God bless America.

Better yet, I could carry her over the threshold of one of those thatched huts that sat over a perfectly clear blue sea, untie each one of those strings slowly . . .

"I just have to tell you what a fantastic job you did with Miss Sylvia. It looks just like her. We really thank you." Jessica Borden was talking to someone, and the sound of her voice brought me out of my daydream.

One step to the doorway, and I saw she was talking to Delilah, who had cocked her head to one side, looking like a parakeet with her dark, beady eyes. "I'm sorry. I wasn't able to take care of Miss Sylvia myself. My new assistant, Presley Cline, did that."

"Presley Cline is your *assistant?*"

"Sure is." If Delilah's pride swelled up anymore she'd float out of the house. "She knows all that fancy Hollywood stuff."

Interesting. Presley said Delilah didn't like her, but the savvy hair dresser wasn't afraid to claim responsibility for hiring her and thus her talents.

"Well, you must've told her about that awful cowlick Miss Sylvia has because I could never get her hair to do right when I went by the nursing home to comb it."

For some reason that stopped me. One of the reasons I never did hair and makeup was because I didn't understand all of the fussing women did with their hair. And Presley wasn't back there for the typical trial and error. She must be a genius with hair.

I milled through the visitation on autopilot, thinking of why Presley was there, why she was good with hair, how long she might stick around, and whether I should follow Armando's advice and ask her out. I was so preoccupied, I forgot one of my cardinal rules of life: Avoid Jessica Borden at all costs.

Someone tapped me on the shoulder, and I turned around to face the first in a long line of people I'd disappointed. To make matters worse, we were outside the room in the hall with no one to rescue me.

Professional. The only thing to do was to be very professional. "Ms. Borden, is there anything I can do for you?"

"No, I just wanted to say that this is all so lovely." She sniffed and dabbed at her now red-rimmed crazy eyes. "Miss Sylvia would be really proud of all the things you've done tonight."

I placed a platonic but reassuring hand on her shoulder and immediately regretted it as her eyes lit up with something akin to worship. "Well, thank you. Let me know if there's anything else we can do."

She threw her arms around me and squeezed with all her might. "If I think of anything, you'll be the first to know."

I extricated myself gently and looked around for her husband. "Where's Bart this evening? I thought I'd talk to him about coaching a girls' softball team again this year."

She smiled, her eyes twinkling for her relatively new husband. "Oh, he couldn't make it tonight, but I'll be sure to tell him you could use his help."

"You do that." I turned to go, but she grabbed my arm.

"Declan, I—"

Out of the corner of my eye I saw a pair of legs I would recognize anywhere. "Have you met my girlfriend, Presley Cline?"

What the hell possessed you to say that? What if she contradicts you right here? Could you screw this up any more?

Presley stopped dead in her tracks, but turned around with her megawatt smile.

"Darling, could I introduce you to Jessica Borden?"

I looked back at Jessica, but her expression held neither rage nor disappointment. She did let go of my arm, though. "We were in the Miss Ellery pageant together, weren't we?"

"I still don't know how I beat your flaming baton act," Presley said as she put her phone to her shoulder. Based on her straight-faced delivery, there was no way this woman should give up acting.

"I couldn't compete with your dramatic monologue," Jessica said.

"You're too kind, and it's so good to see you again, but I have to take this. Please excuse me." She kissed me on the cheek, and the touch of her lips made my heart race. "See you in a few, dear."

I watched her sashay—there was no other word for it—down the hall, and my mouth went dry at the sight of her short skirt and tall heels.

"Well, I'm glad you've found a good woman, Declan," Jessica said. This time I thought I could hear disappointment. "I sure hope she deserves you."

"Oh, more than—" I started to say, but Jessica Borden had slipped into Miss Sylvia's visitation room.

I checked the other to make sure everything was going okay with Miss Belmont's visitation. Soon enough, it was time to usher people out the door.

As the last few folks were going out, a tall man with a shaved head brushed past them to enter. "Mr. Anderson?"

I wondered what gave me away. The black suit? The fresh flower pinned to my lapel? "That's me."

"We're going to need you to evacuate the premises."

The fake smile went to my lips automatically as I led him away from the people and into my office. "I'm sorry, but we're finishing up two visitations, and I'd really like to not cause a panic. Could you please tell me who you are and what this is all about?"

"I'm Frank Davenport from the Building and Zoning Department. We're going to have to revoke your Certificate of Occupancy."

This really was the day that would not end.

"Mr. Davenport, I think we're all under a little stress from the tornado. Yes, we are missing our chapel. Yes, there are boards loose on the porch. I have patched up all of those things and—"

"Your porch is unstable and that doorway is a hazard. There's no telling what other problems I'll find when I come back tomorrow for a more thorough inspection."

Bullshit. The house was solid. I'd hoisted some six-by-six posts to support the overhang, but it was really only a matter of reflooring the porch and adding back the decorative railing. The chapel was a mess but could easily be cordoned off. Damage to the portico was worse than it looked, and the prep room was solid.

Ah. This was Potter's latest trick, no doubt.

"I know it doesn't look pretty, but we wouldn't do anything to endanger our patrons. This is a strong old house. I've got some concrete steps out front and we can wheel anyone who needs it through the side door. The tree guys are coming tomorrow, and then we can triple-check the roof and work on the back parking lot. We can't delay these visitations."

"Well, you're going to have to because I'm about to walk out there and declare this building unsafe. Tacked up the notice before I came in." He leaned across my desk, daring me to say any differently.

He was tall, but I was taller. I moved around the desk so I could stare him down, lowering my voice to the dangerous level we used with the real crazies. "You will not evacuate the building when we only have fifteen more minutes of visitation to go.

Once everyone leaves, I will make arrangements with area churches for the actual funerals, but you are *not* going to cause a panicked stampede over this bureaucratic bullshit."

"You're just an undertaker. What do you know?"

And then he did something even more stupid than calling me an undertaker: He tried to stare me down.

I stared back. It just so happened, I'd worked many a summer with my uncle Eldridge building and repairing homes. In fact, I was halfway to becoming a licensed contractor—only the exams to go—when Sean left, forcing me to go back to the funeral home full time.

My stare must've held all of my frustrations because Mr. Davenport gulped and finally looked away. "Okay, Mr. Anderson. As long as you guarantee there won't be anyone in here tomorrow, then I'll leave you for the night. But if you try to pull a stunt like this again, I will arrest you, close the place down, and lace it with crime tape."

He turned on his heel and stomped down the hall.

Caroline poked her head in the door. "What was that about?"

When I nodded my head, she shut the door. I collapsed into my chair. "Oh, our Certificate of Occupancy has been revoked."

When I looked up, her lips had thinned to a dangerous line. "My father."

"Funny, that's the conclusion I came to."

"My father sent that man over here. He's still trying to shut us down so he can be the only show in town. Just like him to strike while his opponent is weak." She paced the tiny office, two steps in one direction and then two in the other.

"Come on, Caroline. Surely he doesn't have enough time on his hands for all that. He has to be just as busy as we are."

"Yes, but he's on the other side of town and has hardly a scratch to that new monstrosity he built in front of Memory Gardens."

I raked my hand through my hair. "We should've sold to him last year."

"No!" She screamed the word then blanched, no doubt at the

thought that someone outside had heard her. "Your father wouldn't have wanted that."

Didn't I know that firsthand.

"Okay. Fine. Let's say he's that big an asshole. I told the Davenport guy that we'd arrange for funerals at local churches. Miss Ginger explicitly wanted her funeral here. We're going to use the Freesia Room, since it was the old chapel. Most of the folks will probably show up for graveside service at the County Line cemetery instead and then the wake at The Fountain anyway."

"What are you going to do if he tries to evacuate again?"

"I don't think he has the stones to disrupt an actual funeral. If he has a problem, I'll tell him we're playing by the rules from then on out."

Caroline sighed deeply.

"It's all going to work out," I heard myself say.

If only I could believe my own words.

"Yeah, you're right, of course."

"Once more into the breach," I said. It was one of my father's favorite things to say, something he'd cribbed from Shakespeare. I reached to open the door, but Caroline tackled me with a hug. "You're a good man, Declan Anderson. Just like your father."

My arms hesitated only a second before wrapping around her. All these years, and she'd never said anything like that to me before.

Presley

Actually, I'm dating Presley Cline.

What was Declan Anderson's game?

I stalked down the hall to the kitchen, letting my hips sway for Jessica's benefit. And Dec's, to be honest. Around the corner I went, then I stopped dead in my tracks: There at the kitchen table sat Uncle Hollis in his shirtsleeves, a line of ghosts stretching into the prep room across the way.

I grabbed a fan from the table and gave the address to Ira in a shaky voice. He was carrying on about a different part. Something about a movie better suited to me. I felt a twinge of foreboding that Ira was suddenly hot on something other than the fairy godmother movie, but I thanked him and hung up so I could stare at the scene in front of me.

The Colonel stood at the head of the line, directing ghosts to take the chair across from Uncle Hollis. I watched as he listened intently to a little girl with a side ponytail and an arm full of jelly bracelets. He said something to her and she disappeared in the white light behind his shoulder.

He rubbed his eyes, his stubble-ridden face haggard.

"How do you do that?"

He sat up ramrod straight. "Do what? I don't see anything. Do you see anything? Oh, it's you."

"I wish I could make the light like you do. Ghosts have always followed me, but I can't make them go away unless I do something for them," I said as I dragged a third chair to sit at the end of the little table.

"Typical ghost behavior," he said. Suddenly, he grabbed my wrists and looked deeply into my eyes. "You can't ever tell anyone what you see. If you tell them, they'll think you're crazy. They'll send you away."

My heart broke for the older man. And thudded faster for me. So my instincts had been right. I couldn't tell Declan what I saw or he would kick me out at best or have me locked away at worst. Goodness knows, LuEllen wouldn't help me out. She and Granny had refused to believe a word I said when I was little. They told people I had imaginary friends.

At least Granny had to admit I was right in the end.

Not that it did me much good, since she couldn't tell LuEllen.

"Promise me!" Uncle Hollis's plea brought me back to the present.

"I promise," I whispered.

"It's a tough job, but someone has to do it."

"But how? Why so many ghosts here?"

"They say—"

A ghost lady already sitting at the table cleared her throat and stomped her foot impatiently. Uncle Hollis cut her a hard stare that had her clutching her wispy purse.

So much for "You can't take it with you."

"As I was saying," he said, addressing me, "the Colonel and I think this funeral home was built on an old burial mound, one next to a stream considered sacred. You know about the Hickman mounds not far from here, and they found some interesting artifacts when they added this kitchen on back in the forties. Anyway, there's something that keeps spirits here. We've always had to help them along. I tried to teach Sean once."

His gaze traveled out the window wistfully.

"Who's Sean?"

"He's Dec's younger brother. He ran off to Atlanta to go to mortuary school there. But he should've been back by now."

I swallowed hard. That had to be hard on Dec, and something about Uncle Hollis's tone told me there was more to the story than that.

"Then they sent Hollis to the sanatorium," the Colonel cut in.

"Sean went and told Declan everything," Uncle Hollis said as he buried his face in his hands. "Just too much for the boy."

Based on the number of ghosts I'd seen, I could believe it.

"Hollis, you need to get on with it, son. Visitation is almost over, and you know we'll have to take a break then until everyone is asleep."

Hollis rubbed his hands over his face, "Now, where was I? Yes, Mrs. Lynch, how can I help you?"

Mrs. Lynch told a sob story about fighting with her husband and then getting into an automobile accident. She wanted to apologize before she left.

"Why, my dear, you need to go tell him yourself. He passed away not long after you did."

Her face brightened and she disappeared in a whirl of light over Uncle Hollis's shoulder.

"That was easy," I murmured.

"Don't get cocky," he said.

"But how do you do it?"

He looked deeply into my eyes. "You don't have much belief in happily ever after, do you?"

I laughed. "Not really."

"Well, you're going to have to let go and let God if you want to learn to make the light."

"Whoa, stop. Nobody said anything about bringing Jesus into this."

"At least you need to believe in heaven," he said.

"But how do we know that such a thing exists?"

"We don't. We've seen the light, but that's it. The ghosts have to be going somewhere, right?"

"I guess?"

Uncle Hollis put his hand on mine. "Looky here, if you want to make the light you gotta believe in the light. Picture that ghost in front of you walking into the light, into heaven, into joy. Imagine a world where everything makes sense and turns out all right in the end."

"But things don't always turn out all right in the end," I said. He should know that. He worked in a funeral home, for heaven's sake. How many children had he buried? How many funerals for teenagers who wrapped cars around trees? Or servicemen and women who had to come home in a body bag? There were no happy endings, at least none that I could think of.

"Okay, okay, fine," the older man said. "Can you be compassionate? Can you hope for things to turn out right for folks and for God to take care of things rather than taking matters into your own hands?"

"Maybe?"

He sighed in exasperation. "Well, you're not going to make the light until you believe in the light, I'll tell you that."

"But what about the people who should go to hell? Do they get to walk into the light, too?"

"Not for me to decide. I gotta wish them all well. Even the assholes."

Even the assholes. That was a tall order. "But then how did some of the ghosts I met end up going into the light?"

"Did you fix something for them? Did you feel some compassion for them, maybe want to help them out?"

"Yeah," I admitted grudgingly. And sometimes that good will was grudging for them, too.

"There you go. You watch me tonight. Tomorrow it's your turn."

Ghost after ghost told his or her story, and it became apparent that they wanted someone to hear them out. Maybe that was the only compassion they needed. Uncle Hollis listened to their stories, nodding and jotting down notes on a yellow legal pad.

One lady wanted to make sure someone fed her Chihuahua. A

teenager wanted Uncle Hollis to tell his parents he was sorry for driving like an idiot. A little girl broke down into tears because she was afraid she would get to heaven and her grandmother would be mad at her for running away. A bedraggled wife came forward and wanted us to press charges against her husband. She wanted someone, anyone, to know he'd beaten her to death.

"This would drive anyone insane," I muttered under my breath as Uncle Hollis ushered her on. Despite his space cadet demeanor, he had a mind like a steel trap when it came to ghosts, easily remembering who had passed on and when except for the few years he'd been away.

"It's not easy," he said. "It wasn't so bad when I could help them one or two at a time, but now we're really backed up. I must've seen twenty people already."

"Are none of these easy?"

Uncle Hollis shook his head with a sad smile. "Oh, no. Those who die with an easy conscience are most likely to float off into the ether. Those folks, of course, are few and far between. Most of us spend a lot of time worrying about something, don't you think?"

"Yeah, I guess so." I spent a lot of time worrying about whether I'd done LuEllen proud, whether I'd made a mistake following Pinup Betty's advice, whether I'd get the fairy godmother part, whether I'd ever get married and have a family, whether someone would find out I spoke to dead people. The list never ended.

"I see young master Declan headed this way," the Colonel said abruptly. "Away, all of you!"

"He was the consummate funeral director, wasn't he?" I asked Uncle Hollis as the ghosts disappeared in wisps of light and the Colonel followed them.

"No, he was a mortician," Uncle Hollis said with a chuckle. "Back then, mortician was a fancy name, and that's the one he chose. In those days, people didn't fear death like we do. No, they understood death was around every corner. They embraced it."

Embrace death? Just when I thought Uncle Hollis couldn't get any crazier.

Uncle Hollis leaned back in his chair. "Think about it. All the old monuments with weeping angels, urns, and shrouds—those were people who understood death could snatch your youngest child in a heartbeat. They mourned their loved ones. Heck, they made jewelry from their hair and took pictures of their dead bodies as memento mori. These days, we try to scrub death out of every aspect of the funeral business as though we could somehow conquer it."

He yawned and got to his feet. "Caroline goes to all of these damned conventions and comes home with all of this nonsense. We're supposed to say the person's name instead of referring to a body or 'the deceased.' We have to say 'casket' instead of 'coffin' and put them in a 'memorial garden' instead of a 'cemetery.' It's all a bunch of hogwash. Ashes to ashes and dust to dust. And I'll be damned if I'm going to call anyone's ashes 'cremains.'"

Someone clapped, and I turned to see Declan leaned against the doorway. "On your soapbox again, Uncle Hollis?"

"No, calling it like it is," the older man said as he brushed past the younger.

So, no love lost between Declan and Uncle Hollis, although how on earth had the older man ended up in assisted living when he could have such clearly lucid moments?

"If I'd known he was back here, I would've warned you," Declan said as he reached in an upper cabinet for an amber beverage that looked suspiciously alcoholic.

"I don't mind," I said.

The kitchen seemed smaller now that it was only the two of us. I wasn't going to make it any easier for him, either. "So, you have something to explain to me?"

Declan

Well, she didn't waste any time.

I froze where I stood in front of the cabinet with one hand on the bourbon and the other on two mugs.

Get it over with.

I put the bourbon and two mugs on the table. "I was wondering if you would like to go out with me. On a date."

She paused for so long I started counting the ticks of the clock on the wall.

"That's very kind of you, Dec, but I'll be leaving again soon. I don't think it'd be a good idea."

I shrugged and forced myself to smile. "Never hurts to ask."

"I don't mind if you tell Jessica that we went out, though."

Bourbon now poured, both of us had a hard time finding an excuse to leave.

"Is there anything to eat around here? I'm starving," she asked.

"Take a look in the fridge," I said. "But check the dates. I think it was my turn to clean out the fridge last week, and I didn't do it."

"Now would be a good time," Caroline said as she paused at the door to the prep room. "You'll lock up?"

"I always do," I said.

"Easy on the whiskey, too, hotshot."

"Yes, ma'am," I said. Caroline disappeared and that left me alone with Presley once again. She'd found the remains of a fruit-and-cheese platter of questionable origin.

"It's not moldy," she said with a shrug. "Can I have a little of that?"

"Sure." I poured a finger of bourbon into the mug that said, All the coffee in Colombia couldn't make me a morning person.

"Cheese?" She held out the tray, and I took a cube of pepper jack. How could she be this nonchalant? "You mean you don't have a real girlfriend to scare Jessica off?"

"Not much of a casual dater."

"Cold feet to go along with those cold fingers?"

I winced.

"Sorry," she said. "That really gets to you, huh?"

"Not my favorite nickname, no."

"I wonder who started that rumor."

I closed my eyes at the thought of it. I hadn't always been Cold Fingers. In fact, everything had been just fine until my senior year. The next thing I knew, people were snickering when I walked by. I'd seen Lacey Hutchens twice, but she dropped me like a hot potato. I didn't think to ask any questions since I was off to college. It was only later Sean told me "The Legend of Cold Fingers."

Someone had started the rumor that my hands were always cold thanks to the work I did with dead bodies. To make matters worse, Dad died suddenly about then, and everyone became really standoffish. At that point, my cold hands also became cursed.

When I had to quit my architecture degree at UT Knoxville and go to mortuary school in Nashville, then come home to work at Anderson's, the snickering and whispering hadn't stopped. I'd thought the whole thing would blow over once I graduated, but after the second girl I asked out said, "No offense, but I'm pretty sure your family is cursed" I gave up on that idea. Thus began my career of sidestepping goth girls and old ladies.

"Man, I'm sorry, Dec. I didn't know it bothered you that much," Presley said. She reached across the table to squeeze my hand. Ironically, her fingers were chilly.

"I'm fine. It's been a long day."

I felt bad the moment I said it. The woman had lost her home and her car in less than twenty-four hours, and she was sitting in a funeral home kitchen, a kitchen that, by poor design, was way too close to the prep room. Fortunately, it had been a pretty calm day in the olfactory sense.

"I'm sorry I said that. I know you've had a rough time of it."

Presley took back her hand and chugged the rest of her bourbon. "The funny thing is, I made a bigger mess of things out in Hollywood. What do you make of that?"

"I hate to ask what happened there then."

She laughed, a rich sound that bubbled up from her belly. "Oh, I messed up royally. You saw the magazines, but you didn't see how I was dumped by my boyfriend for a newer model. Or how he took my life savings when he left."

"How? Why?" They were the only words I could form. Presley wasn't yet twenty-five. How much newer could the guy get? And why? Was he blind? Then to take her money? My hands formed fists. "I want to pummel him on your behalf."

"And I would love to let you, but I think he went to the Caymans. Turns out he bilked quite a few other folks, too. I can't imagine they were as naïve as I was, though."

"You probably weren't being naïve. There are a lot of good con artists out there." I hesitated, but I needed to know. "But do you like living there? Acting?"

She shrugged.

That's when it hit me: I didn't dislike working at the funeral home. I resented it because my father had made me promise to work there and because I'd had to cut short my degree when Sean took off. There were *parts* of the job I disliked, but I didn't *hate* my job.

If I kept working part time, then I would still have the money to pay off the chapel loan—so we could get another one. I didn't have to have the house on Maple Avenue. There would be other houses.

Presley, on the other hand, disliked her job more than she was willing to admit to herself. For just a minute I envisioned her staying behind here in Ellery. I could pass the funeral home off to Sean, and she and I could renovate the Maple Avenue place together.

"You know, you really are good with hair."

Why did you say that? It's not like she's going to give up acting to cut hair.

"I've always liked styling hair and playing with makeup," she said with a smile. "Not that big a fan of Delilah, mind you, so it's a good thing I'm only here until the new year."

All of my Maple Avenue plans went up in smoke. Ridiculous, really. It's like I was the one with the biological clock and she was the one with wild oats to sow. I had to corral my thoughts to another place.

"Delilah's not so bad when you get to know her. You'll see."

She yawned and stood. "Guess I'll have to find out tomorrow."

"Stick a fork in me," I said as I stood. "I've got a date with a lumpy pillow. Thanks again for playing along to get Jessica off my back."

"Not a problem," she said. "It's the least I could do considering you're letting us stay here, although she's always seemed like a nice girl to me."

"It's complicated. And she's married."

"Still, I appreciate your help. Now you know how bad it really is."

"I have a feeling you're going to make it all work," I said.

She frowned, and I wondered what she was thinking. "I hope so."

She walked down the hall in what I was beginning to think of as her Sexy Funeral Director costume, and I enjoyed the view.

That old suit coat looked better on her than it ever had on me, and I itched to follow her. Down the hall, back to California, maybe even to Timbuktu—it didn't matter where.

But, no, I was stuck here.

Leave it to me to start falling for a girl who wasn't.

Presley

The chain saws started their buzzing before seven. I groaned and pulled the pillow over my head, but it was no use.

"Presley, baby, I can't find my pills," LuEllen whined.

"That's because you took too many yesterday so I hid them."

"Ungrateful turd."

"That's a great way to talk to your only child, the one who will be looking after you in your golden years." I yawned and rolled out of bed. The bedroom where we were staying looked over the back parking lot so I could see them removing the tree bit by bit. I winced as they pulled a branch off the top of my car. The roof had caved in; the windshield had shattered. The insurance company was probably going to make me total it.

"It hurts! Where are the damned pills?" Whining led to coughing, but at least that distracted LuEllen from the hiding place I'd found. "Here are two. I'll come home at lunch to give you another dose."

"Don't bother. I'll just curl up and *die*. Then you won't have to worry about my golden years."

"Always the drama queen. I'm going to work."

After a quick shower with no ghosts to be seen, I went through my duffel bag and found I had precisely one clean outfit: halter

top and tight capris. And the only shoes that went with that outfit were a pair of improbably comfortable wedge sandals.

Well, if I wanted a new wardrobe, I was going to have to get a
paycheck, now wasn't I? It wasn't like I couldn't make the dollars
stretch at the ol' Goodwill. But first I had to have some dollars to
stretch.

And a way to get to the Goodwill.

One thing at a time, Presley. One thing at a time.

Making something out of nothing with my hair and makeup
proved difficult. I finally decided to go light on the latter. I
grabbed my purse and tossed Dec's suit coat over one shoulder
and headed down the stairs.

I walked into the kitchen, and he froze with the coffeepot in
hand. "You do know a cold front went through, and it's only
thirty-seven degrees out there, right?"

"I did not know that." I looked out the back door and winced
at the destruction to my car—it was even worse up close. "It's
only two blocks. I won't freeze in that amount of time."

"Don't you have winter clothes?" he blurted.

"Most of my clothes were burned to a crisp, I'm afraid."

"Well, at least let me drive you to work. We can get to the
truck now, and it has a heater."

A heated truck sounded nice, but he'd just poured a cup of
coffee. "I'm sure you have things to do, and I'll warm up as I
walk."

"Go get in the truck."

"Aren't we bossy this morning?"

He scowled, and I wondered what'd happened to the man
who'd *asked* me on a date last night. "Would you get in the truck,
please?"

Declan

That had come out more irritably than I would've liked, but I didn't want Presley to get frostbite, and I was mad at myself for liking her so damn much. Out of habit, I took the route that would take me past the house on Maple Avenue. Since I wasn't going to be able to buy it, I needed to get out of the habit of checking on it. I told myself not to look, but I saw the FOR SALE sign out of the corner of my eye.

"Oh, that house is lovely."

"The yellow one?"

"Yeah, I've always liked it." She hugged herself, and suddenly I wanted to buy my dream home and give it to her even before she added, "I've always wanted a house like that."

"You sure? It's pretty beat-up."

"But look at that big porch and all of that pretty stuff around the top of the porch. There's that gorgeous tree in the front yard, and the picket fence. It's perfect."

Yeah, it was.

I'd had plans for that old house from the Victorian era. It was an Eastlake, with a hint of Queen Anne, and no doubt imperfectly designed by the man who built it, one of the early mayors of Ellery.

"I was going to buy that house."

Why had I said that? No one knew that outside the family.

Her head whipped in my direction. "You were?"

"I was."

"What happened?"

"Well, now we need to replace the chapel."

"Oh." She slumped in the seat, and I could feel her disappointment for me. "I bet it has one of those awesome staircases and at least one beautiful fireplace."

"Original curved staircase, a fireplace in almost every room."

"Nice backyard for a dog?"

"Actually, yes. And the fence back there was in better shape than the picket fence up front."

"Someday I'm going to buy a house like that," she said. "I've lived my whole life in a trailer or an apartment, but someday I will have an honest-to-goodness home to call my own."

By that time I'd parallel parked in front of the hair salon. I needed Presley Cline to get out of my truck before I said something stupid.

"Have fun at work," I said instead.

She made a face at me and disappeared inside Delilah's shop. The last thing I saw through the beauty shop window before I pulled away from the curb was Delilah's hands on her hips as she berated Presley for who knew what.

The rest of the day passed in a blur. I had to direct the tree guys. Then I called Roy Vandiver to come take a look at Presley's car. I mean, I couldn't buy her a house, but I had a sneaking suspicion Roy could put the Firebird to rights. Then I had to deal with my new friend, Inspector Davenport. He still wasn't budging on the Certificate of Occupancy. If anything, he seemed more unwilling to help me out even after we bonded over crappy furnaces.

He'd renovated a house over on Second Street and had a furnace just like the one at the funeral home with many of the same issues. Since he kept politely dodging my requests for a return inspection, however, I got the impression Arwin Potter might be the one funding his furnace repair.

Then there were all the calls to make to move visitations as well as funerals to area churches. Finally, I got to step outside the funeral home and see if Uncle Eldridge shared my opinion on things.

He informed me, in his usual laconic way, that he was doing me a special favor by coming to the funeral home first. I informed him, in my usual way, that I was grateful and would say it with money once all was said and done.

And there went more of the money I'd saved for the Maple Avenue place.

Uncle El and his crew got to work. I'd been looking forward to fixing things up myself, taking my time and doing it right. Mr. Building Official had robbed me of that. All around me, men hammered and sawed. I itched to join them, so I made myself go back through the front door.

"I can't believe the nerve you have coming here."

That was Caroline.

"Well, missy, you had your chance with me, but you chose to throw your lot in with that hippie Anderson. I'm giving you one last chance not to go down with this ship."

And that was Arwin Potter, her father.

"You sent the Building Official, didn't you?"

I got to Caroline's office just in time to see Mr. Potter's wolfish grin. "Sent him to your place first chance I could. Now, if you'll just hand over those bodies you have in the cooler, I'll take care of them from here on out."

"That won't be necessary," I said. Both sets of eyes turned to me. "I've already made arrangements with First Methodist and First Baptist. Uncle El will have us open again before we need to have any more visitations."

"That's not good enough," Potter snarled.

"Good thing it's not up to you," I said. "You're not taking anyone who already had plans with us. I heard about what you did to the Petersons, bleeding them dry. Hiram had to take a job at Walmart. He's seventy."

Mr. Potter shrugged. "He wanted his wife to go out in style."

"Get. Out." Caroline's voice shook, and the peonies trembled in their vase from where she was clutching her desk.

Mr. Potter stopped right in front of me. He was a short man with a Napoleon complex if I'd ever seen one. He glared at me, but then looked over his shoulder at his daughter. "My offer still stands."

Caroline swallowed hard but shook her head no.

"Have it your way," he said blithely before strolling down the hall and out the front door.

"What in the blue hell was that all about?"

Caroline slumped down into her chair, defeated and deflated. "He knows."

I crashed into the seat opposite her. "He knows what?"

"He knows we're scraping by and that the tornado damage is the . . . is the . . ."

"Nail in our coffin?"

She gave me an "Eat shit and die" look for using a death-related pun. "He knows and, as you can see, he would like to help us along. I guess we'll have to let Armando go."

"We're not laying Armando off. He's better at this job than I am."

"Dec, we're losing our shirts on these burial plans your father and grandfather sold. That account lost tons of money when the stock market crashed."

I stood. "But it's coming back, and I'm not charging those people extra money. They paid in good faith thinking they were doing their loved ones a favor. It's not their fault Dad didn't use the right kind of account or charge them enough to make up for inflation."

She sighed, a jagged breath. "We've got more than enough business to stay afloat, but if the next year looks like most of this year has, then we'll have to sell."

Dammit, my promise to my father had been that I would never sell Anderson's. He knew I didn't want to run the place, but he also knew I would be the one person who made sure the funeral home stayed in the family.

Still a shitty predicament to put a teenager in.

"No," I said softly.

"No?" Caroline slumped forward on her desk. "Fine. I'll have to go work for . . . him."

"Hell no!"

"Maybe I could do some good over there. Stop him from bilk-ing everyone who walks through the door." She steadied the pink peonies of shame, now drooping a bit. "We have to do something."

"I'll think of another way. I may already have an idea or two."

"Next, you're going to have to pay Eldridge, and we both know the insurance isn't going to cover the cost of having him rush the job. Hell, we pay the minimum so it probably won't cover all of the repairs. We've been running this place by the skin of our teeth, Declan. Something's got to give. If I go . . ." Here she paused for a breath and probably some courage. "If I go back to Potter's then that's one less salary for you to worry about."

"He's not going to pay you what you're worth."

"Declan, sweetie, Anderson's doesn't pay me what I'm worth."

"Fair enough. But we have extra business, so that has to help, right?"

"Don't forget the two indigents—"

"But still, we're okay for now, right?"

"For now. For this minute. Maybe."

She didn't look convinced. It was time to break out the big guns. "What if I were to tell you I had saved up enough money to pay off the chapel loan?"

"But, Declan, that's *your* money."

"It doesn't matter. I can pay off the chapel tomorrow and put down enough money for the loan we'll need to rebuild, *but* . . ."

"But what?" Her eyes narrowed.

"But if we do that, we need to think big. We need to add a cre-matory because that gives us an advantage over Potter. And we need to build a new prep room that isn't so close to the kitchen."

"Declan, about this crematory business, I just don't know."

"Think about it before you say no. It would give people a more affordable option. Might keep some folks from going into Jefferson."

"I'll think about it," she said, but her tone of voice suggested she was far from convinced.

"While you're thinking, consider adding a furnace just for pets." I knew I was pushing the issue, but Mrs. Morris really had got me to thinking.

"What?"

"Hey, folks love their pets, too. It wouldn't be the same oven."

"Oh, good heavens! Don't you have some work to do?"

Didn't I always?

But, first, I needed another cup of coffee. I walked into the kitchen and found Uncle Hollis talking to thin air.

He might be a lunatic, but he did work cheap.

Come to think of it, weren't we paying for his assisted living? If we kept Hollis home, that would save us a significant amount from our personal funds if not from the business side of things.

"Why so glum, chum?" Uncle Hollis asked. I wasn't sure if he was talking to me or to his imaginary breakfast companion.

"As Dad would say, we're in a mell of a hess, Uncle Hollis," I said as I poured another cup of coffee.

"We always are, my boy. Now, if you'll excuse me, I have work to do."

I watched the older man enter the prep room while humming "I Guess That's Why They Call It the Blues." He closed the door quietly behind him. How could he be so damn crazy one minute and so sane the next? Maybe Sean had been wrong about him. After all, I was beginning to think I'd been wrong about Sean.

I sat down at the table and cradled my coffee. Maybe Caroline was right. Maybe we should sell the place. I could keep my money, go buy the house on Maple Avenue.

I wasn't Patrick Anderson, that's for sure.

No, but I was Patrick Anderson's son, and he had taught me that someone had to take care of people when they couldn't take care of themselves—and Potter wasn't about to do that.

Presley

"About time you showed up."

"Good morning to you, too, Delilah."

She turned from her customer and took in my outfit. "What in heaven's name are you wearing?"

"I haven't had time to shop for winter clothes."

Nor the money.

"Well, then go down to the armory. Folks have donated plenty of things for the people who lost everything. I hear they have more than they'll ever use." Delilah turned back to the man sitting in her chair and put down the clippers in favor of scissors.

But I haven't lost everything. Almost, but not everything.

I picked up a broom and waited for her to finish so I could make myself useful and sweep up. It was a menial task, one that took me back to my first days in beauty school when I'd finally admitted to myself I'd have to take a second job while I waited to hit it big.

Still waiting . . .

Delilah finished up with the gentleman I didn't recognize, and I started sweeping while they talked money. No one else waited in the shop, but that didn't surprise me in the least. Most folks were still either cleaning up or helping a neighbor clean up. Thank goodness, not that many people had died, but there was one heckuva mess in town. Haircuts weren't exactly high on their list of priorities.

When I put away my broom and looked up, Delilah was smiling at me. It was scary.

"I didn't expect to see the high-and-mighty Presley Cline ever take up a broom."

"I'm not high-and-mighty," I said.

"Not now that you've been caught showing your drawers to the world," she said with a snort, "but that's how you acted back in high school."

My face burned hot. Would anyone ever forget about those pictures?

Delilah headed around the corner, motioning for me to follow her. On the other side of the wall was a setup that mirrored hers. "This will be your station. Decorate it however you want. Until you start getting your own customers, though, you'll be sweeping up, washing towels, and just about anything else I ask you to do. Got it?"

"Yes, ma'am."

"And don't call me ma'am."

Yes, ma'am.

She disappeared around the corner, and I wondered what I was supposed to do when it was slow like this. I wandered back to a tiny closet just big enough for a washer and a dryer. A quick sniff of the towels in the basket on the dryer told me they needed to be washed, so I started a load.

The rest of the day, I had one customer, swept up after several of Delilah's, and ran another load of towels. When I got back from the last load, Delilah was holding the ugly case I'd taken to Anderson's the other day.

"We've got another call," she said with a sinister smile. "This time you're headed to Potter's."

Potter's Funeral Home was everything Anderson's was not. The modern brick building still smelled of new carpet. Everything inside was sleek lines and glass tops instead of the dark, somber wood trim and antique furniture at Anderson's. Potter's also had no Christmas decorations. Not even the green garland or a tiny Nativity scene like Caroline had put out.

"Ah, you must be Presley." An older man in a tailored suit stepped forward, offering a hand. He had to be a good six inches shorter than me—definitely more after you took the wedge sandals into account.

"Yes, sir."

"Oh, call me Arwin. Let me show you back."

He was being perfectly nice, but something about his smile reminded me of a shark, and all the hairs on my neck stood on end again. I looked around nervously for ghosts, but I didn't see a one.

"Delilah tells me you did excellent work for Anderson's the other day," he said as we entered a large chapel then exited through a side door. "How long have you been working with the deceased?"

Pretty much all my life, if you think about it.

"Not long." As we walked through the chapel and entered the prep room, I realized the prickles on my neck had a lot more to do with a *lack* of ghosts than an overabundance of them. After the mass of souls at Anderson's, Potter's seemed downright lonely.

"I only have two customers today," Arwin said, chuckling at his own joke. "They're two ladies from the nursing home, and they are going to be a challenge."

Yes, they would be because I did not see a ghost anywhere to help me out.

To make matters worse, Mr. Potter—Arwin—didn't leave. I finally managed to ignore him enough to figure out how best to take care of thin, brittle hair and some unsightly age spots.

When I finished, Arwin came over to inspect my work while I cleaned up. "Hmm. You do excellent work. You can work on my dead ladies any time."

"Um, thanks."

I nodded and turned to go.

"Come and pick up your check. I'm sure Delilah will be looking for that."

Mr. Potter led me through a maze of rooms and back to his office, an airy space almost as big as one of the rooms they used for visitations over at Anderson's. "Let's see . . . Here we are."

He made a production of taking out a book of oversized checks, flipping through them, and double-checking something. "Normally, Debbie writes the checks, but she had to pick up her daughter from school early today."

I nodded.

"So I heard you were in Hollywood."

"Yes, sir—I mean, Arwin."

"Saw your IMDb page."

Oh, good. He'd seen my roles as "dead blonde," "dead brunette," and "mouthy hooker," among other equally prestigious roles.

"Saw your latest magazine photos, too."

I took in a shaky breath. Nothing to do but endure. Before I left Hollywood, Ira told me not to say any more than I had to because I didn't want anything incriminating to come back to me one day. With each mention of the tabloid, I itched to defend myself, but I said nothing.

He put down the pen and looked up from the checkbook, steepling his fingers as he did. "Thinking about going back?"

I swallowed hard. "Absolutely."

"Waiting for things to blow over, I see." He pointed the pen at me. "That's smart."

I shrugged.

"Well, I don't understand why you aren't a bigger star. You're certainly pretty enough."

What the hell was I supposed to say to that? "Thank you."

"You know, if you ever find yourself short on funds, I'm sure I could find more odd jobs around here." His eyes raked over my outfit. The shark's grin was back as well as the urge to grab the check and flee.

"That's very kind of you, but I'm doing just fine."

"Oh, I don't think you would be working for Delilah if you were 'just fine.' I think you would find I can be very generous."

Dear Lord in heaven above, he is propositioning me. I pasted on a smile and reached for the check. "I'll keep that in mind."

He laid his hand on top of mine. "You do that."

His eyes bored into me, and his smooth fingers stroked the top of my hand for a few seconds that felt more like minutes. Finally, I drew my hand out from under his and took the check, forcing myself to rise and walk out of his office at a normal pace.

"Have a good day, Presley," he said as he leaned back in his chair and clasped his hands behind his neck.

I didn't bother to answer. I also would *not* be coming back to his establishment for any reason. I'd rather deal with the ghosts at Anderson's.

When I reached the parking lot, I remembered that I'd arrived by cab. I dug around in my purse until I came up with my cell phone, but it was dead. I sure as hell wasn't going back in to Potter's to call for a taxi, so I started walking.

How far could it be?

I hadn't gone a mile before a minivan with clip-on antlers and a red nose on the grille whizzed around me and skidded to a stop with a squeal of tires. Out stepped my worst nightmare: my former BFF, Kari.

"What the hell do you think you're doing?"

"Hi, Kari, how are you?"

"Listen, bitch." She caught up to me, standing so close I could watch her nostrils flare. Her curly red hair billowed around both of us while she searched for a follow-up. "You stay away from my husband."

"What are you talking about?"

She poked at my shoulders, causing me to back up in the direction of Potter's Funeral Home, a place I did not want to go. "Of all the mechanics in all the world, why did you have to call him?"

"I still don't know what you are talking about. When I left this morning, my car was totaled. I had to call a cab to get here."

Dec. Even as the words spilled out of my mouth, I thought of how Dec had looked so pensively at my poor messed-up car. He, of course, would call the best mechanic in town.

Wait. Stop.

"You *married* Roy Vandiver?"

"Yes, I married Roy," she snapped. "And you aren't going to steal him away from me this time. We have kids."

"I'm not going to steal *Roy!*"

"Of course you're not! Wait. What's wrong with him?"

For a moment I saw insecurity flash behind her green eyes. I wanted to laugh at the thought of my stealing Roy Vandiver from her, but I stifled the urge. You didn't trifle with a woman like Kari. "Nothing. I honestly had no idea the two of you got married. That's great!"

Cars whizzed by us so fast that we both almost lost our balance on the sloped shoulder. Kari crossed her arms and stared through me as though gauging whether or not I was telling the truth. "Then how did your car end up at the garage beside my house?"

I shrugged. "Dec must've called."

"What? You've been in town less than a week, and now you're going after *him?*"

For crying out loud, I had made her madder. She leaned toward me. "You listen here. I don't know what kind of game it is you like to play with men, but you leave Declan Anderson alone. He is a good man, and he doesn't deserve to be stuck with a bag full of crazy like you."

True.

"Look, I had a job at the funeral home when the tornado hit. My car got smushed. He must've called Roy. That's all."

But why am I telling you this? It's none of your damn business.

"Whatever," she said pivoting and heading back to her van.

"Are you seriously going to leave me here on the side of the road knowing I don't have a car?"

"Damn straight I am," she said before climbing into her mini-van and leaving me to, for all she knew, walk to Ellery in the rapidly approaching dusk.

A hysterical giggle pushed its way to the surface. She still thought I'd stolen her boyfriend and done lewd things with him.

At least I knew Roy Vandiver could keep a secret. And that my former best friend was married to one of the best men I knew.

I dug my cell phone out of my purse. Nope. Still dead.

Surely it wasn't that far back to town. So what if it was getting colder? I didn't need all ten toes anyway. I drew Dec's suit coat closer around me, but he hadn't worn it in so long it didn't smell like him anymore.

Declan

Caroline and Hollis took the service at First Baptist for Miss Sylvia. Armando and I held Miss Ginger's service in the old chapel—the Freesia Room—and then another one for a tornado victim at First Methodist. We even had to put both hearses into service, the new one and the antique I'd foolishly kept because it reminded me of Gramps. I let Miss Ginger take her last ride in the old fin tail. I had a feeling she would've approved.

By the time we all got back to the eerily quiet funeral home, it was dark. So we locked the doors and brought the Woodford Reserve to the now empty Lilac Room.

Caroline downed a shot's worth and held out her mug for more.

"Hey, that's the good stuff. You're supposed to savor it," I said.

"Still don't know why we're drinking Kentucky bourbon instead of Tennessee whiskey," Uncle Hollis said as he stared contemplatively into his Santa Claus mug.

"Or why you won't spring for the Chivas," Armando added with a grin. He was the only Mexican I knew—granted, I knew about five—who didn't like tequila. He preferred scotch, and he liked for it to be expensive and to share the name of his favorite soccer team from back in Guadalajara. Of course, Manny liked tequila enough for the two of them.

"Well, while we're having this impromptu staff meeting," I said, "we need to talk."

"No! We need to raise a glass to Anderson's!" Caroline interrupted hastily. Her look told me not to say a word.

"Here, here," everyone said with a clink of their glasses.

Uncle Hollis looked at the doorway. He nodded and smiled, and I sighed. He was crazy, no doubt about it. Even so, I wasn't sure I wanted to take him back to assisted living. I'd kinda missed the old bastard.

"*Híjole*, what a week," Armando muttered under his breath.

"And it's not even over yet."

"The Fitzgeralds said they wished cremation had been an option," Uncle Hollis said.

"That's the third request this month," Caroline mused.

I gave her a pointed look.

"Okay, fine," she said. She drained her mug and held it out again. I poured. "Declan was just saying earlier that he thought a crematorium would be a good idea. I mean, it's the only thing Dad—Potter doesn't have."

"Don't we still owe on the chapel? You know, the part that just blew away?" asked Armando.

"I have the money to pay that off and a little extra to put aside for a new loan," I said softly.

"Will that be enough?"

"No," Caroline spit, and the spit made her giggle. We'd skipped lunch once again, and all the alcohol was going straight to her head. One of the hazards of being a funeral director: not getting to take advantage of the mouth-watering potluck spreads the ladies of the church would put out after a funeral. Dad had always said to sit and eat with our clients would be "unseemly."

"This crematorium idea *es* good." Armando's English was more heavily accented from the bourbon.

"Yes!" Uncle Hollis's eyes lit up, but he was still staring at the doorway with an eerie grin. "The Col—I mean, I think it's time we looked into new ways of doing things."

"Since when?"

"Since about five minutes ago." Uncle Hollis studied his drink.

"We need an investor," Caroline said even as she extended her mug again. I poured less than a finger and gave her the "This is the last one" look. After all, we had three more funerals tomorrow. I put my own mug down on the table. Someone had to be the designated driver in case we got a call. Armando's eyes met mine, and he put his cup down, too.

"An investor. We need an investor," Uncle Hollis was saying as he stroked his chin and stared into the distance.

"I think I have a solution," Armando said. "I could get together about a hundred thousand if you were to make me partner."

The rest of us gasped.

And to think Caroline had been ready to let him go earlier that day! Right then I could kiss him.

"Armando, I would be honored to add Cepeda to the funeral home name."

He looked up with a grin. "Care to shake on it?"

We met in the middle of the room. I jerked my hand back at the last minute. "Anything I should know about this money?"

"No, *cabrón,*" he said with a snort. "This is my second job. The landscaping company has prospered and my brother, Lorenzo, he has been doing very well with his plumbing business. It's all good money."

"Sorry, *cabrón más grande.* I have to know these things." I extended my hand, and he shook it.

At first I thought he was still offended, but then he smiled. "Apology accepted, partner. But you are assuredly the bigger asshole."

Fair enough.

For the first time, I felt like I was in charge of this motley crew even if Caroline held the official title. "Okay, people. No more bourbon until we get everyone safely taken care of. Armando, partner of mine, we are on call since we're the least sloshed."

"Of course, Mother Hen." Caroline planted a sloppy kiss on my cheek.

"You're not driving, are you?"

"I think I'd better walk," she said. Since her little bungalow was around the corner, that would probably be okay, but still . . .

"I'll take you home," Armando said. I nodded my thanks to him.

That left Uncle Hollis.

"Headed upstairs, Unc?"

"I think I'll sit here for a few minutes and ruminate, if you don't mind."

He was frowning at the doorway instead of smiling. That man had the weirdest mood swings.

"All right, well, I'm headed to my apartment."

I didn't get two steps before LuEllen appeared at the bottom of the stairs. Thank God she was wearing clothes. "Have you seen Presley?"

Not since this morning when she stepped outside looking like a lost nymph of spring. "No. I figured she was already upstairs."

LuEllen shook her head with enough force to shake her whole body. She was also wheezing as if she'd run upstairs instead of coming down.

"Are you okay?"

"I need my oxygen. And she was supposed to have been back at lunch to give me a new round of pain pills. Instead I took some Benadryl and fell asleep, and now I don't know where she is."

"Did you try calling her?"

"It went to voice mail."

Tears slipped down her cheeks, but I couldn't tell if she was worried for Presley, wanting her meds, or some combination of the two.

But now I was worried about Presley. Adrenaline kicked in. I did *not* want to imagine Presley Cline laid out on a slab like a blue Sleeping Beauty who wouldn't wake up. "You have a seat in the room. I'll go find her."

I called Delilah, who'd already gone to bed even though it was only seven thirty. "I called a taxi to send her to a job at Potter's, but she never came back. Lazy heifer."

I took a deep breath to keep from saying something to Delilah that I would later regret and thanked her instead. I really, really didn't want to call Potter.

He answered on the second ring. "Well, well. Ready to sell the place, Declan?"

"No. I'm here with Presley's mother, and she's worried since Presley hasn't made it home yet. She isn't still with you, is she?"

Potter paused for longer than I would like. He preferred his women young. Based on what had happened between him and Lisa Devlin, he also enjoyed keeping them in the lifestyle to which they would like to become accustomed. Presley was desperate for cash, but I hoped to hell she wasn't his latest conquest.

"She was here for quite some time this afternoon," he drawled, intentionally pausing to let me think the worst. "But she took off so fast she didn't even call for a taxi."

I wonder why.

If I didn't like him before, I hated him now.

He chuckled. "She's a looker, now, isn't she?"

And you were hoping she'd get tired of walking and come crawling back to you.

"Thanks for nothing, Potter."

I hung up on him.

Bastard.

I turned to LuEllen. "I think she's walking home. I'm going to see if I can find her."

Presley

Seven miles was a helluva lot longer than I'd thought it would be.

My wedge sandals had rubbed blisters I could hardly feel since I was losing feeling in my toes. My teeth chattered, and my stomach growled with a painful reminder that I hadn't had anything for lunch but an apple. You'd think someone would stop and offer me a ride, but the closest I came were some rednecks who whistled as they went by.

With Dec's coat over my capris, I probably looked like a sad bag lady. As I finally left the highway in favor of a mostly dark side street that would take me into town, headlights approached. The antique hearse stopped just in front of me, its engine rumbling with power.

There was Dec Anderson rolling down the passenger window. "Hey, little girl, want some candy?"

I wanted to hug him. I wanted to kiss him. I wanted to pay him to massage my feet.

"I am so happy to see you," I said as I slid into the passenger seat and put my case on the floor.

"Now, that's not something I hear a lot—especially not when I'm driving this old thing." His smile didn't quite reach his eyes. No, I suppose most people didn't like to see him coming.

"What a day," I said as I leaned back into the seat.

"That's been the consensus," he said as he whipped the

hearse around to make an improbably graceful U-turn. "What happened to you? Your mama's worried sick about you."

"Well, Delilah sent me out to Potter's. He creeped me out so bad I forgot to call the cab company before leaving. My cell phone was dead, and I wasn't going back in there, so I decided to walk. Then Kari showed up, yelled at me a bit, and left me on the side of the—"

"She did what?"

So I told him. Well, I didn't tell him *everything*, but I told him enough.

A muscle twitched in his jaw. "She and I are going to have words tomorrow."

"Don't." I laid a hand on his arm. "I deserved it."

"You deserved to be left on the side of the road in the cold and the dark?"

I lay back and closed my eyes, willing my growling stomach to shush and my toes to quit burning from the heat now blowing directly on them. "Yeah. Totally deserved it."

We traveled in silence for only a few seconds before my stomach roared again.

He chuckled, a low rumble that vibrated through me. "I'm guessing you haven't had supper."

"And only an apple for lunch."

He narrowed his eyes at me.

"What? A girl's gotta keep her figure."

"A girl's gotta eat something. I think Burger Paradise is still open," he said as he reached into his pocket for his cell phone. "You ought to call your mama, though."

LuEllen recovered quickly enough to ask for a burger and fries. And to tell me to hurry because she needed more of the pain pills. She probably hadn't eaten all day, either. Hopefully, she didn't have the shakes from nicotine or alcohol withdrawal. Not that some detox wouldn't do her good.

Dec pulled into Burger Paradise, and we took a booth in the back. When the waitress asked what I wanted, I started to order a salad and a Diet Coke.

Eff it. If I get the part, great. If I don't? At least I will have enjoyed one of the best burgers in the state.

"I'll have a cheeseburger, fries, and a Coke."

Dec stuttered a little as he placed his order as well as a to-go order for LuEllen. When the waitress left, he said, "You were very, um, vehement with your order there."

"I have decided not to diet today."

"Well, okay then," he said as the waitress slid our drinks in front of us.

"As bad as my day was and as far as I walked, I think I'm entitled to a cheeseburger. To cheeseburgers!"

I lifted my glass, and he clinked his with mine. This time his smile reached all the way to his eyes, and he said, "What am I going to do with you?"

"Love me," I said as I batted my eyelashes. That had always been my customary response whenever Granny had asked it.

When I looked up from my delicious full-calorie fountain Coke, Dec's serious brown eyes seared me as if he could see straight to my soul. The idea sent a jolt to my stomach, and I wanted to run far away. I had no business turning him down one day and then joking about love the next. I needed to form the words to tell him I wasn't a good bet. I mean, I wasn't stupid. I looked pretty enough on the outside, but I was a hot mess on the inside. He needed a girl who would settle down with him, not run off to Hollywood the first chance she got.

Only his eyes were telling another story.

I'd seen that look many times before. Men wanted me. It was a blessing and a curse because I now knew there was no way I could give them what they wanted most. I'd tried, though, really I had.

"Don't look at me like that," I whispered.

For a minute I thought he was going to say what they all said, something along the lines of, "I can't help myself. You're just too beautiful." Instead he cleared his throat and looked past me to the waitress. "Sorry."

And then, inexplicably, my stomach dropped down to my still-aching toes as the waitress slid my food in front of me. What the hell? Why did I want *this* man to tell me I was beautiful? Why did I want *this* man to protest? He was older than me, more sophisticated. He deserved a woman more polished than me.

Oh, hell, Presley, just say it. He needs a woman who can at least do the deed.

I blushed so deeply, I could feel both the heat in my cheeks and the pulse of my blood there. I was not about to pursue this . . . whatever . . . any further. No, no, no. I'd tried relationships. They were not for me. I was going to start early on my spinsterhood with a collection of cats. Heck, maybe a bunch of cats would finally chase Pinup Betty out of the apartment.

"Tell me something funny," I said, my voice coming out far gruffer than I'd intended.

"Well, I know a few funny tales," he said with a grin. "If you promise not to tell anyone why we're laughing here in the corner."

I crossed my heart with my finger before picking up my burger and taking a huge bite.

"So, you know the Mortons, right?"

I nodded. I knew of them.

"Their daughter Kelly passed away right after they'd had this nasty divorce—"

"This doesn't sound like a funny story so far," I said, even though my mouth was full.

He frowned. "No, it's not. At least not yet. Stick with me. Anyway, Mr. Morton passed away after he moved to Nashville, but he was cremated and wanted his ashes to be scattered over Kelly's grave—"

"Still not funny."

"Mrs. Morton found out about it. The next day she went over to the County Line with a leaf blower and blew every last one of his ashes off Kelly's grave."

My eyes grew wide with horror but then I thought about tiny Mrs. Morton with a leaf blower, no doubt almost blowing herself backward as she got rid of every last vestige of her husband from her daughter's grave, and I giggled. Then that giggle became a very unladylike snort.

"See? It's not funny, but it kinda is," Dec said with a lazy grin as he dragged a french fry through ketchup. "People do all sorts of stupid stuff, but we all find the same end. There's no need for such drama."

We sat in silence for a few minutes, but then Dec got that mischievous twinkle in his eye. "Couple of weeks ago we did a graveside service. We finished up everything, and I noticed a man kneeling by an older grave. He was crying, beating the tombstone while moaning, 'Oh, why? Why did you have to die?' I had to know, so I asked him, 'Sir, I'm a funeral director, and rarely have I seen such a display of emotion. Who has passed away? A child? A parent? Your wife?'"

Dec paused here and took another bite of hamburger to let me stew on it. Finally, I couldn't take it anymore and had to ask, "Who?"

"Well, the man stood up and tried to put himself together, then said, 'It's my wife's first husband.'"

I spewed my Coke, and he grinned.

"Dec, you're pretty funny."

His eyes grew serious. "Well, you know why they build fences around graveyards, right?"

"Noooo."

"People are just dying to get in."

It shouldn't have been funny since I'd heard it so many times before, but his deadpan delivery was too much.

The waitress put the bill down on the table. I reached for it, but Dec was faster. "Dec, I can pay my way."

"You could," he said, "but I think you need to save your money for some pants. It's getting pretty cold."

He slid out of the booth and headed to the register, and it hit me. This was the best date I'd ever had, and it wasn't even a real one.

Declan

Logically, I knew our trip to Burger Paradise was not a date, but when I delivered Presley to the back door of the funeral home and unlocked the door for her, I wanted more than anything to kiss her good night. She hesitated on the top step for a moment and leaned toward me as though she were thinking what I was thinking.

Before I could stop myself, I kissed her cheek. "You know, just in case Jessica Borden was looking."

"Of course," she said. "I wouldn't put it past her to hide across the street in those bushes."

When she put it like that, the idea was ludicrous. Now I had no good excuse to kiss Presley on the lips, so I took a step backward instead and held out the bag with her mother's supper.

"Good night, Miss Cline," I said. "And lock the door behind you."

I waited to make sure she did just that, and walked across the back parking lot to the carriage house where my apartment was.

Yes, my bachelor pad was another obstacle to dating.

As if it weren't bad enough to live behind the funeral home, rumor had it that my mother had hung herself in the garage underneath my apartment. Rumors being rumors, no one other than Kari had ever bothered to ask me to my face. I would've told them that she'd actually hung herself in the cellar. One of the reasons I'd moved out of the funeral home and into the carriage house apartment was to get away from the place that had taken my mother. Of course, that damn furnace kept bringing me down to the cellar whether I liked it or not.

I took the stairs two at a time and let myself in. It was a tiny place, one room that was bedroom, living room, and kitchen all in one with a tiny bathroom to the side. What would I have even done with a whole house on Maple Avenue?

Fixed it up, painted it in Victorian colors just to tick off the neighbors, gotten a dog.

Yeah, and that kind of house begged for a wife and kids with a swing set in the backyard and bicycles and toys in the front. Try as I might to picture a wife other than Presley, I couldn't.

Surely you'll be able to think of someone else once she goes back to California.

The whole damn thing was more depressing than it ought to be, so I went to the fridge and reached for a beer. Then I remembered I was both on call and had to be up early in the morning, so I put the beer back and got a glass of water instead.

It wasn't the same.

I slumped into the recliner between my "bedroom" and the "kitchen." I kept coming back to the wounded expression on Presley's face when she told me not to look at her, then the sparkle in her eyes after I kissed her cheek. Someone had hurt her, and that made me want to hurt someone.

Only I didn't know who to hurt.

It was ridiculous. Her mother mooched off her. Delilah had given her all the crap jobs. Potter had obviously hit on her, and Kari had left her stranded on the side of the road.

And what did you do, Dec? You hit on her, too.

Any man with a pulse would. At least I backed off when she asked me to.

Yeah, well, you may need to back off some more. Even if she weren't bent on leaving, being Mrs. Anderson hasn't worked out so well for much of anyone, so that's not something you should offer.

Presley

I slipped in through the back door to find Uncle Hollis holding court with the ghosts. He was down to a line of thirteen—and the Colonel, of course.

I rushed the food upstairs, where I found LuEllen asleep. I tapped her and pointed at the greasy bag, but she waved me off. I saw she'd figured out my hiding spot for her medication, so I took her food back downstairs.

"Where've you been?" asked Uncle Hollis as I put the sack in the fridge.

"Long story," I said, pulling up a chair.

He let me sit down before asking, "Think you could make me some tea? You make it so much better than I do."

Yes, because boiling water and sticking a bag in it takes great skill.

I sighed, but kicked off my shoes and went to the stove barefoot. As I filled up the kettle, I thought about what he'd told me the night before: To make the light, you have to concentrate on heaven. You had to think on it and be compassionate and want the best for the person opposite you. You had to visualize that person walking into that ball of light that separated here from wherever and whatever there was.

You had to not worry about hell or whether the person deserved to go there because that wasn't your job.

Once I coaxed the water to boiling and arranged tea bags in cups with the proper amount of sugar, I took the steaming cups to the table and sat down just in time to hear the tail end of a haggard older man's story. ". . . and that's how I ended up walking into the middle of the four way drunk and got hit by that semi."

"Well, that's no reason to still be hanging around, now is it?"

"Well, there oughta be a light there and not just stop signs."

Uncle Hollis studied the man shrewdly and then took his pen to the yellow legal pad. "I'll write a sharply worded letter to the Department of Transportation. Happy now?"

"Guess I can't ask for more than that," the ghost grumbled.

"Now Presley here's going to make the light. Aren't you, dear?"

"Me? Oh, yes. Sure." I studied this Leroy character carefully. Something about him looked familiar to me, but I shrugged it off and concentrated on seeing him step into the light. I closed my eyes and thought of that bright circle with the hazy edges, smiling when I felt its warmth. I envisioned Leroy walking into the light, and, as he did, he got younger and younger, stopping when he was a bearded hippie in ragged bell-bottoms with a concert T-shirt and a trucker cap. He stopped to wave at me before he disappeared into the light.

When Uncle Hollis clamped a hand on my arm, I opened my eyes to see him smiling. "Good job, girl! You're a natural."

I grinned. And I didn't have to go on some fool's errand! Of course, Uncle Hollis had written down an idiotic request, but who knew if he would actually go through with it. Did he need to? "Is it possible ghosts are paranoid?"

"Beats me," he said with a shrug. "Next!"

"Are you really going to write that letter?"

"Eh, maybe," he said as another ghost took a seat at the table.

Well, I'd never thought about *lying* to the ghosts. I suppose I should have. I wonder if it might work on the mysterious Private Banks. Surely, a little white lie would be better than having him spend all eternity hanging around the back door of the Holy Roller.

That's what I should do with Pinup Betty, too. Of course, to lie to her, I'd have to figure out what she wanted to hear.

And I still had to deliver Miss Ginger's message to Beulah. I shivered at the thought because I wasn't looking forward to that little trip.

We helped twelve more spirits cross over, high-fiving over the last one. Uncle Hollis wiped his brow and said, "I think that's everyone."

"What about the woman in the red dress?"

He frowned. "I haven't seen her. At least I don't think so. I've ushered a lot of people to the other side, you know."

I started to question him again, but the Colonel came to stand over us, striking the pose of a man with both hands behind his back, only the one sleeve dangled empty. He wasn't giving off the warm fuzzies.

"Hollis, you must speak to Declan about the Mexican. I don't want his name on this place."

I looked from the Colonel to Uncle Hollis. Obviously, I'd missed something.

Uncle Hollis leaned back and scratched the top of his bald head. "Well, would you prefer for the place to go under?"

Thinking of Dec's dark humor earlier, I giggled at his choice of words. Both man and ghost glared at me.

"The funeral home going under," I said. "It's funny. Like six feet under?"

The Colonel cleared his throat. "I will deal with *you* in a minute. Now, Hollis, you know those greasers killed my father. I never even met him!"

I flinched. It wasn't like I hadn't heard every racial epithet in the book, but that didn't mean I had to like it.

Hollis sighed deeply, rubbing his forehead in a way that made me think he had a headache. "I think it's time for you to go into the light, Gramps. Then you can meet your father."

The Colonel leaned back and crossed his good arm over his chest. "You people couldn't run this place without me!"

"What you mean is we can't run it the way you want it run . . .

without you," Hollis said gently. "Remember when you didn't want us to do a funeral for the Stovall kid just because he was black?"

The Colonel had the good grace to study his ghostly spats with a harrumph. "Old habits die hard, I'm afraid. I was wrong about that. He served our country, and he deserved a proper burial."

"See?"

"He should've gone over to the Young Funeral Home and let his people bury him."

Hollis let out a scream and banged his fist on the table, sloshing his tea. Then he composed himself and sat up. "Don't you think it's a little bit ridiculous to hold a grudge for well over a hundred and fifty years?"

"I know what I know. I don't like the idea. I don't trust him. You heard Declan ask him if his money was good."

Uncle Hollis snorted. "Dec was joking. We would've already been bankrupt without Armando. He's helped keep the place afloat while I've been locked up—thanks to you and Sean, I might add!"

"I don't like it, Hollis, and I can't help it if you and this woman here are the only people who can see me."

Now Uncle Hollis leaned forward, putting his elbows on the kitchen table and his chin in his hands. "How about a friendly wager, Colonel?"

"I'm listening."

"How about if it turns out that Armando is a stand-up guy and we're solvent, say, we are turning a profit by this time next year, then you will step into the light."

"And what if I'm right and he's a Mary-lovin' sonuvabitch?"

Both Hollis and I cringed, but there wasn't a lot you could do to chastise a hundred-and-fifty-year-old ghost.

"If he's shady, then I'll see if I can talk Caroline into turning the place over to Dec like you want me to."

The Colonel nodded, and the two of them shook hands or, rather, tried to shake hands. Uncle Hollis shook all over as the

Colonel's hand went through his, which made me feel better about getting the willies anytime a ghost touched me.

"Wait. What's wrong with Caroline?"

Hollis turned to me. "The Colonel never did think much of suffragettes, and he doesn't think a woman ought to be in charge of the family business. He would prefer Dec. Or Sean."

"Perhaps, if we convince Caroline that her working here is completely unladylike, then Sean will come home and take his place alongside Declan. He is of age now," the Colonel said.

"What about what Dec wants?" I asked.

Both men laughed.

"That's not funny."

"Oh, but it is. The Colonel doesn't care what anyone *wants*," Uncle Hollis said.

I opened my mouth to protest, but I realized LuEllen had never asked me if I *wanted* to be an actress. She had simply signed me up for every kind of entertainment class under the sun and then pushed me in that direction. Kinda made me even prouder of my decision to eat that cheeseburger. Except for the part where I hadn't eaten anything with that much grease or salt in so long that my stomach was unhappy with me.

"Now you, young lady," the Colonel said. "You are a fine example of why women should not be allowed to vote much less work outside the home. What do you think you are doing conducting yourself in such an immodest way?"

Immodest? Me? I was the most modest person I knew. I burst out laughing. "Is this because Dec kissed my cheek?"

Uncle Hollis clapped his hands together. "He did? That's wonderful!"

"She's acting like a trollop. Did you not see what she was wearing last night? My long johns cover more."

"It's a new millennium; you do know that, right?" I asked.

"Do you not have anything to cover your bosom? Maybe a fuller skirt to cover your legs? In my day just the sight of an ankle was scandalous."

"Oh, for crying out loud! Y'all obviously do not have cable in here, do you?"

"Nope," said Uncle Hollis as he sipped his tea. "Too expensive."

"The Colonel needs to get out more," I said.

Uncle Hollis nodded in agreement.

"Here comes Declan now. See if you can restrain yourself," the Colonel said to me, then pivoted sharply and walked down the hall.

Dec entered wearing a different suit from the one he'd been wearing when he picked me up. "What are you two doing still up?"

"Couldn't sleep," Uncle Hollis said. "Presley here was kind enough to make me some tea."

Dec grabbed the key ring by the prep room door. "I was about to call Armando, but do you mind the ride along, Uncle H? I just got a call for a removal."

"Hey, don't you need some sleep?" I asked.

"Nah," he said, his eyes twinkling over the massive bags underneath. "I can always sleep when I'm dead."

"I'm still not tired," Uncle Hollis said. "I'll come with you, and we'll let Armando be."

Uncle Hollis brushed past Dec while singing "Goodbye Yellow Brick Road." Dec smiled at me and shook his head with a "What can you do?" expression.

I stared at the closed door, the funeral home the quietest it had been since my arrival. Now that almost all of the restless spirits were gone, the place had a peaceful feeling. If I didn't know what lay beyond in the prep room, I'd think I was in an ordinary house. It could be Anyhouse, USA, with its harvest-gold refrigerator and mismatched chairs at the table.

I leaned back in one of those chairs, nursing my tea as I thought about the way Dec had looked at me earlier. I kicked myself for the knee-jerk reaction of "Don't look at me that way." I wished I could go back in time and take back those words.

What if I'd blushed instead?

What if I'd taken it a step further and brushed my leg against his under the table?

I could've been in his bedroom when he got that call.

The thought sent a zing through my body. I buried my face in my hands. I could not seriously be thinking about sex with Declan Anderson.

Spinsterhood isn't realistic. You're going to have sex with someone someday.

What the hell was wrong with me?

Maybe it's not me. Maybe I just had the wrong guy last time.

No. This is ridiculous. No more horizontal tango with anyone.

Maybe a woman. Women are gentle, right?

Right?

Way to be stereotypical. And the way you respond to Johnny Depp movies suggests you're heterosexual anyway.

The idea of spending the rest of my life celibate was making me a little antsy.

Face it, you have a crush on Declan Anderson, and it could be the death of you.

Declan

If I never had to do another pickup like Bart Borden, it would be too soon. By the time I got there, Dr. Malcolm had called it. In addition to his practice, Doc had been the medical examiner for Yessum County for at least twenty years and didn't move as quickly as he once had. Since the doctor lived next door, he beat me to the scene.

"Some kind of food poisoning, and he was already having digestive problems," Doc said as he scratched his head. "I thought he might be getting better when I saw him day before yesterday, but I don't see anything untoward. Jessica says she doesn't want an autopsy."

Oh, it was definitely food poisoning.

Uncle Hollis, as unflappable as always, helped me get Bart out of the little brick ranch he shared with Jessica and her parents. She kept sniffling, her own eyes red. She had already excused herself once, no doubt the victim of food poisoning herself since she was still in her robe and sipping from a can of ginger ale.

"Take good care of him, Declan," she said from the front door as we maneuvered the stretcher into the back.

I couldn't help but feel a twinge of sympathy for the woman. Especially when she ran from the door with a hand over her mouth before I could answer her.

"Just when I think I've smelled all the smells there are to smell," Uncle Hollis said once he'd closed the door behind him.

"I know that's right." I rolled down the windows.

Once we got back to the funeral home, we worked together that night to make the process quicker. "Hey, Unc, you ever seen anything like this?" I asked as I held up Bart's hands to show him the sores and the scaly underside.

"Probably eczema," he said.

"This man looks awful for someone who's not even thirty," I said.

"Yeah, well, he looks about like I feel."

"Feeling feisty tonight, aren't we?"

Uncle Hollis sighed. "I think I might be getting too old for this."

"Oh, no. You're not getting out of this one," I said. We'd already done the bathing and initial prep work. We were over halfway there.

Once ol' Bart was clean, Uncle Hollis took the lead on skincare. In this case we didn't need Presley's skill since we were aiming for "lifelike." I started working on his raggedy nails.

"Man, look at these spots," I said.

"Just do the work, Declan," Uncle Hollis said.

And that is how we put Bart Borden to rest—or almost rest. We still needed a suit, but that could wait. Once we'd cleaned and sanitized everything, I was free for a shower.

I was ready for bed, but the sun was coming up.

"I think I'm going to burn this suit," I said.

"Burn mine, too, while you're at it," Uncle Hollis said with a yawn. "And tell Caroline we aren't coming in until noon."

"Ha! Like that'll work."

"Okay, *I'm* not coming in until noon. You're young. You do what you want."

Uncle Hollis disappeared, and I soon heard his feet on the stairs.

Cleo yowled from behind the pantry door. No way could I leave her unfed.

"Spoiled kitten," I said. "I think it's time you went to live with Miss Caroline, what say you?"

She meowed and rubbed against my legs, purring. I thought I was going to trip over her before I put food in her bowl. Suddenly, she looked over her shoulder at the doorway to the kitchen and all the hair on her back stood up and she hissed at nothing.

"Whoa, now. I know you're a cat, but you still need to not bite—or scratch—the hand that feeds you. Maybe you should stay in the pantry a little longer."

She gave an unearthly low growl that seemed incongruent with such a little kitten, and I looked at the door but didn't see a thing.

"Weirdo." I moved her food and water bowls and shut her up in the windowed walk-in pantry and walked across the parking lot for the world's longest and hottest shower. Suit burning optional.

By the time I made it over to the funeral home, Caroline was in the kitchen with the kitten in her lap while she ate her lunch.

"Slow day?" I asked as I put on a pot of coffee.

"I don't know. You tell me, Lazybones." She said it with a twinkle in her eye so I knew she didn't mean it.

"You missed your biggest admirer this morning," she said.

"I meant to," I said as I willed the coffee to percolate faster. It wasn't working.

"Smells awfully cinnamony in here today."

Thinking of how much of the industrial-strength disinfectant we'd had to use, I had to chuckle. "It's an improvement, let me assure you."

I took the pot before the coffee finished, and a few drops sizzled on the warming plate before I could get it back in place. "What have we got today?"

"*You* don't have anything. Well, I suppose you'll have to be on call. Armando and I will handle the two pro bonos today, then we have the two visitations tomorrow. Think you'll have the Building Official off our tails by then?"

"I should be able to. I don't know what he's looking for. Honestly, Uncle El took care of everything that *had* to be done. He's got the chapel sealed off and the porch fixed. It *should* be easy."

Caroline just looked at me. Just because something should be easy didn't mean it would be. A lot would depend on what Potter had told the illustrious Mr. Davenport. I didn't want to think that a Yessum County official would accept a bribe, but far stranger things had happened.

The doorbell rang, and she pointed at the kitten snuggled in her lap.

"I'll get that," I told her, "but you need to understand that cat has another side to her."

"I don't believe a word he's saying," she said to the cat as it leaned up into her palm and kneaded her lap.

Muttering under my breath about never getting to finish a damned cup of coffee, I clomped down the hall, mentally preparing myself for a return visit from Potter or Davenport or maybe even Jessica.

Instead, I opened the door to my punk-ass little brother.

I made like I was going to close the door in his face, but he pushed through and wrapped his arms around me as though he'd been afraid he would never see me again. "Saw the tornado on CNN. I was worried about you, bro."

I finally forced some words over the lump in my throat, but they went straight into Sean's shoulder. Had he grown taller? "We've been worried about you for the past two years. It's not that far from here to Atlanta."

"Sorry about that," Sean said as he pulled away. "It's just—"

"Sean? Is that you?" Caroline barreled down the hall and wrapped her arms around her favorite son. Then she stepped back and smacked the back of his head. "You've worried me half to death! How hard is it to tell me when you're coming home? They make phones for that, you know!"

"Okay, okay. Bad son. I get it." He took a deep, shaky breath. "There's someone I want you to meet, someone I don't want to freeze to death in the car."

Caroline nodded, then looked at me with a giddy expression. I could see visions of grandchildren dancing in her eyes. Sean soon returned with a short, doe-eyed man.

"This is Alan," he said. "My husband."

Well, that was different.

Huh. Actually explains a few things.

The corners of my mouth turned up at remembrances past when Caroline would lecture me on how Sean always had a girl on *his* arm. She had frozen in place, but I extended my hand. "Nice to meet you, Alan. Come on in out of the cold."

"You have to be Dec," Alan said. "I've heard a lot about you."

"Only about half of it is true," I said with a sweeping motion to the Lilac Room. "Could I get you some coffee? I just brewed it."

"No, no, I'll get it," Caroline said. Her eyes glistened with unshed tears.

"She didn't take that as well as I had hoped," Sean said, once she had hurried back down the hall.

I cuffed him on the side of the head. "You ran out of here like a bat outta hell, only called when you needed money, and then didn't warn the woman you were married? To a man? I think she's taking it as well as can be expected."

I cuffed him again for good measure.

"You never called?" Alan's mouth hung open in shock. "You are a bona fide dumb-ass."

I liked this guy already.

Sean walked into the Lilac Room and flopped down on one of the overstuffed Victorian chairs. "I had to work through some shit, Dec."

"Obviously. Considering you can *text* someone in a matter of seconds, there's no excuse for surprising people."

"I didn't know what you'd say. I thought about not coming back."

I stared through him. "This is the twenty-first century. What the hell did you think I would say?"

"Well," Alan said. "My mother fainted, and my dad kicked me out of the house at gunpoint, so . . ."

I stared, not able to find the words.

"Obviously, we worked things out," Alan said, his tone even but his eyes shining fierce.

"Fair point, but Sean ought to know me better than that."

Caroline returned at that moment with a tray full of coffee and such. All traces of her tears were gone, but her eyes were still red-rimmed. I gave my brother a "Now, see what you've done" look.

Caroline took a deep, shaky breath and extended her hand to Alan. "I'm sorry I didn't introduce myself properly back there. I'm Caroline, Sean's mo—stepmother."

"It's a pleasure to meet you, Caroline," Alan said. "And everything I heard about you is good."

Caroline took a seat. "It was . . . it was a bit of a shock." She turned to look at Sean. "I wish I had heard more about you."

Sean took a legal-sized envelope from his coat pocket. "I've got something you might want to see."

Caroline looked warily from him to the envelope and back. She understandably wasn't too keen on surprises. When she finally pulled out the contents, she started crying again. "You've graduated!"

"With honors," Sean said. "From Gupton-Jones in Atlanta. Just like you. And that's where I met Alan."

Caroline's smile faded slightly, but she was bursting at the seams with pride for her youngest. I had to leave UT mid-degree to go to mortuary school in Nashville instead of Atlanta, and I did not graduate with honors. Mainly because I didn't want to be there. Considering my father had been president of his class, a few of the teachers had been disappointed. They weren't anywhere near as disappointed as I had been about having to leave UT behind.

"Oh, is Alan going to work with us, too?"

One corner of my mouth twitched. We already had two more funeral directors than we could pay, and the whole thing seemed oddly hilarious. *Forget about too many cooks in the kitchen, we have too many embalmers in the prep room.*

Alan's smile faded. "Actually, I've decided the funeral business isn't for me. I'm training to be an EMT."

"Thank God," Caroline blurted before adding, "I mean, we were this close to firing someone, so we really can't afford to pay anyone else."

"Please fire me," I said, thinking of the night before. "Especially now that Sean is here. Just go ahead. I need a vacation."

"About that," Alan started. Sean put a warning hand on his knee. So weird. I'd seen Sean go to the Junior/Senior Banquet with a cheerleader on his arm.

"Well, I suppose the two of you can take the green bedroom. Presley and her mother are in the blue one, and Uncle Hollis—"

"Uncle Hollis?" All of the color drained from Sean's face.

"Well, at the time we were shorthanded. Now it seems we have too many cooks in the kitchen," Caroline said.

I choked on my coffee, remembering my own thoughts on the matter.

"Actually, we checked in at the hotel across town," Sean said, but he craned his neck to look around her.

Alan added, "Yes, we're only staying through Christmas and—"

"You're what?" The words came out before I could stop them.

Sean glared at Alan, then finally looked at me. "Alan's father offered me a position at their funeral home in Atlanta."

Dear God, I am going to be stuck here for the rest of my life!

I closed my eyes. "Is it a good position?"

Alan threw out a yearly salary at least ten thousand more than what I was making. With room for advancement. "Well, I guess you better take it."

"Where are you going?" Sean asked. I hadn't realized I'd gotten to my feet.

"I think I need to take a walk. Maybe clear my head."

"In thirty-degree weather?"

My only answer was to walk out the door.

Presley

As I walked to work the next morning, I steeled myself to ask Delilah for an advance on my check. I *had* to get my car back from Vandivers' Shop. I *had* to get some winter clothes, I *had* to pay Dec back for the prescriptions, and I *had* to get LuEllen out of the funeral home before she went on a bender. She'd called a cab to take her to a convenience store for Virginia Slims and Natty Light—I still had no idea where she'd found the money. So far, she'd been smoking outside, but it was only a matter of time before she tried smoking out the bedroom window instead. No doubt the Anderson hospitality would only extend so far if she started smoking and drinking in front of their patrons.

I couldn't ask Dec for money—not now that I knew he was just as strapped for cash as I was.

In my zeal to collect a paycheck, I got to the Holy Roller too early. I did the "I'm frozen" shuffle outside the front door until Delilah pulled up to the curb in her gold Buick. She grunted as she eased out of the passenger seat onto Main Street, staring down a car that wanted to pass but couldn't thanks to her open door.

"You're here early," she huffed.

"I didn't want to be late again," I said.

She opened the glass door then the wooden one behind it before tossing me her keys. "There's a black trash bag in the trunk. Get that for me, would you?"

Yes, Master.

My frozen fingers fumbled the keys, dropping them to the pavement. I had to work through a couple before I found the right one for the trunk. Finally, I found the bag she was describing. I considered hefting it over my shoulder and hunching over in the style of Igor, but I walked inside and put it carefully in one of the dryer chairs instead.

"Open that," Delilah said as she rummaged through her drawers and put change in her zippered bank bag.

The trash bag was full of clothes, winter clothes. Picking up a beautiful turquoise sweater, I saw that it was about my size. "For me?"

"Call it an early Christmas bonus. I can't have you walking around half-naked and freezing your . . . your fanny doodle off, now can I?"

"Thank you, Delilah!" Tears pricked at my eyes. Never in a million years would I have thought Delilah would ever do something nice for me.

"There are some at the bottom that should fit your mother," she added gruffly.

I threw my arms around her in a thank-you hug, but she stiffened. Just as I was getting ready to release the hug, she brought her arms around me and returned the embrace. It was the hug of a woman who hadn't received many hugs in her life, the embrace of someone who didn't know how to accept one.

To tell the truth, it felt pretty damn good to me, too. So good, in fact, that I decided not to ask for that advance. After all, I had the clothes, and I didn't want to ruin the moment. I still had over a week to get my car back.

When was the last time someone had taken the time to look out for LuEllen and me? Besides Dec, no one since Granny, and I'd been taking care of LuEllen for far longer than that.

From the looks of it, I hadn't done too well.

"Oh, get off me and get to work," Delilah said.

But the rest of the day she had a tiny smile that made me think I'd started to win her over.

Declan

When I came back from my walk, Alan was sitting at the kitchen table with the cat. Sean and Caroline were having a discussion in her office that we could all hear.

Alan gestured to the empty chair, and I took a seat.

"Is this some kind of rebellious phase you're going through?" Caroline was asking.

"No, Mom. Everything *before* Alan was the phase."

"Did I do something wrong?" Caroline's voice trembled.

"I'm not an ax murderer!" Sean huffed. "I thought you, of all people, would understand. And here it's Dec who doesn't seem to care."

Well, that's because I didn't. It's not like Ellery was some kind of reverse Narnia with people coming out of the closet left and right, but several of the churches in town had the place in a stranglehold. Who knew how many people were too afraid to be true to themselves?

You mean like how you're working at this funeral home even though you used to say that was the last thing you'd ever want to do?

Sean walked into the kitchen, saw me, and stopped. "Dec, can you tell this woman that being gay isn't some kind of communicable disease or death sentence?"

"Being gay isn't a communicable disease. Or a death sentence," I shouted over my shoulder before turning to him. "Why don't you come help me out instead of arguing with Caroline all day?"

"You going to pay me?"

"Yeah. With Monopoly money."

"Fine. Whatever."

"We'll start with the Building Official and then set up for tomorrow's visitations."

"That's assuming you get the Certificate of Occupancy thing straightened out," Caroline said from the doorway.

"I'll handle it," I said. This visit was supposed to be a technicality, but I wouldn't rest easy until I had the new certificate in hand.

"Don't mind me. I'll just entertain the cat," Alan said drily.

Sean tossed him the motel key. Of course, the lone motel in Ellery didn't have key cards yet. "Dec can bring me back later," he told his husband.

He didn't say anything else until we got in the truck. "You going to light into me, too?"

"No. I am wondering when you were going to tell me your plan to leave me high and dry, though," I said as we drove past the house on Maple. I didn't look at it.

"Dec, I didn't mean for things to go like this, I swear."

"You told me you would take over. You told me I could partner in name only. You stood in the damn Freesia Room and told me you would handle day-to-day operations if I held down the fort while you were gone."

"I—"

"You made me a promise, little brother."

"But—"

"You said, and I quote, 'Uncle Hollis and I will take care of everything.' Then you convinced me Uncle Hollis was off his nut and needed to be sent to assisted living. And you left."

"I got in over my head, all right!" Sean roared the sentence and it reverberated through the truck cab.

I jerked the truck into a parking space behind City Hall and slammed the driver's side door before heading for the back door of the building. At the sound of Sean's footsteps behind me, I bubbled over. "Got in over your head? Is that a euphemism for coming out?"

And my punk-ass little brother punched me.

My fists curled automatically. My arm reared back.

Then I did what I always did: I stopped, held it all in.

I probably deserved that for being an insensitive ass.

"God, Dec, I was only twenty-two, and I'd never even been outside the state. Living here is like . . ."

"Like living in a bubble?"

"Yeah." His eyes met mine, but he hadn't figured out yet that sometimes I didn't like the bubble any more than he did.

Maybe he was too young back then to accept all the responsibility I had wanted to give him.

You had to take over when you weren't much older.

Yeah, and that had turned out so well for me, hadn't it?

I worked my jaw back into place, reached up to the corner of my mouth, and my fingers came away with blood. Great. The Building Official would be really convinced the Amazing Fighting Andersons had their act together.

"Haven't you been in love?" he asked.

"Never been afforded the luxury," I mumbled.

"Dammit, Alan keeps me sane. I know who I am with him."

"Well, if he keeps you sane, then I guess we'd better keep him around."

"Stop it! Stop trying to make me feel worse than I already do. I didn't tell Alan's dad that I would take that position for sure. I'll come here. I'll make things right."

I turned to face my brother just outside the City Hall door. "Look, you've been offered a good job. If it will make you happy and if Alan makes you happy, then *that* is what you need to do."

"Do you mean that?"

"Yes."

He followed me into the Building Official's office. Turns out, Sean had played baseball with Davenport's younger brother, and the two of them hit it off. As always, Sean smoothed things over for me. People might not like me, but they liked him, so we at least got our Temporary Certificate of Occupancy with a promise of a permanent one in time for the ornament ceremony on the twenty-second.

I turned in the direction of the motel, but Sean spoke up. "Go back to Anderson's. I gotta talk to Uncle Hollis anyway."

"What for?"

"I was wrong to tell you he was crazy."

I snorted. "But he *is* crazy. Certifiably bat-shit crazy."

Sean winced. "But not dangerous crazy."

All right. That I could give him. I parked out back, and Sean went in ahead of me. I went into the prep room to casket our latest guests. Poor ol' Bart would have to wait a couple of days since we were one chapel short and still hadn't heard from Jessica about what he would be wearing.

I tidied up in the prep room, but there was Sean in the doorway. "I've got one more thing to say to you."

It was on the tip of my tongue to sarcastically thank him for all of his help, but I decided to hear his one thing.

"Look, I'm not perfect. And I'm never going to be as good as you, but at least I cared enough to come back and tell you."

Wait. Not as good as me?

"Mom has always wanted you to be in charge anyway. I know I said I'd take over, but I was wrong. I don't belong here. I belong in Atlanta."

"What the hell?"

He'd been pacing, but he stopped and turned to me. "You think I didn't notice how Mom always runs the numbers by you? How she always made you go over all of the conference notes with her when she got back? How she asked *your* opinion on which hearse we should buy? I'm not dumb, Dec."

And I laughed.

"It's not funny." He looked like he wanted to punch me again. If he did, I was going to punch him back this time.

"But it is funny, you little asshole! The whole time she was running numbers by me, she was grooming you to talk to the public. She pulled you aside and taught you how not to lose your cool, how to guide a client to the right choice while making it seem like his idea. All this time I've thought she loved you best, and she's been playing us both."

"That's ridiculous!"

I let that exclamation echo around the prep room. It echoed off the tiled walls and floors and ricocheted off the large drain in the floor, the one that took away everything unsavory about life and death.

Finally, he laughed. "I'm such an idiot. *We* are idiots. She wanted us to work together—for you to tend to business while I worked with people."

"Pretty much."

His smile faded as he realized he was the one who was breaking up the perfect partnership. "Why don't you let Uncle Hollis do what Mom meant for me to do?"

I looked at him. There were several reasons. One, Uncle Hollis was older and didn't have the same longevity as, say, my punk-ass little brother. Two, I wasn't sure our clients wanted to be serenaded with Elton John. Three, the man deserved to retire if he wanted to.

"Do you have to send him back?" My almost-twenty-six-year-old brother sounded like a kindergartner asking for a puppy. Did I really scare him that much? Did I hold some kind of parental sway over my brother that he felt he had to plead and beg?

"I'd already decided I wasn't going to send him back. The last time I visited him, he wasn't singing. He doesn't sing when he's not happy."

"Thank you." He hugged me fiercely, and all I could think was, *When did my brother get to be taller than me?*

Well, that and I was pretty sure Sean was hiding something from me, something about Uncle Hollis.

We stepped back from each other and cleared our throats.

"So, you have a movie star living upstairs. How'd that happen?" he asked.

Presley

The trash bag was so heavy that my arms ached and I was out of breath by the time I reached the funeral home. Still, I ran upstairs to find LuEllen and share our good fortune.

Halfway up the stairs I ran into Sean, who insisted on carrying the bag upstairs for me. For a minute I thought he was yet another ghost, but then I recognized him. We'd been in high school together, even went out once. At the top of the stairs, we did this awkward dance around my bag so he could go down and I could find LuEllen.

"You aren't going to believe this!" I exclaimed as I opened the bedroom door and dumped the clothes on the bed. LuEllen wasn't curled up there as I had expected. Instead she sat primly on the edge of a chair in the corner clutching the cell phone I'd left charging.

"When were you going to tell me?"

My heart hammered so loudly I could hardly hear her. "Tell you what?"

"That you got the audition."

"It's about fairy godmothers, and I don't know if I have the part. They're making the announcement soon."

"Fairies?" LuEllen frowned as though I were speaking to her

in a foreign language. "Well, your agent called, and this came in the mail."

"It's about time," I muttered, reaching for the phone just as LuEllen dropped a thick envelope on the bed in front of me.

"Some guy named Carlos wants you to audition for some kind of *Lolita Ann* movie in California. Sounds like some kind of *Hee Haw* thing to me, but Ira swore up and down that it was going to be huge."

"Wait. What? And why were you talking to my agent?"

"The phone rang. I answered it," she said with a shrug.

But at the thought of Ira I couldn't properly swallow. My agent, the long-suffering fellow, had sent me to a party where I had met Carlos Alba, a producer who had several projects in the pipeline. The only one that interested me was the fairy godmother one, but he had others.

My fingers hesitated over the phone. I could vaguely remember how Carlos commented on my accent, how he mentioned something about a classic book that he was going to set in the South. That was before I steered his attention back to the movie I wanted.

And also before my attempt to seduce him, quite ironically, went south.

"I'm not going to call him right now."

I ripped open the envelope. The title of the script clearly said *Lolita Ann*. I dropped the papers, my hands shaking. *Don't freak out. This could be a good thing, a better thing.*

"Presley Ann Cline, I did not raise a coward." LuEllen stood, her wasted body shaking with rage.

Hysteria came out of nowhere. "Maybe I should just quit. It's not like I have a car to get there or money for a plane ticket." Ignoring the script, I sifted through the clothes on the bed, putting what was obviously meant to be mine to the left and LuEllen's clothes in a stack to the right. Underneath the used sweater and a pair of elastic waistband pants, I saw clothes that still had the tags on them. Surely, Delilah hadn't—

Delilah had bought new clothes for us and then hidden them underneath the older stuff. Tears pricked at my eyes.

LuEllen dropped a wad of cash on the blouse in front of me. "That ought to do it."

"LuEllen, I can't take your money."

She pressed the cash into my palm and closed my fingers around it. "But it's your money, every penny of what you've been sending me for the past few years. Well, except for what I spent on beer and ciggies."

"What? But how?" At this second display of generosity, the tears came hot and fast, and my short little mother hugged me. "I cashed those checks you sent me and put that money straight in the lock box so I wouldn't touch it. Good thing, too, with that fire."

I opened my mouth to speak, and she said, "I know! Don't smoke near my oxygen. I'm gonna quit. First thing in January when I can get a new tank."

I'd believe that when I saw it.

She hugged me. "Don't give up now, baby. Not when you're so close."

But close to what? Dread settled at the bottom of my stomach, an inkling that Ira had news but it wasn't the news I wanted.

"Okay, Mama. I'll think about it," I whispered into her thin, brittle hair.

I closed my eyes against the possibility of showing my face to Carlos after I'd run from his bedroom gathering my clothes as I went. He had done nothing to stop me. Hadn't said a word. How in heaven's name was I supposed to face him again?

"Presley, baby, what happened?"

"You saw how I embarrassed myself," I said. That was part of it. I was mad at Carlos. I was mad at myself. I was mad at Pinup Betty for telling me every day that I was being childish and naïve to not use my body to get what I wanted. She told me I would never get anywhere in Hollywood if I didn't sleep around. That's the way it had been when she got there, and that's the way it still was. "You've got to give a little to get a little, honey," she used to tell me.

Then there was what Ira said when he called to tell me he got me on the guest list at the party. "Kid, this is pretty much it. If you can't swing this, I don't know where to go next."

And it had been two and a half years since any big parts had materialized, so I believed him.

LuEllen pulled me to arm's length, her eyes hard. "It's not the end of the world. I didn't want you to sleep around, but it's human nature, I guess."

The tears came so fast, I couldn't see. I couldn't get the words to come out in anything other than a whisper. "Even worse. I couldn't. Not all the way. There's something wrong with me."

I expected LuEllen to slap me, but instead she sat down on the bed and pulled me close. "Oh, baby. There's nothing wrong with you."

"Oh, there's something wrong with me." My throat burned.

"Was it your first time?"

"Yes."

"Did you love him?"

"No."

"Well, there you go. You just need the right man. Or at least the right reasons. And to be married. Knowing he can't up and leave you is really good."

"But you told me that if I spread my legs for some man I might as well piss away all of my dreams. That the only way to make sure I didn't get pregnant and end up like you was to just not have sex."

LuEllen stopped rocking. "I said that?"

"Yes, you did."

She sighed. "I was so worried you'd make the mistakes I did. You're so much prettier, so much smarter, and I only wanted you to come out all right. I should've told you to be careful. I should've warned you that the first time usually ain't that great no matter who you're with, but I shouldn't have told you that."

"But now you can see why I can't go back!"

"Of course you can. You go in there and you hold your head high. What's the worst thing they can do?"

"Tell me no."

"That's right. I'm proud of you for sticking to your guns as long as you did. I always knew you were a better girl than I deserved." And then my mother kissed the top of my head just like she used to do when I was little. I didn't feel better, though, just . . . restless.

"So you don't think there's something permanently wrong with me?"

LuEllen held me at arm's length again. "No, baby. Have you been to the lady doctor?"

"No. I hadn't had sex, so why should I?"

"Oh, Lord have mercy. That doesn't mean you don't have lady parts. We'll send you to the lady doctor, and you'll know you're okay. But first you need to call that nice Ira fellow."

I smiled at LuEllen. Not many people considered Ira to be "nice." Tenacious, maybe, but not "nice."

I also knew I wasn't going to the "lady doctor"—at least not yet. For one thing, I didn't have insurance. For another, I was embarrassed, and nothing was going to change that. As much as I would like to tell myself Carlos had taken advantage of me, he had made neither threats nor promises. I was the one who'd shown up at that party looking for him, and everything about that night said he was looking for a one-night stand. I had merely played the part of a willing accomplice.

At least right up to the moment of truth.

"You are going to take this part if they offer it, aren't you?" she asked as she pushed the thick script into my arms. "So the world can see what I've always known?"

How could I say no to that?

"Of course."

She squealed. My odd little mother squealed, hugged me tight, and then wished she knew a nearby place to get some champagne.

"I've always wanted to try some of the fancy stuff," she mused.

I was afraid she already had me walking down red carpets and putting her up in a mansion, but I didn't say a word. If Ira was calling me early *and* talking about a different movie altogether, then something had gone wrong.

Declan

"It's a long story."

"Oh-ho. Mr. 'never really been afforded the luxury'!"

"Keep it down! I kissed her cheek. She kissed mine. I don't think she's interested." I shoved my hands in my pockets. Not much else to do with them.

"Oh, I'll be the judge of that."

"Maybe I'm not interested. Did you ever think of that?"

Sean just looked at me.

"Fine. Can't you just let it be?"

"Nope. Now spill."

So I told him about the tornado and how her trailer blew up and about going after Presley the night she had to walk home from Potter's. Somewhere in the middle of my explaining to Sean how it was a good thing that Presley only seemed to be interested in kissing, Caroline called for us.

Just like that we were back to business. Afterward, my day fell into a familiar routine: two visitations that dragged on past eight and a ridiculous urge for bourbon. I wandered back to the kitchen, wondering who else might be back there, hoping for someone in particular. As I rounded the corner my eyes were drawn under the table to a pair of long, shapely legs that I knew very well.

I reached for the top cabinet and removed the big plastic container of sugar so I could get to the bourbon. "Didn't expect to see you up so late."

"I can go," she said flatly. She had a huge stack of papers in front of her and appeared to be about halfway through reading it.

Something was wrong. I'd never heard Presley be anything but cheerful or at the very least resolute. Tonight, she sounded . . . defeated? "Well, you know what they say: Never drink alone."

The corners of her mouth twitched. "I suppose I could stick around if it would help you out."

"It would." I held up the bottle of bourbon. "Want some?"

"Got any Coke?"

I poured a couple of fingers in each mug and then got a can of Coke from the fridge. "Amateur," I said as I slid her drink in front of her.

"Proud of it," she said with a sad smile.

I thought of how LuEllen had huffed and puffed through the funeral home the other day with her case of light beer. Yeah, I could see where drinking might not be high on Presley's list of priorities. "So, shitty day?"

"I think I got an audition for a pretty big role," she said.

"That's awesome!" I sat down across from her. When she didn't respond, I added, "Or not."

"Maybe awesome? It wasn't the part I wanted, and I embarrassed myself with the producer. Now I have to go back and see him again, and he's the one who has a lot of say in whether or not I get either role," she said with a sigh before taking a gulp from her mug.

A stab of hot jealousy went through me, but I fought it off. I had no claims on her. It was crazy to think she didn't have thousands of men following her around in California. "It can't be that bad."

"It was bad." Her cheeks burned bright red just thinking about it.

"Aw, it can't beat some of the things I've seen."

"Wanna bet?"

"Last spring I had to dress a twenty-seven-year-old woman in a Tim McGraw T-shirt and a bright green thong for her viewing. Because that, according to her mama, is what she liked to wear to bed."

She spewed her drink. "That's bad."

"Hon, that's the tip of the iceberg." I saluted her with my mug and took another generous swig.

"Wow."

Yeah, there wasn't much to say to that. I had to shake my head to get rid of the memory.

We drank in silence, awkward silence.

I finished my drink and put it by the sink. I was about to tell her good night when she finally spoke. "So, you're a guy."

"Last I checked." I didn't turn around because it seemed she found it easier to talk to my back.

She took several deep breaths before continuing. "If a girl tried to have sex with you but couldn't and then she ran away, would you hate her forever?"

The hell?

Now I had to turn around. "I'd probably wonder what was wrong with me."

"Really?"

"Yeah. But maybe I'm not the best person to ask."

"I think you may be the only person I could ask."

Her eyes met mine and, like that, I was a goner. It had been attraction before, but this was something different, something powerful. I wanted to be the only person she could ask for the rest of our natural-born lives.

"Are you in love with this guy?" I had to ask. I didn't know who he was, but I wanted to kill him. Not very fair, but true.

"No, no," she laughed. "Oh, no."

I sucked in a breath and leaned back against the sink. I'd been about to go blue in the face waiting for her answer.

"It's just . . . Have you ever found yourself doing things you really didn't want to do?"

I snorted. "Every damn day."

"Then why do you do it? Why can't you stop?"

Well, that's the million-dollar question.

"I guess because I don't want to let anyone down."

She smiled knowingly. "So when do we stop living for other people and start living for ourselves?"

"I don't know, but maybe we should start."

She scooted her chair back and stood, taking one step toward me and then another. I stood up straight, wondering what she had in mind. She was chewing on her bottom lip when she stopped in front of me, and it was the hottest damn thing I'd ever seen.

Presley

I'd just read the scene where Lolita Ann seduced Hubert just as he had given up on his own plan of seduction. This damned movie was not only going to require a love scene, but it'd also require me to seduce a man. I'd have to take the initiative in ways I'd never had to do before, since my specialty, to date, had been playing dead bodies.

I stood in front of Dec, but I hesitated. What was I going to do?

You're going to get to living, that's what.

So I pushed Dec against the kitchen sink like the wanton woman my mama didn't want me to be. It felt so weird to be almost eye level with a man. Often I towered over them, especially when I wore heels, but I had Declan Anderson backed against the counter, and it felt good.

Then I lightly brushed my lips against his.

That felt better.

Dear God, the electricity that rippled between us at the touch of my lips to his. I groaned aloud, and he took it as an invitation. His arms wrapped around me, and he took the kiss from chaste to French.

I'd always been pretty good at the kissing, but this was the most engaged I'd ever been in a make-out session.

He tasted like the smoky bourbon and Declan, and that only made my pulse race more. His tongue met mine measure for measure while his hands roamed over my back, my hips, cupping my ass until I couldn't get any closer to him unless I took my clothes off.

A thrill raced through me. I *wanted* to be that kind of close.

I rubbed against him, and he groaned. Having power over this man felt good, heady even. Feeling a confidence I'd never known, I put one of his hands over my breast, and he gasped.

So did I.

"Do you want to take this over to my place?" he growled.

This is what you wanted, isn't it? To prove to yourself that there's nothing wrong with you? To show that you could play the part of Lolita Ann?

But what if LuEllen was wrong? What if there really *was* something wrong with me? Could I stand to be embarrassed in front of Dec the way I had been with Carlos?

That would be a hundred times worse.

I jumped backward.

Dec's brown eyes widened.

"I can't do this," I muttered.

I tried to run, but he grabbed my arm lightly. The hairs on the back of my neck stood up, and this time it was a ghost of a memory of being in this same situation as a teenager. I'd explored my feelings and gotten to this point exactly only to tell Lon Higgins the same words.

Nausea pitched in my stomach. Lon had said, "You can't leave me like this—I'll get blue balls," and then put my hand down his pants. If Dec said something similar, I would die right there in the kitchen.

Instead, something in my eyes made him drop my arm and hold his hands up in surrender. "Honey, you don't ever have to do anything you don't want to do."

Knowing that I didn't have to, I burrowed into his embrace.

Declan

I was suspended somewhere close to heaven with Presley in my arms, still buzzing from having had her kiss me, but then she sniffled, followed by a hiccup and the telltale shoulder movement of a woman trying to hide her sobs.

If there's a man out there who can stand to see a woman cry, then *he* needs to hand over his man card and let me keep mine. I'd rather know too much about flowers and not hurt women than be some kind of knuckle-dragging Neanderthal. Maybe I liked fruity drinks and pop songs and there was nothing wrong with that.

And maybe I was thinking of something, anything, other than the beautiful crying woman in my arms. So I said the seven words I was still too much of a man to *want* to say: "Do you want to talk about it?"

"No."

Thank God.

"But you don't hate me?"

I held her out, trying to thumb away her tears, but they were coming too fast. "Hate you? Why would I hate you?"

I never even allowed myself to hope we'd ever get that far.

"Because I led you on and then stopped."

Realization smacked me.

"I'm going to guess that was because some guy was an asshole. By the way, I'm going to need a name, an address, and I'll be back when some knees are broken."

She laughed. Well, more of a hiccup really, but it was a good sign. Then she started talking even though she said she didn't want to, but I took that as a pretty good sign, too.

"Why don't we go over to my place where the chairs aren't so hard?" I held up my hands palm out. "No funny business."

She looked at me like I'd lassoed the moon and then took my hand as I led her across the parking lot and up the stairs to my apartment. Of course, once we got there, I realized the only place two people could sit was on the bed. She got a little concerned when I took off my shoes, but I fluffed some pillows up against the headboard and patted a spot beside me.

She took the seat tentatively, sure to leave at least six inches between us.

"So," I prompted.

"So."

"I wasn't kidding when I said I would inflict bodily harm on someone." I wanted to grab her hand, but the space between us told me to bide my time.

"Fine. Lon Higgins put the moves on me. More than once. Talked me into doing things I didn't necessarily want to do with him."

He needed to watch out. His ass was in the phone book.

She took a ragged breath, quiet tears falling down her cheeks. "I mean, we didn't have sex, but it was pretty close. He *wanted* me to have sex with him. Told me he would . . . hurt if I didn't and that it would be all my fault."

I itched to wipe away her tears, but I handed her the box of tissues instead. "Presley, that should've been a *him* problem. I'm so sorry."

"That wasn't even the worst of it." She blew her nose, then paused for so long I didn't know if she would continue. "I was scared to death I was pregnant, and—"

"I thought you said you didn't have sex!"

She studied her feet, and her hand landed on the bed a couple of inches from mine. "LuEllen didn't want me to take the county's sex-ed classes. Said she'd teach me herself. She told me all of these tales about girls who got pregnant from being naked in a hot tub with a boy. Or the kids who were fooling around and *somehow* his sperm got inside her. Bam! She was sixteen and pregnant, her life ruined forever."

"Call me a skeptic, but I think those kids were liars."

She rolled her eyes. "I know that now. Heck, I think I knew that then, but there was an irrational part of me that feared pregnancy. LuEllen always made such a big deal out of how I didn't want to end up like her."

I couldn't help but wonder if things would've been much better if LuEllen had spent that time improving herself as an example to her daughter.

"Funny story," she said. She threw her hand up to gesture. When it came down, her fingers touched mine. Such a simple touch, but I had to tell myself to concentrate. "After I kicked Lon in the nuts and told him to get out of my . . . home, he told everyone at school that I was frigid and that they shouldn't vote for me for Homecoming Queen. I panicked. LuEllen would've had a flying duck fit if I hadn't at least made court."

"This is a funny story?"

"Yeah. I talked Roy Vandiver into telling everyone we'd had sex and that it had been fantastic."

"Kari's husband?" I almost broke out in a cold sweat thinking of how mad Kari must've been.

"That's kinda why she left me on the side of the road. He was her boyfriend at the time."

"Still not seeing the humor." My fingers hooked on to hers. She looked down for a minute but then eased her hand into mine. Up until that point, I'd always thought hand holding to be overrated.

"I deserved it and probably more. Stealing Roy from Kari two weeks before the Junior/Senior Banquet was a really crappy thing to do."

"I'm surprised you're still alive."

She stared ahead into my little kitchenette, and I studied her profile. So beautiful, so damaged because of it. "But that wasn't the worst thing I did."

"Which was?" Why did I suddenly feel like a priest hearing confession?

"I . . . I decided to seduce this producer to get a part I really wanted. Instead, I got scared and ran away, but those pictures?"

"I've seen them." *And I won't think about them right now because you have a very attractive ass.*

"Those pictures made it *look* like I slept with him, so that's what everyone assumes. That's why I had to come home for a while to hide out. Now they want me to play this character who's a real seductress, but I don't know how."

No, the problem was she didn't have any idea just how seductive she could be.

"But you don't have to know how," I said. "You're an actress!"

She laughed, but it came out half hiccup and half sob. "I tried out my skills on you, and look what a mess I made of it."

My insides went cold. She'd been acting? She hadn't felt what I'd felt? Not even a little?

Know what, Dec? This isn't about you.

I couldn't help but touch her face. "You worry too much. You are a beautiful woman who's waiting for someone worthy of her affections."

"But what if Lon was right? What if I am a frigid bitch?"

"You are not a frigid bitch." I squeezed her hand and calculated the odds that anyone would suspect me if Lon Higgins were to disappear.

"How do you know?"

"I just do?"

"Maybe you could prove it to me someday?" she asked, all sleepy and shy.

"I should be so lucky," I said as I opened my arms. She hesitated but snuggled against me. I gently rubbed her arm, closing my eyes to remember the moment, the feel of her body against mine, her head tucked under my chin, and the scent of honeysuckle from her hair.

She sat up straight. "I've got to call Kari and apologize!"

I pulled her back down against me. "Not at three in the morning, you don't."

"Good point." Then, exhausted from crying and "confessing," she fell asleep while I held her in my arms.

Presley

At the banging on the door, my first response was, "Ten more minutes."

Then a muffled voice shouted, "Presley. Ann. Cline. If you are in there, you had best come out now!"

I sat up, disoriented because sunlight streamed through the small window my mother was staring through, and I was in a strange room. Dec's room.

Shit. LuEllen.

I jumped out of bed and opened the door. Dec gave a groggy, "Wha?"

I opened the door and stepped out so quickly I forgot my shoes.

"Look, when I told you it was okay, I didn't mean for you to go jumping in the bed of the first man you could find!"

Shushing LuEllen was doing no good, so I started walking. Dec didn't need to hear anything she had to say. It was early enough that we could hopefully sneak upstairs before anyone came to the funeral home. What time was it? I fumbled for my phone in my back pocket and checked the time. Blessedly, I had an hour before I had to be at the Holy Roller.

LuEllen hadn't quit talking yet. She was beginning to wheeze. "Really. I thought I'd scarred you for life, but apparently not. I can't believe that you would do this to me, that you would do this to yourself when you are so close—"

When she had to stop for a coughing jag at the back door of the funeral home, I said, "Can you at least shush until we get upstairs?"

"No, I will not shush," she said as we walked through the kitchen past Caroline and Uncle Hollis, who stared at us in wonder. "I will not shush. I did not raise you the way I did to have you throw it all away by sleeping with that Anderson boy."

I almost ran into Jessica Borden, who was standing in the hallway, wearing her best Sunday black.

"I'm sorry about this," I said to her, knowing I'd also have to apologize to Caroline later. "LuEllen. Mother. If you want to tear into me, it can wait until we are upstairs, but you do *not* know what you are talking about."

"The hell I don't!" But she blessedly had to stop yelling because she couldn't go up the stairs, yell, and breathe all at the same time. I had never been so happy about her smoking habit.

Once I got her into the bedroom, I closed the door and wheeled on her. "Look. What's left of the cherry that you are so concerned about is still in place, all right? And I think I might be falling for that man, so I would appreciate it if you wouldn't yell and make a scene in front of his entire family when they have been kind enough to take us in when we didn't have anywhere else to go!"

LuEllen coughed and wheezed, coughed and wheezed. Finally, she found some words. "Falling for him?"

Yeah. Falling for him. I hadn't realized it either until the words came out of my mouth, but, yeah, I was falling hard for Declan Anderson. I had been ever since he'd shielded my body in the closet. Maybe ever since he'd tutored me in geometry.

"Yes, with him," I hissed. "Why not with him?"

"But he's a . . . funeral director." She wrinkled up her nose.

"Oh, and I suppose they don't deserve to fall in love, too?"

She took a few more deep breaths, making that odd throat-clearing "ah-hem" sound she made as she got her breath back. "When you put it like that."

"I don't care if he's a garbage collector, a proctologist, or the guy who scrapes roadkill off the highway, and it shouldn't matter to anyone else, either."

LuEllen regarded me, her head cocked to one side. "Well, he is a kind man. And a handsome one, too."

"Don't you get designs on him, and it's time for you to stay out of my business. I'm almost twenty-five, and you can't even quit trying to kill yourself with nicotine or alcohol or tanning or whatever else you do when I'm gone."

"I'm not trying to kill myself," she said, but her voice was small and her eyes were big.

"What I'm saying is that I'm an adult now. I'm going to do what I want to do."

"What about the audition?"

"Screw the audition!" I rummaged through the stack of clothes for something to wear and headed to the shower. I had had enough of LuEllen for one morning.

When I stepped out of the shower with nothing around me but a towel, I screamed because the Colonel took up most of the space in the tiny bathroom.

"Get out!" I whispered.

"No. Is it true that you lost your virtue to young Declan?"

"No, I have not. Not that it is any of your business!"

"Presley, are you okay in there?" Caroline asked from the other side of the door.

"Um, it was a . . . a . . . a spider," I said. "Just shocked me. I'm fine."

"Okay," she said.

I waited for the sound of her sensible heels clomping on the steps to fade away before I turned back to the Colonel. "Look. My virtue is my business, so get out."

"Your virtue is *my* business if we extend you hospitality only to have you leave your chaperone and act like a common whore."

A hysterical laugh bubbled to the top. "I am the farthest thing from a whore, I can assure you."

"You were in a most compromising position, and I must insist that you and Declan marry at once."

"Colonel, this ain't the eighteen sixties. If you have such a problem with the situation, go talk to Declan. Takes two to tango, you know."

"You know as well as I do that the boy can't see me! Besides, it is up to the lady to keep herself chaste since we men are privy to certain carnal desires and—"

Oh, the more things change, the more they stay the same.

"Know what? If you are really concerned about my modesty and chastity and whatever, then you need to get out of here because I am about to drop this towel and get ready so I'm not late for work."

"You wouldn't!"

I dropped the towel, and he vanished.

Declan

"Wha? What the hell just happened?"

I had been getting to my feet when the sunlight coming through the door blinded me all over again. I heard voices outside and went around the bed only to trip on Presley's shoes. Through the paper-thin walls I could hear LuEllen saying, "Look, when I told you it was okay, I didn't mean for you to go jumping in the bed of the first man you could find!"

I wanted to hear Presley deny it, to say something nice about me, but instead the voices got quieter, which meant they were walking away. I held up Presley's shoes and laughed a little. Kinda like Cinderella, but not.

I looked out the window and saw LuEllen giving Presley what-for at the back door. It might be better to let that argument run its course. Then my phone buzzed, and I drew it out of my pocket.

Declan Anderson, front & center. Now.

Well, hell. If Caroline had sent me a text, it had to be bad. It took her forever to type one out since she still had a flip phone and had to hit each button several times to get the right letter.

Even so, there was no need going over there and not being ready for the day, so I prolonged the inevitable by showering and shaving and getting dressed. I knotted my tie and grabbed

Presley's shoes before I walked across the parking lot and into the lion's den.

"Okay, Caroline, here I—Jessica, I didn't expect to see you here so early. I'm glad to see you're feeling better."

"Much better," she said with a small smile that acknowledged her husband hadn't been so lucky. She held Cleo close and laid her chin lightly on the kitten's head. Cleo closed her eyes, purring so loudly I could hear her from where I stood.

"I told Mrs. Anderson that I needed to come by early today to make final arrangements because I still have to take Daddy to the doctor this morning. I'm glad I got to see you," she said with a pretty blush.

"Er, me too," I stammered.

Caroline and Uncle Hollis were both looking at me with a mixture of disapproval and . . . amusement? Caroline didn't take her eyes off me as she said, "Hollis, would you be a dear and meet Miss Borden in the Lilac Room to discuss arrangements. I need to have a word with *my son*."

"Certainly. Miss Borden?" Uncle Hollis ushered Jessica, who was still holding the kitten, down the hall. Caroline craned her neck to look down the hall so she could see when they disappeared around the corner.

"I don't know if I want to smack you or hug you," she whispered fiercely.

"It's not what you think."

"Then why are you carrying her shoes?"

"I'm Prince Charming."

She pinched my cheek. "I know you are."

Then she smacked me and grabbed me by the ear. "Next time set an alarm so Presley is back in the house before we open for the day so her mother doesn't yell down the hall about the two of you sleeping together."

"Ow, okay." I stepped back and straightened my coat and tie. "But, for the record, we didn't sleep together. I mean, we *slept* together, that's how we lost track of time, but—"

"You're so cute when you're twitterpated." She patted my

cheeks. "And now you have two pretty girls after you. When it rains, it pours, eh?"

"Coffee. I need coffee."

Before I could take even a step toward the coffeepot, Presley appeared at the door and blushed bright pink. "I was just coming for those."

I gestured that she take a seat. "Milady?"

She couldn't meet my stepmother's eyes without blushing, but she let me slide a flat on each foot. "Thank you, but I think I'd better run for work."

"Where's your coat?"

She waved my concern away. "I don't have one, but this sweater should be plenty."

I didn't think so, but she was in a hurry to go, and I didn't want her to have to face the wrath of Delilah. "Need a ride?"

"Not today."

I started to go after her, but Caroline put a hand on my arm. "Let her go. It's not so cold she's going to get hypothermia, and she obviously wants to get out of here."

I looked after Presley, and Caroline sighed dramatically. "You are too cute! I don't know if I want to gag or celebrate."

I leveled a hard look at her.

"Your father used to make that same expression when he was irritated at me!" she sniffed.

I made for the coffeepot. "What're we doing today?"

"Well, we have the two visitations, but they're both going to be church funerals tomorrow, so there are some details I'm going to need you to iron out. Bart Borden's visitation is tomorrow. Then let's say our prayers that we make it through Christmas."

I nodded, but we both knew the chances that we would make it through Christmas without losing someone were slim to none. Those funerals were among some of the hardest we did. No one wants to lose someone during what's supposed to be the happiest time of the year. "Ornament ceremony still on the twenty-second?"

"Right?"

"Good. We're supposed to have our official Certificate of Occupancy by then."

"Well, let's hope so," Caroline said.

For the past few years we'd put up a Christmas tree and let folks bring ornaments that represented someone they'd lost that year. A few people kept coming back, like Mrs. Morris, who'd lost her husband on Christmas Eve two years ago.

"Do we need anything for that?"

"No," she said slyly. "But I was wondering if you were planning to go Christmas shopping now that you have a girlfriend."

"Maybe."

"A-ha! So she is your girlfriend."

I gave her the Anderson look. "I'm going to my office to get those details in order."

"Oh, and call your uncle El. He said he wanted your input on some renovation ideas and to talk about your, and I quote, 'hare-brained cremation idea.'"

I grinned. "That and he wants to be paid for what he did the other day."

"Naturally."

I'd just sat down when the cat flew down the hall, hissing.

I didn't want to know.

Presley

No matter what I'd told Dec, I could've used a coat. I wasn't about to stay in the funeral home another second, though. Between the Colonel and LuEllen and not knowing how to act around Dec, just no. So I decided, in light of my recent windfall, to treat myself to breakfast at the Calais Café. The diner made up a corner building on Main Street less than a block from the Holy Roller, and I had thirty minutes to kill.

I walked through the door and wondered if the universe was having fun with me that day because Kari sat at a booth by herself. Might as well apologize while I was having a day of being embarrassed.

I stepped up to the table and waited for her to look up.

"Oh, you have some nerve coming over here," she growled.

"I need to apologize to you."

She turned back to her menu. "It's six almost seven years too late for that."

"Well, I'm going to say it anyway. I am sorry. What I did was inexcusable and selfish." I leaned in to whisper the last part: "And I promise Roy never had sex with me. He just said what he did to get a bunch of jerks off my back."

I turned to walk quickly to the other side of the café, but she yelled after me, "Hey! Come back here!"

No doubt she was talking to me. Kari Vandiver. It still didn't sound right. She'd always be Kari Land to me.

She might not be the president of the Presley Cline Fan Club, but her husband did have my car. I dug deep for a smile before I turned. "Yes?"

"You might as well sit with me. There's nowhere else to sit."

That part was true.

"I have something I want to say to you, too."

Kari had green cat eyes—either homicidal or content—hard to tell which, but a quick glance showed me chairs in the café were hard to come by. I still needed to eat and run. Surely she couldn't poison me while I was sitting across from her.

I slid into the booth, reminding myself the place was also full of witnesses if she decided to assault me.

"I'm sorry for leaving you on the side of the road." She stared through me, daring me to scoff at her vehement apology. "I shouldn't do that to my worst enemy, much less someone I once considered a friend."

It took me a minute to play back the apology in my head. Kari had always been fiercely loyal, but apologies weren't her strong suit. On the other hand, I tended to apologize for things that weren't my fault. "I really am sorry for what I did back then. I wasn't thinking about anything other than how LuEllen would chew me out if I didn't at least make court for Miss YCHS."

"And that was so important you had to steal *my* man right before the Junior/Senior Banquet?"

I winced. "I told you, though. Roy and I never—"

"I know that. Figured that out on our wedding night." She rolled her eyes.

The waitress slid a Belgian waffle in front of Kari. My stomach growled, and my mouth watered.

Audition. Now you have an audition, so no carbs for you.

"What can I get for you?" She took out her pad and licked her finger so she could turn the page.

I sighed. "Egg-white veggie omelet and a coffee, black."

The waitress looked at me as though I had five heads, but she wrote it down. "Coming right up."

"Again, I'm sorry. It was such a stupid thing to do. I'll understand if you keep hating me, but—"

"You think *that's* the reason I'm mad at you? I got Roy, and it was obvious he hadn't slept with *anyone* before he slept with me."

"Then why?"

She ate for a few minutes, but stopped to consider me. "I don't understand why you didn't tell me. I was your best friend. I could've been in on the joke instead of on the outside looking in."

My rumbling stomach folded over in a pang of sadness. Why hadn't I told Kari?

Because she was far more worldly than you, and she would've laughed at you for making such a big deal out of sex.

"I tried to tell you. I guess I didn't try hard enough."

Kari grinned. "I guess I did throw things at you."

The waitress slid a cup of coffee and a questionable omelet in front of me. I reached for the hot sauce by the napkin dispenser. "Well, I ran off to California before you could take a softball bat to my car."

"You left without saying good-bye," she said quietly.

"I'm sorry about that, too," I said as I picked up my fork. "I learned quickly how hard it was to find a good friend."

"Ain't that the truth," she said as she took another bite of her waffle. "Look, I saw you drooling over my strawberry waffle, and I could probably use some protein. Wanna share?"

That was Kari's peace offering. Her anger had blown over, and it was possible we could be friends again. Not quite yet, but soon. "I can't go halfsies, but I'd love a bite of the waffle."

We maneuvered our plates around to share our breakfast, just like we used to do.

"So is it too much to hope that you didn't put sugar in my gas tank?"

She waved the thought away. "Nah. Roy told me not to touch that car because it's a classic. In fact, I think it's almost ready."

"Really?"

"Oh, yeah. It already looks like new because Roy's brother took it over to the body shop first. Now Roy's tinkering with the engine. They both sit out there orgasming over the thing. I think Roy loves it more than he loves me."

Yeah, and he might end up keeping it since I had no idea how much it was going to cost to fix it or if I could ever convince the insurance company to reimburse me since they were in California. "I'm not even sure how I'm going to pay him."

Kari's grin spread wide. "I'm always looking for a good baby-sitter."

"Really?"

She brought out her phone to show me pictures of two impish girls. The oldest had Roy's features, but Kari's wild red curls. The younger one had Kari's face, but the black hair Roy used to sport before he shaved it all off. "They're beautiful, Kari."

I should've been an honorary aunt to those girls. I should've been taking them shopping and buying them things they didn't need. If I'd stayed home, I'd probably be married with kids of my own.

And who's to say your husband wouldn't have run off and left you, just like your father left LuEllen?

Kari snatched the check while I was mooning over her kids. Apparently, loving her daughters was the quickest way back into her good graces.

"Hey! I was going to pay for that!"

"Come by the shop sometime and pay me back in juicy gossip," she said as she grabbed her purse. "I gotta open up in five."

"I need to be at the Holy Roller in five, too. Maybe I'll bring lunch one day."

"I'd like that," she said, her smile suggesting she was just as surprised as I was that she wasn't still mad at me.

Honestly, I was jealous of her. She'd known exactly what she wanted back in high school, and she'd already made it all happen: Roy, kids, take over the florist. Done.

I'd been so caught up in myself that high school had been a blur. After being a big fish in a small pond, California was a disorienting ocean. I'd always been working two or three, sometimes four, jobs just to survive. Day in and day out, I was told I was too tall, too plain, too girl-next-door, too sexy, too old, too young—it was always *too* something.

Almost all of my "too"s had been positive in Ellery: too pretty, too talented, too good to stick around. Of course, I suppose those "too"s had their downside: too consumed with her appearance, too conceited, too big for her britches. All these years, I'd been afraid that the people back home would only see my failure to be what I said I would be. Most of them, like Kari, had been too busy living their own lives to even give me a second thought. Now back in the pond, I was a smaller fish than I had been.

And that was okay with me.

The universe, however, wasn't done having fun with me yet. My phone started to buzz, and I looked down to see a picture of Ira's smiling face.

Declan

"Look here, son, this crazy idea of yours would take some doing."

Uncle Eldridge, the middle of the elder Andersons, dealt strictly in pragmatism. "You're going to have to get a zoning permit and convince old man Dandridge to part with a slice of that pasture that backs up to the carriage house. Then, you're going to have to tear down the carriage house so you have a place to put the damn thing. It's ridiculous. Burning people to a crisp."

"But what if we made this additional parking and moved both prep room and crematory to where the carriage house is now with a covered walkway here." I pointed to the blueprints, but Uncle El was already shaking his head.

"No, no, no. Forget about Dandridge and work on Mrs. Little for the lot by the portico. Put the crematory, chapel, and prep room there and put the parking where the carriage house is."

"And you think Mrs. Little will sell us the lot where the little store used to be?"

"More likely than that asshole Dandridge giving you anything. If you or Sean go over there, she'll sell. It's getting the permit you need to worry about."

I am beloved by goth girls and old ladies. "I'll talk with Mrs. Little, and maybe Sean can go work on the proper people to get the permits approved."

"Good luck," said Uncle El. "I'm not doing the first thing until I see the permit itself. Same goes for this money you're telling me about."

"If Armando says he has the money, then he has the money."

"What do you want to do with the chapel in the meantime?"

"How bad is it?"

Uncle El leaned back, stroking his chin in a way that reminded me of Uncle Hollis and my father. Of course, Uncle El wore Wranglers and plaid shirts instead of suits, so the effect was a little different. He still had all of his hair, too, something neither my dad nor Uncle Hollis had been able to accomplish. "Your pews are all broken up, but the Baptist church over at Loganville is getting new ones, so we could probably buy theirs for a song to use until we got everything else in motion. I can get the boys to clean it out and get a working roof that won't break the bank—as long as you're sure you want to do this expansion. Whole thing's liable to go bust, you know."

Maybe more pessimist than pragmatist.

"It'll work," I said. "People will be able to come here instead of having to drive into Jefferson for cremations."

"Yeah, and people need cremations like they need a hole in the head."

"If we add together the insurance money, what I have, and what Armando has, we can make this work."

"Yeah, well, what are you going to do about the house on Maple?"

I looked away. Uncle El was the only one who knew how much I wanted the house because I'd had him walk through it with me to make sure that it was structurally sound and to get his opinion on some of the changes I wanted to make. He'd agreed with me that it had a lot of potential and was also likely to be auctioned off cheap. "I'll have to give up on that. Sean's going to work in Atlanta anyway, or did you hear?"

Uncle Eldridge stared at me. "I heard."

"If I'm going to keep working here then I won't have the time or the money to fix up a place. I'll need something that's pretty much ready to go."

Uncle Eldridge grunted his agreement of my assessment. "If you're sure this is what you want, then I'll get everything started as soon as you do the funeral on the eighteenth, right?"

"Yes, sir."

"Maybe you'll get a chance to come out and get your pretty-boy hands dirty for a change."

"Maybe." But I doubted it.

He turned to go, but he stopped at the door. "You know, I was looking forward to having you come work for me again."

High praise from him. I smiled. "I was looking forward to working with you, too, Uncle El."

Uncle El looked like he wanted to say something else, but he left shaking his head instead. I caught snippets of his conversation with Caroline. No doubt he was looking in the fridge for some sweets. People brought them from time to time, sometimes for grieving families and sometimes for us. It was the South; people expressed sympathy with sugar.

"Dec! You still haven't cleaned out the refrigerator," Caroline called from the kitchen.

"I'll get it this evening. Promise."

Caroline appeared in the door and waggled her eyebrows. "Maybe your girlfriend can help you."

"Are you my mother or my twelve-year-old sister?"

She blanched. "You called me 'mother'!"

I shuffled some of the papers on my desk. "Well, that's because you are."

She came over, ruffled my hair, and kissed my cheek before leaving. Her own cheeks were pink with excitement. I guess I should've called her mother sooner if I'd known it was going to make her that happy. Instead I said, "Do you mind? I have to make some calls now."

She left, but poked her head through the doorway one more time. "Remember. The refrigerator."

Yeah, yeah.

But first I needed to order some flowers for a certain lady.

Presley

I tossed an extra couple of dollars on the table for a tip and went outside to answer the call.

"Okay, Ira, what happened to the fairy godmothers?"

"I'm fine. How are you?"

Usually, Ira was too busy to answer the phone with pleasantries. He'd often pointed out to me that he was agent to some very important people with an unspoken admonition that I, too, could be one of those very important people if I would just work a little harder. If he was stalling with pleasantries, that meant he knew I wouldn't like his news.

"I'm fine. And the fairy godmothers?"

He sighed, then paused so long I thought the call had been disconnected. "After all of the media attention, Carlos didn't think you would be a good fit for a children's movie. But, hey, there's some good news!"

I stopped where I was on the sidewalk and someone almost bumped into me. I felt tears pricking and swallowed a few times to keep my throat from closing up on me. "One isolated incident and now I've been branded as too slutty to be in a children's film?"

"Well, that and they got Reese Witherspoon."

I'd always known they were looking for a bigger actress, but I'd hoped . . .

"I know, kid. What can you do? It's all bullshit."

"It's not bullshit. It makes sense." I ducked down the alley between the Calais Café and the next block of stores that made up Main Street's business district. Phone conversations with Ira often became . . . spicy. Best to take that conversation away from Miss Lottie and Miss Georgette, both of whom were ambling in my direction. "But, Ira, I don't know about this part. I started reading the script the other day and—"

"Presley, I'm going to tell you straight. You don't try out for this part? I wash my hands of you."

I rounded the back of the florist as I spoke. Tears rolled down my cheeks. Keeping my throat from closing was no longer an option.

He sighed, and I could picture him pinching the bridge of his nose. I'd made him do that a lot over the past few years.

"Presley, how long have I been your agent?"

"Three years," I croaked.

"And a half."

"Have I found you work?"

"Of course."

"Have I gotten you some big auditions?"

"Yes."

"This is your best opportunity yet."

He was right, of course. He'd found me bigger auditions for more commercial movies, parts where I'd been unceremoniously passed over for someone with a bigger name or a different look. *Lolita Ann* was going to be a smaller film, and they couldn't afford big names even if they wanted them. This was the type of movie that won critical acclaim, maybe even an Oscar.

"Ira, the script says they're looking for someone who can look fourteen to sixteen years old. I'm way too old for that part. And probably too tall."

Ira didn't say anything for so long I was afraid we'd been cut off. Finally, he sighed heavily. "I don't pretend to understand what goes through some of these people's minds. All I know is this is the best shot you've had yet."

But I had a secret: my famous *Arsenic and Old Lace* performance when I was in high school? The one that had sent me to Hollywood in the first place? That hadn't been me. The ghost of the old high school drama teacher had taken up residence in my body for three nights and let the lines flow from my body in a way that I hadn't been able to duplicate since.

I was a has-been long before I was a somebody.

"Pres?"

"I'm still here."

"Look, you've always had everything you needed except for one thing."

"What's that?"

"Confidence."

I squeezed my eyes shut.

"Look, I know the two of you bumped uglies and—"

"Ira!"

"Come on! Thanks to those photos, the whole world knows. Besides, Carlos told me everything."

Obviously, he didn't tell you everything.

"He doesn't care about any of that."

"He doesn't?"

"No, no, and no. Make sure you're here on the twenty-third ready to do your thing. If you get the part, great. If you don't, I'll see if I can get you some commercials and bit parts to keep you on your feet for a while. Simple as that."

I couldn't afford to turn down bit parts, and what would LuEllen say if she knew I'd turned down a chance like this? After all, I'd promised her.

"All right, Ira. I'll do it." I had a hard time getting the words out. My throat burned.

"Come on and say it. . . ."

I had to smile. "You're the man, Ira."

"Of course, I am. Oh, and Pres?"

"Yeah?"

"Carlos said to tell you he found your innocence charming. That's what actually got you an audition for this part. He also said he'd love to pick up where you two left off."

And he was gone.

My insides froze. I could not. I would not. Was Ira suggesting the part was mine as long as I—?

I couldn't. Just the thought of facing Carlos had me blushing, and I was on the backside of Ellery where I knew he couldn't see me.

Ira was right about one thing, though—I needed more money. Thanks to LuEllen, I had the gas money. Lord willing, I'd have enough for the car. Then, I still had to find a way to pay Dec back for her prescriptions and the Andersons' hospitality.

But how was I supposed to play the part of a seductress if I'd never had sex?

Easy. You've been seducing people since you were plopped down in your first baby beauty pageant.

Yeah, but baby beauty pageants didn't have filmed love scenes, and I'd royally botched last night's attempt. I might've felt naked during the swimsuit competition once or twice, but I'd never actually been naked in a room full of people.

Then I thought of waking up beside Dec, of the intimacy of sharing a bed.

No. You are not going to ask Declan Anderson to be your hands-on sex-ed instructor.

Oh, but I could do a lot worse. I couldn't help but think back to my *Lolita Ann* experiment in the kitchen. I had never felt that attracted to anyone before, and now that I'd spilled my guts to him about my past experiences, it was like I didn't have anything to fear. He'd still held me through the night, never judging.

Who knew? Thanks to how LuEllen carried on that morning, the whole Anderson clan might kick us out before supper. I wouldn't blame them if they did.

I'd been so caught up in my thoughts, I'd walked directly to the back entrance of the Holy Roller, the one I'd been avoiding ever since I met Private Banks. Great. He was in his usual spot at the back door. That's what I got for walking around the back-side of the building. I should've just cursed in front of the busy-bodies and been done with it.

Wait, I could do this now. I could help this young man into the light. I swiped away the last of my tears.

"Hi, Blake," I said, digging deep for the confidence Uncle Hollis always showed. "Time to go into the light."

He held up one hand. "Whoa, not yet. Did Delilah say any-thing?"

Oh, she says lots of things. "About?"

"My kid. Did she find my son? Is she taking good care of him?"

"Well, I haven't quizzed her on the subject, but she did give me her word."

He shook his head. "Not good enough. She's as stubborn as a mule. I want to know where my kid is, what his name is, and that he's all right. Then I'll go. I swear it."

"I'm sure she has everything well in hand. Why don't you go ahead?" I closed my eyes and imagined Private Banks walking into the light.

He must've reached for me because I felt the cold, shivery ghost touch go through my shoulder. "Wait!"

"Gah, will you stop that?" I looked up and into his eyes, those familiar eyes that I couldn't place.

"I want to go into the light, really I do. I can see that it both-ers you I'm here, but I need to know for sure."

I exhaled shakily. Getting close to Delilah was going to be tricky. "Okay."

I reached for the back door, caught movement out of the cor-ner of my eye, and narrowly sidestepped his hand.

He grinned sheepishly. "Sorry. I was just wondering what your name is."

"Presley."

"Like Elvis?"

"Oh, yeah. My mom loves Elvis. My granny did, too."

He tilted his head to the side and smirked. "Presley. It suits you. And thank you for coming back. Who knows how long I would've been here without you."

This time, when I reached for the door, he didn't try to touch me.

But I had to face something even scarier: Delilah.

Declan

Trying to get Kari to put together a bouquet of flowers normally wasn't this hard.

"Look, do you have the flowers I requested?" I asked as I cradled the phone on one shoulder and shuffled through some paperwork that needed my attention that afternoon.

"Well, yes, but coral roses? Come on, Declan. What gives?"

"You're nosy. Make it happen or I'll call the other florist in town."

"Ha! You will not because you know they have supermarket flowers."

I made another stack of papers that could be handled later and noticed Caroline leaning in my doorway. "You are a flower snob."

"Hello, kettle? This is pot, and you are black. Now, who is the lucky lady?"

I took a deep breath. I hadn't fully thought this through. Kari had left Presley on the side of the road. "They are for Presley Cline, to be delivered to the Holy Roller."

Nothing but silence.

"Is that going to be a problem?"

"No problem," she said, suddenly all business. "What do you want on the card?"

"Thinking of you and my name, but not in that forged signature you like to try."

"I'll type it."

"Perfect. And this isn't a problem? I thought flowers. I thought you. I forgot all about the intricacies of women and how you left Presley on the side of the road. Don't do that again, by the way."

"No worries. We're all made up."

I could *feel* her smile coming through the phone. "All made up?"

"She came by this morning and apologized. Thinking about having her babysit the kids sometime."

Well, this was a mistake. The only thing worse than Kari coating Presley's flowers with a poisonous substance might be having Kari tell Presley everything she knew about me. Too late to turn back now.

"So you like her, huh?" Kari asked.

Caroline motioned for me to get off the phone.

"May be a flower-loving guy, but I'm not talking feelings with you, and I have to go. Duty calls."

"I'll send you a bill, then, Mr. Desire."

"You'd better behave or I will direct our patrons to the supermarket flowers."

"You wouldn't and you know it. Now get back to your duty."

As I hung up the phone, I couldn't help but think I had just made a terrible mistake.

"Yes, Caroline?"

"The furnace has died again."

I pushed back from the desk and started rolling up my sleeves. "I swear that's the only reason you keep me around here."

"That and the scrambled eggs," Caroline said, hugging herself in the chilly hallway. "Thank you in advance."

I walked down the hall, out the back door, and around the house. I took a moment to steel myself before I opened the cellar door. Every time, I reminded myself I wasn't going to see my mother. Every time, I held my breath until I saw the cellar was empty except for some old quart jars and my nemesis, the furnace.

Then the oddest thing would happen when I stepped down into the cellar: I felt a crazy and unexpected peace. Sometimes I'd catch myself humming while I worked—which I was doing today—and it was almost always an easy fix—just as it was today. Sometimes I didn't even need a part to get things running again. When the furnace started again, it was always with a sigh rather than a cough.

The furnace hummed to life, and I gave it a pat on the side for good measure. I had the craziest urge to linger in the cellar for just a few minutes more. Either I was going insane or I had a morbid curiosity about the place where my mother chose to hang herself. Maybe after all this time I was still searching for answers.

Presley

It didn't take my resolve long to crumble. Delilah was in a pretty good mood, and I questioned the wisdom of riling her up to get Blake's answers. Just as I was working up the courage to ask her about his kid, the bells above the door tinkled. I looked up to see Tiffany Davis toting flowers. "Hey, you!"

"Looky here! It really is you. Welcome back, cuz." Tiffany set the flowers down and hugged me tight. LuEllen's sister was Tiffany's mother, but no one had seen her in years. "And these flowers are for you."

"For me?"

"Ha! I'm only surprised we haven't been delivering more, Miss Movie Star."

My smile slipped a notch. "I don't know about that."

Tiffany waved away my concern. "Don't you worry about those magazines. You know you haven't hit it big until *someone* catches you in a compromising position."

My heart swelled at the acceptance from my cousin.

I thanked her for her trouble before she left. Delilah's eyes narrowed, but I couldn't tell if she was displeased with Tiffany's baby bump or that I had flowers. I walked around to my station to put the bouquet on a little shelf above the sink. They were a lovely mixture of purple and white flowers with peach roses. I'd never even seen a peach rose before.

I slid the tiny card out of the envelope. On the front it said, *Thinking of you, Dec.* On the back it said, *Girl, we need to talk. Kari.*

I frowned at the card. What was that supposed to mean?

Dec had sent me the flowers, but why had Kari felt the need to write a note on the back? I mean, guys just called up and said, "Pick out something pretty," didn't they?

I did a lot of sweeping and towel washing that day, but word was getting out that I was there. I did a wash and set, then wrote down an appointment from the mother of a teen girl who wanted something "Hollywood." I even caught myself humming as I worked, occasionally sneaking back to sniff the flowers Dec had sent.

Finally, I got to my last appointment before lunch. I was too distracted for my own good and needed the break since I had come way too close to nipping the ear of Gigi Neil's rather energetic two-year-old. In my defense, cutting his hair was a lot like trying to hit a moving target. At least I got the bowl cut just the way she wanted it in the end, and no ears were harmed in the making of a tiny Beatle.

"Who gave you the flowers?" Delilah asked once she got back from lunch. I knew she'd been wanting to ask me for a while, but this was the first time we'd been alone since they arrived.

"Dec Anderson," I said. My cheeks heated in spite of my best efforts.

She muttered something unintelligible, and I didn't press for details. Instead, I ducked out for my own lunch break and walked next door to the florist where Kari was arranging potted poinsettias.

"There you are! You—" She pointed at me. "You have some splaining to do."

"I like him a lot."

"And?"

"I may have kissed him?"

"And?" She took a seat on the stool behind the ancient cash register on the counter.

"And he sent me some really pretty flowers."

"Oh, no. No, no, no. Dear, sweet, naïve Presley. Declan Anderson does not send flowers to just anyone."

Well, I would sure as heck hope not.

"This shop used to belong to his mother, and—"

"Caroline?"

"No. His mother. Caroline is his stepmother. Anyway, this shop belonged to his mother, the one who killed herself—"

His mother had killed herself? Was she the woman in the red dress? I'd only seen her once, but I sometimes still got that feeling someone was watching me.

"—And she taught him all about flowers. If he sends flowers, he's careful."

"I really think you're overreacting here, Kari."

She didn't get a chance to answer me because a lady came in to order some flowers for her daughter who was turning sixteen that day. Once her order was finished, Kari's eyes practically shuttled the woman out of the shop. "White carnations mean sweet and lovely. Orchids, refined beauty. Baby's breath represents innocence, and coral roses mean desire."

Innocence? Carlos had said he found my innocence "charming." Why did all of these men see me as innocent when I felt anything but?

And why did that one jump out at me first? I should have been focused on desire. I swallowed hard.

"He's fallen for you," Kari said. "Hard."

I couldn't breathe. The feeling could be mutual.

Her smile faded into a stern frown. "But you had best not play him and then dump him."

Like you did with the other boys. She didn't say it, but I knew what she meant. I had used Roy, and I wasn't too proud of that. I'd broken it off with plenty of other boys, too, always careful to keep the relationship from getting too physical—especially after

Lon. "He asked me out, and I turned him down. So can you chill?"

"Well, you did something," she said.

Yeah. I unloaded all of my baggage at his doorstep.

"When did you and Dec get so chummy?" *And when had I become so jealous? Get a grip, Presley.*

Kari either didn't hear the snark or didn't care. "Look, when Dec's mother killed herself, a lot of people around here speculated that Mr. Anderson killed her. You know, small town, not enough to do, and then he married Caroline Potter not too long after. But then *he* died and people just steered clear. Fine to let the Andersons bury you, but don't get too close. It was like people thought they were cursed."

She reached under the counter and pulled out a dog-eared spiral notebook and laid it on top. "About the time Mr. Anderson sold this place to my parents, I found this under the cash register."

I hesitated to touch the notebook because the faded cover barely hung on.

"Go on," Kari prodded.

I opened to a random page and saw a whole list of flowers that started with D. Who knew dandelions symbolized faithfulness? Or that dahlias represented dignity and elegance? I flipped back to the cover and saw where *Lucy Anderson* had been written in a loopy cursive. "I don't understand."

Kari smiled at my confusion. "When I found the notebook, I took it to Dec. I was just nine, and he was already in high school. He was so nice to me, though, and thanked me. He must've studied it frontwards and backwards looking for some clue, any clue that would tell him why his mother did what she did. He was grasping at straws. He still missed his mother and didn't trust Caroline because she was a Potter."

"Wow." Creepy Potter was Caroline Anderson's father? Weird.

"Yeah. Dec memorized this entire book. When I worked in the shop as a teenager, I would occasionally get a customer who cared about flower meanings. I remembered the notebook and would call him up to ask him to look things up, like a flower for "congratulations" or "friendship." I could use the Internet now, but back then we still had dial-up. It was long distance and slow and, anyway, he showed up one day and handed me the notebook. Said he didn't mind me calling him at work—I was all of sixteen so he had to be lying—but why bother when I could go straight to the source. I think he'd given up on figuring his mother out. Since then we've had to work together on so many funerals and things that we became friends. I've never forgotten how he was nice to me when I was such a little kid."

My heart ached for him. At least I had LuEllen, such as she was.

"Why didn't you tell me this when he was tutoring me?" I asked.

"Hey, maybe I had a little crush on him, too."

"You could've fooled me with all the grief you gave me. He gets along with Caroline now, doesn't he?"

"Now. He told me his father died when he was just a senior in high school. Tough time to be left with a new stepmom and a little brother."

Yeah, and I could guess the only thing that would drive someone to read up on flower meanings was a way to figure out why his mother hadn't loved him enough to stick around. When I was little, I would've done anything to know who my father was. Especially when I was a teenager. At one point I'd thought about how my father might come out of the woodwork if I were to be famous enough. But what then? Would he only beg me for money? And that was just an idle daydream, a reason I told myself to keep going when LuEllen's insistence rankled.

"Earth to Presley!"

"Sorry, what?"

"I was saying, you'd best give that man another kiss. He thinks you're beautiful, lovely, and innocent. And he wants you."

"You're getting all of that from a bunch of flowers?"

She smiled as she nodded. "The few times he's sent flowers to a girl on Valentine's Day? I can tell you they weren't red roses, and I doubt it's because he knew they were more expensive on that day than any other."

Even I knew red roses meant love.

Love.

I hadn't thought about love—not until my accidental confession to LuEllen.

I'd been too busy thinking about sex.

And why did I feel a pang that he hadn't sent red roses to me, either?

Because love was scarier than sex. After all, what was there to keep a man from running away as my father had? Why take the cow once you'd had the free milk? That's what LuEllen would say.

"Why are you muttering about cows and free milk?" Kari asked.

I hadn't realized I had been talking aloud. "Um, I don't think Dec's interested in a relationship."

"Are you?"

"No, not really." I mean, it would be impractical to say the least. I'd already promised Ira I would go back and audition for this *Lolita Ann* thing.

"Then enjoy the moment," Kari said with a tone of voice that suggested I was a complete idiot.

"You just told me not to play him and dump him!"

She rolled her eyes, and it took me back to high school. "I said not to play him. I didn't say you couldn't have some adult fun."

"It's just things are . . . complicated."

She arched an eyebrow. "I don't suppose you'd care to elaborate on that cliché?"

"Not today," I said as I forced a grin. "I have to finish up work today, then I just might give a very thoughtful man a kiss."

She grinned back, obviously delighted with my response and not seeing it as the deflection it was.

Well, well. I might have what it takes to be an actress after all.

Declan

The fridge was full of disgusting things. It took all afternoon, a roll of paper towels, and a ridiculous amount of disinfectant to get everything cleaned up and thrown out. On the plus side, I re-stocked all of the soft drinks and found a brand-new carton of Rocky Road in the freezer. Hard to tell who bought it, but I might have to sample the ice cream later. You know, quality control.

At least my reward for finishing up the fridge was to close the door and find Presley. She didn't say anything, just wrapped her arms around my neck and kissed me soundly. "Thank you for the flowers."

"You're welcome."

"Declan, visitation's in an hour. Presley, upstairs and out of sight, yes?" Caroline had taken to mothering Presley, too. At least she didn't seem to mind, too much. I minded, but then what could I do? Duty called.

I went across the parking lot to shower off all of the furnace grime and to change into a fresh suit, making a note that it was past time to go to the dry cleaner's. When I came back, Presley had disappeared, so I went about my business taking care of people. For once, it didn't feel like a burden. It wasn't so hard to give a smile of encouragement. By all rights, I should've been more depressed than ever because I knew Sean was going to leave everything to me in just a couple of weeks, but I wasn't.

I watched my brother across the way, offering an arm to an older lady who was walking to a casket to pay her respects. She started sniffling, and he produced a handkerchief, an honest-to-goodness handkerchief. She looked up at him with the same moony eyes of a preteen at her first boy band concert. I had to chuckle.

You are not alone in old lady love.

Circulating the next room, I replaced an empty box of Kleenex, answered one lady's question about the antique chair she sat in, then found a Dr Pepper for Mr. Love's grandson. He had been standing there receiving visitors for so long that it seemed such a small thing to ask.

By the time we closed the door on the last visitor, my feet were aching. Caroline clapped a hand on my arm. "You did really well tonight. Better than I've seen in a long time."

"Felt better than I have in a long time," I said. "Hey, Sean, thanks for the assist."

"You're welcome," he said. He was putting on his coat to drive back to the hotel.

"It's really silly of you two to stay out there when we have another bedroom upstairs," I said. "Surely Alan doesn't think we have cooties since his family is in the business."

"Okay. Maybe we'll come over tomorrow," Sean said. "And save some money. I guess we weren't sure we'd be welcome."

"Now *that* is the stupidest thing you've ever said." Even as I said the words, I could feel Caroline's disapproving glance. It would take time for her.

Uncle Hollis brushed past in pajama pants as Caroline and I walked to the back door.

"How did he change so fast?"

"He left ten minutes before the last guest," Caroline said with a laugh.

As we entered the kitchen, I heard the hiss of the kettle and Uncle Hollis singing about how he was still standing.

"So it's going to be all Elton John all the time now?" I asked Caroline. "What happened to the Dolly Parton?"

She shrugged. "Did you clean out the fridge?"

"Yes, I cleaned out the fridge."

"Did you tell Presley to make sure she was back in the funeral home long before we opened?"

"No, I'm not sure that's a conversation we have to have."

Caroline smiled. "I am. I can see her sitting at the top of the stairs waiting for you."

I looked through the glass panes of the back door, and there she was sitting at the top of the stairs of the carriage house.

I gave Caroline a kiss on the cheek. "Night, Mom," I said as I headed out the door.

"You called me Mom! That's twice in one day."

I paused to look over my shoulder. "You made me clean out the refrigerator. Such a mom thing to do."

As I crossed the parking lot, Presley stood. The crazy woman still wasn't wearing a coat.

I took the stairs two at a time. "I hope you haven't been waiting long—it's still cold out here."

"Just a few minutes. I figured it was safe when Uncle Hollis came back upstairs."

Caroline stopped, halfway in her car, to yell, "Remember what I said!"

I waved her off. "Caroline said to make sure you're back upstairs before we open. I think she's giving you a curfew."

Presley smiled. "Okay then. So she's not too mad about this morning? I apologized this afternoon, but she seemed to still be mad at me."

"Hard to tell with her," I said as I opened the door. "As long as you don't frighten any other patrons, she'll be fine."

She followed me inside, and I yanked off my tie and tossed my suit coat on the recliner and started rolling up my sleeves. "So, what brings you over to my humble abode?"

"I have a proposition for you."

Presley

It wasn't until after the words came out of my mouth that I realized just how slutty they sounded. He stared at me for so long I was afraid he was about to usher me out the door. He stood there with rolled-up sleeves and his hands on his hips, those suspenders making him look like a hero from a black-and-white movie. Finally, he spoke. "And what is your proposition?"

I took a deep breath. "If I'm going to do this movie, I'm going to have to shoot a love scene. Several, actually. I think I've made it obvious I don't know what I'm doing."

I sound like a complete idiot. This is the stupidest thing I have ever done.

Yet my pulse was racing at the thought of it.

"So you're not looking for a relationship?"

How to answer this question . . . yes but no? "Well, I will have to go back to Hollywood before the end of the year."

"And that would be it?" His eyes bored through me, and I couldn't read his expression. Dec Anderson would make one helluva poker player because I couldn't tell if he was going to toss me out on my ear or take me up on my offer.

"Yes, I suppose so."

"No strings it is, but why?"

I swallowed hard. This wasn't anywhere near as easy as I'd pictured it in my mind. "What do you mean 'why'?"

"Why me? How do I know I won't be another guy you regret?"

"Because I trust you." The words came out of me before I realized they were true.

He chuckled and looked away, running a hand through his hair. "I am trustworthy. And dependable. And loyal. I am, I think, a dog."

How did I go wrong with trustworthy?

He plopped down in his recliner. "I'm the one to 'show' you things? The older man you can think of fondly later in life after you've moved on to a younger conquest?"

"No, it's not like that at all."

"Then what is it like? What do you want?" His dark eyes flashed, and his words held an edge.

"You," the word came out on a whisper.

"What?"

"You. I don't know the how or why of it, but I just want you. Back when you tutored me, I remember wanting you to brush against me. When we were stuck in that closet, I thought I would die if you didn't kiss me. I know I turned my head because I got scared, but everything scares me. Still, I keep coming back to . . . you."

"Why?"

The man was honestly baffled.

"Dammit, you are gorgeous. I don't know how you can't see that. And you're funny. And you're good at what you do. I've always had a crush on you."

He smiled, and it was that shy smile that took my breath away, the one that would have all the women in Ellery after him if he were to smile like that every day. "You're the gorgeous one, not me."

"I'm a blonde with a pretty good metabolism," I said, "but you are the definition of tall, dark, and handsome."

I walked toward where he sat in the recliner. His fingers clenched the armrests.

"I know I've made mistakes. I know I'm scared, and that I've run. I know that I'm not . . . pure, but—"

"No one's pure."

"You're the only man I have ever even wanted to have sex with."

"We may need to get your vision checked," he said. He wouldn't meet my eyes. He was trying to play it off, but I saw it. He was damaged, too. First, wondering about why his mother had committed suicide. Then having to deal with the Cold Fingers rumors. All of it had taken its toll.

I put my hands on the arm of the recliner and leaned forward. "My vision is a perfect twenty-twenty. And you desire me. Your flowers told me so."

I was daring him to kiss me, holding my lips not far from his in that special place where attraction lingered like two magnets held not quite together. The first time we kissed, I'd been the one to initiate the contact. This time, I wanted him to kiss me.

He gave in with a growl and pulled me forward. Even as he kissed me, though, his hands stayed perfectly at my waist as though he knew he had to drive with his hands at ten and two. I kissed him back, but those hands wouldn't move. The frustration of it began to eat me alive, but it was a delicious frustration, one that made me want him all the more for the restraint he was showing.

He broke off the kiss, his forehead still touching mine as we both gasped for air.

"You deserve better than me, than this," he said, his hand waving around to indicate his shabby apartment.

"But I won't be able to find anyone with a greater this." I put my hand on his chest above his heart, and he picked up my hand to kiss my palm.

"And you're sure?"

"Very. I want your hands all over me."

He started tracing his fingers up and down my arm. "That makes two of us."

When he gathered me up in his arms, I squeaked. "You're going to hurt yourself!"

"Ah, but I've moved bodies that weighed two or three times what you do. I have to confess, though, it was nowhere near this much fun." He tossed me on the bed and kissed me, disappearing in the little bathroom and opening the medicine cabinet.

"You have got to be kidding me."

I sat up. "What?"

He sat down hard on the edge of the bed. "Do you want to know how pathetic I am?"

"You're not pathetic."

"Oh, I'm sad. All of my condoms have expired."

I waited for him to suggest that we try them anyway. I would have to tell him no. The idea of condoms alone scared me, but expired condoms? That was just asking for trouble. No way would I risk unprotected sex, either. LuEllen would keel over if she knew I had, much less if I turned up pregnant.

"Of course, there are other things we could try," he said.

"Other things?"

He gave me a wicked grin. "You said you trusted me."

I swallowed hard. "I do."

"Then how about we explore all the way up to third base?"

I exhaled, still scared, but nowhere near as scared as before. I hated myself for the sense of relief that I felt. Something about Declan made me not want to hold anything back, but I'd been holding so much of myself back for so long that it was nearly impossible to let go. "Hey, batter, batter, swing?"

He laughed like I was the most brilliant woman he'd ever met, and then he took me on a tour of all the bases but one.

Declan

When my phone alarm went off the next morning, I had to pinch myself. Then I leaned over to kiss Presley's head. Honeysuckle. So strong, sweet, and almost too good to be true. "Presley."

"Mmm?"

"You'd better go slip inside before Caroline comes in."

She rolled over and nestled into my chest. "Five more minutes."

I carefully unwound her arms and stepped out of bed. "No more minutes."

"You are mean," she said with a mischievous smirk. It was a sentence she'd said more than once the night before. I was pretty sure she didn't mean it.

"Presley, you gotta go."

"The sun isn't even out."

"I regret that you force my hand." I yanked the sheet off the end of the bed, and she shrieked at the cold air left in its wake.

"That was cruel and unusual," she grumbled, but she got up and changed out of my T-shirt before putting her own clothes back on. It took her a few minutes to realize I was watching her.

"What are you doing?"

"It's not as much fun as watching you undress, but it still has its perks," I said.

"You'd like to watch me undress?"

Every day for the rest of my life. "Yes."

"Maybe I'll do a little striptease for you."

"Don't make promises you can't keep," I said.

"You were more fun last night," she said with a sigh.

"Maybe I'm only fun at night," I said as I handed her my suit coat from the day before to use as a jacket.

"Then maybe I need to visit you again tonight."

"Oh, you better believe that I will be prepared if you do. It can't come fast enough," I said as I leaned in to kiss her.

She turned her head. "Morning breath!"

I turned her back to face me. "I don't care."

Then I kissed her and sent her on her way.

Every day for the rest of my life, I thought to myself again as I watched her stumble across the parking lot. I was going to have to tamp down those feelings because she'd made it clear that she wasn't interested in the long haul. I couldn't blame her. What did I have to offer her compared to Hollywood?

I flopped backward on the bed and one of the slats clattered to the ground.

Dammit.

Damn the Andersons and their mate-for-life-bald-eagle ways.

I wouldn't do it. I wouldn't tell her. If I told her, then she might stay out of guilt. I knew way too much about that. Nope. I would enjoy these moments. I would do my best to make love to her as she deserved. Then I would send her back to California and wish her all the best.

Presley

I felt boneless. Even the cold morning air couldn't take away what I'd felt with Declan. He was patient. He was funny. Just thinking about him made me wish it were night again already. If I couldn't have sex with this man, then it just couldn't be done. Maybe I'd go to the drugstore, too. Just to be on the safe side.

I tested the door, then brought out my key when I saw it was still locked. The kitchen was still dark, so I turned on a light and put Dec's coat on the back of one of the chairs where he would find it. Humming all the while, I put on a pot of coffee.

A throat cleared behind me, and I jumped out of my skin.

When I whirled around, I saw the Colonel. "By my count that is twice you have spent the night in a bedroom not your own. Tell the boy to marry you."

"Look, I can't really tell Declan what to do," I said. "And those rules were for a time when women couldn't take care of themselves. I'm handling it."

"You are living under *my* roof," the Colonel roared. "So you must have him make an honest woman of you."

I giggled. "I am an honest woman."

"You are a whore."

It was such an ugly word. I knew what they said about sticks and stones, but words could harm me. "Take it back."

"I will not. Your actions are not those befitting a lady."

"Well, you aren't acting like much of a gentleman."

He was taken aback. I had managed to insult a ghost. "If you were a man, I would call you out for a duel."

"No, you wouldn't. You're an intolerant bully who refuses to accept change."

"The insolence! The nerve!"

"Presley's right, Gramps."

God bless Uncle Hollis.

I closed my eyes in relief as Uncle Hollis took a seat. "Would you mind scrambling me an egg?"

"Sure, not a problem," I said as I began opening cabinets to look for a skillet.

"Mark my words," the Colonel said. "Some things need to change around here or I will lay waste to this place no matter if I did build it."

"Actually, one of the university folks built this house," Uncle Hollis said. "You just moved the business here back in the thirties."

The Colonel disappeared suddenly, which I thought was unusual until Sean and another young man appeared at the door.

Uncle Hollis rose to greet them. "Oh, good! Are you two going to stay with us for the holidays?"

"Well, you know Caroline has only the one bedroom," Sean said as he put down his suitcase.

"And the hotel here in Ellery is . . . interesting," the other guy added.

"Oh, where are my manners. You know Presley, right?"

Sean grinned. "A year ahead of me in school and a movie star!"

"Hardly." I nodded to him then extended my hand to the shorter, stockier guy when he held out his. "I'm Presley."

"I'm Sean's husband, Alan. Nice to meet you."

"Nice to meet you, too. Anyone else want eggs?"

And that's how we settled into a lovely breakfast with eggs, toast, coffee, and laughter. With such good company, it was easy to forget about the Colonel's warning.

In all of the excitement about the flowers the day before, I'd allowed myself to chicken out of asking Delilah about Private Banks's—Blake's—child. I knew I'd have to ask her eventually, but the Holy Roller had been blessedly busy all day. Word had spread there was a new hairdresser in town.

I did a blue rinse and another wash and set, but most of my clientele were younger women asking if I could give them one of the new styles from Los Angeles. I was happy to oblige, and they were excited to ask me all sorts of questions. I kept saying the same things over and over again.

"Yes, it's a big city." *And it's expensive. And sometimes dirty.*

"Yes, it's sometimes scary—but only if you wander into the wrong parts of the city." *Like the actual Hollywood Boulevard before they cleaned it up.*

"Yes, I once met Brad Pitt." *Only because I was sent to get his coffee.*

"No, I haven't met either of the hot guys from *Twilight*."

"Yes, I have an IMDb page." *Please don't look at it.*

Finally, my last customer of the day, P. J. Willis, sat down.

I ran my fingers through her long straight hair. "What are we going to do today?"

"Cut it all off."

"Are you sure you won't miss it?" Something about her disgusted tone suggested this wasn't a happy decision. Truly, I was a little jealous of her thick hair, a natural brown but with strands of blond and red.

"Not a bit," she said with determination. "Can't we donate it to a charity or something?"

"Absolutely." I opened my mouth to try to talk her out of it again, but the woman staring at me from the mirror was resolute. This had to do with a man. "Boyfriend doesn't like long hair?"

"Ex-husband *loves* my long hair," she spat.

"Well, in that case, let's cut it off."

I pulled the hair back into a low ponytail and made the cut, depositing the hair in a plastic bag.

"I feel lighter already," she said with a sigh. "Trust me on this: Don't ever give up one ounce of yourself for a man."

Dec came to mind even as my hands and scissors flew. I'd tried to give him more than an ounce of me. Well, the physical me.

P. J. seemed to be talking about something else.

I looked at her face, how her brow was smoother and how the corners of her mouth kept quirking up. Getting her hair cut was the right idea. By the time it grew back she could decide whether *she* liked it long or short.

But something was missing.

"Chin down," I ordered.

In a matter of minutes, I'd taken the bob up even more in the back and worked with the natural angle of her hair so it was longer at her chin. The result was a sleek yet sassy bob that perfectly suited the shape of P. J.'s face.

"Oh, I love it!" she said when she looked up. She swished her hair from side to side. "You are a miracle worker."

"And you are welcome," I said as I picked up the broom. She paid me—including a generous tip—and practically skipped out of the shop. I chuckled to myself as I swept up the hair. My feet ached, but the quicker I swept up the sooner I got to go home.

I came around the corner to see Delilah hunched over her broom, still sweeping.

"Let me get that for you," I said, taking the broom before she could protest. "Your feet have to be killing you."

For once, she didn't argue. Instead, she sat in one of the dryer chairs.

"If I were to get a movie part, would I still have a job when I came back?" I couldn't meet her eyes.

"If I fired you, I'm afraid the town would boycott me," she said.

Oh, thank goodness. Now for the hard question.

"Did you find Private Banks's kid?"

She stiffened.

Great, Presley. Way to ruin things when the two of you were having a civil conversation.

"Yes, I did. Everything is just fine," she said softly.

I finished sweeping and took her hamper of towels to the laundry room, then went back for mine.

When I came back, she was gone but had left a note for me to lock up when I left.

I didn't think too much of it; after all, I was on a mission to the drugstore next door.

Declan

That day we had two funerals for the last of the tornado victims. They both went smoothly, and we made it back early to prepare for Bart Borden's visitation. I was excited enough about the possibility of a visit from Presley that I wasn't even that nervous about running into Jessica.

She showed up early with a plate of her specialty, what she liked to call an apricot salad. Over the years, she'd brought no fewer than ten of the concoctions made of Jell-O, sour cream, and pineapple. "I made this one just for you, Declan. I know how much you like them."

I smiled and said thank you even though I really wasn't a fan. Tossing it, however, would be so much easier than continuing the conversation.

She smiled quite prettily. "I wanted to do something to thank you for everything you've done for our family over the years."

I closed the fridge and turned to go, but she had me cornered. Without warning, she hugged me tight and planted her lips on my cheek, leaving them there a lot longer than I would've liked. When she let go, her cheeks were pink once again. I wish there was a way I could convince her not to be so uncomfortable around me, because then I wouldn't have to feel so uncomfortable around her.

"Well, uh, thank you, Jessica."

She gave a little wave as she went down the hall.

The sound of a paper towel being ripped from the roll snapped me out of my catatonic state. At the sight of Presley, though, my panic increased. "That was not—"

"I know," she said with a huge smile. "The deer-in-the-headlights look you have going on told me everything I need to know."

Thank God.

"You do, however, have ugly orange-red lipstick on your cheek, I'm afraid." She dabbed the paper towel under the faucet and wiped away every last trace of Jessica Borden. "You know, you might want to stick with her instead," Presley said solemnly. She left me hanging for quite a few seconds before adding, "I don't know the first thing about making Jell-O salads and hers has won awards at the County Fair."

"I could give a rat's ass about Jell-O salad."

Of course, Caroline arrived in time to hear me cussing in the funeral home. First, she pointed to Presley. "You, upstairs or outside." Then she pointed to me. "Watch your language and get back to the Lilac Room. We're still having a visitation, you know."

"I was—"

"Don't care," Caroline said, hands on her hips.

I reached into my pocket for my keys and pressed them into Presley's palm. "Please tell me *you* had time to—"

"Done and done," she said with a grin before sneaking out the back door.

Caroline and I stood at the doorway where we could look down the hall, smiling our deranged "Everything's fine" smiles while we had a discussion.

"Look, Mrs. Borden brought one of her Jell-O salads and felt the need to thank me in a very personal way. I needed a minute."

Today Caroline was channeling demonic Barbie. "Oh, and I'm sure Presley just *happened* to be there."

In my best overenthusiastic-game-show-host expression, I said, "Oh, I'm pretty sure the show was for her."

"I don't care. Get down to the Lilac Room and make sure everything's going smoothly."

So down to the Lilac Room I went. Armando had everything running perfectly. Sean and Uncle Hollis were standing in opposite corners looking bored. I caught Caroline out in the hall. "Look, I don't even think you need me here tonight."

"Nice try," Caroline said. "Mrs. Borden specifically requested that you be in charge. As far as she's concerned, you are."

Dammit.

With a deep breath I shifted into funeral director default mode. My eyes scanned the rather large crowd for people in need or people about to lose it. I saw neither. I did see a need for more chairs, so I went to get more of those. I changed out the jug of water for the cooler, and directed an older lady to the bathroom. I answered a young man's question about when the funeral home was built and brought Jessica a Coke.

Slowly but surely, people began to leave. Armando left to take care of paperwork, and Sean watered the plants. Uncle Hollis had disappeared again, but who was I to begrudge him his pajama pants? Caroline spoke with one of Bart's sisters by the guestbook, and that left me alone with Jessica. Again. Seeing her walk in my direction, I headed out of the room and into the hall. No way did I want to be left alone in a room with her again.

I caught Caroline's eye, and gave her the "Do not leave me alone for any reason" look. She nodded back.

"How are you holding up?" I asked Jessica.

"It just doesn't feel real yet," she said sweetly. It chilled me to my soul. "I'm so glad you were here tonight. For you to be here after all you've been through helps me know I'm going to be okay, too."

"That means a lot to me," I said. "And if I haven't said it before, I'm sorry for your loss. Bart was a really good man."

"That, he was," she said as she reached for my cheek but stopped short of actually touching me. "If there's ever anything I can do for you, please call me, you hear?"

I nodded, and she turned for the door.

Caroline was telling Bart's sister, "You and Jessica have such a long day tomorrow. Why don't you try to get some rest?"

Caroline saw them to the door and locked it behind them. She waited a good ten beats, then turned on me. "Next time, you take the woman who never stops talking, and I'll take the cute blushing widow."

"I'm not asking for her attention!"

"Between her and Presley, I'm beginning to think you've been passing out some kind of love potion." She snapped off the hall light.

"Trust me when I tell you I haven't," I said as I fell in step with her on her way to the back door in the kitchen.

"Yeah, yeah. I saw you pass your keys to Miss Thang." Caroline stopped in her tracks. "Are you going to make an honest woman of her?"

"What?" Her voice had sounded different, guttural and forced. She blinked repeatedly. "Did I just say that?"

"Yeah, you did."

"Why did I say that?" She rubbed her temple.

"I don't know." *And please note how I'm not answering your question.*

"I've got to get some sleep," she said, walking down the hall. "You remember the rules now."

"Back well before sunrise or we all turn into pumpkins."

"And I will smash you." Her tone went from devilish to angelic. "Night night."

With those cheery words Caroline was gone, but Uncle Hollis was staring at me blankly. "Are you?"

"Am I what?"

"Are you going to make an honest woman of her?"

I could almost feel each hair on the back of my neck rise because his tone of voice had sounded almost identical to Caroline's. "What's gotten into all of you tonight?"

Uncle Hollis shook his head in confusion. "That was odd. I'm sure you have business to attend to, though, so good night, Dec!"

He turned his attention back to the stove and whistled "Step into Christmas" while he flipped a grilled cheese.

Now that was officially the craziest thing I'd seen Uncle Hollis do.

I started to question him, but I could see a light on in my apartment. I'd just chalk it up to sleep deprivation doing weird things to a person because, for once, I had places to go and *living* people to see.

Presley

I lay in Declan's bed wearing nothing but a smile.

I was done being a good girl because my mother told me to. This time I was prepared. This time I was in love, even if I wasn't planning anything permanent. This time I was going to have sex, and I was going to enjoy it like a normal, reasonable woman.

At least I would if Declan would hurry up and get here.

When he finally came through the door, he took one step inside and stopped. "Are you . . . ?"

"In my birthday suit? Yes. I thought you could do a striptease for me and then maybe I would return the favor sometime soon."

"Presley."

"Declan."

"Believe me when I tell you that sliding under those sheets would be a dream come true, but—"

"No buts. Just please."

He shrugged off his coat and reached for his tie, and my breath caught in my throat.

Declan

I am not a saint.

Every fantasy, every dream I'd ever had was waiting for me under those sheets, and she'd just used the magic word. So, I did as she asked. I stripped off all of the garments that defined me, climbed into bed with a willing woman, and I lost myself in curves and long legs and the heavenly scent of honeysuckle.

Somewhere along the way I must've missed a signal, must've missed a cue, because when I came back to earth, I looked down at this woman without the words to tell her how hard I had fallen for her. She caressed my cheek, but the only word I could find was *you*. Then one look in her eyes and everything magical and perfect crumbled and fell away.

Presley

I was with him, I was with him, and then my body revolted.

Don't. Stop, I told myself.

It's Dec, I reminded myself.

For the love of all that is sacred and holy, relax, I screamed at myself through the pain.

But I didn't.

I froze.

You will not stop him, and you will make it through this. Any minute now it will be magic. That's how it works.

With trembling fingers I reached up to touch his face as he slumped over me.

"You," he panted, his face full of wonder.

Don't cry. Whatever you do, don't cry.

But the hot tears slipped down my hairline and into my ear, and all of the wonder in his expression turned into horror.

Declan

I'd hurt her.

"Oh, God. No. Why didn't you stop me?"

"Not your fault," she choked out.

"Of course, it's my fault!"

I pulled her to me, trying to protect her—from what? Me?

She wriggled free and disappeared into the bathroom.

How had the most wonderful moment of my life so far just turned into the absolute worst?

Goddammit, you sad sonuvabitch. I pounded the pillow in frustration, as if that poor bastard had been to blame. On the other side of the bathroom door, Presley sniffled. I took care of the condom and paced away from the door and then back to it again, not sure what to do. Just as I was getting ready to take the door off its hinges to get to her, she emerged, her eyes and nose red from crying.

"Are you okay?"

"I'm fine."

As if there had ever been a woman alive who was actually fine when she said she was. "Presley."

"I'm not talking about it right now." She stepped into her underwear, then her pants, and then her top. She crammed her bra into her purse with shaking hands.

"But you will talk about it later?"

She wouldn't meet my eyes and moved for the door. I quickly blocked it. "Please don't leave like this."

She crossed her arms but looked at the wall to her right, her eyes glassy and threatening to shed tears again. "I need to go right now. Look, this is obviously my fault, but I have to leave. I need . . ."

When it became obvious she wasn't going to finish the sentence because she didn't really know what she needed, I took each of her hands and brought her knuckles to my lips. The gesture shocked her enough that her eyes met mine. "I'm sorry. Next time—"

"I don't know if there'll be a next time."

Her words were a punch in the gut. No next time? If there were no next time, then I couldn't fix this. I had to fix this. Of all the wrongs in the world, this was the one I had to make right. "You have to let me make it up to you. Please."

"Remember what you said to me earlier? I don't *have* to do anything I don't want to." She wrenched her hands from mine. "Now, move, please."

Shocked by how she'd used my own words against me, I moved to the side. I watched her walk across the parking lot, but instead of going inside, she rounded the corner and started walking down Maple Avenue in the opposite direction.

What the hell had just happened?

Dammit. Crazy woman. I couldn't let her walk around in the cold like that.

She told you to leave her alone.

Yeah, and she'd also told me to make love to her, and making love to her had been perfection. Right up until the moment it wasn't.

Anger flared.

No. She wasn't going to tell me to have sex with her then not tell me she was hurting and then blame me for the whole thing. No.

Stop, Declan. Think.

I replayed every intimate moment between us. The moment in front of the kitchen sink when she said, "But you don't hate me?" Then when she'd told me every last detail of, essentially, why she was afraid to have sex with me and ended with "But maybe he was right. Maybe I am a frigid bitch."

She might be ready to give up, but I wasn't.

Okay, Dec. You can do this.

I grabbed my pants and my keys. She wasn't going to get rid of me that easily.

Presley

At first I didn't know what I was doing or why I was walking around town in the middle of the night. Then I turned left on the street where the Vandivers had their shop, the cold weather having made me as numb on the outside as I was on the inside. I needed to get away, and to do that I needed my car.

Up the street I trudged, willing myself not to think of how I'd failed once again. If I couldn't have sex with Dec, then I was truly broken. He twisted my stomach in knots. At times when he kissed me, it felt as though there was no such thing as close enough to him. The night before? We'd had a grand time. But when it came to actually having sex, I apparently couldn't unclench.

Well, you sure as heck aren't a virgin now.

Fat lot of good that did me. Maybe I could tell the director of *Lolita Ann* that I would like for all of the sex scenes to be changed to "fooling around" scenes. I'm sure that'd work oh-so-well.

Once I reached the chain-link fence around the Vandiver repair shop, I realized how stupid my nonplan was. Who would be at the shop at that time of night? Was my car even in any condition to be driven? I tugged on the padlocked chain that held the gates together. My breath rose in front of me, and I shivered.

Next to the fenced-in shop was a small brick house that the

Vandivers used as a sort of office. I walked across the lawn and sat on the concrete steps that led to the porch, hugging myself against the cold.

No two ways about it, I would have to get that part because now I'd ruined whatever I had had with Declan through my inability to be a normal, functioning adult. Even if I didn't get the part of Lolita Ann, Ira would find me enough bit parts to survive for a while—especially with any on-set jobs doing hair and makeup.

So you're going to run away from Declan now? Do you plan to keep running for the rest of your life?

The pain between my legs had subsided to a dull ache, but the humiliation, disappointment, and the wound to my pride were going to take much longer to heal. I felt like I wanted to cry, but I couldn't find the tears. I couldn't stay there on the porch or I would freeze to death, but I sure as hell couldn't go back. Not after what I'd done.

Or what *he*'d done.

I had trusted him. I had thought he would know.

That's why you're really upset. You thought he would be able to heal you magically, that it would be different from how it had been with Carlos. I guess it was different since I hadn't chickened out and run into the night with my skirt caught in my underwear.

I closed my eyes and buried my face against my knees, but I couldn't forget his horrified expression as he'd asked why I hadn't stopped him. I was mad at him, but I was also mad at myself because it felt like some kind of failing on my part. I mean, I was sexy. *Maxim* had said so.

Sexy people were supposed to have sex. It had to be true because everything in the commercials and the movies and the romance novels said so. Those movies and television and novels made it all look so easy. All you had to do was be pretty and you would find the man of your dreams. You would have this moment when he first thrust into you that was painful, but it would be quick and magical and then you would climax together. Then, on television especially, you would be able to have sex with all sorts of people, and it would all be good because you were all so damned sexy.

But I, Presley Ann Cline, was sexy, and I couldn't have sex.

My hoarse, hysterical laugh echoed off the metal shop next door. If I couldn't have sex, then why be sexy? Screw all those early-morning runs. Screw Pilates. Screw all those nasty veggie-and-egg-white omelets and salads and all the times I'd done a juice fast. Screw it all. It turned out that sex was like Hollywood: It looked glamorous and like everything you'd ever wanted but instead was awkward and awful and liable to fuck you over in the end. So screw sex and screw Hollywood and screw being sexy.

See? When you really wanted to curse something, when you wanted to use the one word your mother told you never, ever to use, you used a word for sex.

Fuck it all, I'm going to go back and eat that pint of ice cream I saw in the freezer.

Declan

I looked everywhere for that woman. I drove up and down each street. I woke up both Kari and Delilah. I called the funeral home and woke up Uncle Hollis and LuEllen. I checked the bus station, both gas stations, the playground, churches, the Holy Roller.

I had parked in front of the Holy Roller and was about to call Jefferson hospitals and then the police. Sean called me as I had my fingers poised over the numbers.

"Dec? You might want to get back over to the funeral home."

"I'm not on call tonight," I said.

"No, Presley just came back in, and she isn't acting like herself."

I started the truck and sped the two blocks, taking one corner on two wheels. When I came through the back door, Presley was eating straight from the carton of Rocky Road ice cream while LuEllen, Uncle Hollis, Sean, and Alan looked on. The bottle of bourbon sat beside her.

"Y'all, go to bed," I said.

"No, stay," Presley said with her mouth full. She took a slug straight from the bottle. "I am getting unsexy. It's so much more fun than getting sexy, let me tell you."

I gave the group crowded in the door the infamous Anderson

look, and they scattered. When I'd first seen her, all I had felt was relief. The longer I watched her the angrier I got.

"Grab a spoon, Dec," she said.

"I was worried about you. I saw you walking down Maple and then I couldn't find you."

Her spoon paused midair. "I'm sorry about that."

"You're sorry?"

She jabbed the spoon in the ice cream and gulped from the bourbon before slamming it on the table. "Yes. I. Am. Sorry. I am a fucking failure at everything, and I am sorry to have dragged you into my orbit of suckitude."

She picked up the spoon again.

"Don't do that. If you mix that much sugar with the bourbon, it'll be the worst hangover you've ever had."

She laughed. "Never had a hangover. I've been too busy being good. Never had too much to drink. No cigarettes, no drugs, no fatty foods. Not even one speeding ticket. I didn't sleep around and I did exactly what my mommy always wanted, and it has all made me so *fucking* happy."

Every time she used the word *fuck* I cringed, and I realized she didn't even cuss that much. Or hadn't. "Seriously. Let's put away the ice cream. You can take an aspirin and drink some water and sleep this off, and then we'll talk about it in the morning."

"I'm bad for you. I'm poison," she slurred. "I'm done talking. We're done talking."

"The hell we are!" My voice roared across the kitchen, and I waited for the patter of feet to come down the stairs. They didn't, and I took several deep breaths before I continued. "You know what you are? A person. You are a beautiful person, but you're not perfect because no one is. And I'm not asking you to be. I'm only asking you to be mature and to work through this instead of running away or whatever *this* is."

"Oh, this? This is me giving up. I'm going to get fat and live in a van down by the river." She slapped the top on the ice cream. "But you're right about the sweet stuff. What I really need is a pizza."

She crammed the ice cream in the freezer and took out her cell phone. She swayed a little as she dialed, and I could see the bourbon had gone straight to her head.

"Hello, Giovanni's? Oh, good! You still have the same number. Yes, I need a large pizza with every meat you can find. Except anchovies. Gross. Yes. A large. And I need you to deliver it to Anderson's Funeral Home. No, this isn't a joke. I'm at the funeral home, and I need a pizza. Hello? Hello?"

She cradled the phone and looked back at me. "They hung up on me."

"Because you are drunk."

She held up one finger, but both she and the finger listed to one side. "I have not yet begun to drink."

I ran my hand over my nose and mouth. I had seen some weird shit in my life, but this night was topping it all. "Presley, what are you doing?"

"I told you," she said as she opened the fridge. "I'm getting unsexy. What'd you do with the cheese?"

"I threw it out. Stop, you're going to make yourself sick."

"I've been sick my whole life. Now, I'm getting well. What's this orange stuff?"

"It's a Jell-O salad. There are crackers in the cabinet—that would be better."

She closed the fridge and went to the cabinet. I put a hand on her shoulder, and she flinched. She *always* flinched and that made me mad, so mad at myself and at every other asshole who had ever hurt her. So I lost my temper for the second time that night. "I am not going to hurt you!"

But you already have.

"I mean. I am not going to hurt you again. I swear it."

She turned around. "Why with the again? I'm broken. I can't be fixed. I told you it wasn't your fault."

"You keep saying that, but I know you trusted me. Thing is, I was trusting you, too. I know I hurt you, but do you think you can trust me again?"

She nodded.

"Will you let me try again? To show you that it's not you?"

She bit her lip and nodded, the tears coming again. I pulled her close. "Besides, you might as well stop trying to be unsexy because it's not going to work."

"It'll work if I get fat."

"I would still love you if you were fat."

She looked up at me. I had used the word *love*. It had slipped out so naturally, I hadn't even realized it until she looked up at me. Fortunately, I doubted she would remember my slipup.

"What if I really can't have sex?"

I sighed. "Then I guess I would have to take matters into my own, um, hand."

"You would do that for me?"

"I'm beginning to think I would do just about anything for you."

She buried her face in my chest, her tears soaking through my white undershirt. I held her. "You do, however, owe me a strip-tease. Someday."

She laughed a little, and I took that as a good sign.

"All right. Water, aspirin, and sleep. Do you want to go upstairs or do you want to come with me just like before?"

"Just like before?"

"Before tonight, before last night. When you slept and I held you."

"That."

So we cleaned up the mess in the kitchen, and I took her across the parking lot and upstairs for aspirin, water, and some much needed sleep.

In the light of morning, she tried to sneak out of bed, but my arm closed around her like a vise. "I am not done spooning. Dammit."

She laughed nervously, then swallowed hard in a way that made me wonder if the aspirin and water trick had worked. "What was the 'dammit' for?"

"The dammit makes the spooning more manly," I said as I pulled her closer.

"We broke Caroline's rule again," she whispered, cutting the last word short like she had to shut her mouth or else. Oh, yes. It was coming.

"Caroline needs to lighten up. As long as LuEllen doesn't come over here and pound on the door then yell at you all the way across the parking lot and through the funeral home, I think we'll be okay."

We lay like that for some time, and I had almost drifted back to sleep when she said, "I don't understand why this can feel so right, but I can mess up the other so badly."

This didn't feel totally right. I needed to pee like the proverbial racehorse, but I wasn't ready to let her out of my sight. "Because practice makes perfect?"

At that she bolted for the bathroom and heaved up last night's Rocky Road. Lucky for her, I had a cast-iron constitution, which made me the perfect person to hold back her hair. "Never had a hangover before, huh?"

She groaned.

"Well, achievement unlocked," I said. "There's a toothbrush in the medicine cabinet, and I think I have something bland for you to eat."

She nodded. When I came back from the kitchen, she had thrown up again.

"*You* are going back to sleep," I said.

"I think I'm going to die."

"Nope. Just feels that way. I'm a funeral director. I would know." I extended a hand, and she took it. Instead of going to bed, she started putting on her pants.

"What are you doing?"

"I have to go to work."

"Woman, it's Sunday."

"Oh, thank God." She kicked the pants off and lay back on the pillow, completely missing the irony of her response.

"I am putting Coke, crackers, and water here on this table. You need more water than Coke and more sleep than anything else."

"Sir, yes, sir."

I showered and was out getting dressed when she asked, "What are you doing?"

"Getting ready for work."

"But it's Sunday."

"Fish gotta swim, birds gotta fly, folks gotta be buried." I added my cuff links, then tied my favorite tie. I leaned over to kiss her forehead, and she hooked one finger around a suspender and snapped it at me.

"Why are you being so good to me?"

"I think you need to ask yourself why other people haven't been," I said as I tucked the blanket around her. "No running off."

"I couldn't run off if I tried," she moaned.

"Good," I said. "I'll be back after the funeral. It'll be a while."

"I'll be here," she said.

I paused at the door to look at her once more before I left. Yeah, I loved her. She was the absolute last person on earth I should love, but there she was in her hungover, skittish, going-back-to-Hollywood-whether-I-liked-it-or-not glory.

Oh, Declan, you sad sonuvabitch. You always did know how to pick 'em.

Presley

If I could dig a hole and bury myself in it, I would.

I had screwed up screwing, been mean to Dec, got drunk and yelled at everyone, and then had to throw up while he held my hair. Seriously, I would move back to California right then except for the part where the sun hurt my eyes and my head felt as if it were being repeatedly hit by Thor's hammer.

The only answer was to lie here until I died. Surely, Dec would plan something nice for me.

When I woke up, the sun had shifted to a mellow winter afternoon sun. The new hearse wasn't back, so I knew Declan wasn't, either. Maybe it would be best if I showered and got a change of clothes before he saw me again.

I tiptoed into the quiet funeral home and noticed that LuEllen was still in bed, too. Trying not to wake her, I got clean clothes and headed for the bathroom. I contemplated going back to Dec's apartment because I didn't want a return visit from the Colonel, but I showered and he stayed away. It smelled so rank in there, I would've stayed away, too, if I could have. Someone upstairs had experienced a violent digestive reaction, but I managed to clear out the worst of it between the Lysol and the fan.

I peeked in on LuEllen, her hot-pink cast hanging over the

edge of the bed in what had to be an uncomfortable angle. It was quiet, too quiet. I crept up to the bed to wake her up.

That's when I saw her eyes were open, and I screamed.

"Oh, for crying out loud, don't be so dramatic."

There in the corner sat my mother, but not my mother. She looked like her teenage self, with impossibly puffy hair that stood up away from her face. She wore a chartreuse midriff with black suspenders and acid-wash jeans. With her blue eye shadow, shiny lip gloss, huge hoop earrings, and a million jelly bracelets, she looked . . . young.

"Mama!" The tears came hot and fast. I remember chastising her for trying to kill herself, but I never expected her to succeed. No, I wasn't ready.

"Oh, come on, baby. You knew it was going to happen sooner or later." LuEllen sat down beside me and tried to hug me, but instead her ghostly arm went through me, causing that awful shudder. I jumped to my feet.

"Are you—? What happened?" I asked as I swiped away tears. I hadn't lost her yet. Not entirely.

"I don't know, but I feel *so* much better. I can breathe! Well, I don't need to breathe, but no aches, no pains, and I'm so damn cute. Look! You can't touch this." She stood up and did some kind of dance move. "Look at me Cabbage Patch! Running Man! Roger Rabbit!"

I made a sound that was somewhere between a giggle and a hiccup. No woman should ever have to see her mother as a teenager. Then she gave me a radiant grin, and I saw she had done her dance moves just to cheer me up.

"LuEllen. Seriously. You couldn't give me a warning or something?"

She shrugged. "I didn't know. I got this horrible stomach virus thing, and the next thing I know I'm looking down at my own self and thinking how pathetic I was."

"You're not pathetic," I said. More tears slid down my cheek, but they weren't the kind that caused my throat to cramp up.

"No, but I *was* pathetic," she said. Despite how young she

looked, her eyes held an eerie wisdom. "I don't want you to do what I did."

"It's okay. We used a condom, and—"

"You did what? Those things tear! And you are so close to your audition. Are you insane?"

I held out my hand to stop her only to remember she couldn't hurt me—at least not in the traditional sense. "LuEllen. Mama. I am an adult. I am allowed to have sex." *Even if I can't seem to.* "And I'm not sure I want to audition for the part. I don't think I can do it."

"But you have to! This is it. You are so close, Presley, baby. You can't give up now!" She reached to cup my face, and I flinched, but her hands hovered just around my cheeks, which somehow gave a sensation of warmth instead of the icy prickles I was expecting.

"I'm beginning to think that's your dream, not mine." My voice came out strong and unwavering. Did my mother have to die for me to feel like I could speak my mind?

"My dream?"

"Look, I know I ruined your life, and I'm sorry about that, really I am, but I can't keep doing this just because you want me to. Soon you're going to go into the light—"

And there I went with the crying again.

"Baby girl, this was *your* dream. Since the time you were three, you told me you wanted to sing and dance and act in plays. You used to put on these shows for me and Mama." She smiled at the memory. "They were so cute! You would line up all of your stuffed animals to be an audience."

It was suddenly very hard to swallow. "But I always felt like I had to get the lead role in the play or make the Miss YCHS court or win the Miss Ellery pageant or you would be mad at me."

"Mad at you?" She put her hands on her hips. "You're the best thing I've ever done."

I'm the best thing she's ever done?

I couldn't stop the sobs. If I didn't get it together, I was going to drown in my own personal Presley Ocean. Why had LuEllen had to die for us to have this conversation? "I've always thought I was the one who . . . ruined your life."

Her eyes widened. "Oh, sweetie, no. I did that all by myself. I—"

The silence stretched between us while she thought about what she had been about to blurt out. "I ruined my life. Your father, well, he wouldn't have gone away if I hadn't said some of the things I had—"

"You made my father go away?"

She winced. "Yes and no. Kinda hard to know what he was ever going to do."

"Who is he? Where is he? Can I find him?"

"No, baby. I promised I wouldn't tell."

"But you're dead! What can it matter if you're dead?"

"It'll matter a whole heckuva lot to the person I made that promise to," she said. "How do you think I paid for all of the singing and acting and piano lessons? Or the softball equipment? Or the pageant dresses?"

"You told me you got them from Goodwill." My life had been a lie? I'd felt guilty for years about what I thought was LuEllen's selflessness, and now she was telling me that she had help along the way?

"Oh, I did get a lot of that from Goodwill or rummage sales, but sometimes you can't find what you need in those places. That's when I had to ask for help."

I swiped at my tears with the heels of my hands. "And you won't tell me who this fairy godmother was?"

LuEllen laughed. "I swore I wouldn't tell you, but I will say a more unlikely fairy godmother you'll never meet. Now, come on, baby, it wasn't that bad, was it?"

"Staying thin wasn't that much of a problem because I didn't often have much to eat. Do you know I spent my first two years sleeping on other peoples' couches? The other women were so hateful, sabotaging me in any way they could. And the men? They only wanted one thing. I don't have to tell you about that."

"Was it all bad?"

I took a deep breath and thought for a minute. There was the famous actor who brought me a coffee because a cold rain had set in on the soundstage where I was playing dead that day. I did make some friends at beauty school and with some of the makeup artists on the last shoot where I was cutting hair. Some of the ghosts had been all right. Even Pinup Betty had been trying to look out for me in the only way she knew how. But, yes. It had mainly been hard and humiliating. "Not all bad, but mostly bad."

"But you'll try one more time? For me?"

"Why is this so damned important to you?" I shouted. I clamped my mouth shut and listened for evidence that people had come home and finally caught me talking to my "imaginary friends."

"What are you so afraid of? Do you know how many people would kill for this kind of opportunity?"

Oh, I knew, all right. I could think of at least three other actresses who would slit my throat in my sleep if they thought it would mean they could try out for the part of Lolita Ann.

"Are you afraid of this Carlos fella?"

"Yes." *No.* What else could he possibly do to me at this point? He'd seen all of me there was to see.

"You're afraid of something," LuEllen said.

I started to sit on the end of the bed, saw LuEllen's body, and took a seat in a chair instead. "I'm afraid of everything. I'm afraid of letting you down, of sex, of Delilah, of making people mad, of living in a trailer, of never finding love, of losing love, of getting this part, of not getting this part."

"Look at me." LuEllen pointed to her body, the empty wasted vessel where she used to be. "Do you see that? I'm dead. And I'm not coming back, and I'm kicking myself for all the things I didn't do because I was afraid. I was afraid of going back to school, of dating again, of what people thought of me and said behind my back, and I was afraid *for* you—afraid you would make my mistakes, afraid I wasn't feeding you enough, afraid you weren't getting the right lessons or the right clothes, afraid you were starving in California or that someone was taking advantage of you. I was afraid of so much that I forgot to live. You'd—"

"Better get to living?" I said, remembering what Miss Ginger had said to me the night of the tornado: *I would tell you life is short, but I made a pretty long go of it.*

"Yes, exactly!" LuEllen rewarded me with a grin.

I thought of Dec. I thought of the house on Maple Avenue. "What if I want a home and a husband? What if that's how I want to live?"

"That's something I always wanted," LuEllen said wistfully, "but you also don't want to be wiping butts and wondering how things could've been different if you'd only *tried* to get that part. I saw this thing on Dr. Phil once. I think you're afraid of success."

"That's ridiculous!"

"Sounds ridiculous, but it's true. You know what it's like to do the things you've done so far, but what if you get that part and what if people start expecting a lot from you? I think that's what you're really afraid of. What did I always tell you about all of the contests and pageants?"

"You know you won't win if you don't bother to enter," I replied dutifully. It was the Cline family motto, after all.

"Go. Please promise me you'll give it a try."

I took in a shaky breath. "I already did."

"Whew. Glad we got that settled because I think I just heard the hearse pull up. I'm going to disappear, and I suppose you're going to have to give a performance of being distraught. It'll be good practice."

"What?" I already felt dehydrated from all of the tears I'd shed, and I hadn't been doing so hot in the first place thanks to the hangover.

"Can't have people thinking you're talking to ghosts, now can we?"

I pointed at her in victory. "Ha! And now you know I was right the whole time."

She shrugged. "Other people still would've said you were crazy."

"Wait! You aren't going into the light, are you?"

"No, baby, I'm going to stick around at least until you come back and tell me about that audition. Unless I can somehow follow you, in which case we can be besties forever!"

Now there was a thought even more terrifying than LuEllen going into the light without saying good-bye.

The back door opened, and I went to that sad place I used when I needed tears, the one where I imagined meeting my father and his laughing at me and telling me he had never cared what happened to me. "Someone call an ambulance. I think there's something wrong with Mama!"

To my surprise, acting scared and shocked and heartbroken wasn't hard at all.

Declan

I'd been looking forward to talking with Presley that night, maybe getting some supper. I certainly didn't have ambulances, Dr. Malcolm, or laying LuEllen out on the slab in my plans.

Presley was oddly subdued about the whole thing. She was crying silent tears, but not agitated or sobbing and moaning. I wondered if she was in shock.

She answered questions from the police and Dr. Malcolm. In the end, Doc determined that LuEllen had probably died from a heart attack. Since he saw no evidence of foul play, he handed the body over to us.

"Bet this is the shortest call you've ever been on," he said in a wry voice only I could hear.

I looked at Presley's solemn face, thinking about all that we already had between us. "Shortest, but definitely not the easiest."

He clapped me on the shoulder. "It'll all work out. It always does."

No, it didn't. I liked to believe that things always worked out, but I'd seen a few too many incidents to the contrary. I nodded to Sean, and he guided Presley toward me. Since Caroline and Armando had already gone, it was up to those of us who were there. "Presley, do you want me to take care of LuEllen, or do you want me to stay with you?"

"Stay with me," she said.

"Okay. Do you want to say any good-byes?"

She shook her head yes, more tears coming to her eyes. Sean nodded at me, this time asking without words if he was to take lead. I nodded back. Caroline really had taught us to be a team, even if we had missed it at first. I would miss him when he went back to Atlanta. Hopefully, he wouldn't stay away for so long next time.

Uncle Hollis, Sean, and Alan stepped aside and let Presley have a moment with LuEllen. I closed my eyes, but I didn't have a prayer in that moment. In December in particular, we always prayed that everyone would keep on living. At least one person always failed to get the memo. This particular unanswered prayer had come at the worst time possible.

Sean leaned over to whisper in my ear: "You're still going to need to get her to fill out the paperwork basics, but Uncle Hollis or I will take care of LuEllen."

I clapped a hand on his shoulder. "Thanks, man. I don't know what I would've done without you here."

He gave me that sad smile that looked a little bit like my own. "You would've made it. Like you always do."

Presley emerged from the bedroom. She took my hand, but she was looking over her shoulders as though looking for someone or something.

"Do you want to bring your things over to my place?"

"Could I?"

Like she had to ask.

"Do you want to get them now or come back later?"

She looked over her shoulder again and then to me. "Later."

We went down to my office and filled out the bare minimum of paperwork. I never wanted to use my serious, quiet voice with Presley ever again. Never. Now that we'd come to this moment, though, I didn't know how to get back to where we had been before.

Time. Time was always the answer.

Unfortunately, time was the one thing we didn't have.

She linked her fingers in mine, and I led her across the parking lot as the sun was setting. She didn't say anything, and I didn't make her. I fixed us supper, and I put her to bed. I sat in the recliner for the longest time. Could I slip into bed beside her? Should I?

Before I could answer the question, I must've dozed off, but she cried out in her sleep so I crawled into bed and held her.

Presley

The next morning I wanted to go back to work, but Delilah wouldn't let me. I told her I needed something, anything, to occupy my mind. Once I went over to the funeral home, but there were so many people there, I couldn't have a discussion with LuEllen for fear someone other than Uncle Hollis would hear me. So I packed up my things and moved over to Dec's apartment.

Ira called to make sure I was still coming for the audition.

Two days. You have two days to figure this out.

It felt disrespectful to have LuEllen's funeral so soon, but she was the number-one person wanting me to make my audition. Not that I could tell anyone else that.

Kari came by to express her condolences and to tell me my car would be ready the next day, and I sincerely hoped so.

I looked over the script, trying to get my mind to concentrate on the lines and not wander. I still couldn't believe that the lead, Lolita Ann, had been highlighted. I'd casually mentioned to Carlos that I was interested in the smaller part of Charlie, Lolita Ann's mother. Ira had suggested I was getting a little too long in the tooth to play a nymph, and I'd agreed. In this Southern rendition of the story, Charlie was blindly devoted to Hubert and spent most of her days chain-smoking and drinking while trying to make their trailer into something more Martha Stewart. Charlie reminded me of LuEllen, so I'd felt as though I had a real handle on that part.

But Lolita Ann? She was innocent—and not. She struck me as entirely too stubborn, and I had trouble finding sympathy for her because she had given away so freely what I had spent so long trying to keep. That said, I could see why Carlos might want me to play the part. I had seduced him and then fled with what he probably thought were childish dramatics.

"What are you doing?" Dec had returned, although he was still looking at me as though he had to walk on eggshells, and I hated it. Every kiss went to my cheek or to the top of my head. Every touch was light, as though I were made of glass. Every word he said was soft, and his patience was so infinite that I wanted to throw things, to rail at him, to say mean things so he would forget about me and I wouldn't have to worry about when he inevitably brought up his plan to show me that sex wasn't so bad after all.

"I'm studying this part for the audition."

"I'm glad you've decided to go," he said as he hung up his suit coat and took off his suspenders. Then he yanked off his tie and took off the cuff links to put them in the bowl on the table by his bed. He walked just out of sight, and I knew he was changing into lounge pants and a T-shirt. As if he needed to shield me from a body I'd already seen.

I wanted him to beg me not to go, but I also wanted him to kick me out.

If I were being honest with myself, I wanted him to fall to his knees beside me and beg me not to leave him, to tell me he couldn't live without me, and to promise his undying love. And I hated myself for wanting that. Hadn't LuEllen thrown her life away pining for a man she'd somehow sent away? Everything about modern life told me I needed a man, *but* I had better not limit myself to needing a man.

You've got daddy issues.

Hell, yeah. I didn't even know who the man was. I grew up in the estrogen trailer with no one to model a loving relationship. I grew up so scared of sex that I still couldn't unclench to save my soul. I made Lolita Ann look well adjusted.

Dec came around the corner giving me the pity look I hated so much. "What are you thinking about over there?"

How screwed up I am. "Just this part, and how I should probably be pulling my weight around here."

He kissed the top of my head on the way to the kitchen. "You don't have that much weight to pull. But I did order a pizza with all of the meats but anchovies."

So damn thoughtful. Why did he have to be so damn thoughtful? Why was it so hard to go back to where we were before? "Thank you."

He came back with a beer for each of us. "Want me to read any lines for you?"

I considered it. I didn't want him to play Hubert, not even for a minute. "Maybe later."

I pretended to read while we sat in silence, still not sure what to say or how.

"Pres, I'm worried about you. I'm beginning to wonder if we need to find you a counselor or—"

I laughed out loud. In order to grieve, I had to lose LuEllen, and she was still in the funeral home waiting for me. I'd already caught her singing "Don't Go Breaking My Heart" with Uncle Hollis over breakfast. Of course, he and I were the only ones who could hear LuEllen's part. But I couldn't tell Dec that. He'd think I was off my rocker. I finally settled on "LuEllen and I weren't that close."

"The two of you were closer than you think," he insisted, as he crossed his arms over his chest.

We stared at each other, and I couldn't take it anymore. "I want things to be like they were before."

"Before we had sex?"

"Yes. No. I don't know."

"I shouldn't have given in," he said. "I should've known you weren't ready."

"I should've told you," I said. I laughed, but it had no humor. "Coulda, woulda, shoulda."

He started to say something, but a knock at the door told me the pizza had arrived. I knew I shouldn't eat it since my campaign for being unsexy *should* have been suspended until after the audition, but it tasted divine. I could only handle one piece because, like the meal from Burger Paradise, the pizza had more grease than my poor stomach could imagine. Over supper, Dec asked questions about the role, and I told him about spoiled, precocious, stubborn Lolita Ann.

"That doesn't sound like a very uplifting story," he said.

"It's not."

We watched some television and brushed our teeth and went to bed in a way I imagined old married people did. Declan rolled over. Our eyes met in the dim light of a full moon filtered through curtains. We just looked at each other for the longest time. Finally, he kissed my forehead.

"Don't."

"Don't what?"

"Quit kissing me on the forehead and the cheek and the top of my head. It feels as though you're patronizing me."

"That's not what I mean to do."

"Well, that's what it feels like. It feels like you're afraid to touch me."

"I am!"

So, like Lolita Ann, I touched him.

He grabbed my wrist. "No, not like this, not right now."

Embarrassed and angry, I rolled over to face the window, but he pulled me close into one of his manly spoons.

Declan

I almost kissed Presley's cheek before I remembered what she'd said about it being patronizing.

I kissed her lips, and her eyelids fluttered open.

"Morning, Glory. Delilah called and said for you to not even think about coming into work today," I said.

She closed her eyes again. "The funeral's at ten o'clock this morning, right?"

"Right."

"I'll be there at nine thirty," she said as she rolled over and went back to sleep.

I closed the door behind me and started walking across the parking lot.

Normally, I was a patient man.

In my line of work, there was no room for impatience. Anger only led to mistakes. Practice had taught me to tamp down the emotions, but I still wanted more than anything for this day to be over. Unfortunately, Presley would leave tomorrow which meant I had little time to try to make things right between us.

You know she won't want to have anything to do with you if she gets this part and makes it big.

Yes, I did know that. I also knew there was no way I would ever ask her to give up the opportunity. Here I was still doing the thing I'd once said I would never do. I'd already given up on the house on Maple. I'd given up hope that Sean would take my place. I could switch positions with Armando, but it was only a matter of time before Uncle Hollis would have to retire, which would put me right back on the roster. I could sell the place to Potter, but then it would become a part of an unfeeling corporation and not be the business that had served Ellery for over a hundred years.

I had also made a promise to my father.

I stopped in the kitchen to put on a pot of coffee, thinking of the day I lost my father. I was impatient—the last day I tried that emotion out—because I wanted to take Lacey to the movies for our second date. Dad was upstairs in the room where LuEllen and Presley had been, the old master bedroom. He'd caught the flu but appeared to be on the mend, especially as he explained to me that I would just have to reschedule with my girlfriend.

"Look, Declan," he said as he dug into his dessert, "I know it's Friday night, but I need you on call because I'm not a hundred percent. Hollis needs someone to ride along with him. That's all I'm asking."

"Dad, can't Unc handle one night by himself?" I wanted to take Lacey to see *The Saint*. She had a thing for Val Kilmer, and, for our first date, we'd rented *Tombstone*. I'd managed to round second base. She had to work on Saturday night, so if we didn't go then it would be a whole week before we had another chance.

"Son, I'm sending you off to college in a few months, so do you think you can do this for me? Caroline's back still isn't one hundred percent, Sean is too young, and I'm as weak as a kitten. I need you to step up." He gave me the Anderson look.

"I guess we can go to the movies next week."

"Thank you." He set his bowl down on the nightstand. "Look, I count on you to help me keep things running. I know you think you want to be an architect, but this is an important business. Potter sold out to some corporation, and he's worse now than he's ever been. Ellery needs us just as much as we need Ellery."

"I know, Dad. I know."

"Woe is my world-weary teenager! Oh, to be eighteen again," my father mocked. "Heaven forbid something happens to me or Caroline, I don't want you to sell to some big business based in Texas. If they're in Texas, I don't think they care what happens to someone all the way over here in Tennessee."

"I know, I know." I had heard this speech many times before.

He clamped down on my wrist. "You don't know, not yet. You remember your mother's funeral, don't you?"

"I was eight. I remember."

"Of course you do. Funerals are for the living. We take care of people because this isn't a job—it's a calling. You'll understand one day what it means to have someone give the people you love the proper send-off."

Little did either of us know I'd only have to wait another three days.

That Friday night I was on call, but I sneaked three streets over to Lacey's house, confident that I could be back to the funeral home on time if needed because I had my handy-dandy pager. When it went off that evening, I didn't even bother to call back first. I put on my shoes and jogged all the way back, cutting through Mrs. Morris's yard and yanking on my suit coat as I went. When I saw the ambulance in the back parking lot, my first thought was how much trouble I was going to be in because someone had hauled the body there in one of those expensive things. My next thought was that Caroline had thrown her back out again.

When I came through the back door and saw Uncle El patting ten-year-old Sean's shoulder, I knew something was very wrong. Uncle El was a bachelor, and he didn't know the first thing about kids. That's when the stretcher came past me. Dad was still alive, but he wasn't conscious. He died on the way to the hospital.

Uncle Hollis did the embalming himself, but he called on some of the guys from Young Funeral Home to help us run visitation, the funeral, and the graveside service. It was three days later when I learned funerals really are for the living. My dad wasn't the richest person in Ellery by a long shot, but he did belong to every civic organization in town and quite a few state-level organizations. Shriners, Lions, Masons, Rotary Club members, ministers, veterans, softball coaches, members of the senior citizen center, town councilmen, and the members of the Chamber of Commerce all showed up. Many had come to pay their respects to my mother not too many years before. Everyone came for my father.

Even at eighteen I was beginning to know my kind, and, whether I liked it or not, funeral directors were my kind. In addition to all of the locals, several out-of-towners showed up in their pristine black suits, looking so polished and comfortable in their formal wear that I knew they, too, were in the business. They circulated through the crowd doing imperceptible little things to make everything easier. Trash disappeared from the floor. Chairs were magically unfolded in rooms that became too crowded. Empty boxes of Kleenex were replaced. Hands clasped shoulders and an unspoken goodwill broke through the shock and sadness.

Patrick Anderson's funeral procession stretched longer than any I'd ever seen before or since.

And the flowers. For months Anderson's Funeral Home looked like a jungle habitat. Several of the peace lilies were still strategically placed throughout the funeral home. Sometimes Caroline would move them all to a room for a visitation if the flower offerings for that particular person were especially sparse.

Seeing all of that love for my father didn't bring him back. It didn't even make it that much easier that he was gone, but at least I knew he meant as much to other people as he had always meant to me.

The coffeemaker had quit gurgling, and the silence brought me back to the present. I knew I needed to start the scrambled eggs everyone would be looking for, but I couldn't get out of my chair. Fatigue? Frustration? Having to watch another person I loved suffer? Who knew what was keeping me in my chair?

Morning check. I still had to do the morning check.

Coffee was on so that meant prep room next.

When I opened the door, I heard Uncle Hollis singing "Tiny Dancer."

A call must've come in the night before, and he had an infant. The baby girl was already in the casket and everything had been cleaned up and put away, but Uncle Hollis was singing Elton John's ballad like a lullaby, his arms cradling an imaginary child as he rocked her to sleep. His song tapered off, and he opened his arms and lifted his palms, murmuring, "There you go, my sweet."

My dad had always said that if you ever completely lost your heart, you needed to get out of the business. Looking at the little one, I knew I still had the heart. As for Uncle Hollis, I was afraid his might be a little too big. "Unc?"

"Declan, my boy." He swiped at a tear as he turned around.

"What were you doing?"

He clapped a hand on my shoulder as he left the room. "Sometimes the spirit needs a little help, that's all."

Presley

It's hard to be solemn at your mother's funeral when her ghost is standing in the aisle beside you pointing out one guy's hot or that woman isn't her friend at all or she'd heard that couple over there was into the kinky stuff. I feigned a coughing fit so I could give her a dirty look.

The Andersons laid her to rest in Ellery City Cemetery. Caroline was the one to do the research and find an old burial policy, or I wouldn't have known how to begin to pay for even the simple service I chose. Caroline also took me aside and showed me all of the paperwork that had to be done when a person died, an insult to injury, if you ask me.

Not many people came to the little service. I was surprised to see Delilah, who hugged me and whispered cryptically in my ear, "You take your time, but be sure to drop by before you go. I wrote out a check for what I owe you so far."

"Thank you," I said.

"Hateful biddy," said LuEllen. It was all I could do not to turn to her and give her a dirty look.

Kari, of course, was there. The woman who used to work at the convenience store with LuEllen came as well as a few people I didn't know. All in all, it was a tiny ceremony, and the Andersons almost outnumbered actual mourners. Counting the minister, people conducting the service were definitely in the majority.

After lunch Dec dropped me off at Vandivers' Shop to pick up my car so I could drive to the airport in Memphis. I had retrieved all of LuEllen's money from the bank and only taken out what I needed to get to California. I put the rest of the cash on Roy's grubby counter. "This is all I have now, but I'll pay you the rest as soon as I can. I know it'll be a while before I even find out about this part, but Delilah says I can keep working at the Holy Roller."

"Shoot, Presley, I oughta pay you for letting me work on that old Firebird. Don't you ever sell that thing without asking me first, either."

"I won't. How much is it going to be?"

Roy quoted a number that made me want to faint dead away. Instead, I called upon my acting skills to give him a smile. Then I made sure I could set up a payment plan.

"Tell Kari bye for me," I said.

"Ain't you gonna be here for Christmas?" Roy asked as he picked up his cap and scratched his shaved head.

"I think so, but you never know how the flights will go, and last time I got in trouble for not telling her good-bye, so I'm covering all of my bases," I said. "So please make sure she knows and tell her I'd still like to babysit those kids of yours one day."

"You say that now," Roy said. "That little one is hell on wheels."

I couldn't resist. "Takes after her mother?"

"You know it! Now you be safe," he said. "I think you'll like how she drives now."

And I did. The Firebird purred.

"I've missed this old thing," said the teenage version of my mother.

When I managed to crawl down from the ceiling of the car, I looked over at LuEllen. "What are you doing here?"

"Just wanted to see what you were up to."

"I thought I told you that following me wasn't cool," I said.

We'd discovered LuEllen *could* follow me when she magically showed up in Dec's apartment the morning of her funeral where she'd made some comments about his physique that I was still trying to unhear. Then she'd followed me to the funeral. Now, apparently, she'd decided she was going to follow me everywhere. "It's creepy, and you may see some things you don't want to."

"Oh, if you and Declan start playing kissyface, I'll leave," she said.

I wished I believed her.

"Car sure runs good," she said.

"I think Roy and his brother can add 'miracle worker' to their resumes," I said.

For some reason, I couldn't find any parallel parking on Main, so I pulled around to the back of the Holy Roller. Well, well. It would be interesting to see how Private Banks and LuEllen reacted to each other. I giggled a little at the idea that they might end up having some kind of ghost love connection.

I parked away from the shop in an area with no cars around me. Roy's brother had not only fixed the roof and the windshield, but he'd also beat out every other dent and buffed and polished the old car. If I could make it at least one day without any dings, that'd be great.

I got out of the car. LuEllen followed me, chattering about how she wished she had a ghost version of her car to drive around. I could see Private Banks against the wall, but LuEllen hadn't noticed him yet.

"What's so funny, you?"

"Nothing."

"LuEllen?" Private Banks's voice cracked, and the ghost of my mother froze.

She turned slowly. "Blake?"

The two of them ran for each other, and I looked around to make sure no one else was around. When I got to the back door, Private Banks was kissing my mother, his hands clenching her ghost butt.

"What the hell, Mama?"

LuEllen turned around but she was still clutching Private Banks's hand like she thought he might go away. "Presley Ann Cline, this is your daddy, Blake Banks."

I couldn't move. I couldn't breathe.

"A baby girl. I would've sworn we were going to have a boy." He grinned, and I realized why those eyes and that smirk were so familiar: I saw them in the mirror each morning.

"But you said he went away. That he left."

"I did," he said as he stepped forward to look me over. "I joined the army when LuEllen told me she was pregnant. Figured that was a good way to make some money to take care of the two of you. I didn't count on being in a car accident on the way home from boot camp."

He turned to my mother. "Guess you were right about how I shouldn't have gone off, huh?"

"Honey, I'm always right," she said with the most beautiful, dazzling grin I'd ever seen. "But I know you were trying to do what you thought was best."

Blake Banks was my father and Delilah's brother. I was adding two and two and coming up with five. LuEllen's words made a lot more sense now: *Nope, your best bet is Delilah. You tell her that I sent you. Hateful biddy.*

"Delilah is my aunt?"

Private Banks/Blake/Dad laughed. "Yeah. Imagine that?"

I wished I were imagining.

"Oh, look at that!" LuEllen said.

I looked over my shoulder to see the light, the one that appeared when I appeased some crazy ghost.

"No! Wait! You can't go yet. I just found you."

"And we found each other, which means it's time to go," LuEllen said as she looked at my father.

"We sure made an awesome baby," he said.

"You have no idea."

"Tell me all about it on the other side?"

"You know I will," she said before turning to me. "Presley Ann, you go show the world what you can do, you hear?"

"Wait! What am I supposed to tell Delilah?"

My father laughed. "Call her *Aunt* Delilah—she deserves it."

My parents were being drawn into the light.

"Wow, it's beautiful over here," my mother said. "I love you, Presley, baby. And no matter what, I'm proud of you."

My father ripped his gaze from my mother long enough to look at me. "I'm glad I got to meet you!"

The universe zipped itself up and I was looking at the dingy backside of Ellery. Someone left through the back door of the drugstore. They probably wondered why I was staring at them.

"I'm glad I got to meet you, too, Dad." The light might be gone, but I was left with a gaping hole inside. I'd now unexpectedly lost LuEllen twice in three days. I'd finally found my father only to lose him just as suddenly.

You shouldn't be this sad. At least you helped them find each other.

True, but I was alone. Completely and utterly alone.

Well, not entirely. I still had Dec, and I'd just discovered I had another aunt.

I could hardly wait to tell her.

Declan

The baby girl's name was Sarah, and I watched her funeral service that afternoon with new eyes. I'd been a participant during LuEllen's funeral that morning, holding Presley's hand. In the afternoon service, I had only minimal duties, which meant I could watch Armando, Caroline, and Uncle Hollis at work. Even Sean pitched in because, as he said, "Why not? I'm still on the payroll."

Sometimes the spirit needs a little help, that's all.

I didn't think Unc had been talking about my spirit, but he could've been. One touch on my shoulder along with just the right words, and some of that fatigue and frustration I'd had in the kitchen had melted away. Sarah's parents were young and alone in spite of the number of people around them.

But we were there.

Caroline, staid and calm, looked away while the mother composed herself. Armando slipped the father a tissue when he started to cry. Sean somehow managed to make both of the parents smile. Uncle Hollis directed the huge crowd with an impossibly deep and quiet voice, and we got that baby to the cemetery and her parents, hopefully, to a place where they could live on, even if nothing was ever the same.

Then, gutted, all us Andersons congregated in the Freesia Room.

The fancy grandfather clock said we had ten minutes before we could close the doors and fight over who was going to be on call. I already knew it wouldn't be me, because I'd taken a hundred call shifts for each of them. Now they knew I needed to take care of Presley, so someone was going to take that shift for me.

"Caroline, before today I thought I'd lost my heart," I said.

"A day like this?" she said. "If you can't find your heart, I need to send you to law school."

"The law is safe from me," I said. "Although having a lawyer in the family wouldn't be the worst idea."

Everyone murmured their agreement, and we watched the minute hand move a little closer to the twelve.

"I thought you promised me cheer," Alan said to Sean. He'd been reading in the Freesia Room, waiting for us to return. "I distinctly remember you saying cheer."

"Oh, it's another fun, old-fashioned Anderson Family Christmas," Sean said as he slapped a hand on Alan's shoulder.

"I've seen that movie," Alan said. "I'm leaving."

"No, no. We're all in this together," I said with a grin, ready to recite Chevy Chase's impassioned speech.

Cleo came streaking through with a yowl, her hair on end.

"Electrocuting the cat is taking the *Christmas Vacation* homage too far," Caroline said.

"I do not know what's gotten into that cat," I said. "I think she needs to go live with you now."

She shrugged. "She's a grief therapy cat."

"I don't think grief therapy cats should hiss," Sean said.

Uncle Hollis started singing Elton John's "Honky Cat" and about the time he got to the part about drinking whiskey from a bottle of wine, the grandfather clock chimed the hour.

"Bourbon day?" Armando asked.

"Bourbon day," I said.

"What's bourbon day?" asked Sean.

"A day in which we consume bourbon," Caroline said as she stood. "I'll get it, but, out of my love for all of you, I declare myself on call."

"I'll be on call with you," Uncle Hollis said before he went back to humming "Honky Cat."

"*Gracias a Díos*," said Armando.

He had three girls himself, one not much older than Sarah. I couldn't imagine the toll today had taken on him.

The doorbell rang, and we all froze.

"I'll get it," I said. When I got to the door and looked through the peephole, I saw Jessica Borden.

"Is everything okay? Come on in?"

"Oh, no, I can't come in."

Thank God.

"I just wanted to drop off another little token of my appreciation. I needed to keep my hands busy today, and a little birdie told me you liked coconut cake."

"I do." And that reminded me that Mrs. Morris had never delivered on her promise, which could only mean she wasn't feeling well. I needed to check on her.

"Enjoy," Jessica said, her cheeks pink.

"Thank you," I said, marveling at how easy that had been as I watched her go. Maybe in another year or two we'd be able to have conversations that weren't awkward and full of her blushes.

Balancing the cake with one hand, I closed the door and put the dead bolt back. Poor Jessica. I wasn't about to eat this cake. One look in the mirror that morning, and I'd decided I needed to start some kind of workout if I wanted to keep up with Presley Cline. No beer, no bread, no sweets—that would get me at least five or ten pounds off. And no bourbon.

Well, after this round.

"What's that?" Uncle Hollis asked.

"Coconut cake from Jessica Borden," I said. "Seems cold. I'll go put it in the fridge."

The cat followed along at my heels, mellow again. I put the

coconut cake under the apricot salad, which was missing a hunk, and I fed the poor kitten, which purred its gratitude.

"Who's been into the Jell-O salad?" I asked as I held out my mug for some bourbon. "Anyone care if I throw it out?"

"I'm not eating that," Alan said. "I'm pretty sure it has sour cream in it."

"Lactose intolerant," Caroline and Sean said in unison. Then they giggled.

"I do not eat horses' hooves," Armando said.

"I'm not sure they still make Jell-O from horse parts," I said. "Unc?"

"I don't like pineapple," he said with a sniff.

"Okay, then. I'll toss it out," I said as I sat in one of the over-stuffed chairs. "Tomorrow."

Caroline snorted. "Sure you will. After I remind you twelve times."

I lifted my mug in salute. "Eleven more to go."

"While I have you all in here, ornament service tomorrow," Caroline said. "Company Christmas party tomorrow night."

"You make it sound so fancy," Armando said. "Company Christmas party."

"*Family* Christmas party," Caroline said. "How about that?"

"I like it."

I guess that meant I had to go shopping tomorrow morning—especially if I wanted to make sure I had a gift for Presley when she came back to pack up the rest of her things.

One by one, the others filed out. Caroline and Armando each went home. Uncle Hollis ambled back to the kitchen. Alan followed Uncle Hollis after Sean gave him a pointed look.

"So what's going on with you, big brother?"

"Things."

"You look like Eeyore."

"Thanks."

Silence stretched between us.

"Something happen with the movie star?"

"Good guess after the other night."

"Want to talk about it?"

I gave him the Anderson look.

He held up his hands in surrender. "Just thought I'd ask. You know where I am if you decide to talk or, heaven forbid, ask for help."

I almost laughed at the idea of asking Sean's advice on this particular matter, but I didn't want to insult the brotherly olive branch he offered. Might as well spill my troubles. We had bourbon. I could pretend he was a bartender.

So I told him the basics.

He whistled. "Didn't see that coming."

"Tell me about it."

"Easy fix," Sean said as he stood.

"What?" Not an easy fix, not an easy fix at all. I knew all about easy fixes, and this wasn't one.

"Google, you dumb-ass. Anything you could ever want to know is on Google."

I am *a dumb-ass.*

I stood, and he pushed me in the direction of my office. "Go, use the Google for nefarious purposes!"

"It's not nefarious. It's altruistic. Charitable, even."

"Ha, and a little self-serving," Sean said. "Oh, hey, and one more thing."

He looked up and down the hall, and, even though no one was there, he whispered something in my ear.

Presley

After hours meant the Holy Roller was empty.

I swallowed the lump in my throat and forced myself to walk closer to Delilah, who leaned against the front window watching the cars go by on Main Street.

"Good evening, Aunt Delilah."

She wheeled around to face me, her eyes wide. "How did you find out?" Her eyes narrowed to a murderous glint. "It was LuEllen, wasn't it?"

I hadn't thought this through. It wasn't like I could say, *Hey, I commune with the dead—I figured it out when your brother grabbed my mother's ass.*

I squared my shoulders. "LuEllen kept her promise, but I pieced it together. I guess it explains why you used to hate me. At least, I hope you don't hate me anymore."

"I don't hate you," she said, but the words sounded like they came out painfully.

"Thank you for everything you've done for me."

She looked up. "You're going to thank me?"

"Well, you gave me this job, and I know you bought some of those clothes new even though you tried to hide them underneath the others. And I hope I can still come back to work if I come back."

"Yes. Of course."

"So, thank you."

Delilah trudged across the shop, looking older than her years. I didn't understand how my father could be her sibling because she looked so much older than he had. Of course, LuEllen had reverted to a teenager in her ghostly form, and my father had never had the chance to age.

My aunt took a seat in her chair and gestured for me to have a seat in the dryer chair across from her. "Your father was my little brother, Blake. I was the oldest kid of the bunch, and he was a surprise. Mama had me practically raise him, and I spoiled him rotten."

I opened my mouth to defend the father I'd never known, but she held up a hand.

"By the time he got to high school, our parents were too worn-out to make him behave, and he sure as heck didn't want to listen to me. He took up with LuEllen, and I made a mistake."

She paused, looking up at the sky. Then my scary aunt started to cry. "I caught him kissing her, feeling her up, really. I told him to stay away from her. I *forbid* him from seeing her. I told him I would tell our parents what I caught him doing if he didn't straighten up."

Now she looked down at her hands and sighed. "Which made him want to see her all the more."

I wanted to speak, but I didn't have anything to add to this story. The only thing I could do was sit on the edge of my seat, hoping to hear the part I needed to hear: why I'd never been allowed to meet this Aunt Delilah, why I'd been denied an entire side of my family.

"One day Blake announced he was joining the army. I chewed him up one side and down the other. If I'd known he was trying to be a man about it all, I would've offered to help him so he could go to college. But he didn't trust me because I had been trying to make him do what I wanted him to do."

Silence stretched between us. The hum of the fluorescent lights was enough to drive me out of my mind.

"He died in a car accident on the way back from boot camp, and it was easier to blame LuEllen than myself. That's why I told her I'd give her money if she would never tell you who your daddy was. I never thought about how much you might look like him. You're his spitting image. Looking at you reminded me of him and how I'd made him go to extremes, and I hated you for it.

"But then you told me about him." She gulped for air. "I thought LuEllen had decided to go back on her word and was putting you up to it, but then you started singing the Elvis song he used to sing to me and I knew something was up. Those aren't even the real words to that song. So I hired you in spite of myself. And I was wrong, so wrong about everything."

She buried her face in her hands and cried.

Delilah, known throughout town for having no mercy, cried.

I sat, stunned for a few minutes. Finally, I walked over and stood behind her chair and leaned over to wrap my arms around her shoulders. She might have spent most of my life hating me, but, when all was said and done, she was about the only family I had left. "I'm glad I have an aunt."

She clamped down on my arms to pull me closer, and we cried together.

I didn't feel like driving after leaving the Holy Roller so I went next door on the off chance Kari might still be there. Fortunately, she was.

"Hey, lock that, will you? I was just getting ready to leave," she said as she grabbed her purse. "We can go out the back door."

We reached the little break room at the very back of the building, and she took a seat at a wobbly table with mismatched chairs. "I have ten minutes before I have to pick up the girls, so how are you holding up?"

I thought of LuEllen and Blake—my mom and my dad—fading into the light together. "Much better."

Kari cocked her head to one side. "That smile actually looked genuine."

So I hadn't fooled her the other day. *That's me, Presley Cline, world's worst actress.*

"I found out who my dad is today."

Kari's eyes widened. Back in the day, we'd speculated on the topic a few times, usually when she was two or three wine coolers in and I was still nursing the first one to make sure I never actually got drunk.

"Don't leave me hanging! Who?"

"Delilah's little brother." The words still felt foreign. "She's my aunt."

"That old biddy's your aunt?" Kari clamped a hand over her mouth. "I'm sorry. That just slipped out."

I laughed. "No, she really is an old biddy." *My mom even said so.*

"How did you find out?"

Way to go, Presley. Now what could I say? "Um, Delilah told me." *Kinda.*

"Wow. That's just, wow."

We sat in silence for a minute, but Kari couldn't hold it in any longer. "So. You and Declan?"

"I don't think it's going to work," I said. Last night he'd stopped short of sex yet again. Not that I blamed him.

"And just why the hell not?"

"You know, he's older—" *And more experienced; probably prefers women who perform like porn stars.*

"What, eight years? That's not that much older."

"He's serious." *About me.*

"That's funny." She said with a snort. "Girl, don't throw Declan Anderson away. If there's another man on the planet I would trust as much as my Roy, it would be him. Be good to him."

"Hey! How do you know you don't need to be telling him to be good to me?"

Kari's smile faded. "I know you both. You like to hold your cards close to your vest, and there's something you're not telling me. Maybe you've never really had a relationship with a guy—they're not all wine and roses. Maybe you're looking to make something perfect that can't be—I've seen you do that a few times, too. Either way, make it right."

"Easier said than done," I muttered.

"Easy things," she said as she put on her coat, "aren't worth having."

Declan

I watched Presley packing, my stomach somewhere around my toes. Time to shove her out of the nest, so to speak. What did I have to offer her here? A dingy apartment over a garage and behind a funeral home?

Part of me wanted to beg her not to go. I told that part of me to shut up because I wasn't about to be the reason anyone gave up a dream. I'd wanted to be an architect, but I left UT early and went to mortuary school instead. Then I had wanted to be a contractor. That simply wasn't in the cards, either. Thanks to the things I'd seen today, I was beginning to understand I was exactly where I needed to be, but that didn't mean Presley had to be stuck with me.

"I think I miss you already."

She smiled. "For the third time, this is just an audition. It doesn't mean I get the part."

You'll get the part. They would be a fool to give it to anyone else.

We went through the ritual of getting ready for bed, even sharing the sink as we brushed our teeth. She smiled at me in the mirror, and I smiled back. We still weren't to the place where we'd been before. Tonight I dreaded she might ask me again, but I was also hoping she would. I was prepared this time.

"Declan?"

"Mm-hmm?"

"I can't sleep."

Did I dare? I shouldn't. I should wait until she came back, if she came back. The "if" was making me weak. I didn't want her to go out to California with *that* as her last memory of me.

"I don't think I can do this tomorrow," she said.

Oh, that.

"Of course you can," I said.

"No, I mean I don't think I can face him unless . . ."

I rolled over to study her. "Unless you knew a different man might've changed the outcome?"

"Yes, exactly."

In a perfect world, I would have planned on candlelight, steaks, and wine. In my mind, I'd already put together a playlist of music. Then she kissed me, and I knew I had everything I needed as long as I never lost sight of how everything I needed was her.

"Do you still trust me?" I asked.

She nodded yes, and something inside me cracked. How could I have thought "trust" was boring? Trust was right up there with love, perhaps even more precious.

So I showed her.

Patient didn't begin to describe me, and in my line of work I have to have an eye for detail. Google had given me over seventy-five million results for "how to make love to a virgin," and I read at least fifty of them. If there was a technique, I tried it, and when the time was right, I put her on top.

Presley

Oh.

At first I thought Dec had lost his mind when he pulled me on top, but no. By God, for the first time in my life, I was in control. I was calling the shots. I could stop or go. Sensation built— something new but also different—and I chased it. My body took over, my mind now only aware of . . . the sublime. The orgasm caught me by surprise, washing over me in a combination of confidence and relief.

I giggled as I collapsed over Dec.

"Well, that wasn't quite the reaction I was looking for," he said as he stroked my back. He kissed my hair, and I didn't mind so much. To be honest, I didn't mind much of anything at all.

"What if I told you I was more likely to repeat the experience?" *And, in fact, I may insist.*

"Giggle away, then." He gently moved me aside to take care of the grittier aspect of sex, yet another part the books and the shows and the movies don't bother to tell you. He returned quickly, though, and wrapped his arms around me. "See? You *can* teach an old dog new tricks."

"All sorts of tricks, wonderful tricks." If I'd learned where all of the portrayals of sex had gone wrong, I'd also learned all of the places where they were right.

"I may have more tricks."

"More?"

"Yes, more. If you ever come back, I'll demonstrate each and every one of them."

"Come back? At the moment I'm not sure I want to leave."

"But you have to go," he said as he lazily traced the jagged scar on my thigh. He didn't have a problem with it, unlike all of the photographers who complained about having to airbrush it out of photos.

"You know, I could stay here." My heart pounded as I said it. Maybe it was just the sex talking, but I didn't think so.

He rose up on one arm, his expression now serious. "I can't let you do that."

"What do you mean you can't 'let me'?"

"Fine. I can't make you do anything, and I wouldn't want to. But if you stay, you'd always wonder what if, and I won't be the reason the world is deprived of Presley Cline. Besides, we said no strings. Remember?"

"But what if you marry another girl while I'm gone and I miss out on all of your tricks?" I teased.

He closed his eyes. "Being Mrs. Anderson isn't all it's cracked up to be, so no strings for me."

No strings. My gut hollowed out. Had I really been so confident that he would be the one who wouldn't want to let *me* go? "But what about what you want?"

He laughed and rolled over on his back. "As the great philosopher Mick Jagger once said, you can't always get what you want."

"But what if you did?"

He paused. For a split second my heart hammered against my chest because I thought for sure he was about to say that he wanted me, but he took his time and measured his words carefully. "If I could have the things I wanted, I would have a house like the one on Maple Avenue. I would figure out a way to work here without it consuming me, and someday, by God, I would visit Tahiti and stay in one of those little huts they build over the ocean."

I forced a smile to my face. He hadn't put me in those plans. I guessed I should console myself with the fact he hadn't excluded me, either.

It was my turn to kiss Dec's forehead on my way out the door. I let my lips linger in good-bye even though I had to leave at an obscenely early hour to make my early flight since the closest airport was two hours away in Memphis. I drove through town past farms and swamps and through other little towns. In the past, my heart had grown lighter with each mile between me and Ellery. Not so that morning.

I had to ask myself if I really didn't want the part or if I was afraid of running into Carlos. Was I really sick of acting or did I see staying with Dec as the easy way out? Here I was already arguing the merits of acting versus marriage, and it was quite possible that Dec had simply checked something off his bucket list: have sex with actress.

No. That's not right. That's the LuEllen side of you talking.

And maybe that wasn't fair to LuEllen. Sure she'd been the most vociferous, but hadn't the overall message to all of us girls been that we had to control ourselves around the boys? Weren't we taught that boys are selfish and can't be expected to stop themselves, so we girls would have to do the stopping for them? Weren't we taught that if we gave into our desires that we'd make stupid decisions, so we would just have to be smart enough for both us and the boys? And then there was the position I found myself in now: to give in to love would mean giving up my vocation.

On the one hand, I admired Declan for wanting me to go. On the other, I wanted him to at least acknowledge that I'd been willing to stay behind for him. The whole thing was confusing. He and LuEllen had one thing right, though: If I didn't at least try, then I would never know.

And all of this worry when I certainly didn't know I had the part. This could end up being a really expensive trip for nothing.

Declan

I didn't get up when Presley left, but I should have.

Instead, I lay there kicking myself for not telling the truth when she asked me what I wanted most. I wanted to share the house on Maple Avenue with her, to kiss her when I got home and have her tell me it would all be okay if I had a particularly rough funeral. I wanted her to go to Tahiti with me and to wear a patriotic bikini like the one she'd worn in that magazine. I wanted to make love to her in one of those huts over the ocean while the water lapped gently below us. I'd told her that Ol' Mick said you couldn't always get what you wanted. He'd also said that if you tried hard enough, you sometimes got what you needed. With Presley the line between "*want*" and "*need*" was a tad blurry.

When the first pink rays of sunlight seeped through the window, I forced myself to get up and prepare for the day to come. Through the morning ritual I went: coffee, cat, prep room, locks. The kitten insisted that she be fed before I went on my tour of the place. That morning, the gray sky looked about as cheery as I felt. The prep room was blessedly empty, and I said my December prayer that it might remain that way.

Sean and Alan came downstairs, and we fixed breakfast together.

"Where's Uncle Hollis?" I asked.

"No clue," Sean said.

Just then the furnace cut out. "Again?" I added a few other words I wouldn't be able to say once the doors opened for the day. So far, I'd had to change the filter, replace the lighting element twice, and relight the damned pilot light so many times I'd lost count.

"This furnace isn't long for the world," I said as I put on my coat to go outside. "I've about had it."

"Want me to help?" Sean asked. He was still wearing his pajama pants and had no shoes.

"No. I've got this. Why don't you see where Uncle Hollis is?"

Out the door and around the house I went to open up the side doors that led down to the cellar and the bane of my existence. "Come on, you old piece of shit. I finally decide I like this place and you want to make it hard on me to keep it?"

The furnace cut on, and I took a step back. I hadn't touched it. I gave it a gentle pat. "Sorry I called you a piece of shit, I guess."

Confused, I shut up the cellar and went back around the house. When I came back in, Sean stood at the door, his face white. From somewhere down the street I could hear sirens.

Caroline came in behind me, pushing me out of the way. "What's going on here?"

"It's Uncle Hollis."

I heard Sean tell me that he'd gone to wake up Unc only to find him nonresponsive, but I felt a million miles away. Paramedics rushed through the funeral home, and I grabbed Cleo and held her to my chest to keep her from running out the door.

I closed my eyes and whispered a prayer. *Please, God, don't take Uncle Hollis, too.*

Presley

After a restless night's sleep in my curiously empty apartment, I walked into my old friend, the casting studio. The routine felt like home: turning in the head shot, filling out the information, and taking my number.

Times like this I wish I read, but I wasn't much for sitting still. One of the things I'd always enjoyed about cutting hair was the movement and the people. Waiting was hard.

"You look like your dog died."

If I had never heard that brash New York accent again, I would've been quite all right. I moved to a corner alone and opened my script so I could pretend I was reading my lines. "Betty. And to think I thought you'd finally gone into the light. What are you doing here?"

She was just as I knew she would be, chestnut hair in Victory rolls wearing a polka-dot dress with a sweetheart neckline and the reddest lipstick imaginable.

"I got bored at your place and thought I'd see if they had ghost casting today for once. The neighbors had a ménage last week. Bet you hate you missed that."

"Not really."

"Oh, that's right, Miss Virginal here. Next time you let me talk you into sexing someone, you might want to give me a head's up on that one, hey, doll?"

I looked up sharply. "How'd you find out?"

"Your producer friend walked past a few minutes ago and mentioned it to the woman walking beside him. She giggled."

My face burned hot. Surely he wouldn't have called me all the way out to California just to make fun of me. Surely.

"Would that have really changed your advice?"

"Of course! If I'd known I was hanging out with the Last Virgin of Hollywood, I would've sent you to someone who could do it right. Shame ol' Mick Rooney's passed away." She took a moment to look heavenward but then focused her eyes on me. "Or maybe seen if we could sell you to the zoo as the endangered species you are."

"You're always so nice to me, Betty. Yeah, that's what I've missed. I'll have you know I don't qualify for that zoo exhibit anymore."

"Come on, honey. That thing with Carlos hardly counts."

"I'm not talking about Carlos." Why was I telling her this? This is how I got into trouble with Betty before. We shared an apartment and a profession, often talking together at home and in the older studios where she'd once worked. How sad that I would've rather talked to a ghost than have nothing to do.

"Well, well, who's the lucky guy?"

"You wouldn't know him. He's back in Tennessee."

"So that's where you went! Where in Tennessee?"

"Ellery."

"That close to Memphis? I knew a guy from Memphis."

I looked over at Pinup Betty. She'd always wanted to be an actress, but the best she'd done were a series of pinups to boost military morale during World War II. She wasn't even a Betty. Her real name was Liesel Applebaum. "Betty, what's your story? Aren't you tired of hanging out here?"

"Doll, I ain't going nowhere."

That almost sounded like a challenge. I opened my mouth to ask her more, but they called my number.

"Break a leg," Betty said.

I smiled my thanks, and just a few minutes later I had a slate and was waiting to enter a room that had Carlos on the other side of the door. They called me in and there he stood with a man and a woman, one of whom was probably the director. I forced myself to make eye contact with him, but he didn't acknowledge me. I knew he wouldn't.

They wanted me to address the camera, no surprise there. I said and spelled my name and gave my phone number and then nodded to the stand-in on the side to let him know I was ready. I schooled my face for "confused nymphet." In real life, I was the opposite of this role: older but more naïve. I was the anti–Lolita Ann.

The stand-in started with the audition scene, one actually at the end of the movie where Lolita Ann is pregnant with another man's child. "It's only twenty-five steps to my truck. Just twenty-five. Come with me, Lolita Ann. Right now."

I shivered a little, feeling what Lolita Ann might've felt. "You mean you'll only give us the money if I go with you to that motel and spend the night?" She considered leaving with the man who'd once schemed to steal her innocence, weighing the pros and cons. Even as I read the lines, I wanted to shout no, but I had to consider just as Lolita Ann would.

"No, no, darlin', I mean we'll tear out of here. You'll come live with me and die with me and everything in-between."

It wasn't a stretch to say, "You're crazy."

"C'mon, Lolita Ann. Just like before. But better."

In my mind I was back in the funeral home kitchen and Declan was saying, *All right. Water, aspirin, and sleep. Do you want to go upstairs or do you want to come with me just like before?*

Hangover or not, I liked that before more than this before.

"Would you like to do another take?"

The question jarred me back to reality, and I did another take. Neither Carlos nor the other man or woman said a word. I knew better than to expect them to betray any sort of emotion, but the effect was still unnerving, especially considering I knew Carlos had seen me as naked as the day I'd been born.

"There's something I would like for you to do cold," the woman said. She directed the man who'd been reading my lines to bring in a chaise lounge in front of the camera. "The scene in the motel."

My heart was beating double time. Of all the scenes, the one in the motel was the one most like what had happened with Carlos. Maybe this was his revenge? His way of getting back at me? Or maybe they really wanted to see what I'd do with the scene.

The stand-in had the chaise, and I looked him over.

"He is sleeping, and you sneak up on him and seduce him."

I crept up on the stand-in and delivered Lolita Ann's line: "I know what you want. Want me to show you?"

The script called for me to straddle Hubert. I hesitated, which was completely wrong for Lolita Ann. Aside from the technical difficulties of trying to straddle someone on a chaise lounge, I didn't want to straddle the nice young man who'd been reading lines, and he didn't look as though he wanted to be straddled.

But I did. I looked into his eyes and tried to convince myself he was Declan and that he had just introduced me to this very position. I kissed the actor underneath me. "I was a daisy-fresh girl and look what you've done to me."

I delivered the line as coy, almost a tease.

"And thank you."

Once again, I forced myself to make eye contact with Carlos and then the others in nothing more than acknowledgment.

"We'll let you know in about a week," the woman said. She was already looking down at her tablet.

Of all the times I'd ever auditioned, this was the first time I'd had the urge to hold my middle finger high on my way out the door. When I first read the script, I couldn't shake the image of Carlos in the part of Hugh Hubert. After the audition, I knew I'd been wrong. He wasn't Hubert; Hollywood was. Hollywood and the idea of fame had seduced me, seduced my mother, seduced countless others. All of the focus on beauty and fame led to baby pageants and skimpy clothes for girls and children becoming worldly before their time. Hubert saw Lolita Ann as a girl placed on earth to gratify his needs, then he blamed her for tempting him. That's how people like Carlos saw me: an object to satisfy their lust, but then it was my fault if I got caught and damaged my own image.

"How'd it go, honey?"

Pinup Betty followed me out the door. I waited until I was in the rental car to tell her everything.

"Wow. They're serious," she said.

I didn't want to think about my audition. "Speaking of serious, what are you looking for, Betty? Why stick around here?"

She said nothing as we drove back to the apartment we shared. I let her stew until we reached the Ten. "Come on, you know all about my sex life. The least you can do is let me help you cross over."

She laughed, but the sound was rough instead of the tough she usually went for. "You'd miss me when I was gone. Besides, you can't make the light. I've seen you try."

I couldn't help but smile. "Maybe I've learned a trick or two while I was away. Tell me what I need to do to find you some peace. We'll consider it an early Christmas present."

We rode in silence until I reached our apartment. Her overconfident smile faded as we climbed the stairs to the second floor and walked through the door. "Please don't send me. I can't go."

I'd never seen this Betty before. "And why not?"

She began to weep. I had the urge to wrap an arm around her shoulders, but, of course, I couldn't. "I did something I regret, and I don't want him to ever know."

"What are you talking about?"

"Ralph. We were going to get married just as soon as he got back from the war only he didn't come back."

"That's an easy fix! I bet he's waiting for you on the other side." I could already feel the light blooming behind me as I envisioned being able to give Betty a happily ever after.

"No! No! Stop! I was supposed to have his baby, and I—I—

chose not to have it so I could keep working as a model and actress. I had to eat, and I foolishly thought we could make another baby, but we never had another chance."

The light had bloomed to a full portal behind me. I could feel its pull, and I knew Betty could feel it, too, but she kept her eyes on the floor, refusing to look. I looked over my shoulder for her. There at the edge stood a handsome man in World War II pilot's gear. "Betty. I think that's Ralph," I said softly.

"I can't face him. I deserve to be stuck here."

"Betty, he's motioning for you to come on."

She shook her head no, and I ached inside at having made the tough Brooklyn girl cry. "I think he already knows, and he's been looking for you anyway."

"No, no, no!"

The sounds of Glenn Miller's "Little Brown Jug" wafted through the portal, and all of the hair on my neck stood on end. Betty looked up. The pilot—it had to be her Ralph—held out a hand as though asking her to dance. Slowly, she walked toward the light. Then she stopped and took a few steps backward. "It's a trick, a mirage. I'll go straight to hell."

"I don't think it works like that," I murmured.

"Liesel Applebaum, get your cute little booty over here so I can give you that dance I owe you!" he said in a familiar accent that warmed my heart. Of course. She once knew a man from Memphis.

Betty looked at me, torn between the man she loved and the fear that she'd hurt him.

"Go on," I urged.

She ran into her Ralph's arms, and the portal exploded with light and love and laughter. Before it snapped shut, Pinup Betty—Liesel Applebaum—turned to me and shouted, "You better hang on to your Tennessee boy!"

Ah, but my Tennessee boy didn't want to hang on to me.

Declan

It took twenty-four hours, one year shaved from my life, and two IV bags' worth of fluids, but Uncle Hollis was expected to make a complete recovery. The ER doctor on call and I commiserated about the number of stomach maladies going around that winter.

"Flu season has hardly begun," he said. "And to have whatever stomach virus is going around on top of everything?"

I nodded knowingly.

He clapped a hand on my shoulder. "No offense, but I'm hoping not to see you again anytime soon."

I smiled. "Sometimes I don't even want to see myself coming."

"You Andersons are all right," he chuckled before going off on his rounds.

Steeling myself, I stepped into the tiny hospital room. "How're you feeling, Unc?"

He lay back against the hospital bed, looking every bit of his age and then a few years more. "Like shit on a stick. Without the stick."

Okay then. Unc's cussing meant it was bad, but he did have his color back. "Well, you look better."

He sighed, and I knew he wouldn't be singing any songs today. "I think I'm a notch or two above dead. How's that?"

"I'll take it," I said as I took a seat.

"What are you doing?"

"Sitting here with you."

"Who's holding down the fort?"

"Armando and Caroline."

"Where's my pretty actress?"

I looked out the window. "Back in California where she be-longs."

Uncle Hollis snorted. "Nah. I think she belongs back here. She improved the decor considerably."

Among other things.

"You don't have to sit here and babysit me," he said irritably.

"Nope. Sure don't." Leaning back, I picked up a celebrity rag that Caroline had left behind. In a small picture up top they had reprinted the photo with Presley's butt hanging out. As shapely as her rear was, I still wanted to punch the paparazzo who'd em-barrassed her.

Yeah, and if those pictures hadn't come out, she would've never come to Ellery.

On second thought, maybe I should send a thank-you note.

"Declan, would you leave this old man in peace? Make your-self useful and go do some Christmas shopping for me."

I didn't look up from the magazine. "I think I'd rather sit here with you than brave the mall so close to Christmas."

"Please?"

I could understand when a man wanted to be alone. "Fine. Caroline will be here in a couple of hours. You tell me what you want, and I'll go get it for you—but absolutely no dying on me."

"Wouldn't dream of it," the old man said, even though his eyes were already closed. He did, however, tell me what he wanted me to buy, and I went off to the mall, gritting my teeth and hoping for the best.

We'd had to cancel the ornament ceremony, although I did happen to be there when Mrs. Morris stopped by. Then we post-poned the family party until Christmas Eve afternoon so Uncle

Hollis could join us. He'd improved quite a bit but was still eating only broth and Jell-O.

"See? Cheerful," Sean was saying to Alan.

"This is much better," Alan said as he squeezed Sean's hand. My brother's smile went all the way up to his eyes, and I realized how long it had been since I'd seen him that happy.

Usually, we piped hymns through the speakers, but I'd set up a mix of classic Christmas carols so we were enjoying Bing and Ella and Nat and the Rat Pack. We'd finished off the old bourbon, but Sean had given me an even larger bottle. Being the kind soul I was, I was sharing.

For Armando, I'd dusted off my architecture skills and sketched the funeral home—only I'd changed the sign to read "Anderson-Cepeda." We still had to get the permit and sort out the insurance money for the chapel. Then we'd need to get a loan from the bank, but the sketch was a sign of good faith.

I got Caroline a new e-reader. Woman was always reading something. Sean and I exchanged the same St. Louis Cardinals cap but different gift cards. I didn't know what to get Alan since I'd only known him for a few days, so I got him a gift card and a T-shirt that said I'M WITH STUPID. For Uncle Hollis I got some CDs. He refused to embrace MP3 players, and we all needed some variety in his repertoire.

"Well, we all chipped in and got you a little something," Caroline said. I had noticed not many gifts had come my way, but I hadn't thought much of it. Last year's haul had included cashews and argyle socks, so I hadn't expected much this year.

She passed me a little box. I was expecting my customary can of cashews, but inside was a key ring with a couple of shiny new keys. "What's this?"

"Your uncle El was at the auction last Saturday," Caroline said. "Your house on Maple Avenue went for a song. We all chipped in to get the five thousand he needed for intent to buy. It's yours, if you want it."

New keys for an old house. My vision blurred. "I don't know what to say."

"Well, even your uncle El was pleased with the price."

That was impressive. Uncle El thought everyone was out to swindle him.

I swiped away a tear, a manly tear, dammit. I thought of how Presley and I had talked that night about living for other people. They'd been paying attention all along. The house wouldn't be the same without her, but it was a nice consolation prize since fixing it up would give me plenty to occupy my time.

Caroline's voice got gruff at the sight of my misty eyes. "I sign your paycheck, and I think you can swing it if you want it. If you don't, Uncle El's going to flip it."

"I . . . Thank you."

"You gave up your money to make this place better," Armando said. "You invested in us. Now we invest in you."

I turned the keys over in my hand, and the teeth bit me in their newness. Like a kid with a new toy, I wanted to check out my ramshackle dream house. "I don't know what to say, other than thank you."

"You are welcome," Caroline said. "I'm glad you're going to stick with us."

I grinned up at her. "I do make this suit look good."

"So, you are staying?" Uncle Hollis asked even though he was looking at the door.

"Yeah. I've fought it long enough. This is where I belong, although it's going to be harder without my people person."

"Nah, you don't need me," Sean said. Was that a hint of a blush I saw?

"I might not *need* you, but it would be a helluva lot more fun with you around."

The light in the hall flickered and then exploded.

"Something similar happened the other day," I said.

"Did it, now," Uncle Hollis said.

"Might need to double-check the wiring," Caroline said. "We can't have that kind of thing happening when we have patrons."

"Cat's acting crazy and lightbulbs exploding? Sounds like you've got a ghost," Alan said matter-of-factly.

"Nonsense," said Caroline.

"Of course there are ghosts," said Armando. He stood and put on his jacket. "But it is past time for me to be home, so you can hunt for them yourselves."

"I'd say the person is mad, too," Alan added.

"What do you think, Hollis?" I asked.

Uncle Hollis stared hard at the hallway as though mad at someone standing there. "If it is a ghost, I think he has worn out his welcome."

Just the sort of response that would normally make me think Uncle Hollis was crazy, but his eyes were stone-cold sober.

Presley

My apartment felt empty without Betty.

The past few years I'd seen her as nothing more than an annoyance, but I couldn't get the image of her crying out of my mind. Never in a million years would I have guessed she was sticking around to punish herself. She'd always seemed so confident, arrogant even.

It had all been a façade.

I'd been packing up my things since the audition and telling myself not to check for a last-minute Christmas Eve flight. I'd been dithering the whole time about whether to stay or go, then reminding myself I didn't have the part yet anyway. Besides, Dec had said "no strings." Did he really mean that? Was I confusing sex with love because I hadn't experienced a lot of either?

My cell rang, and I fished it out of my pocket, hoping it was him. My heart sank at the sight of Ira's name instead of Dec's.

"Hey, Ira. What's up?"

"Well, kid. You're going to be Lolita Ann. That's what's up."

I couldn't find the words. My whole life I'd been waiting for this moment. I should scream. I should cry. I should do . . . something.

"Kid?"

"I'm here, Ira. I'm overwhelmed. I think I need to sit down."

"Yeah, you do." Then he told me a number that represented more money than I'd made the last three years put together.

"Thank you," I said, my eyes misting. I wanted the part, but I didn't want the part. The thought of playing Lolita Ann made me queasy.

No. You'll take the damn part and get paid enough that you never have to take another part again. I'd keep my promise to my mother. Then I'd make another promise to myself that I wouldn't do another thing I didn't want to do.

It didn't hurt that all of those zeroes would help me pay Roy for the rest of the car repairs and Dec for my mother's medicine.

"When does filming start, Ira?"

"March, I believe. In Atlanta. Want me to see if I can get you some gigs on that vampire show or that zombie show they're filming there?"

I couldn't help but grin. Atlanta wasn't that far away from a certain tricksy man I knew. "Ira, that would be perfect."

"Welcome. I always knew you had it in you. Somewhere."

Well, it wouldn't be Ira without a backhanded compliment. I murmured my thanks and wished him happy holidays.

Then I pulled out my phone to check for any available flights to Memphis. Nothing left that day, but there was one seat left on a Christmas Day red-eye flight. The amount of extra money I'd need to pay to switch my flight was more than the flight originally cost. Despite the dizzy nausea of spending so much money, I pulled the trigger. After all, I had a check with a lot of zeroes headed my way.

Declan

It might be Christmas Eve, but I was having a hard time getting into the spirit. After the party broke up I'd decided to go through the mail. Our Certificate of Occupancy had been denied. Again.

That's when a blind fury carried me to Potter's Funeral Home and then to The Fountain after his secretary informed me he wasn't in but that he might've stopped by there on his way home.

Funny, how The Fountain wasn't anywhere near his swanky in-town home.

When I walked into the cinder-block bar, conversation stopped. I immediately spotted Potter, sitting along the wall with my good buddy Inspector Davenport.

"Well, I hope the two of you are having a wonderful Christmas," I said. "Is this where you usually meet to discuss new ways to destroy my business?"

"Now, Declan," Potter began in his greasy tone. "Let's not jump to conclusions."

"How much is he paying you, Davenport? Any hope I could outbid him?"

The inspector had the decency to look sheepish, but he didn't admit anything. "Maybe I'd better get home to the family. Thanks for the beer, Arwin."

"Least I could do," the older man said before turning his

hawk's gaze on me. "What are you going to do, boy? You've never had the stomach for this business."

My fists curled by my side.

I will not hit an old man, even if it's Potter.

"No, up until a couple of days ago, I didn't have the heart, but now I do. What is it going to take to get you to live and let live?"

He laughed bitterly. "That's a funny thing to ask, considering we both cater to the dead."

"No, we respect the dead but work our hardest for the living," I said quietly. "And that's why we Andersons are better at what we do than you are."

He stared at me agape. The Andersons and the Potters had always had an unspoken rule: Do not denigrate each other publicly. Never say what you are actually thinking.

Some rules are meant to be broken. "What is it you want from us?"

"I want my daughter back," he said before closing his mouth tightly in a failed attempt to keep the truth from me. My bold question had elicited an honest answer, a sad answer.

"Well," I said, my anger dissipating like air from a tire with a slow leak. "You have a funny way of showing it."

"If I were to buy you out," he said, "then she'd have to come work for me again, wouldn't she?"

I shook my head. "I don't think so, Potter. In fact, I bet she would quit on the spot. Maybe you ought to look into apologies. Or maybe flowers—she really likes those."

He nodded and pushed away from the bar, tossing a crinkled ten on the ledge.

"I'll go now," he said grudgingly. "I'll talk to Davenport about the inspection."

"You do that," I said. Even though I wasn't as angry as I had been, my heart raced. Adrenaline surged even though I didn't need it anymore.

"Ho there, Declan. Want a beer before I close up?" Bill had leaned back and held on to his suspenders.

"No, thanks, Bill," I said. "I'd better get on home. Tell Marsha I said hi."

"Will do," he said with a nod.

I walked out of The Fountain and looked at the old hearse in the parking lot. That was going to start some rumors. Colorful Christmas lights from inside The Fountain blinked around me, and the noise inside had once again reached a dull roar. For a minute I wanted to join them, but then I remembered how they'd all stopped what they were doing when I walked through the door.

Instead, I walked around to the driver's side of the hearse, giving her a pat on the hood before I climbed in and drove myself home.

When the doorbell rang the next morning, my first thought was of Presley. I tamped down any excitement, though. Calls on Christmas Day were never a good thing. Imagine my surprise when I saw June Cleaver's greatest admirer, Jessica Borden, complete with a cake plate.

"It's so kind of you to bring another cake, but we haven't finished the first one."

"May I come in?"

"Of course. How can I help you?" I shut the door to keep out the cold and turned around to the barrel of a gun.

"I came by to say Merry Christmas," Jessica said. "And goodbye."

"Let's not be hasty," I said, my hands automatically going up in surrender.

She paced the foyer as if she hadn't heard me. "All I've ever wanted is for you to love me. That's all."

I didn't like the way this conversation was going. I put my hands down and backed toward the umbrella rack, my fingers closing around the Colonel's old walking stick. "I thought we were getting to a place where we could be friends."

She snorted. "I never wanted to be friends."

"Okay. Maybe we can be more than friends." Or prison pen pals.

Her blue eyes widened, then narrowed. "You're just saying that. I don't believe you."

She cocked the pistol, an old one by the looks of it, and aimed it at my heart, but her hand shook. "Why couldn't you just eat the Jell-O? Or the cake?"

"Maintaining my girlish figure?" What in the blue hell did cake or Jell-O have to do with any of this?

Oh, dear God, no. How the Jell-O salad showed up after Jessica heard LuEllen berate Presley for sleeping with me. The hunk of Jell-O salad that went missing before LuEllen's death. The piece of coconut cake that Uncle Hollis ate. Bart's sores that Uncle Hollis dismissed as eczema.

"You poisoned them."

Her eyes flashed with anger and she straightened her aim.

"I thought I had a chance with you again, but then I saw your blond slut at the corner gas station. This has gone far enough."

Presley? Back in town?

I stood taller and straightened my cuffs, an almost Pavlovian response to a stressful situation. "I don't think shooting me is going to help."

"Well, if you're not going to be with me, I'm certainly not going to let you be with *her.*"

I resisted the urge to laugh hysterically. I'd just sent Presley away a couple of days before and doubted very seriously that she could already be back.

"It would've been a relatively painless death if you'd eaten the cake," she added as she set the empty plate on the steps.

"I don't buy that for one minute. I've seen a lot of gastric distress in the past few days."

"Fine. Less pain than the slow agony I put Bart through."

"You're insane!"

"And you're an idiot! When your father died, you were supposed to have time to go out with me!"

My blood turned to ice in my veins as I realized what dessert my father had been eating just before he died: a bowl of Jessica

Borden's award-winning Jell-O salad. She'd killed him, too! My fist tightened around the cane, but I didn't dare make a move.

"But why? Why the others? Why now?"

"I did give up on you for a while," she said, the pistol never wavering. "That's when I married Bart, but he just wasn't you. So I told myself I'd poison him slowly while I waited for you. After a respectable time to mourn, we'd both be ready. Then *she* showed up."

Down the hall, I saw Caroline. I'd never taken Caroline for a ninja, but neither Jessica nor I had heard her come in through the back door. Cleo leaped from a nearby chair and went to Caroline with a mew, but my new nemesis kept her eyes on me.

Caroline needed to know Jessica Borden had a gun. I let go of the useless cane and held up my hands, palms out. "Go ahead and shoot me."

"What?" Jessica's hand wavered. Clearly, she hadn't expected that response. I'd shocked Caroline for a second, too, but she'd gone back to digging in her purse quickly and quietly. I knew she would. Jessica wasn't the only one with a gun; Caroline had an almost unhealthy love for her Smith & Wesson.

"Then again," I continued, stalling for time, "I've lost the girl. Maybe you should let me live and be miserable."

She considered it, but then her eyes narrowed. "I think you're bluffing."

"Declan, surprise!" Presley sang from the back door.

Jessica's eyes narrowed with hatred, and she shot me.

Presley

The first gunshot went off as the back door closed behind me. Then came the second. I ran down the hall. Caroline stood shaking with a handgun out. Jessica Borden lay on the floor sprawled backward, a gun at her side, and—

Oh, God.

He lay on the ground, a bloom of scarlet coming from his chest. Caroline was still staring at the gun in her hand. She had been the one to shoot Jessica Borden, whose body lay sprawled in the hall. Jessica's ghost stood to the side, stunned.

"Call nine-one-one!" I shouted to Caroline as I slid beside Dec.

All the blood.

The police procedurals had taught me nothing about what to do with the blood. I pressed down, but then Dec coughed with a gurgle.

"Do something!" wailed a woman from behind me. I glanced over my shoulder to see the lady in red.

"Mom?" asked Dec. I looked from him to his mother. She had to be, with that dark hair and sad smile.

Uncle Hollis stepped gingerly down the stairs. "Colonel!"

The Colonel appeared in the foyer, his military boots just inches from Dec's head.

"Fix it!" Uncle Hollis yelled, his voice hoarse.

Caroline ran up the hall with her cell phone to her ear. This wasn't the time to play coy about ghosts if the Colonel really could help Dec. "Help him," I said. The moaning ghost on the other side of Dec echoed my pleas.

The Colonel looked down at Dec with the dispassion of a man who'd seen war. "He's too far gone. Nothing I can do."

Uncle Hollis stood. "You can take his place."

"She can take his place," the Colonel spat as he pointed to the lady in red.

Dec's mother looked up at the Colonel. "I'm not anywhere near as strong as you."

"I tell you now, jump in there and take his place or we're going to lose him!" Uncle Hollis was standing face-to-face with the Colonel. Blood oozed through my fingers. Caroline tossed me towels, oblivious to the ghostly discussion going on in front of her.

"Tell me something, Gramps. You're staying because you think your way is the best way, aren't you?"

"That's right."

"Because your way is the more Christian way?"

"You know it is."

"So you love Armando like yourself?"

The Colonel sputtered.

"What about the Young brothers and Presley and Sean?"

"That's different," the Colonel said. "They aren't doing what they're supposed to do."

"Well, Declan loves Armando enough to promote him, the Youngs enough to trust them when we need help, his brother enough to accept him, and his movie star enough to let her go. That's a lot of love. What do you have to give?"

He loves me enough to let me go?

Dec shuddered underneath my hands, and I whimpered. Declan's mother wailed in the corner while she wrung her hands. Jessica stared down at her mortal form in disbelief. In the distance I heard sirens.

"If I go, I won't be able to come back," the Colonel said slowly.

"And we'll miss you, but, at some point, don't you have to trust that you've taught us the way to go?" asked Hollis. "If not for us, then for Dec. He doesn't deserve to die, does he?"

"Very well. I can see I am no longer wanted," the Colonel said. "I'm going to attempt this, but I make you no promises."

Then he poured himself into Declan, causing the body to shake in what almost looked like a seizure.

Declan

I had to be out of my mind with pain because I saw my mother to one side and some old dude arguing with Uncle Hollis. Scariest of all, there were two Jessicas. One lay on the floor, and the other looked down at the body.

The old guy melted into a hypnotic wisp of light, then floated into my body. For such a tiny strand of soul, I felt like I had something inside me trying to burn its way out. Then the old guy reappeared, drawing my breath with him and making me arch off the floor. "I can't do it."

"Dammit, we're losing him," Uncle Hollis said. "Come on, Gramps. You've seen Dec the past few days. We need him around here, especially with Sean leaving."

Muttering curses, the Colonel dissolved again into what looked like a plume of smoky light and sank into me once again.

EMTs rushed through the door, and everything became a blur of light and sound. The world spun, and some force reached deep inside me even as my soul rose and I could look over the shoulders of the EMTs as they ripped apart my shirt to get to the wound.

Caroline paced nervously. Uncle Hollis gesticulated from the foyer. Presley held my hand, and my mother wept at my side.

Jessica looked up at me and said, "I never really wanted to hurt you."

Farther and farther, I floated away down the hall, the world becoming smaller and smaller like the view from a telescope with the circle of vision narrowing until nothing but blackness remained.

At first I thought I'd shown up for my own embalming.

After all, I was flat on my back with tubes, but the beeping wasn't in time with any Elton John song I knew. Well, that and my right carotid artery felt intact. I had reached up to the spot where I would've made an incision to drain my body. Nope. Still good. Blood still flowing inside these vessels.

But, holy hell, lifting my arm hurt. Why did I do that?

The world had a hazy feel, and I wanted to sit up to clear my head, but my body was not responding to that particular request. Instead I dozed off and zoned back in a few times until the shadows on the walls told me morning had faded into evening.

And then I smelled honeysuckle.

I opened my eyes to see Presley, Sean, and Caroline talking to a doctor.

"I can't explain this one," the doctor was saying in a whisper. "Based on the trajectory of the bullet, it should've gone through his heart, but it went north instead. He is one lucky man."

One lucky man.

Now there were some words that hadn't been used to describe me in quite some time.

Presley looked over at me, then did a double take as she realized my eyes were open. She grabbed my hand and rained kisses on my face, her hot tears sliding down my cheeks. "Thank God, you're alive!"

I opened my mouth to speak, but the words wouldn't come out.

"People, you've already been here for ten minutes. Time to go," a portly nurse instructed from the doorway. The doctor held out his hand to silence her.

He gently shoved Presley to the side and went through all of his doctorly questions about fingers and days and presidents. "Well, Mr. Anderson, we might be able to move you to a regular room sooner than expected."

I nodded.

"Two more minutes, folks," the doctor said with a smile that lingered a little too long on Presley. "But I'll see what I can do to have him moved."

Caroline came first, squeezing my hand and blinking back tears. She brushed my hair back from my forehead, and it didn't feel weird. She'd been my mother for more years than she hadn't, after all. "You get better, Declan."

"You scared us, man." Sean didn't know what to do so he awkwardly patted my arm.

Finally, Presley took his place, and Sean ushered Caroline out of the room.

"You came back," I said. Well, that's what I tried to say. It was a lot of mumbling ending with "back."

"Of course I came back," she said. "And if you're going to land in the hospital every time I leave, then I'm not going to leave any more."

"Have to," I said, trying to tell her to go for it, to take the part, and to take the chance.

She frowned. "You once told me I didn't have to do anything I didn't want to, and I'm going to hold you to it."

The nurse was back in the doorway, so Presley kissed my forehead and left, leaving only the sweet scent of honeysuckle behind.

Presley

When I was little I would wake up at three o'clock on Christmas morning and run to the living room of the trailer to see what Santa had brought me. Considering Santa never actually brought me what I asked for, it took me a ridiculous amount of time to figure out the truth about him. I wanted to believe. I needed to believe there was an entity out there that cared about what I wanted.

Instead I got the fake Barbies whose hollow legs would split open at the seams long before the year was out. Then there was the time I got a clearly used bicycle whose streamers had been cut off from the handlebars. Or the Hot Wheels sleeping bag when I'd asked for a pink canopy to go over my bed. Sure, a canopy wasn't a practical idea since I slept on a mattress on the floor and wouldn't have had a place to put it. Heck, I probably wanted a real bed more than the canopy.

Then there was the year LuEllen came in late from her convenience store shift, totally sauced, and handed me a bag of sour gummy worms for Christmas. She gave Granny an air freshener for our car, the one that had just been repossessed. That was the Christmas I stopped expecting gifts, or even wanting them.

On this Christmas night, I prayed for one thing and one thing only: for Dec to live. I might still be wary, but it looked as though he was a gift I'd get to keep. His color looked a hundred times better, and he'd insisted I go home for sleep, a shower, and for the presents he'd left for me on his kitchen table.

First, I looked in the bag. He'd found a sign that said, I'M A BEAUTICIAN, NOT A MAGICIAN. I laughed. Putting the sign down, I picked up the large box and ripped into the paper around it.

A coat.

A gorgeous turquoise wool peacoat.

My throat closed up. How could someone who'd only known me for a couple of weeks have picked out things I both needed and wanted when my own family had never done that? My grandmother's standard Christmas gift was a crisp ten-dollar bill. And thank the good Lord Dec hadn't bought me an off-brand Barbie. I'd had enough of those.

But I had nothing of substance to give him.

I had hastily drawn a coupon for a trip to Tahiti, but I hadn't been able to actually buy anything since I hadn't been paid yet. The coupon in its little box seemed so childish and insignificant.

But there was one other thing I was good at doing, something that might be helpful to both Dec and the tortured ghost who had to be his mother.

I walked across the empty parking lot and let myself into the funeral home. It was dark and eerily quiet. I almost missed the Colonel, but he'd been so brash and so loud, he'd almost hidden someone else from me.

Before I formally met Dec's mother, however, there was the matter of Jessica Borden.

I walked through the funeral home until I found her sitting on the stairs. She stared at the spot where she'd lain after being shot. In the hubbub of getting Declan to the hospital, she'd almost been forgotten. Here she sat, an afterthought in death as she had been in life. I would've felt sorry for her if she hadn't been a serial killer.

"I'm going to send you into the light," I said with a confidence I didn't quite feel, "but before I do, I'm curious as to exactly how many people you killed."

She smiled. "Oh, about six. Declan would've been seven and then I planned to shoot myself to follow him."

Then she told me about her husband, her in-laws, Dec's father, her cousin, and LuEllen—although that had been an accident. "I was working on my own parents, too. They were just so old and miserable."

Once I worked through my disbelief and disgust I asked, "How did you even learn about such things?"

"My grandmother," she said. "She knew all about rat poisons. Said she learned it from her grandmother before her. The poison isn't as easy to find as back in her day, but it's amazing what you can buy on the Internet."

I shivered in spite of myself. Imagining a heaven for Jessica Borden was going to be difficult, but I had to close my eyes and try.

"Hey! What are you doing?"

Ignoring her, I tapped into the one thing we agreed on: her taste in men. It was truly sad she'd never felt enough love and acceptance to keep her from killing others.

"I'm not going!"

Her tone wasn't convincing, so I thought harder on that portal of light, reminding myself that I didn't have to be judge and jury. I wished her well. I wished she would find whatever she needed in the life after this one.

She gave a little scream.

I opened one eye and then the other. The staircase was vacant, and I could feel a peace that told me she was gone.

Down the hall I strolled, drained enough to want a cup of tea before I faced Declan's mom.

"I know you're here," I said once I'd gone through the comforting ritual of boiling the water and steeping the tea. "I'm going to take a seat at the table, and I'll tell you how Dec's doing if you'll come out."

She appeared slowly, not in a flash like the Colonel often did. She sat down across from me, and I studied her face. There was a hint of Dec's nose and the shape of his eyes, but he must've gotten all of his other genes from his father, although he did share the same eye color and the same dark hair of this woman. She wore a red dress with a peplum and the world's largest shoulder pads. She fidgeted with a set of bangles on her wrist, and I wondered if that was a habit she'd had in life.

"Please tell me how he is."

"He's doing much better," I said. "The doctors claim it had to be a miracle because they can't explain how he's living and breathing much less doing so well."

"Oh, thank God."

"Don't you think it's time for you to move on?" I asked gently.

"I couldn't," she said. "I left my little boys once, and I don't think I could do it again."

"They're fine," I soothed. "They have Caroline, you know."

She sighed, more mannerism than anything since she had no breath. "She has done such a good job for them. So much better than I did."

"Would it help if you sent a message?"

"Well, I . . . maybe? I guess I never thought about it. I knew Hollis would be able to see me, so I steered clear of him because I was afraid of what he might say. He has every right to hate me. They all do. He loves those boys. Especially since he never had any children of his own."

I remembered my conversation with Kari about flowers and how Dec knew all their meanings, how he'd searched through his mother's notebooks to try to figure out why she'd done what she had done. "Why don't you say it with flowers?"

Her eyes lit up, and she told me what to put in the bouquet as well as what to write on the card. She told me other things, too, because she didn't want to leave and because she needed to tell some stories about her son to someone who loved him as much as she did. Then she allowed me to imagine her walking into the light, and that's just what she did.

I savored the tranquility of the funeral home for just a few minutes. Convincing Kari to open up her shop for me on the day after Christmas would take some doing, and it would probably involve holding the phone away from my ear for some yelling.

Declan

The next day they moved me to a regular room, and my nurse for the day, Mario, liked to sing "Baby, It's Cold Outside." He was surprisingly good at both parts.

"What's up, Miracle Man?" he would say when he checked my vitals. I had to admit I liked "Miracle Man" a lot better than "Cold Fingers."

"Feeling better by the minute," I said.

"Good, good. Did Santa Claus find you, or were you a naughty boy?"

"I'm hurt you think I would've been naughty," I said.

"I saw your girl coming through here. I was *hoping* you been naughty," he said with a grin that took up most of his face.

"A little naughty," I admitted.

"All right, that's what I like to hear. I'll be back in a while," he said as he went off singing, "I've got to go away. . . ."

I know that's right, Mario.

In breezed Presley in the blue coat I had bought her. I knew she had to have it the moment I saw it, and it did look perfect on her. She was also carrying an arrangement of flowers.

"Thank you for my presents," she said shyly. "I, um, don't have much to give you, but this was waiting for you at the funeral home."

She put the arrangement on the rolling tray beside me. I studied the bouquet out of habit: pink carnations, amaryllis, a few red roses, white heather, and a few of the pink peonies, although they had seen better days.

Odd. I reached for the card. It said:

I'm sorry I broke the furnace all those times, Mom

I looked at Presley, and she looked back at me.

Pink carnations could mean many things, but in this case I was going with "a mother's love." The pink peonies of shame were, of course, an apology. Red roses for love and amaryllis for pride. A few sprigs of white heather suggested "Dreams do come true."

"She wanted some sweet pea and purple hyacinth, but Kari didn't have those."

Of course, she wanted the purple hyacinth because—

"Wait. How?"

So I had seen my mom? And another ghost, too?

"I don't get it."

She took a deep breath, and I could see she was nervous.

"Dec, I can see ghosts," she said. "So can Uncle Hollis."

I stared at her for so long she had to add, "I promise I'm not crazy. Jury's still out on Uncle Hollis, though."

And it all made sense. That's how she'd known how to do Miss Sylvia's hair, why she'd spent so much time with Uncle Hollis, why she hadn't been surprised to see my mother or the old soldier like I had.

"Can I see her? Again?"

She shook her head, biting her lip. "She went into the light."

Sweet pea. She'd wanted the sweet pea for departure, for good-bye.

"But I only saw her the once."

She shrugged. "Maybe because you were dying? That's your miracle, you know. Your great-grandfather saved you. Somehow."

"So the old soldier guy was Great-Granddaddy Seamus. I'd always wanted to meet him."

"You saw him?" she asked.

"Yeah. And for a minute I saw my mother."

Presley shifted in her seat. "She said to tell you she's sorry, that she wasn't thinking straight and she should've gone to the doctor instead of, well, you know. She also told you to be nicer to Caroline. I had to leave a bouquet of dark pink roses in full bloom for her."

Gratitude.

"Kari, by the way, said to get well soon and, at this point, we owe her the Jack."

"I can do that."

"I really do appreciate your gifts," she said. I noticed she hadn't taken off her coat yet. "They're the nicest presents anyone has ever given me."

I would've done better if I could.

"You deserve even more," I said.

"Well, I have one more present for you," she said shyly. "And I really hope it's something you still want after my little confession there."

Please let it be something skimpy under her coat. Please let it be something—

She handed me a tiny box, and I opened it to see a slip of folded paper. I looked at her, and she nodded, so I unfolded the paper and read aloud, "'Good for one trip to Tahiti to stay in a hut over the ocean.'"

"You got the part, didn't you?"

She nodded. "Filming starts in March, but Ira said he might be able to find me some small parts in the meantime."

"Congratulations," I said, trying to hide my disappointment that she would be leaving me again soon. "I always knew you could do it."

"So you're not freaked out by the fact I can see dead people?"

"Well, Dad always did say life held too much mystery to be explained by science alone." I yawned in spite of myself, the painkillers kicking in once again.

Presley took my good hand and squeezed it. "Don't worry. I'm staying for a while."

I wanted to tell her not to stay. I wanted to tell her to go on and live her life, but the words were already lost to me, and her hand felt so warm in mine.

Presley

While I was waiting for Dec to heal, I had one other thing I had to do: deliver Miss Ginger's message to Beulah. I'd heard she wasn't playing at The Fountain anymore, so I decided to take my chances with Miss Ginger's place. Sure enough, piano music wafted through an open window. I took a deep breath and rang the doorbell.

Beulah came to the door, and I almost didn't recognize her. Her jeans were a second skin, but her sweater hung loosely. She'd thrown her hair back into a ponytail and wasn't wearing makeup. She looked so young.

"Can I help you?" she asked, keeping the door cracked.

"Presley Cline, I was a couple of years behind you in school."

"I know that. And?"

"This is going to sound weird, but I'm just going to blurt it out." I took a deep breath. "Miss Ginger said to tell you to make up with your mother and to do it for yourself because she'd already used up all of her favors. She said to call you Beulah Lou so you'd know I'm not crazy."

"You're flippin' insane!"

And then she slammed the door in my face.

Well, that could've gone better.

No matter. I'd done my part by delivering the message, and I felt much lighter for having done so.

Dec progressed nicely, and we got to take him home sooner than expected. Apparently, the wound had looked much worse than it was, although the doctor said I had done some quick thinking in applying pressure. The doctor also kept tossing around words like *miracle*. I knew the truth, but I wasn't about to try to explain to people the role the Colonel had played. It was enough to be grateful things had turned out the way they did. I mean, I would've preferred to catch Jessica Borden before she poisoned half the town and shot Dec, but she had us all fooled. I suppose Colonel Mustard was right: The female of the species *was* more deadly than the male. Or was he quoting someone else?

Anyway, as I was helping Dec up the stairs to the carriage house, my phone rang.

True to his word, Ira had found some bit parts for me in Atlanta. The only problem was I needed to leave in less than a week if I wanted to take advantage of them. Ever since my realization about Lolita Ann, I'd been formulating a plan.

"We need to celebrate," Dec said, his eyes sad despite his smile. He'd overheard enough to know I'd been offered some additional little roles—one a recurring role on the vampire show.

"*You* need to take a nap."

"Even better. We can celebrate with a nap."

"Celebrate with that nap. Then you need to see your brother off, and he's not going to leave unless you look better," I said as I helped him take off his shoes and ease under the covers.

"You're going to take the part, right?" he said from where he lay back on the pillow.

"Maybe I want to stay here with you," I said. "Do I really want to play a vampire, a zombie, and then an oversexed girl? I'd rather play Wonder Woman."

"She's a brunette."

"That's what hair dye is for," I said.

"Sacrilege," he said, but his eyes were already closing. "Presley?"

"What?"

"Go."

I stared at him, watching his chest rise and fall with breaths that looked so much calmer than the ones I felt. How could he dismiss me this way? "No."

His eyes flashed open. "What did you say?"

"I said no. That's what I said."

He tried to rise up on his elbows, but I pushed him back down using his good shoulder. "In fact, I'm going to call Ira right now and tell him to forget the whole thing."

"You wouldn't!"

"Oh, but I would."

He shot out of bed far quicker than I expected, far quicker than he should have, based on his grimace of pain as he took my cell phone away from me. "Don't get stuck here like I did."

"Remember when you told me I didn't have to do anything I didn't want to do?"

He lay back, my phone still clutched in his hand, and groaned. "That again? I wish I'd never said it."

"I, for one, am glad you did," I said. "Because I'm going to tell you what I want to do and how it's going to be."

His eyes bugged out.

"First, I'm going to stay here for a few days and nurse you back to health. Then I'm going to fly back to Hollywood long enough to pack up my stuff. I'll stop by on the way to Atlanta, but then I'm not coming back until I'm done. When I do get back to Ellery, I'll have enough money to take you to Tahiti. Think you can heal by then?"

"Yes, ma'am."

"Good. Now listen to this next part very closely," I said as I sat down on the bed beside him. "I would like for that trip to Tahiti to be a honeymoon, so—"

"Being Mrs. Anderson—"

"Blah, blah, blah. I'm keeping my name. We can *not* get married, if you'd like, but I'm in love with you and there's not a whole helluva lot you can do about it."

He lifted his hand to cup my cheek. "I only want the best for you because I love you."

"We're on the same page then." I put my hand around his and leaned into his palm.

Remorse for being so bossy hit me as I looked down at my pale Miracle Man. "I mean, you do want to be with me, don't you?"

"Only since the moment you showed up on my doorstep in the middle of a dark and stormy night," he said.

"Because you don't have to do anything you don't want to do, either."

"Oh, the things I want to do," he said with a sigh. "The mind is willing, but the flesh is oh so weak."

"When you're healed then," I said, telling my breath to come and go evenly again. After all, it was going to work out. We were going to make it work out.

His hand dropped, and I knew his painkillers were kicking in. He swallowed hard, his eyes already closed. "I just have one thing to ask of you."

My mouth went dry. "What's that?"

"Can I pick out the bikini for the Tahiti trip?"

Declan

Reader, I married her.

Oh, sure, I waited until she finished shooting her movie, but that was partially so I could propose properly with my mother's ring. Then we went to Tahiti: warm, clear water and sun and little thatched huts and Presley in that American flag bikini.

While Presley was off being an actress, I worked hard to make Anderson-Cepeda profitable again. I spoke with Mrs. Little, and she sold us the strip of land for a fair price. Getting approved for the crematorium wasn't too hard since Davenport and Potter knew I could turn them in for bribes. Even better, I didn't have to rely on Sean. I went to that city council meeting myself. We broke ground about a week ago, and sometimes, if business is slow enough, I go out to help Uncle El and the guys.

We're even on our way to the pet crematorium—the local vet, Dr. Winterbourne, and I have come to a mutually beneficial agreement, and the new facility beside his rural office will be up and running in six months.

In the evenings, I work on the old Maple Avenue place. It's habitable, but we're still fixing this and that. Presley's hinted at some new ideas on how to be unsexy now that she's decided to take a hiatus from Hollywood and cut hair with her Aunt Delilah. I'm not opposed to the practice required, but I want to keep her to myself a little longer even if I'm not a spring chicken, as Caroline informs me almost daily.

I'm too busy taking life one day at a time, one second, one breath. Sometimes, I forget. I start looking ahead so far I forget about the days that are right under me. Just as soon as I forget, though, I'll have to go pick up someone else who might've forgotten. That helps me to remember.

I look down at the grave of my father—and my mother. "Well, I'm keeping my promise. Hell, one day we may make enough money that I'll buy out Potter."

"*Oye, Jefe, ¿listo?*"

"*Ya voy, ya voy,*" I say. Manny has been helping me with my Spanish. Armando, too, but he's busier now that he's a partner. I walk up the knoll to take a look at Manny's work. It looks pretty good in the fading afternoon light.

"I feel like a cheeseburger," I say.

"And tequila?" asks Manny.

"Maybe," I say. But probably not, because I have a certain duty to the folks in town. I can't be downing shots of tequila and then tooling around town in a hearse. People need to know they can trust me.

No, I'll have that cheeseburger and toast Grandpa Floyd with my sweet tea. Then I'm gonna go home to the old house on Maple and kiss my wife full on the lips. I might even get to show off some of my tricks.

After all, an Anderson always keeps his promises.

BETTER GET TO LIVIN'

Sally Kilpatrick

ABOUT THIS GUIDE

The following discussion questions are
included to enhance your group's reading of
Better Get to Livin'.

Discussion Questions

1. One inspiration for this novel was the movie *It's a Wonderful Life*. What allusions to the film did you catch? Did you see any similar themes?

2. Do you believe in ghosts? Why or why not?

3. Who was your favorite character in this story and why? Your least favorite?

4. At the beginning of the story, Dec mentions that Caroline has been up to something on the computer. What do you think it is? Hint: You can ask the author on Twitter (@Super WriterMom) or on Facebook (https://www.facebook.com /SuperWriterMom/).

5. Presley has a breakdown because she looks sexy, but she has difficulty embracing her sexuality. She also talks a lot about purity and innocence. Do you think it's fair that she's expected to look sexy but to not have/enjoy sex by some, yet others, like Potter, assume she'll have sex indiscriminately because of the way she looks?

6. In his memoir, *The Undertaking*, Thomas Lynch talks about sex and death as "existential bookends" of life. Do you think pairing the seemingly unlikely relationship between sex and death works well in *Better Get to Livin'*?

7. Do you think LuEllen did her daughter a disservice? In what ways was Presley more of a mother than a daughter?

8. In what ways is the Colonel a relic of the Old South? Since he sacrifices himself to save Declan, do you think Dec represents the New South? If so, how?

9. At one point LuEllen says, "I was afraid of so much that I forgot to live." How do her words relate to the overall theme of the book? Which other characters talk about fear, and what are they afraid of?

10. Dec tells Potter that the Andersons "respect the dead, but work [their] hardest for the living." How does that theme play out in the book?

11. Another theme of the book is promises made to parents. Do you think LuEllen should've made Presley go for the audition? Do you think Dec's father should've made him promise to keep the funeral home in the family?

12. How does Presley change from the beginning of the story to the end? How does Dec change?

13. Is there anything you're afraid of, anything holding you back? How can you better get to living?

Aunt Dot's Apricot Salad

10 ounces 7 Up (or any other lemon-lime soda, but southern
   ladies have their favorites)
1 package (3 ounces) apricot Jell-O
8 ounces sour cream
1 can (15¾ ounces) crushed pineapple, drained

Bring 7 Up to a boil. Stir in Jell-O until dissolved. Add sour
cream. Mix well. Add pineapple. Mix and gel. "Mix and gel" is
shorthand for put the concoction in the fridge once it's well
mixed and leave it there until it's congealed.

*This recipe comes from Dorothy Louise Patterson Warbington and has
been a family favorite forever. For some reason a holiday just isn't a
holiday without apricot salad. If you haven't had a Jell-O salad in a
while, give it a try—just don't add anything extra.*

Don't miss these other Southern novels by Sally Kilpatrick!

THE HAPPY HOUR CHOIR

Sally Kilpatrick's debut novel is a hopeful tale of love and redemption in a quiet Southern town where a lost soul finds her way with the help of an unlikely circle of friends. . . .

Life has dealt Beulah Land a tough hand to play, least of all being named after a hymn. A teenage pregnancy estranged her from her family, and a tragedy caused her to lose what little faith remained. The wayward daughter of a Baptist deacon, she spends her nights playing the piano at The Fountain, a honky-tonk located just across the road from County Line Methodist. But when she learns that a dear friend's dying wish is for her to take over as the church's piano player, she realizes it may be time to face the music. . . .

Beulah butts heads with Luke Daniels, the new pastor at County Line, who is determined to cling to tradition even though he needs to attract more congregants to the aging church. But the choir also isn't enthusiastic about Beulah's contemporary take on the old songs and refuses to perform. Undaunted, Beulah assembles a ragtag group of patrons from The Fountain to form the Happy Hour Choir. And as the unexpected gig helps her let go of her painful past—and accept the love she didn't think she deserved—she just may be able to prove to Luke that she can toe the line between sinner and saint. . . .

"It is hard to believe that this is Kilpatrick's debut novel. The characters are honest, lively, and heartfelt. Beulah deals with a number of relatable challenges. No character is wasted, and they remind the reader that anything worth having is not easy. A good takeaway is that family is what we create, not restricted to bloodlines. Kilpatrick mixes loss and devastation with hope and a little bit of Southern charm. She will leave the reader laughing through tears. This is an incredible start from a promising storyteller."
—*RT Book Reviews*, 4.5 Stars

BITTERSWEET CREEK

From the author of The Happy Hour Choir *comes a Romeo and Juliet story with Southern flair—witty, warm, and as complex and heart-wrenching as only love and family can be.*

For a century and a half, the Satterfield and McElroy farms have been separated by a narrow creek and a whole lot of bad blood. Both sides have done their share of damage. But the very worst crime either family can commit is to fall in love with the enemy. As teenagers, Romy Satterfield and Julian McElroy did exactly that. Then, on the night they were secretly married by a justice of the peace, Julian stood Romy up.

Ten years later, Romy is poised to marry the scion of one of Nashville's most powerful families. First she has to return home to Ellery to help her injured father—and to finalize her divorce. For Julian, seeing Romy again brings into relief the secrets he's kept and the poison that ran through his childhood. Romy has missed the farm and the unpretentious, downright nosy townsfolk. In spite of her efforts, she's also missed Julian. But though she suspects there's more to that long-ago night than Julian ever revealed, the truth will either drive her away for good, or reveal what is truly worth fighting for. . . .

"Kilpatrick's sophomore effort is a Southern take on *Romeo and Juliet*. The reader may believe they are listening to a tale from their favorite country neighbor! The story explores nature versus nurture in chapters told in alternating POVs. The characters deftly illustrate that leaving the bitter in the past can pave the way for a sweet future."
—*RT Book Reviews*, 4 Stars

"Pleasantly engaging. The author adds depth to the love story by incorporating issues of domestic violence and racism. . . ."
—*Library Journal*